Rebellion:

The King's Spy
The King's Captain
The King's Cavalier

By Mark Turnbull

© Mark Turnbull 2021, 2021, 2022.

Mark Turnbull has asserted his rights under the Copyright, Design and Patents Act, 1988, to be identified as the author of this work.

This omnibus edition first published in 2022 by Sharpe Books.

Table of Contents

The King's Spy 1
The King's Captain 119
The King's Cavalier 269

The King's Spy

Mark Turnbull

Chapter One

Naseby.
14th June 1645. Between ten and eleven of the clock.

There were almost three enemy horsemen for every royalist. But Parliament's untested 'New Model Army' seemed no different to their previous armies, and indeed provoked the same churning emotions; apprehension and determination. Fear. Captain Maxwell Walker was not ashamed to admit that to himself. He glanced around at his squadron of two hundred; elite cavalrymen of the royalist Northern Horse. A glance was all he could afford in the brief pause, while the musketeers that interspersed his lines caught up and then took aim at the enemy.

"Give Fire!"

The royalist matchlocks triggered a succession of fiery glows that burned as brightly as the sun. The thudding gunshots merged into a din of trumpet and drum, yells and explosions. Captain Walker led his men forward through the rolling smoke. With the smell of war in his nostrils, Maxwell released all of his emotions in a deep cry, and the fields around Naseby seemed to shudder from the pounding march of man and beast. His heart raced. The royalist left wing of seventeen hundred were pitched opposite an enemy wing of four thousand. This was Maxwell's arena of battle. The remainder of the two opposing armies on the field – seventeen thousand men – were put out of his mind, leaving him to focus on those opposite who began to come on apace.

His carbine jangled from the hook on his belt, as if itching to be used, though it would have to wait just a little longer, until he was closer. The same with 'truth' and 'justice', his aptly named pair of pistols, which sat in their holsters and would be best employed at point-blank range. The six-foot Maxwell, clad in an ochre buff coat, was carried ever closer to the parliamentarians by his black mare.

"Charge!" He bellowed.

The two sides closed up. Maxwell discharged his carbine and then pointed his basket hilt sword at the enemy, all thirty-one inches of its double-edged blade now at one with his outstretched arm. He slashed at one trooper; first from the left, and once their swords met, swung in from the right, but was blocked again. Each clang reverberated in his iron grip. Maxwell's opponent was a blur of blackened armour and buff coat, and now alongside each other, they engaged in a broadside of blades.

"Papist dog!" The parliamentarian yelled.

Maxwell locked his broadsword against his foe's and then reached for a gun, but as he grabbed the butt, his opponent cried out and then slumped dead from another gunshot. Taking advantage of the brief respite, Maxwell drew one of his Dutch pistols, aimed its eighteen-inch barrel at the next oncoming parliamentarian, and sent a ball into him. No sooner had he shoved the pistol back than another foe closed up and their swords clashed and scraped with flashes of silvery steel. This speedy exchange led to Maxwell slicing across the man's flank, but as he did so, two more parliamentarians drew closer. It was no good.

Maxwell turned his horse about and disengaged. He spotted his green pennant and its scrollwork motto 'Cuckold Wee Come' and made his way back towards the taffeta flag to re-join the receding royalist line. He barely made it before being set upon by a pursuing parliamentarian who yelled out, "God our Strength!" Not even the Almighty could stop whizzing balls of lead, nor the skilled eye and co-ordination of Maxwell Walker, who parried the man's attack and then sent him to meet his maker.

As the three-deep royalist line began to waver and gaps opened up, the code word of the day, 'Queen Mary,' was called out. It was desperately repeated over and over. Trumpets screamed at the bloody gashes, deathly thrusts and the gore of faces, limbs and torsos. Maxwell ran one rebel through with a mighty thrust of his sword, only for it to become stuck somewhere within the man's rib cage. Another parliamentarian rounded on Maxwell, who roared with anger, for that was all he had left to counter the blade that was swung at him. An image of Catherine, his late wife, flashed before him for a split second. But the strike against Maxwell's arm thankfully failed to penetrate his deer-hide coat. Finally freeing his sword, he parried a second blow and drew his last flintlock, aiming it at the enemy's triple bar helmet. The man's wide eyes didn't even register with Maxwell as he pulled the trigger. It all seemed in slow motion. The flint struck the frizzen and dancing sparks ignited the priming powder, sending forth a small pistol ball. Yet his opponent remained of this world; Maxwell knew it, for he had shot many a man in many a battle these past three years. A few more slashes and cuts saw the man off, though by now the royalist squadrons around Maxwell were beginning to fall back again. One of their colonels, Sir Philip Monckton, leaped from his dying horse and mounted a replacement, trying in vain to stop the rot. Some royalists fled towards their cavalry reserve, where a splendid red, blue and gold royal standard fluttered, and from whence the King himself watched over his army. The very presence of the monarch, appointed by God himself, would surely see the royalists succeed against all odds.

"Stay! Hold firm!"

Maxwell implored his troopers to remain in the fray. The fleeting thought of Catherine had calmed something deep inside him, as if he no longer feared death. Now Sir Marmaduke Langdale was urging his Northern Horse to hold fast, and his pale features and stern bearing, cocooned within the blackest of armour, demanded obedience. It worked. The steady stream of routed troopers dried up, the inferior royalist ranks held their ground, and their second line came up in support to fill the gaps. Maxwell bellowed encouragement to those of his horsemen who remained with him, but sight of a certain scarlet flag rendered him silent. It peered over the helmets of the rebels ahead, as if it had been dipped in blood, and the emblem upon it – a skeleton wielding a sword – fluttered provocatively. It was the mark of a murderer. One who had killed inhabitants from Maxwell's home town of Selby.

"Gervase Harper," he growled.

Maxwell's head throbbed beneath the ribbed bowl of his Flemish helmet with its single face guard. He moved his horse off, urging his men to follow, and made right for Harper's standard. Having just been spared from death, he assumed it must have been for the purpose of extracting retribution upon this murderous dog. He attempted to carve his way through to Harper, losing himself in a frenzy of blows. He couldn't feel his sword-arm any longer, nor how it ached; in fact, it felt as if his body and spirit had somehow separated. Then Maxwell took a slash to his arm. This time it cut through his buff coat to leave a blood-red edge to the seam, the same colour as the silk sash around his waist. He fought on, determined not to die before he had run his blade through Harper's blackened heart. One opponent's horse was felled by a bullet that peppered Maxwell with warm droplets of blood. He was numb to it all. But then Harper's standard vanished amidst the fluid mass of horses and riders. Maxwell, as if he'd been temporarily deafened this whole time, was now struck by the ungodly noise. His squadron began to break in the face of such relentless odds and there was nothing for it but to sound the retreat.

***

Maxwell fled for his life. His jet-black horse hammered back towards the royalist lines. Into the dip of the land he thundered, which lay between both armies, and then up the incline on the other side. He dared not look back, nor take his eyes off Dust Hill where he instinctively headed, and from where the fluttering royal standard beckoned him.

To his far right was the position where he'd started. He pushed on, gasping for breath in the warm summer air that seemed to smother him, and which whistled past his helmet like the pleas of a hundred dead souls. He now approached a royalist infantry regiment who stood firm. Their resolute blue coats shamed him into slowing his mount, having covered nearly four hundred yards already, and a cursory look over his shoulder confirmed that he was not being pursued. Somewhere within the chaotic tangle of horsemen that he'd left behind, Harper fought on. Both the Battle of Naseby and Maxwell's own conflict were far from over. This was confirmed as he passed the bluecoats and approached Dust Hill where one thousand reserve troops stood poised for their moment, and whom he recognised as the King's lifeguard of horse and foot. Neither was he alone. Nearly a hundred other fleeing horsemen had, like him, drawn rein near the reserves where they began to regroup.

"I'm not finished with you, Harper," he hissed.

"Captain Walker!"

A subordinate rode at him with a raised hand, leading Maxwell to draw up and pull off his helmet. He wiped the sweat from his brow and brushed back his sandy locks.

"What is it?" Maxwell asked. His speech broke, as if slipping into the cracks of his bone-dry mouth.

"It's me, sir, Cornet Durham."

"Well?" Maxwell struggled to think straight, but he recognised Anthony Durham. "Spit it out, man."

"Sir William is gathering survivors."

"How many so far?"

"Most of the two squadrons recently repulsed."

"And Langdale?" Maxwell asked of their commander.

"Still in the action, sir."

The two horsemen hammered towards Sir William Blakiston, who was in the process of firing off orders and receiving updates. First, the death of two majors, then reports of rabbit warrens and gorse hindering both royalist and parliamentarian alike, as well as the most crucial fact of all; Lieutenant-General Oliver Cromwell, in command of the opposing enemy wing, had not even committed his full force. At least a third of his troops were simply standing by and watching the gradual erosion of the royalist left wing.

"Sir William." Maxwell saluted.

"Gather up your men, Walker," Blakiston said, pointing across the horsemen. "Get them ready for another charge."

Maxwell eagerly rode towards the familiar faces. "Let us rally and prepare to re-join our comrades!"

"Huzzah!"

Seizing the opportunity, Maxwell took a measure of gunpowder. His hands shook, though he didn't notice until he attempted to spill it down into the barrel of his carbine. After pushing the ball and wadding down with a short scouring stick, he took the key that was around his neck and proceeded to wind the wheellock's mechanism, three-quarter turns clockwise. The clicking noise was somewhat satisfying. The chain inside wrapped itself around the spindle, making the weapon ready for firing once more. Maxwell, too, was ready to return to the fray. He eyed the mounted melee in the distance and rubbed the carbine's barrel with a hint of pride, as if the bullet it contained was the very one which would blast Harper's skull apart. The gun would be worth every bit of its one pound and sixteen shillings – well over half of his weekly wage – if only it could find its mark.

Maxwell next reloaded his pair of pistols. After that, while his horse snatched at some grass, he finally serviced his own needs and gulped ale from his flask. The awful tepid tang nevertheless steadied his nerves and stimulated part of his mind that had closed off in the fighting.

"Skippon has been wounded!" Sir William Blakiston cheered.

Sergeant-Major-General Skippon's wound would leave a critical absence of senior parliamentarian officers. This good news drew Maxwell's eye to the centre of the royalist army, where the King's veteran infantrymen were proving their mettle. Musketeers blasted gaps into the parliamentarian lines, while pikemen picked them further apart with the steel tips of their eighteen-foot poles. The opposing blocks of pikemen bludgeoned one another in a bid to force the other to give way, and then came together in a crush. It was as if the intermittent flashes of gunfire were sparked by their friction. Both sides resembled scudding storm clouds. Gone were the array of colourful coats, for their dyed wool of red, blue and green were all absorbed by the smoke of battle that turned every man to a mere grey shadow. Standard after enemy standard was swallowed up by the resolute royalists, and with each pennant that bowed out, victory began to look ever more possible.

Maxwell adjusted his seating on his down-stuffed saddle. He glanced further across to the royalist right wing and saw that Prince Rupert of the Rhine, the Commander-in-Chief, was missing along with most of his horsemen. The King's nephew had surprised everyone by leading that cavalry wing in person. True to form, his galloping fist of renowned horsemen must have punched through the enemy lines and chased them off, but now there were few of either side on that far wing. Rupert's absence, and that of his troops, unsettled Maxwell. The King, positioned amidst the reserves with a posse of civilian and military advisors, must have felt the same apprehension. The royalist left wing – Maxwell's wing – was all it took to double that apprehension, upon realisation that this was their Achilles heel. Outnumbered and outmanoeuvred, the left wing was crumbling, which meant that Cromwell's men could soon be unleashed upon the royalist infantry.

"Cornet Durham," Maxwell called. "Enquire of Sir William when we are to move. Time is not on our side."

"Aye, sir."

Maxwell drew his sword, for in his own mind he had already answered that very question. He held the grip firmly within his buff gauntlet and was in no mood to sheath the blade again.

A jangle of weaponry and a unified noise of hooves, along with deep bawls of instructions, cast aside all worry and apprehension. The royal reserves were activated. An energy enthused them. The King's lifeguard of cavalry and infantry, the Newark Horse and the squadrons of Northern Horse that had reformed here, now became as one. The royal standard emerged from the line. The King in gleaming, armour made ready to lead them forward and Maxwell yelled to his men to prepare. The regiment of bluecoats further ahead of them also stood to arms and looked set to join the pending attack which would vanquish Cromwell, Whalley, and all of the rebels who had enjoyed the upper hand on the left wing for far too long.

"We rescue Langdale!" Maxwell yelled.

Another cry went up. It was, though, of a different sort altogether and at odds with the earlier deep, resolute tones. A man had seized the King's bridle. That much Maxwell could make out, for the King's horse suddenly turned aside.

REBELLION

What in God's name ... ? Maxwell could not comprehend whether this was a traitor in their midst.

In that second, like a misfiring musket, the charged might of this reserve seemed to fizzle out. Most turned and left the field with the King, joined by an ever-increasing flood of Langdale's routed horsemen, sight of which robbed many more of their morale. Confusion reigned within the reserves; was the King retreating?

Below them, Parliament's General, Sir Thomas Fairfax, led his reserves forward and the royalist infantry no longer had it so good. In a fleeting moment the wind of victory, which had seemed set to usher the royalists on, now changed tack and blew in their faces like a turncoat. In the blink of an eye everything was transformed. Even Prince Rupert's return was too late to improve anything; his cavalry merely followed the King off the field. The day was lost. The royalist infantry, who had fought the King's corner since the start of the war, would not abandon him now and continued to slog it out until the bitter end. Maxwell gritted his teeth and fixed a glare at the enemy.

"Captain Walker, fall back."

Maxwell turned to see Sir Marmaduke Langdale, commander of the Northern Horse, and nicknamed 'The Ghost' by his men. It seemed as if the entire royalist reserve had been merely an apparition that had vanished into the Northamptonshire countryside.

"What in the name of Christ has just happened, sir?" He asked Langdale.

"Defeat, and we on the left wing shall be blamed."

"We held off twice our numbers ..." Maxwell stammered and realised that Harper had also escaped justice once more.

"This is no time for analysis," Langdale's gaunt face stared at him. "Go to Wistow Hall."

"Where?"

"Listen to me, damn you!"

Walker well-knew the commander's blunt temperament and respected him for it.

"Go to Wistow Hall," Langdale explained that it was a nearby estate. "The King has left some important belongings there. The enemy might have the day, but they must not take possession of these items, too."

"Of course." Maxwell nodded.

"I shall make for Newark. Join me there."

The hot summer's day had given way to a cold and uncomfortable conclusion. Defeat. A double defeat at that. When his darling Catherine had been shot, Maxwell felt as if he'd shattered into pieces, and had collapsed by her side while her murderer had ridden off. Maxwell's beautiful, intelligent and loving wife had been destroyed by the mere contraction of Harper's forefinger; a movement so simple and so easy, which had triggered devastation. Maxwell had been powerless to stop her murderer's flight. Today, Harper was escaping justice for a second time and it consumed Maxwell, almost to the point where he could have ridden single-handedly into the enemy ranks to seek the man out, had he not been burdened with this mission. Maxwell would not die in dishonour. He would accomplish the task for the King and then have his day with Harper.

Chapter Two

14th June 1645. Evening.

Prince Rupert of the Rhine placed his feet onto solid ground for the first time since dawn and brushed back a red cloak that revealed his armour, which sported a flourish of golden enamel across his breast. That morning, he'd been in the saddle marshalling troops long before the battle at Naseby had even commenced. Following their defeat, the royal party had fled from the scene and had not drawn rein since. As he straightened his back, the numerous clicks seemed to count up every hour of his ride. It felt good to stretch. To breathe clean air and tread upon the earth once more began to resuscitate his senses and his steed brayed its own appreciation of the respite. The Prince's horse was quickly taken away and a replacement sought, and he watched the inhabitants of Fawsley Hall welcome the King, raising his eyebrows at the irony; an estate owned by a parliamentarian family, but whose royalist tenant was now aiding the monarch.

He summoned his friend and confidante, Colonel William Legge. "I must talk with you before my frustration bubbles forth. God knows, it has been bottled up within me all through this ignoble retreat."

"The King's bridle, Your Highness?" Will replied with a grimace.

"Aye, you guess correctly."

"The Earl of Carnwath, I believe, felt the need to stop the King riding to his death." Will lowered his voice and stepped closer.

A five-sided stone window, which stretched up the entire side of the great hall, looked as aghast as Rupert, its long window frames like gaping mouths. The last vestiges of sunshine that lit them up were as burning as the words hanging on Rupert's tongue.

"He seized the King's bridle without opposition?" Rupert couldn't quite believe that victory had been snatched away from the royalists not by the enemy, but by one bold and interfering nobleman. "How did a man with no military position lose us the day?"

"He turned His Majesty's horse aside and created confusion. It was thought that the King desired the reserve to fall back."

"Swounds, I'd have cut off the fellow's hand there and then!" Rupert exclaimed.

"Perchance it is a good thing His Majesty does not share your temperament, Your Highness." Lord George Digby paused by the two men. "Such a rash and brutal act would alienate our most loyal supporters and, pardon the expression, give the enemy the upper hand."

"I'd wager even you, My Lord, cannot condone the intrusion of this spectator into such a key battle?" Rupert asked.

"It is not my duty to condone or condemn, sir. I merely do as the King bids me."

"You condemned my opinion when I argued against seeking this battle in the first place?" Rupert's brown eyes fixed upon Digby. "I warned of the rebels' superior numbers."

"They were besieging Oxford, sir," Digby clasped his hands together like a pious monk. "Seeking battle drew them away from our headquarters, which we would otherwise have lost. And besides, it would not have been honourable to simply run away from this *New Noddle Army*." He couldn't help a stray smirk over the nickname.

REBELLION

"Which is precisely what we have been forced to do, all through the actions of the noble Carnwath!" Rupert replied.

"Forgive me, gentlemen, I must see that we do not remain here longer than it takes to change horses." Digby gave a quick nod and then left them.

Rupert rubbed his face as if trying to awaken himself from this nightmare; one where he faced battling not just the enemy, but also a phalanx of senior advisors within the King's ranks. He had known that it would be folly to engage the parliamentarians and had instead advocated a continuance of the march north, to tackle the Scots and regain the northern heartlands. As commander-in-chief his opinion should have prevailed. But, as usual, politicians such as Digby had interfered and opposed a logical military decision. Or more exactly, they had opposed *him*.

"I will be blamed for this defeat, Will," Rupert hissed.

"Nobody can lay this at your door …"

"He will," Rupert interrupted. "Mark my words. I may be Commander of the King's armies, but, by God, I am powerless!"

"If I may counsel patience, Your Highness, and beseech you not to let them divert your Herculean efforts."

"Patience?" Rupert shook his head. "This war will not be won by patience."

Colonel William Legge was nevertheless a calming presence. Rupert considered whether it was his friendly Irish manner that most endeared the man to him, or his very fatherly and sensible advice. After having had his opinions overturned by the King and the council, and having fought non-stop, day after day, in his uncle's cause for three years, Rupert's nerves were flagging. The six-foot-four prince needed more than just a change of mount. He had almost gotten used to the racing heart and dry mouth, symptoms of being constantly at war. He followed after the cunning Digby, a consummate politician with golden locks and a silver tongue. The man had recently been described by a parliamentarian major-general as a poisonous spider, which was very apt, for the King somehow always ended up being snagged in one of Digby's gilded webs.

A small group clustered about King Charles, whose mood seemed as black as the velvet cloak he wore. The monarch's horse was led away with the crimson saddle and its gold embroidered fleur-de-lis' still fastened about it, while a replacement with a plain saddle was led forward. The transformation was in keeping with the devastating effects that Naseby had – and would continue to have – upon the King's fortunes. They had not even the time to partake of any sustenance, lest the enemy catch up and take them all prisoner.

"Pray keep my saddle as a memento, in remembrance of me," the King said to the loyal tenant, who now dropped to his knees.

When King Charles turned to face Rupert, his uncle's melancholy expression almost drove the prince to his knees in sympathy too. The monarch's eyes were without their usual sparkle. It was as if they were clouded by deep-rooted emotions that had been dredged up and his heavy eyelids were almost symmetrically matched by bags underneath. Only his exquisite moustache and the small beard at his chin, which he had sported ever since his youthful trip to Madrid, retained an image of majesty.

"What of my belongings at Wistow?" The King frowned.

"It's already in hand, Your Majesty," Rupert knew well of their importance. "I had Langdale send one of his best men."

"I have also despatched someone, so pray let the Prince and I shoulder this particular burden for you," Digby added.

"My thanks to you both. I will leave the matter in your hands then, gentlemen," the King replied.

REBELLION

"If I may venture, sir, you shall find ours the safest pairs of hands in your service," Digby turned to Rupert and gave a smile of sarcasm.

***

Maxwell was almost out of the woodland, so he finally drew rein and stopped. The furious motion of the ride, and rhythmic thudding of his horse's hooves, continued to affect his exhausted body and mind even when he had dismounted. His face was numb, eyes and mouth dry, and his head ached. Upon sight of the golden sunset rippling across a puddle, he dropped to his knees and began to sup at the water in desperation. His horse followed his lead. The surface soon swirled with an earthy brown tint, but nevertheless, it was balm to his jagged throat, if only temporarily.

"Good, eh?" he gasped and looked at his steed. If he'd had the energy to laugh, he would have done so. Probably manically, at that.

Maxwell had stopped to partake of the remains of a freak downpour before it was siphoned away by the gnarled tentacles of the oak trees that lined his route. He looked at the tangled criss-cross of branches lit up by the fiery glow of the evening sun, which gave the appearance of a hundred burning eyes watching him. Wistow Hall was not far, or so he kept telling himself. But rather than mount up, he paused out of sheer fatigue. The cannons, gunshot and pounding hooves that had incessantly rang in his ears were now banished by bird song; a few glorious chirps silenced his mind for just a moment. A soft breeze wafted the sweet scent of the undergrowth. It had been enlivened by the rain, droplets of which were left studding leaves like quicksilver, and this neutralised the pungent remains of gunpowder. Maxwell was alive. He had survived.

"You smell that?" He asked as his horse lifted its head and snorted.

However, the faint noise of hooves soon began to return to Maxwell's hearing. A soft repetition started to build within his mind, relentlessly creeping up on him once more, and he cursed the way that battles would haunt him. He didn't know if he could cope with it any longer, nor whether it would drive him insane, for in the past such trauma had always been eased by his beloved Catherine. Now every single day without her was a battle in itself. He cursed himself for being weak. Lonely. Self-absorbed.

In his battered state he tried to block all else out by covering both ears, and although the sound abated a little, something deep inside prompted him to remove his hands. He held his breath and listened. The hoof-falls were like a heartbeat. He felt connected to the woodland floor and could have been mistaken for thinking he had sensed the faintest of tremors. Then his mare adjusted her footing. Maxwell squeezed his eyes closed; the sound was real and there were, indeed, horsemen getting closer by the second.

"In the name of Christ!"

He led his horse off the road and down an incline, tethered her to a tree and then hurried some distance from it. Crouching behind an oak, whose cracked bark was like a dragon's scaly skin, he loaded his carbine and wound the wheel lock. The nearing riders caused a rustle from the leafy canopies overhead as birds fled, yet Maxwell had no option but to stay deathly still, coming to the certainty that there were only two horses. At this moment, he wished he was back on the field of Naseby, where he at least had his comrades for support.

Praise the Lord! Maxwell looked up to feel the pitter-patter of another rain shower, which seemed to bring the entire forest to life. Their leaves tremored and rustled from a calm breeze as if heralding the visitors. Two cavalrymen, one with an orange sash, rode by. The raindrops played out a tune on Maxwell's ribbed helmet as he watched the troopers continue along the route and towards the end of the forest. They slowed, however, just before vanishing. It was as if the trees had united and closed behind the pair like a phalanx of pikeman and Maxwell hurried across the cushioned undergrowth to catch a glimpse of where they were headed. The woodland opened onto a field full of vibrant grass, which he soon heard the horses munching at while the two men talked. They had stopped to rest. Maxwell hid behind a sturdy oak and peered through the foliage, holding his carbine to his chest like a baby and protecting the gun from any droplets of rain.

"It cannot be far now."

"Aye, but we must search yonder houses first, for the King and his scurrying rats will hide in any hole they can."

"Surely he would never consider anything less than Wistow?'

"Perhaps, but let us be vigilant. Even if we don't find the King, there may still be ale to be had, amongst other things." One of the duo chortled.

"Good thinking, sir, we can grab the best of it before the others catch us up."

"Aye, you know how the captain likes his food!"

The smell of tobacco wafted through the trees like an apparition that had been sent to stalk Maxwell. The men drew the contents of their pipe bowls, eager to partake of whatever delights the few nearby houses could offer, whether to satisfy their bellies, or their codpieces. Soon enough they were on their way, and Maxwell watched them approach a fork in the road and head off towards the scattering of houses in the distance. He cursed the pair, wishing that he could have cut their throats and rammed their pipes down them, for it was men such as this, lusting after plunder, who had raided his home with Gervase Harper at their head. After giving them a little more time to get out of sight, he mounted up and hammered towards Wistow, the silhouette of which he could now see in the distance against the dying horizon. What didn't register in his mind until he was approaching the hall, was the two men's talk of their comrades who were not far behind them. Maxwell would have to be fast.

***

The night had drawn in cold. After that morning's battle, it was as if the chill of Naseby's killing field was spreading across the countryside in dire warning. Even Wistow's seven windows and their multitude of twinkling panes, lit up by glowing candlelight, gave Maxwell little warmth. He knew just how much the place was at risk and instead of offering respite, the proud, new hall was little more than a grand target; a large bloom upon which a swarm of rebels would soon land.

Maxwell rode up to the red-bricked house, stumbled down from his horse and then tethered her. He took his pistols, rapped upon the door – as much to wake up himself as well as the inhabitants – and made sure to hold the guns out of sight. Eventually an old man appeared, whose piercing eyes examined Maxwell from beneath sagging lids, while a white moustache struggled to hold back the deep lines at either side of his mouth.

"Can I help you, sir?"

"I come with urgent business for Sir Richard Halford."

"Sir Richard isn't expecting anyone at this hour," he replied and would have closed the door, had Maxwell not jammed his foot in it.

"Rouse him! This is the King's business," Maxwell demanded, pushing it open and stepping inside.

"Really, I cannot believe that His Majesty would send anyone with such poor manners!"

"If poor manners are all that worry you, then save your remonstrances for the Roundheads who will be here tomorrow. Now, pray wake your master," Maxwell insisted.

"And more firepower than a frigate, I see?"

REBELLION

The footman eyed each of Maxwell's guns. His sallow cheeks puffed with outrage, yet he slowly headed towards the wide, wooden staircase, where two carved lions glared from the balustrades at the demanding interloper. At the top of the stairs the glow of the man's candle picked out a full-length portrait of King Charles, who looked into the distance as if haunted by the momentous events that were tearing his kingdom apart. The fashionable Wistow Hall was barely twenty-four years old. The King had reigned for twenty of them. Such a short timescale in which so much had changed. The one certainty of this civil war was that life was never going to be the same again, no matter how the conflict ended.

As he waited in the wan light, Maxwell paced to the table and prodded the thick Turkey-work carpet upon it. The colours were bright and extraordinary in spite of the darkness. Above him a white plasterwork ceiling was picked out by the flickering glow and its array of patterned squares, each adorned with decorative flourishes and fruits, was like a large, heavenly cloud. The charred remains of wood in the fireplace coughed up the odd wisp of smoke and gave one last crack as the night took hold. The ravaging fire had burned itself out after consuming all that was available in the grate. Maxwell prayed that this war would also go the same way before it reached his two boys, Thomas and Christopher, who were tucked away in deepest Yorkshire with their Aunt. Catherine's sister could offer them the stability they needed, and the motherly love that had been stolen from them; in fact, it was love that Maxwell wasn't capable of right now, and his heart had hardened in a bid to protect what was left of it.

Once Gervase Harper was dead and hostilities over, only then could Maxwell attempt to come to terms with his loss. But right now, the woodsmoke took him back to that last evening with Catherine, when he had thrown her coif covering to the corner of the bedroom and then playfully tangled his finger around her blond curls. As he had kissed her lips, the entire room – nay the house itself – had fallen away and they had been at one with each other. Not a care in the world. They had whispered their love as if they had still been a courting couple and not eight years into their marriage; the blacksmith and his wife had forged such a happy life together. She was the most beautiful woman he'd ever set his eyes upon.

"What the devil d'you think you're playing at, sir?"

"Sir Richard?" Maxwell turned and gave a deep sigh.

"Aye, an' who be you?"

"Captain Maxwell Walker, of Sir Marmaduke Langdale's cavalry, sir. Sent on behalf of His Majesty."

"You've no right to come bursting into my home no matter who sent you!" Clearly Sir Richard's blood was up. The footman led his master closer, holding up a candle in a bid to illuminate Maxwell's features.

"Spare your anger for the rebels. We are both of the same side in this conflict and I am only here to collect the King's possessions," Maxwell said, and held up his hand. He had little time or patience to listen to the whimsical rantings of a baronet.

"We have nothing of His Majesty's here."

"Please, Sir Richard." Maxwell took a deep breath. "I implore you to let me return the items before it's too late. I *narrowly* escaped two enemy cavalrymen on the way here. Their comrades are not far behind them and they are coming to Wistow."

"How do I know what you say is true?" Sir Richard replied and then a loud knock came at the door.

"You must assure me that the items of which I speak are well hidden," Maxwell whispered, and locked eyes with Sir Richard. "That could be the enemy I speak of." He held both of his pistols close.

"Have our valuables hidden," Sir Richard quietly ordered the footman and then hesitated. He glanced once more at Maxwell's determined expression and in that moment an unspoken solidarity seemed to take hold. "Stand by with those guns of yours."

"Go," Maxwell said, and moved to the side where he would be out of sight.

Sir Richard opened the door.

"Pray excuse this late visitation, but I must speak with Sir Richard Halford on a matter of great importance," the visitor explained.

"I am he."

"My master was one of your most recent guests. He has left one or two items here and wishes to have them returned to him most urgently. I hope, sir, that you may assist me and then I shall be on my way?"

Sir Richard stammered. "Your name, if you please?"

"John Lynch, at your service, sir. I have this note, which will verify all that I say."

It took Sir Richard barely a few seconds to glance at the piece of paper before he hastily handed it back to the man. "I'm afraid you are mistaken. There is nothing that any guest has left here."

"Are you not a loyal subject of His Majesty?" Lynch whispered. "My humble apologies, but I cannot leave without what I crave."

"Who are you?" Maxwell stepped forward and poked a pistol at Lynch. "Get back, Sir Richard!"

"By God, sir, I would ask you the same question!" Lynch held up his hands. "Sir Richard is not your hound to be barked at in such a manner."

"My name does not matter. Now, give me that paper," Maxwell snapped, "or I will blast you back to your master, whomsoever he may be."

"Enough!" Sir Richard intervened. "I will not have any bloodshed in my house."

"I am not one to tell falsehoods," Lynch glared at Maxwell. "I have already stated my case."

Maxwell took the note from Lynch and read it. Sure enough, it corroborated the man's words, but crucially, it was signed by one of the two Secretaries of State, Lord George Digby. Maxwell cursed. Nobody, not least the King, could afford any such delays to his business. This whole task was turning out to be a fool's errand and one which was wasting his time.

"Now, who the devil are you?" Lynch asked again.

"Get inside," Maxwell ordered, "before it's too late."

Lynch removed his felt hat as he stepped into the hall, and his stiffened leather boots clinked across the black and white tiles. He stopped and faced Maxwell who finally gave his name and shared the details of his task.

"Then we are both here for the same reason," Lynch shook his head and turned to Sir Richard. "I trust you can assist me now, and we can let Captain Maxwell get back to his soldiers."

"With respect, I would like to see the King's possessions handed over, and then partake of an hour's rest," Maxwell said. "I'll be gone long before dawn."

"I shall see to this royal matter, sir. I suggest you return to the army, for you have a lot to make up for after today's performance," Lynch replied.

"You are lucky, John Lynch, for if I wasn't too tired, I'd break that jaw of yours for spouting such an insult," Maxwell said and then turned to Sir Richard. "By your leave, I will rest a while in front of the fire."

Maxwell sat on a chair and removed his boots with a grunt of satisfaction, followed by his buff coat and carbine. Then he took the Turkey-work carpet, placed it on the floor beside the fireplace and lay down upon it, thinking of Catherine. In spite of his desire to reconnect with the memories that had earlier filled his mind, Maxwell was almost immediately lost to a deep slumber. So deep that time held no sway upon it.

Chapter Three

Early Hours. 15th June 1645.

A loud bang broke Maxwell's respite. In an instant the noise snatched him away from the world of his dreams and he jumped to his feet. He left his buff coat and boots and in his woollen stockings, crept quietly through the hall. The flickering candlelight almost disguised some faint movement to Maxwell's left, and a groan made him spin around and aim his pistol, only to find John Lynch, who was sat asleep at a table with his head in his arms. Voices murmured from a doorway up ahead, which upon approach, Maxwell found to be Sir Richard Halford and his footman. He watched through the crack of the door as the men placed a small, velvet bag into a square void in the wainscoting that covered the walls and then secured the particular wooden panel back into place.

"Best that gold remains here until Mister Lynch is ready to leave," Sir Richard said.

"Very wise, sir."

"Now, place the King's papers below the floorboard in my bedroom, for those are the most valuable items."

Maxwell returned to where he had slept and got dressed. The time had come to leave, for he felt rested and had no wish to be any further associated with Lynch or his task. The man's haughty manner was just the type that Maxwell couldn't abide, and this mere scribbling secretary had little appreciation of the true dangers of this conflict. Perhaps, if he continued to sleep, Lynch might just get his first taste of war at the hands of the parliamentarians who would, no doubt, be here soon enough.

"You are leaving?" the footman asked as he walked into the hall.

"Yes, if you could open the door?"

"Of course." The servant smiled as if he'd not forgotten, nor forgiven, the manner of Maxwell's arrival, and was only too pleased to see the back of him.

Upon stepping outside and being released from the stuffiness of Wistow Hall, the cool air soothed Maxwell's face as he looked east. The shadowy, grey expanse of meadows led to a horizon of silhouetted trees where black dots of birds darted in search of an early morsel; the only signs of life it seemed, for their song was the sole noise to be heard. To the south-east, upon slightly higher ground, was a village cluster of ten houses, and in the southern distance, a windmill waited to be resuscitated. The crack of orange that broke open the sky made ready to bring the world back to life and Maxwell mounted up, hoping to be well on his way before the labourers began trudging towards the fields. He set off due south, towards Saint Wistan's Church, aiming to avoid the main road.

As he drew closer to the church, however, he spotted two black horses standing out against the ironstone tower. One of them brayed a mocking laugh that seemed to cast scorn on Maxwell's assumption of being the only one up and about at this hour. He dismounted, tied his mare to a tree and carefully approached the church, from where he heard a crash and an exchange of voices. The door was open. He moved slowly, so as not to unnerve the horses.

"Where is Saint Wistan, your Prince of Mercia?" a man yelled. "I don't see his hair growing through the ground where he was murdered, or is that another Catholic lie?"

"This is no Catholic church!"

"Perhaps we should scalp you, bury your hair and turn you into a new Saint Wistan." The man let out a deep guffaw.

"Please, not the communion table!"

REBELLION

There came a crash of breaking wood.

"Why are you so sad, priest? Destroying it will bring your congregation closer to the Almighty."

"I am no priest. I am the vicar, Robert Fryer, and have been so these past eight and twenty years."

"A Popish altar, instigated by a Popish Archbishop of Canterbury, who you have worshipped more than God himself," the man cried. "And that window …"

A prayer book smashed through the stained glass and, after fluttering through the air, it landed in the graveyard with a thump. Shards of glass rained down around Maxwell as he headed to the doorway with his pistols, and from where he saw two parliamentarians in their armour. One used his sword against the face of a statue, while the other flung books at the old vicar and then shoved him backwards and against a tomb. The clergyman's black square hat fell from his head, while his white cassock and puffed sleeves seemed to cocoon the old man as he collapsed. The sight enraged Maxwell, who marched into the church.

"I think you might wish to worship my two guns," Maxwell shouted "Now, kneel before them!"

"Who in God's name are you?" the officer asked with a start.

"I said on your knees!" Maxwell insisted and moved closer.

"To hell with you," The other soldier replied and went to shoot.

Maxwell fired without hesitation. The soldier fell backwards and sprawled across a pew, while a streak of his crimson blood splashed across the officer's orange sash.

"Drop your weapon, or you're next." Maxwell came on relentlessly, taking aim with his other pistol.

"Whatever you say." The officer dropped his blade.

"At least your scarf is now a nice shade of royalist red," Maxwell said with a sarcastic smile.

"Damn you, cavalier."

"If you condemn me for fighting for my King and the laws, then yes, you're correct. Now, tell me where the rest of your men are," Maxwell demanded, and it was only now that he recognised the pair as the men that had passed him in the woods last night.

"You are damned, and not just for your murder of this man. The gunshot will have alerted my colleagues. We, who fight to break free from the bindings of your tyrannical King."

"Where are these other rebels? I'll give you ten seconds to tell me."

"You have no time to give. They will be on their way here at the sound of your pistol."

"Tell me, or to hell with you!" Maxwell hesitated over what to do next.

"Shoot him," the vicar wheezed. "Do it now, otherwise he'll bear witness against you."

Maxwell, shocked that the clergyman was alive, knew that he spoke cold common sense. The enemy troops would no doubt be up and to arms now. He had no choice. When Maxwell squeezed the second trigger that morning, he did so with a deep sense of foreboding, stemming not only from his own perilous position, but due to the fact that he had to consider killing this man before actually doing it. He had calculatingly come to the decision to end the life of another. There was no mask of impulse here. That briefest of pauses had stripped away all excuses and left him looking into the face of a fellow Human Being, whose spirit was soon condemned to mingle with the smoke of Maxwell's gun and dissipate into nothing. Perhaps Maxwell was no better than Gervase Harper.

"Now, give me the guns," the vicar moaned.

Maxwell ignored him and ran to the door, but the vicar continued his weak protests and explained that very soon he really would be beyond the enemy's grasp forever.

REBELLION

"You're wounded?" Maxwell asked.

"My heart. The Lord will shortly take me." He placed a hand to his chest and winced. "The guns, for then it will appear as if I shot them."

"My wife, my dear wife ..." Maxwell shook his head and tears began to well up in his eyes. He looked down at the eighteen-inch barrels and the revulsion that swept over him encouraged his obeyance of the vicar. He knelt down and pushed them into the man's grasping hands.

"Your action ... sprung from an honest heart," Reverend Fryer closed his eyes and struggled for breath. "Think on that."

Maxwell felt the need to speak but could not find the words to say; whether to thank the man, to ask for forgiveness, or seek some final blessing which was clearly beyond Fryer to give. The vicar's emaciated skin was sucked into the contours and voids of his skull. Yet in Fryer's sunken eyes, Maxwell saw contentment. They glistened with all that needed to be said. Reassurance. Love. Peace.

Maxwell hurried out of the church and mounted his horse beneath a glorious dawn. He hammered back up to the house. Quite why he had returned to Wistow Hall was beyond him, and, indeed, he could barely think straight right now. He rapped on the door, calling for Sir Richard Halford.

"You?" The footman opened it.

"They are here. The vicar is dead!"

"Not blessed Master Fryer?" the old man seemed most upset and let Maxwell inside.

"Captain Walker!" John Lynch barked in an accusatory tone. "I heard gunshots."

"The rebels are nearby," Maxwell explained, and then accompanied Lynch, who went outside to look across the meadows. Sure enough, they could see horsemen in the distance.

"The King's items," Lynch hissed.

"What in God's name has happened?" Sir Richard Halford hurried over. "Is the vicar dead?"

Maxwell explained that he had shot two cavalrymen who were desecrating the church and assaulting Robert Fryer, news of which provoked only a slow nod from Sir Richard.

"You must both take off your military attire and change into servant's coats. You are now nothing but stable hands who came here from another estate," Sir Richard called for Peter Irwin, the head groom.

"I need to leave with His Majesty's possessions." Lynch demanded to know where they were.

"If you leave now you will be taken and they will fall into enemy hands," Sir Richard warned.

As Peter Irwin quickly led Maxwell and Lynch away, along with their horses, an unsettling quiet descended over Wistow Hall as its inhabitants prepared for what the day ahead had in store. The windows were left shuttered, Sir Richard remained in his nightshirt and cap, while Peter had his two attendants muck out the horses to get their hands and clothes dirty with the grime of their newfound trade. Meanwhile, the three bodies that lay in the church were covered in golden shafts of morning light. The Almighty had their souls borne to heaven, leaving the carcasses to be discovered by a handful of wary parliamentarians who hurried inside. In their wake, the graveyard's grass was stroked by a calm breeze which lapped it against the gravestones. The two black horses looked on in wonderment.

***

Maxwell attacked the piles of dung with his spade and furiously scraped it across the stone slabs of the floor. The intermittent grating rang throughout the stables as he heaped more dirt onto the rest, for within the pile was his carbine, wrapped in a shroud and buried, but ready to be resurrected at a moment's notice. After leaving the church strewn with bodies, cleaning up this mess seemed to help focus Maxwell's troubled mind, which from necessity blocked out the morning's events. The noise rang in his ears. Even the memories of Naseby had been rendered silent. He could not help but wonder how he had gone from cutting down the enemy one day, to shifting dung the next. In battle he was protecting his family by championing the King and his lawful government. His fight was an honourable one. But now he struggled to understand his purpose here and he'd lost more than enough already without losing that. He was adrift in Leicestershire, while a creeping tide of parliamentarians cut him off from his comrades, and all for some trinket or other that the King had left behind in this grand house.

This had all better be worth it, he thought as he cast more shovelfuls with a grunt and a hiss. Until, that is, a hand grasped his arm. He recoiled.

"Not so viciously," Peter Irwin, the head groom, counselled.

Maxwell paused and then grasped the shaft of the spade by the neck and stood it upright. He remained silent, wiping the irritating sweat beads that were running down his forehead, while his heart thumped out a peculiar rhythm; one which had begun intermittently since Catherine's death, as if it struggled to function properly without her. He laid the spade against the wall.

"It will arouse suspicion," Peter explained, as if searching for a response.

"Come and eat, lass." Maxwell grabbed a handful of hay and fed it to his black mare, who snorted her thanks. Hers was the only interaction that mattered. The girl had braved the horrors with him and been his only companion all the way to Wistow Hall. His large hands patted her in gentle reassurance and stroked her coat, which was so black that it shimmered with a blue edge in certain lights, like the feathers of a crow. He certainly wished he could fly away on her right now. Something was fundamentally wrong with simply waiting for the enemy to seek him out and to make no effort to either evade or fight them. His trembling fingers stroked the black mane but stopped as quickly as he had started.

"Where you from?" Peter persisted, though he did not look up from brushing the horse next to Maxwell. Indeed, he seemed to be attempting to untangle the complex stranger in a similar way to how he coaxed any new horse. "Somewhere north, I'd wager?"

A hiss and some steam took Maxwell's attention as a newly made horseshoe was thrust into some water. As the noise fizzled out it was rapidly replaced by the clatter of horses' hooves, which drew nearer. Maxwell's hunters were approaching.

"You have a trade?"

"Aye, blacksmith." Maxwell sniffed and wiped his forehead, but Peter seized his arm. "What in God's name …"

"What's this?" Peter looked at a wound on Maxwell's upper arm.

"Soldiers occasionally get them."

"Precisely! Now, roll down your sleeves," Peter insisted with an urgency that was at odds with his patient and friendly character. "Quickly."

Gruff voices yelled from outside. The clank of swords, snorts of horses and footsteps led to a repeated thudding on the door to the hall. They shouted out for entry. Threatened to break it down. Next, some soldiers burst into the stables dressed like the two Maxwell had killed, and it was as if their ghosts had led their colleagues to him in a bid to secure retribution. Four soldiers in all marched briskly inside. The leading man had his visor raised and the triple bars pointed accusingly, whereupon Peter stepped forward.

"Will you need your horses seeing to, sirs?"

REBELLION

"You will not leave this stable until Colonel Hopkins has spoken to you all!" the corporal barked, before directing two of his men to take up sentry outside.

"You are from General Fairfax?" Peter asked.

"Silence! What's your name?"

"Peter Irwin, Sir Richard's head groom."

Maxwell watched Peter closely. The man's rather high, arched eyebrows gave him an interested look in whatever was said; a natural expression that also masked most of his actual emotions. Peter was a calm and collected individual with a sixth sense, or so it seemed, that gave him an ability to judge people well. His oval face was exacerbated by a long chin, though any ribaldry of this would, no doubt, be countered by his tall, muscular frame.

"This whole place reeks of cavaliers!" The corporal began pacing the length of the stables, with cursory glances here and there, as though he'd soon find a couple of royalists crawling around in the joints and rafters or scuttling to the corners. "Your old clergyman probably spouted as much Popish shit as this." He spat out a globule of phlegm and pointed at the dung heap as if the very mention of Reverend Fryer had left a sour taste in his mouth. "Murdered two godly men of our troop this morning, he did."

"An old clergyman ..." Peter paused.

"An old man with two damned pistols, I hasten to add. But the Almighty hath cast him to hell for his sins."

Maxwell glanced at Peter. The man avoided all eye contact, but in the fraction of a second's pause, it was clear he realised the truth about this shooting.

"Didn't you hear the shots?" the officer raised an eyebrow.

"With cleaning up all of this," Peter replied and gestured to the heap of manure, "and the noise of old George clobbering his horseshoes out?"

MARK TURNBULL

The officer glared at George and the hammer he held. "Hardly the mighty Thor, is he?" He laughed at the bedraggled old blacksmith and then left, demanding that they all wait.

At the brazier, George thrust a horseshoe into the nest of flames and the embers that enveloped it, and then started sorting through his tools. Peter began brushing the horse again in a series of methodical sweeps. While Maxwell observed all of this a mixture of guilt, grief and hopelessness came over him.

"I always said that Reverend Fryer had a ruthless streak," Peter called out. "What say you, George?"

"Ruthless? I ..." Maxwell shook his head.

"George?" Peter shouted again. "Fryer once threatened to whip you, did he not?"

"Aye," George replied. A man of few words.

"Church is haunted, too," Peter continued and then glanced at Maxwell. "Are you going to do any more work today?"

Maxwell made brief eye contact with Peter. He was struck by the man's tenacity and dogged determination – almost shamed by it – and he nodded his thanks. George began pounding the red horseshoe and the dull clangs reverberated through Maxwell's body, a familiar noise that in days of peace had been as regular as his own heartbeat. It took him back to his hometown of Selby and the warmth of his forge; warm not just due to the crackling fire, but also from the joyful noise of his family. Young Thomas and Christopher would be regular visitors on cold winter days, making mischief with the tools – much to his chagrin – admiring the weapons he had made and playing out their own game of knights with wooden swords. He'd even started to instruct Tom before war had intervened. George's hammering began to sound more like ghostly chimes as Maxwell realised that in his grief, he'd excluded his sons, the people who needed him the most. Closeted in his private sorrow, he had dwelt upon the loss of his beloved wife, and not given any consideration to Tom and Kit's feelings, nor the fact that his beautiful, witty and kind wife was also their mother. Their world. Instead, he had removed himself from their existence and offered little comfort, save for the irregular sums of money that he could send back. He earned two pounds, twelve shillings and six pence per week – often backdated – and even then, given in random lump sums whenever occasion and the paymaster permitted.

"Right, lads, let's have you all into the house now," a corporal demanded from the doorway.

Maxwell had forgotten about John Lynch, who put down a broom and joined the line of stable hands and the smithy. They were led outside and into Wistow Hall like new soldierly recruits. Peter was prevented from removing his boots and their collective footsteps echoed across the hallway, watched by the beady eye of the old servant in the corner, and then into the study.

"Over there." Colonel Hopkins directed the six men to the far wall where they were quickly flanked by two soldiers.

Maxwell watched as the colonel stood behind a wooden chair and rested his hands on the back of it. The backrest was divided into four panels; each inlaid with a flower that more resembled inquisitive eyes, amidst a cross, the ends of which curled like flaring nostrils.

"These are the stable lads and the smithy, sir."

"Right, I want your names, ages and how long you've worked here," Colonel Hopkins ordered, his brisk tone belying an orderly man. He sat down at the table, picked up a freshly cut quill and briefly pointed the end at old George. "We'll start with you."

"George Oswin, sir, but I know not my years."

"Have you no idea at all?" The Colonel sighed.

"My blessed mother once told me I was born not long after the great storm that burst the river."

"Ah, then you are near enough sixty years, just like the old servant," Colonel Hopkins neatly inscribed the figure beside George's name.

"Length of time here?"

"Born, bred and will die here."

"I mean length of time employed by the Halfords," the Colonel waited and then after further delay, looked up. "Speak, man!"

"I am but a humble smith ..." he faltered.

"Oh, come and make your mark," Hopkins waved him closer.

George moved to the desk. He attempted to master the quill pen, a cut and trimmed goose feather, and accidently brushed some papers from the desk.

"Retrieve them!" The Colonel demanded and pointed at Maxwell.

While crouching down and gathering the papers up, Maxwell noticed a flowing signature of Thomas Fairfax, the General of Parliament's New Model Army. As he retrieved the last two, he noted that Fairfax had dated it this morning from Kibworth, a few miles south of Wistow. He guessed they might be headed for Leicester, a town which the royalists had only just captured in a bid to lure the parliamentarians to battle. If only he could read these letters and discover the intelligence they contained; enough, perhaps, to stem the misfortune of Naseby? No sooner had he placed them on the desk and stepped back into line, than it was his turn.

"Name and age?"

"Andrew Walker, sir. Thirty years."

"Length of time here?"

"Arrived five days ago, sir. I'm a blacksmith ..."

"Five days? Where from?"

REBELLION

"Sir William Saville's estate in Yorkshire. He was killed last year and since then many of us have lost our employment. Sir Richard kindly stepped in, for he knew my late master well. I'm to replace that old man," Maxwell pointed at George and recounted the facts Sir Richard had given him.

"I see," the colonel replied and looked Maxwell up and down. "Then you will be able to shoe my horse."

"Of course. I shall see to it after you have finished with us."

"Sir Richard should have letters of recommendation about you." Colonel Hopkins frowned. "Inform the good baronet that I would like to speak with him afterwards," he instructed a soldier.

The colonel continued watching Maxwell. The man's thick black eyebrows added a certain menace to his expression, and his very short hair gave Maxwell nothing else to focus on but his piercing eyes.

"Was that all you wished to ask me, sir?" Maxwell enquired.

Perhaps it had been foolish to remain here he wondered. Though that judgement was based upon him actually having had a choice in the matter.

"Yes," the colonel replied with a deep inhalation and turned to the next man.

"Peter Irwin, sir. Twenty-five years of age."

The soldiers would soon be on their way and then Maxwell could be on his – but General Fairfax's letter, perchance, may contain some very useful scribblings to take along with him. Writing that may just help nudge his commander, Sir Marmaduke Langdale, into seeing what could be done about his arrears of pay, which was as much as he could do to help his boys right now.

***

They had stood before the Colonel for what felt like hours as if they had been nothing more than half a dozen criminals. The scratching of the man's quill had recorded every detail of their responses. It had been the only noise to fill the silence between questions and answers, except when the Colonel had intermittently dipped it and then meticulously wiped the end against the inkwell to make sure the flow was just right. A meticulousness that made Maxwell wary. When Hopkins had finished with John Lynch, who had given over his claim to have arrived with Maxwell from the same Yorkshire landowner, he had ordered them all to be confined to the stables again, penned in there like they were nothing more than animals themselves. It was after half an hour that a knock came at the stable door. The bolts were slid back with a ringing noise and a soldier filled the doorframe.

"Walker?"

Maxwell wiped his hands and headed towards the man, whereupon he was escorted back into Wistow Hall.

"Colonel wants to see you. Wait here," the soldier ordered.

Maxwell's gaze went to the crest on the opposite wall in a bid to distract his troubled mind, which churned over why he'd been summoned again. He looked at the luscious curlicues that flourished around the Halford coat of arms like climbing ivy. In the centre, a lean, black greyhound stood poised for action. Above were three fleur-de-lises, topped by the head of another greyhound with a helmet beside it, as if the dog had just removed it in sheer defiance.

"You will deliver up every blade and gun, or any other such other weapons to my captain, Sir Richard. I am a very fair and reasonable man, yet you have crossed me."

From within the study, the colonel's voice was resolute.

"Even my hunting spear?" Sir Richard asked.

"Everything!"

"Of course, colonel."

"Now, I will ask you one last time. Are you foolishly secreting any more weapons around this house?"

REBELLION

"It was merely an oversight, I assure you."

"Your misguided royalist sympathies are well known …" Hopkins paused, as if he was a judge preparing to pass sentence. "I have a mind to tear this house apart in front of your eyes."

"There are no more arms about the place," Sir Richard assured.

"It's gone beyond that. There is the matter of gold and silver coin, which you also claim is scant to be had, though I am now sceptical of all you say."

"Truly, all I own is already in your possession."

"I am not so sure of that. One thing I will need is your deer," the colonel added.

"Of course."

"My men will be here for some weeks; therefore, we must have sufficient food, and the hides can be turned into buff coats. Nothing will be wasted."

The voices went quiet. Maxwell's heart sank upon the news that these soldiers would be here some time, as well as the threat of the house being searched. The door then opened and Sir Richard Halford stepped into the hall, before closing it again behind him. Maxwell quickly glanced to the main entrance to check that the door was closed and then turned back to Sir Richard, who was brushing his lace collar into place. The man's round chin was lost amidst his rather bulging neck; an appropriate echo of how isolated the baronet seemed right now.

"Sir Richard, may I speak to you about George?"

"Perhaps later."

"He's asked that I turn out nails to repair the fences, but surely I should focus my attention on the hall itself?" Maxwell continued regardless, and then signalled to Halford. "This loose candle mount is a risk." He led Halford towards the far wall.

"Yes, you are correct. See to it."

"I shall see to all threats this house faces. Pray remember my reason for being here, which drives my every action," Maxwell whispered.

Sir Richard stepped back, paused, and then walked away. Maxwell returned to his place outside of the door and wasn't there long before the colonel opened it.

"Come inside."

He followed Colonel Hopkins into what had become the man's oak-panelled headquarters. On the desk was an iron chest, its open lid and the intricate locking mechanism on the underside resembling a gaping mouth full of worms. Whatever military secrets it had consumed, they were consigned to remain there when Hopkins closed it with a bang and then turned the key in the top.

"Andrew Walker."

"Yes, sir?"

"Now that Sir Richard has satisfied me of your origins, I require you to work both day and night for me. I have horses that require shoes as well as arms and armour that need urgent repairs. You will begin immediately." Colonel Hopkins threw a log onto the fire and crushed the charred remains of the last ones beneath it.

"It will be an honour to assist you and your cause," Maxwell replied and nodded his head.

"You move from one royalist estate to another, yet you say such a thing? Do you take me for a fool by paying such fraudulent lip service to Parliament's Godly cause?"

"No, sir. Though they be mere words, I speak the truth," Maxwell replied. "My late master was ruthless with and oftentimes denied us our wage. There were occasions when I was without means to secure food and left to scavenge the very oats from his precious barbary stallions." He paused and looked at Hopkins in silence.

"I see." Hopkins said no more than that, but his black eyebrows rose along with the lines of his weathered brow.

REBELLION

"I can prove where my heart lies in this quarrel," Maxwell stepped forward, making Colonel Hopkins sit up straight. "I know the whereabouts of something that might greatly interest you."

"Is that so?" Hopkins folded his arms, the blue sleeves of which were decorated with rings of gold embroidery. The sparkling strands winked at Maxwell as if encouraging him to continue. The rain then started up again and rattled against the window as though the entire kingdom was shedding tears over the bloodshed that was tearing it apart. To some men their allegiance was as changing as the weather, but to others it ran through their very veins, and only the emptying of them would put a stop to such loyalty.

"I have not been at Wistow long, but 'tis enough time to know that Sir Richard is no different from my last master."

"What is it that will be of great interest to me?" Hopkins asked.

"I have seen where the squirrel doth hide his nuts; inside the oak of this room itself," Maxwell whispered.

"God knows what strange language you use in Yorkshire. Speak plainly, man!" Colonel Hopkins barked.

"Then may I ask for your protection? What I have to say will jeopardise my employment here."

Colonel Hopkins stood and his face flushed. "You must first prove worthy of my protection."

"In the wall, sir, I have seen Sir Richard open a secret panel many a time and will wager all of his hidden valuables are in it." Maxwell pointed at the chequered squares of panelling.

Colonel Hopkins walked over to the wall, his leather soles clipping against the wooden floor. "I knew he had something left to hide!"

Maxwell followed, all too aware of the colonel's piercing eyes that watched his every move. He recalled what he had seen last night and the position in which Sir Richard had stood. He lined himself up with the window.

Colonel Hopkins remained deathly silent. Maxwell placed his hand upon the first panel along and knocked upon it. A dull thud. The next one to the right echoed upon his knuckles and he stepped back.

"That's the one."

"Right," Colonel Hopkins took a long fireiron and began thumping the handle into the segment. The spherical cap soon battered a hole through it and then the colonel ferociously bashed the corners until he was able to get at the contents. He panted as he shoved his hand inside the small void and felt around. As he withdrew a small velvet bag, gripping it by the neck like a dead bird, the door opened, and a concerned soldier entered.

"Is everything ok, sir, I heard noises?"

"Aye, perfectly," the colonel barely looked at them, but instead pulled the top of the bag open and tipped it upside down.

Sir Richard Halford appeared at the door. His eyes burned, lips pursed, and deep creases appeared between his eyebrows. He seemed to fight an internal battle as golden coins dropped onto the table with delicate chimes and tinkled when some settled on top of one another. They lay in a pile upon the desk, like Adamites in all of their naked glory.

"As Master Walker said to me earlier, a squirrel has certainly been hiding some very precious nuts." Colonel Hopkins grinned. "Had these slipped your mind when you gave me your earlier assurances, Sir Richard?"

The baronet stuttered. He looked at Maxwell and then to the colonel. "You traitor!"

"Is that aimed at me, or Master Maxwell?" Colonel Hopkins asked.

"No, sir, at the blacksmith!"

"You will have no need to steal your horses' oats again," Colonel Hopkins took a gold coin and handed it to Maxwell.

REBELLION

"I am sincerely grateful." Maxwell looked down at the hammered coin; a triple-unite of three pounds, and from its marks, minted at the royalist headquarters in Oxford.

"Thirty pieces of silver would have been a more apt gift," Sir Richard growled. "He has no place in my household any longer."

"A wise decision. For he is now in my employ and I need a smithy more than you," Hopkins said and turned to Maxwell.

The rain played on the multitude of small panes like marching drums, while the fire cracked and spat as it consumed its log. The flames danced ever higher. Maxwell nodded his agreement to the colonel's offer. If he did end up making horseshoes for the parliamentarian army, he had no intention of finishing many, for he would be away from here at the first opportunity. Maxwell failed to notice John Lynch appear at the doorway, his teeth gritted and nostrils flaring like one of the stabled horses.

Chapter Four

Three days later, Maxwell sat in a rickety pew. It seemed old enough to have witnessed the last building project at Saint Wistan's, when the west tower was added two hundred years ago. Certainly, it prevented tiredness from overcoming him as he sat uneasily while an army preacher, Hugh Peters, extolled a fiery sermon. The Cornishman's accent and passionate speech were occasionally too strained for Maxwell to understand, even if he had wanted to. Maxwell was no believer in the defeatist Puritan idea that God had already decided who would be damned and who saved – he was firm of the opinion that people earned God's grace through good work, respect and faith.

"O Lord, rebuke me not in thy wrath." Peters pointed at the congregation. "Neither chasten me in thy hot displeasure."

Even the church struggled to retain Peters' words, nor did it amplify them, for the roof was holed and the walls damp, and made even more so by the dog that now urinated against one. The musty smell of the building's rotting carcass – decomposing like one of the bodies in its churchyard – hung in Maxwell's chest.

"I am troubled. I am bowed down greatly. I go mourning all the day long," Peters extolled Psalm thirty-eight.

In the corner the wooden altar rail lay in a heap. Its balustrades resembled a pile of bones and the rail, with its carvings, no longer hemmed the communion table in to the east end of the chancel. The table was free. Soldiers had dragged it into the middle of the church like a dead buck and put it back on show for everyone to see. No more was

REBELLION

God separated from his flock by such woodwork, nor any clergyman who claimed to act as some sort intermediary; a direct link to the Almighty had been re-established. The Book of Common Prayer was nowhere to be seen, statues of Christ had been mutilated and the windows smashed. Green tints of mould crept across the wall like insects come to feast upon the helpless church, which without incumbent or adornment, was left defenceless to everything, especially the Puritan minority.

"I am feeble and sore broke; I have roared by reason of the disquietness of my heart."

Peters could almost have been talking about the church itself, or in fact, Maxwell, whose attention was finally caught by these words. His sorrow had seen him roar for almost one year now and still he had found no comfort. Perhaps he never would. But he could not roar any longer.

"My heart panteth, my strength faileth me. As for the light of mine eyes, it also is gone from me." Hugh Peters' rather rounded face and average height were as plain as his black attire, but his energy and passion abounded. "My lovers and my friends stand aloof from my sore and my kinsmen stand afar off."

Maxwell was as empty as this damp shell of a church. That he knew already. But unlike the building he would not crumble, for within him a fire still burned; momentarily fed by loyalty to his King but burning out of love for his sons.

He thought about Reverend Fryer. Of the man's courageous defence of both his church and his beliefs against those who had invaded his haven, not to mention his selfless act upon the point of death, which had caused his memory to be cursed by many. Maxwell's mind also strayed to the two rebels he had shot here and thence to Naseby, where he had killed many others. Did God put the pistols into Maxwell's hand to do that, or was he little better than a killer? Had he been tainted by hate and vengeance for too long? Fryer's peaceful nature, as well as Peter Irwin's trusting, compassionate character, seemed to offer Maxwell light in his despair. Maybe he could emulate them and live in light instead of darkness. His loss and the resulting pain may even be the Lord testing his faith and now it was time to heal; to heal his sons and through selfless focus on others, repair his own broken soul. Good remained all around Maxwell, even amidst the evils of war.

"I will declare mine iniquity. I will be sorry for my sin," Peters said, his voice climbing. "But mine enemies are lively, and they are strong, and they that hate me wrongfully are multiplied."

Colonel Hopkins sat engrossed. Sir Richard Halford distracted. At the back of the church a gathering of soldiers hung in the corner while the villagers, sandwiched between preacher and troops, said little and moved little.

"O my God be not far from me. Make haste to help me, O Lord my salvation."

With those final words deliberately tailing off, Peters had finished. Yet he continued to stand and did not take his eyes from the congregation. The many wrinkles that contorted his eyebrows were as deep and serious as his beliefs. During this pause, despite his small mouth seeming poised for another sermon, it was the silence that stirred people more than the psalm itself.

Finally Peters called for a hymn to be sung, which the colonel's surprisingly melodic voice dominated. There was to be no musical accompaniment. Maxwell often wondered with some jest whether Puritans would even ban the cavalry trumpet or drumming of orders if they had the chance. When all was concluded, Maxwell, stood and felt a sense of freedom, as if the chains that had strung his heart had loosened. He could breathe easier and think clearer after his soul-searching and the faces of Tom and Kit came to his mind's eye as he made his way to the door.

REBELLION

Everyone filed outside. Beneath the ironstone walls of the church, Maxwell gave a discreet and respectful nod to the lump of freshly dug earth, beneath which lay Reverend Fryer's mortal remains.

"I never thought I'd enjoy one of those Puritan sermons so much," a girl from the village said as she joined Maxwell and Peter. They slowly walked along the grassy path while most of the congregation overtook them.

"Aye, 'twas certainly thought-provoking," Peter tactfully replied.

"I hope the next one is just as appealing to me." Her eyes flicked to Maxwell, before dropping back to the ground.

Peter smiled. "How is the disquietness of *your* heart, mistress?"

"Peter Irwin!" the girl blushed.

"You have no reason to fear, for the good Maxwell is too engrossed with the word of God to notice the chatter of us mere mortals," Peter said.

Maxwell turned to the pair. "Nothing escapes my notice."

"Even the attentions of a young maiden?" Peter raised his eyebrows.

"What?" Maxwell saw the girl look at him. "I will not play games of this sort." He walked ahead, as if the very suggestion had insulted Catherine's memory.

"Master Walker!" John Lynch caught him up and drew him aside. "A word if you please."

"What is it?" Maxwell frowned.

Before he had even registered Lynch's features, Maxwell saw a blur of movement and went to duck, but he was too late. The man's fist slammed into Maxwell's face with a crunch and the force made him stagger backwards, grasping his nose. His face and hands trickled with blood.

"Traitor!"

"You …" Maxwell couldn't speak and coughed on the blood, leaving his voice pathetic and unintelligible.

Lynch stood up straight and took a deep breath as if he couldn't quite believe that revenge had come so swiftly. He glared at Maxwell, but quite unfinished, stepped closer again.

"That, sir, is merely to content my own anger. I will also have vengeance for our master."

Maxwell wasn't sure if he meant Halford, Digby, or the King by that statement, but guessed it was the latter. He expected another assault, but Lynch walked away. Maxwell kept his head but cursed the coward for attacking him while he was so distracted. His pride felt just as wounded as his face. But the most important thing was to ensure that this incident did not cause any deviation from Maxwell's plan, and in fact, it quite worked in its favour. The people whispered about what had just happened but moved on quickly and only Peter Irwin remained.

"Would you forgive me if I say you deserved that?" Peter Irwin's voice was as calm and collected as ever, despite his lack of sympathy.

"Yes."

"Then you deserved that," Peter smiled and shook his head. "Why are you so angry towards people who mean you no harm?"

"The lady?"

"Yes, but also to Master Lynch, Sir Richard's footman, and me, when I first met you," Peter asked with a sigh.

"I lost the person ... closest to me." Maxwell struggled to communicate, and the ridiculous sound of his speech made him shake his head. "My wife."

"My condolences." Peter groaned. "That answers so many of the questions I have about you."

"Shot by a rebel," Maxwell interrupted.

"Then if I may ask, why did you betray Sir Richard, who is a royalist?"

"I have not."

REBELLION

"You led them to his gold. Why help them after all they have done to you?" Peter whispered.

"Sometimes when you lose one thing, you realise the importance of what you have left. Halford knows. They'd have pulled the place apart if they hadn't been abated."

"I admit to being relieved that there *is* more to your actions than meets the eye." Peter said, as if he'd been proved right to keep faith in this complicated character, who for all of his faults was steadfast, principled and determined.

"You'll never understand my reasons. But trust me."

"I can tell you're a man of your word."

"And you're a good man," Maxwell faltered. "A friend, if I may count you as such."

"I would be honoured," Peter replied with a smile, "even if you do sound like you have a musketball in each nostril."

Chapter Five

Lichfield.
15th June 1645.

Prince Rupert approached a doorway to one of Lichfield's tallest houses. Each storey of this wooden structure jutted out further than the last, so that it leaned wearily towards the houses opposite. As weary as the Prince felt right now, having spent the last twenty-four hours or more in the saddle, retreating from Naseby via Leicester and Ashby-de-la-Zouch.

"Your Highness." Sir Edward Walker, the King's Secretary-at-War, stopped him with a raised hand. "His Majesty is touching," he said in a rather hushed and reverential tone.

"What?"

"For the evil," Walker pointed through the part-open door.

Rupert watched as a clergyman from the Cathedral read from the Book of Common Prayer. The words were inaudible, but his tone was even and balanced. A young boy rather awkwardly stepped forward, tenderly watched by a man who could be none other than his father. The boy kneeled before the monarch.

King Charles sat on a plain wooden chair. His Verdigris doublet and the embroidered golden curls that wound their way down his sleeves were tempered by a burnished iron breastplate. From the bottom of the armour flowed a yellow buff coat. The martial adornment reminded Rupert that this was a King on the run, yet a faint smile came to

REBELLION

his lips – one of admiration – that his uncle should, even now, be carrying out such a ceremony. One which every monarch had conducted for the past six hundred years, ever since Edward the Confessor cured the first sufferer.

"The boy's father has donated much to our cause," Walker explained, as if he had read Rupert's expression. "No need for any certificate to prove this is *his* first touch!"

"Indeed."

King Charles leaned forward and extended both of his hands towards the boy as if channelling his divine healing power. All reading of the Prayer Book paused momentarily. The King laid his hands upon the swellings of the boy's neck; the cluster of abscesses and their characteristic light purple hue, ironically the colour of royalty. This briefest of touches reduced the lad to tears. Relief, joy and thankfulness. Rupert had been holding his breath all the while and he only realised it now as a man hurried to the door and blocked his view.

"A coin," Lord Digby said, holding both hands. "The boy needs a touch-piece."

"I have not a farthing," Rupert replied.

"Someone must have a coin. It need not even be gold!" Digby said.

It was an officer standing with the guards who stepped forward, removed his leather gloves and with some difficulty, hastily inserted his plump fingers into his purse to extract a silver shilling. He peered at the roman numerals that denoted twelve pence and then held it out. Digby had taken the coin before the man could proffer any excuse that it was the highest denomination he had.

"His Majesty will reimburse you," Digby turned and headed back into the room, where he handed the coin over to the King.

After a pause, and with the shilling between his fingers, the King made the sign of the cross and then passed it to the boy, explaining that he should hole it and thread a ribbon through, so that it could be worn around his neck. The fact that the piece was no longer a golden angel, which had so long been employed for this purpose, and was merely a coin that had paid a royalist officer, seemed quite indicative of the current situation. Parliament had been in full control of the capital since the very outset of this conflict, and with it the Tower of London mint. Were Rupert to let his mind dwell on this, or the recent defeat, he would have sunk into despair. Instead, the King's stubborn resolve to continue on appealed to his nephew's gritty determination.

Rupert entered the chamber as the boy and his father were shown out. They bowed as they passed, but the Prince's attention was firmly focussed on the King, who washed his hands in a proffered bowl. He looked tired. The heavy lids of his uncle's eyes seemed even more weighty, while his moustache – many times captured by the late artist, Van Dyck – was flecked with silver-grey and not so finely crafted. This change of colour sadly fitted with the falling value of the touch-piece. The King paced to the window, whereupon he gazed out at the dominating Cathedral that loomed over the close.

"To where are we headed next?" he asked. The question seemed almost posed aloud to the Almighty and could have referred to many things, not least their route of flight.

"Wolverhampton, Your Majesty," Digby quickly interceded. "But I beg you take some rest while you can."

"Pray fetch my embroidered nightcap and bible," the King instructed.

"I'm afraid we don't have either of them, sir." Digby paused with a grimace. "We have received confirmation that your carriage was taken by the rebels."

"My letters?" For the first time the King turned around to face the men.

"We must assume they have also been lost," Digby replied.

REBELLION

The King sat down again on the chair and rested his head in one hand.

"When we join Lord Gerard and his two thousand Welsh levies, we shall seek battle with Fairfax once again. And after his defeat, we'll take back all of your possessions, which have been so monstrously stolen," Digby declared.

If only our army was as strong as your delusions, Rupert thought as he looked at Digby.

"What of my belongings at Wistow Hall?" King Charles asked.

"Alas, we have no news, though I have full confidence in the man I sent to recover them," Digby said.

"There are two men, sir," Rupert reminded Digby. "One of our captains was also despatched."

"My cipher is at Wistow. If that falls into the enemy's hands, they shall be able to decode all of my most private and sensitive correspondence." The King stood and signalled his wish to take some rest.

"There is cheese and bread, should Your Majesty wish to partake?" Walker said, but his offer was politely declined.

The monarch walked into the bedchamber – trudged, almost – followed by his gentleman, leaving Rupert, Digby and Walker behind to discuss the movement of the army and assess the losses in both soldiers and baggage. Rupert growled with frustration. The parliamentarians would, no doubt, dance a jig if they ever understood the enormity of the contents of the royal documents, which would most likely reveal the King's unedited opinions; regarding everything from the late peace proposals, or worse still, about the Queen's attempts to drum up foreign support. The propaganda value of the King's letters, neatly penned like lines of well-drilled infantrymen, would be worth the equivalent an entire army. The lack of a cipher could hold off the enemy's codebreakers, but if it was to fall into their hands, every secret would be immediately surrendered up to the rebels.

"I pray God blesses our two men in their endeavours, otherwise the enemy will use those letters to fan the flames of their rebellion," Rupert said. For once the prince and Digby were united in their shared concern.

Chapter Six

Wistow Hall
30th June 1645.

The flames of the forge wisped and flickered. As Maxwell worked the giant bellows, the injection of air fed the fire, and from its charcoal roots it climbed ever higher. He extracted an iron bar from within and began hammering it against the anvil until it began to bend into the shape of a horseshoe. The curve glowed yellow, while the two arms of the shoe burned a glorious vermilion. In rhythm with the chiming hammer-blows, he eased the shoe around the anvil and moulded the shape while sparks burst from it.

"It needs to go in there now," Old George grunted and pointed at the water.

Maxwell ignored him. The man had been watching him intently ever since he had been forced to accept that the small forge was now a shared workspace.

"Remember this all belongs to Sir Richard and not your colonel." George's bottom lip curled over his top one, so firm was he of his opinion.

"Look, I have my work for the colonel, and you have yours for Sir Richard …"

"Sir Richard doth own Wistow!"

"My thanks for the reminder," Maxwell wiped his brow. "Now, please allow me to finish my task."

"I got nails to make," George held one up and ran his finger over the clinched tip that curled back on itself. "The master's enclosure fences need repairing."

Maxwell exhaled sharply. The noise merged with the resulting hiss as he doused the shoe in some water. George's ramblings and jealous protection of his master's interests were frustrating, but Maxwell had a lot of respect for the man, who despite his aging years was still a master smith. Only God knew how many decades George had lived and breathed such work, because nobody seemed certain of his age. He treated the shears, hand vice, chisels and hammers like they were his family, for he had no others, and the multitude of clay pipes that had been disposed of and trodden into the soil floor also suggested that this small area was as good as his home.

"My friend." Maxwell put down the equipment and placed a hand on George's shoulder. "I mean no ill to either you or Sir Richard. I will soon be gone with these soldiers," he assured.

"Then make haste," George replied, "for you are not wanted here."

"Can someone assist us?" a maid appeared at the door. "The laundry press is stuck."

"Let me help." Maxwell took off his apron and followed her, leaving George to his beloved forge and giving them both some respite.

"Goodwife Margaret is in a black mood," the maid told Maxwell. "Apothecary has just been and left us the wrong herbs and plants."

The pair walked to the kitchen, which was strewn with piles of clothes that were both clean and dirty, and amidst this array was Goodwife Margaret, sat on a bench. To say that she was queen of the kitchen was not altogether fitting; more an aging and oppressive general.

"Ah!" Margaret grunted as she forced her overweight body to stand, but even then, she stood only as high as Maxwell's chest. "Undo this press, for she is too weak," she wagged her finger and then placed her hands on her hips.

REBELLION

Maxwell looked at the wooden press, sandwiched between which was a folded linen bedsheet, and the giant screw on the top made it more resemble some sort of torture machine. He took hold of the screw and pushed until it surrendered with a creak and then turned it a couple of times while the maid patiently waited. Margaret's large mouth grinned as the job was accomplished and then she snapped at the maid, who continued to watch Maxwell, instructing her to get on with the task.

"Burdett," Margaret called to another maidservant, who immediately answered to her surname. "Get the master's pill ready," she said, tucking her wiry hair back under her coif. "The one the physician left two day's since."

"Anything else, Goodwife, or am I dismissed?" Maxwell asked. His question prompted some stifled mirth from the girls of the kitchen.

"Be on your way," Margaret waved her hand without actually looking at him. Her attention remained with Burdett. "No, it's the pill coated in gold, for it needs to work fast," she snapped.

As Maxwell was walking back to the stables he paused when the morning sunlight laid its glow across some stone balustrades, picking out a scattering of cobwebs. They sparkled so exquisitely that it seemed as if they could be stitched into a doublet like the finest silver lace. Such beauty as this remained undimmed by the dark hand of war and he thanked God aloud that he had the eye, as well as the outlook, to notice it. This was an encouraging sign, because for too long he had become blind to all things of beauty. Ironically, for all his concerns at being here, his world had been a very dark place before Wistow.

"Walker?" Colonel Hopkins walked towards him.

"Yes, sir, may I help?"

"It's rather fortuitous that I caught you here, where I may speak a little more freely than in the house," Hopkins said, lowering his voice and focussing his attention upon Maxwell's nose. "Does it heal well?"

"Aye, sir, praise be to God."

"The man lashed out due to jealousy, nothing more," Hopkins said, "because the Almighty has led your heart to the cause of Parliament. I would have had him whipped, had not you and Sir Richard pleaded for clemency. But you are one of my men now, Walker, and I look after my own."

"He is but misguided. I pity him enough for that without seeing him punished further," Maxwell replied.

"A gracious remark." Hopkins nodded. "Now, have you overheard anything around the house that might be of use to me?"

Maxwell took a deep breath and considered the lie he had formulated for this moment. "Well, just one detail regarding the King, which is a rumour that he is headed for Oxford."

From the distance a rider came on apace. Silhouetted by the sun, the man and his steed seemed to have emerged from it, as if transported from another realm. Mysterious and solitary, the stranger's approach prompted Colonel Hopkins to stop talking and break away from Maxwell, much to the latter's relief.

"Sergeant, see to our visitor," Hopkins instructed.

As the newcomer drew closer, his helmet, breastplate and buff coat betrayed him as nothing more than yet another cavalryman; a parliamentarian, as confirmed by the sash wrapped around his stomach like a tawny sunbeam. When the man removed his helmet, Maxwell was shocked to recognise him and his face chilled almost instantly. His breath grew rapid and his heart began to pound. It was Gervase Harper.

"Master Walker," Peter called out, "I need to speak to you about the dappled mare."

Maxwell did not hear Peter. Instead, he eyed Harper and the Colonel, who greeted each other with a warmth of expression and pleasantries that belied a friendship. Now deep in discussion, the pair began to amble towards the gardens and Maxwell's direction.

"I need your assistance," Peter said as he approached.

Maxwell had come to recognise the colonel's sense of duty and plain approach, for it was essential to understand the man's character in order to successfully double-cross him. He remained very wary of Hopkins, that was true, but the fact that Hopkins knew Harper somehow changed everything. The two men laughed. It was a hollow, deathly laugh that echoed through Maxwell's mind.

Colonel Hopkins glanced at Maxwell. "Wait a moment, I wish to finish our conversation."

"What is it?" Peter whispered.

"That's him."

"What do you mean?"

"The man who killed Catherine."

"Don't be rash." Peter was forced to retire as the men neared.

Gervase Harper's eyes were permanently narrowed like those of a fox. Wily, exploring and calculating. Their cold expression was enhanced by thin dark eyebrows. His oversized upper lip and the black moustache upon it made his mouth seem to hang rather grimly, while his beard crept up his defined cheek bones to give his long face a gaunt appearance. Above his forehead a pointed centre of hairline gave way to straggling dark locks than hung down to his shoulders, straight and unadorned by even the slightest of curls. This was Gervase Harper. For the second time Maxwell beheld the killer's countenance, one which for so long had consumed his thoughts both night and day.

"This is my smith, but also my hound. He has sniffed out hidden gold, as well as some interesting information," Colonel Hopkins said, holding his hands behind his back. "I *will* hunt down the King and all of his cavaliers."

"God will deliver the tyrant into our hands," Harper replied in a raspy voice. "But it appears your smith will have trouble sniffing out cavaliers." He looked at Maxwell's nose and grinned, revealing a row of yellowing teeth.

"A mark of his honesty." Hopkins explained how Maxwell had led him to a stash of coins and earned the enmity of a colleague.

"The King is not hiding here, then?" Harper asked.

"No, but Halford entertained him prior to the battle," Hopkins replied.

"It's a relief that you are searching for our royal fugitive, because General Fairfax is most assuredly not. He contents himself with the taking back of Leicester before heading off in search of Lord Goring."

"Goring? He'll be off to the South West then?" Hopkins asked with surprise.

"That's right. Whether the King joins his last field army, or not, the defeat of Goring and his troops is essential to our ultimate victory."

"Walker was just telling me about something he'd heard," Hopkins replied and instructed Maxwell to recount the details.

Maxwell couldn't meet Harper's eyes for more than a second or two for fear that it either sparked terrible memories or got the better of his restraint. He tried to focus on what the pair would want to hear and what he might be able to say that would be to the King's benefit.

"The servants here have mentioned the King's recent visit. By all accounts his retinue had been certain that whatever the result of the coming battle, they would head south and back to Oxford, because the rich courtiers feared for their goods and families left there." Maxwell glanced at both men.

Considering the scrutiny he was under, Maxwell thought it a blessing that he had been punched in the nose, for at least it offered him some protection from being recognised by Harper – if, indeed, the man would have retained any memory of the unfortunate people who had crossed his path.

"Interesting," Colonel Hopkins replied. "Typical of the greed of these fellows."

Harper made a short but gravelly hum as he weighed it up. "Not much help."

"Master Irwin had need of my assistance. Would there be anything else?" Maxwell asked.

"We are done now, are we not?" Hopkins looked to Harper for approbation and gained a nod.

Maxwell's skin prickled and his muscles were tense. He walked away in silence, focussing on the stables ahead. The only saving grace about having to interact with them was the confusion he hoped his words might give. The King was not actually destined for the south after Naseby; Langdale had mentioned that the royalists would be heading west, most likely to pick up recruits from Wales.

Soon closeted within the stables once more, Maxwell continued to finish off yet another horseshoe, using his hand chisel and a hammer to create a groove in the centre of the shoe. It was methodical and calming and focussed his mind. The familiarity of the work at times even made it feel like he could be back home in Yorkshire, though a big reminder of his current situation was his injury and the heat that made his nose throb. It would have been a relief to have finished the shoe, had not Gervase Harper appeared.

"We meet again."

Maxwell gripped his tongs. "May I help you?"

Harper paced slowly closer. He watched his feet, sighed, and then stopped next to his horse. "I want her brushed and fed."

"Of course, I shall ask Master Irwin."

"Her oats …" Harper paused. "They are the very best."

"I do not doubt that."

"Her oats, d'you hear?" Harper's mouth widened into a smile. "I hear that you are prone to pilfer from our four-legged friends."

"That was …"

"Consume just one of her oats and I will tear out your insides to get it back," Harper warned and then headed towards his mare.

Maxwell watched as the man patted her head and stroked his fingers up and down her ear. Those murderous hands which had committed such heinous crimes now caressed, and soothed. Then Harper called Maxwell over.

"Shall I fetch the head groom?" Maxwell walked closer, but tried to excuse himself.

"No, I wish for you to feed her."

Harper leaned forward and kissed the side of his mare's head. His greasy black hair hung limply and obscured his face. As Maxwell observed, he remembered that he still held the tongs by his side. He could see the crown of Harper's head amongst his straggling hair; a soft spot that seemed to offer itself as the ideal place to bash a hole through to his brains. The weight of the tongs in Maxwell's hand began to tell.

"You have a love of horses?" Maxwell quickly laid the tongs on the floor and then took hold of a sack.

"I love this one."

"She is a fine example and has a striking coat," Maxwell poured out some oats.

"She's looked after me well. Rescued her from a fat old royalist in Yorkshire. So exceedingly fat that I thought he would burst on the point of my blade," Harper said.

Maxwell made sure to touch the horse gently and gave her plenty of encouragement under Harper's scrutiny. The patterns of white speckles on her dark coat were like the frothy vestiges of a wave upon a beach. Her eyes twinkled as blue as the summer sky. She must have seen many a sight and kept all of her master's secrets. As she began to eat, Maxwell turned to Harper.

"Shall I brush her?"

The question garnered but a nod from Harper, who then finally left. It took some minutes before Maxwell dared turn around after hearing the man's footsteps fade and the door clash. Harper was a calculating and manipulative killer. It wasn't until Maxwell saw that Harper had gone that he opened his dry mouth and coughed. He remained silent and considered what could have happened had he not placed the tongs onto the floor and took some satisfaction from knowing that Harper's life had been in his hands for that moment. He had chosen to spare him. Maxwell had good reason, for to take Harper's life away would be to forfeit his own to the public hangman and die condemned as a murderer, never to see his sons again.

As he brushed the mare's hindquarters, he noticed some saddlebags in the corner. After first checking that nobody was close by, he kneeled down and opened them up. He slipped a hand inside one and finding nothing, was just about to close it again when he noticed a small slit. He inserted one finger, felt a folded piece of paper and then coaxed it out. The remains of a red wax seal – only a few tiny shards – clung to it in parts like droplets of dried blood. He gently peeled the small note apart, no more than seven inches wide by three inches long, to see handwriting that was far from neat. Clearly written in haste, it was almost haunting to read, especially due to his surreptitious behaviour.

The King has been sighted in Lichfield. Suspect he aims to either relieve Chester – which our forces besiege – head for Wales, where he may repair his losses, or some even suggest strike north to Scotland. Whatever he decides upon, I shall continue to shadow him and not rest until I fulfil my orders and bring him to battle.

Your servant, Colonel-General Sednham Poyntz.

Maxwell paused. The potential of the King heading for Scotland came as quite a surprise. But knowledge of the monarch being shadowed by the commander of Parliament's forces in the north was a real shock. No wonder Harper had dismissed Maxwell's lie that the King was heading for Oxford. The door opened at the other end of the stables. Maxwell tucked the paper into his shoe and stood up, for he had no time to replace it in the saddlebag.

"You not finished brushing her yet?" Harper eyed him.

"Not quite."

"Give it to me," Harper strode towards Maxwell with his hand out and then took the brush. "I haven't got all day. I need to get back to the army."

As do I, Maxwell thought. "If you excuse me."

Maxwell headed out of the stables and away from the house – and the soldiers. He could not be caught with this note, but equally didn't want to destroy it. The question was where to put it. Then he saw Saint Wistan's Church, which was very apt, considering his fervent prayer that Harper did not check those saddlebags.

***

The Almighty had listened. Harper had left Wistow unaware of his missing note. That evening, as Maxwell walked through the hall, he spotted John Lynch coming the other way and both men navigated the six-legged table that dominated the centre of the room. The silver candlesticks had been taken by the soldiers, leaving its surface bare. The wood panelling, too, was revealed in all of its amber glory, the tapestries having been stripped from them and burned for being too Popish in their imagery. As he walked up the stairs, Maxwell glanced at the King's portrait in its gilt frame. Sir Richard Halford had intervened with the colonel and given him a small figurine of a horse that he had been admiring in exchange for the portrait being left alone. A hollow victory in this small corner of Leicestershire. Or perhaps it was merely that this painting had become an echo of the past that was fast slipping away and therefore no longer such a threat.

From the top of the stairs, Maxwell noted that John Lynch had remained in the hall, talking to one of the maids, but his observation was soon cut short when he heard Colonel Hopkins laugh. This was not an expression he'd associated with Hopkins, for it seemed jolly; a warm amusement. Maxwell knocked on the door, having been summoned, and hoped that such humour was a portent that the meeting would not cause him any undue concern or difficulty. He waited.

"Who is it?"

"Walker, sir."

"Enter."

Maxwell opened the door and stepped inside the bedroom which had been Sir Richard's until recently; the biggest, and with the best view, though as he turned to Colonel Hopkins, he realised that the man was only interested in one vista. The maid stood over him combing his hair. Her fingers caressed his locks and methodically ran the tortoiseshell comb through them, whereupon it flicked back into wiry curls and resisted her best efforts. The colonel, however, seemed not to have any such opposition.

"Leave us and return in one hour. You can finish this before I go to bed," he told her.

Maxwell turned away, not wishing to pry. His awkward gaze went to the floral silk hangings on the wall, and even the pot of aromatic flowers on the windowsill that would ward off flies – though they didn't prevent the maid from buzzing around the colonel as she tidied up.

"Fetch me some of that fine sack, too," Colonel Hopkins said as she left, and then turned to Maxwell. "From Spain.

If there's one thing these Catholics know, it's how to make a good wine."

Maxwell smiled. "You sent for me?"

"I did, indeed. Now, I have a request to make of you."

"I see." Maxwell didn't like the sound of this.

"Come now, do not take it ill before you know of the details."

"My apologies." Maxwell nodded. Catherine had often commented on his rather telling expressions.

"I need you and Sir Richard to be friends again."

"How so? After what has passed, I am not certain that I could achieve that."

"It must be done," the Colonel said sternly. "We can engineer it. When I take my men onto the march again, I need someone I can trust in this house, who will watch every visitor and overhear every conversation. Sir Richard has hosted the King and may do so again, therefore Wistow could become a trap in which we may, God willing, catch him."

"I can only give it my best attempt, sir, and will see Sir Richard tomorrow. Perhaps I should start with an apology."

"A good idea." Colonel Hopkins' dark eyebrows rose. "You shall be re-established here, and I will pay you handsomely for your good work on my behalf."

A firm knock came at the door and upon the colonel's permission, John Lynch entered the room and held up some wine. "Mary asked me to fetch it, Colonel. She said that she had a few other things to prepare for."

Lynch poured out two glasses as instructed, before Hopkins nodded permission for him to leave. The colonel then began to unfasten the twelve buttons of his russet coat. He enquired whether Maxwell had any questions and if he had understood what was required.

REBELLION

"To speak plainly, sir, I feel our goal with Sir Richard may be made all the harder by Master Lynch and his resentment of me," Maxwell said.

"Ah," the colonel replied and picked up one glass. "I have already told him that he will join my force and tend our horses. I have observed his thorough work and how well he puts them at ease; especially my own."

"I'll wager he was enamoured by that news?"

Colonel Hopkins didn't betray any humour. Instead, he took supped his wine, before gesturing at the other glass and inviting Maxwell to partake. "Let us drink to our plans."

Maxwell stepped forward. He wasn't a lover of wine, but didn't wish to spurn the invitation, therefore he took the glass and held it up. "My thanks."

"Perchance it must be from a different region," Colonel Hopkins said with a frown. "Pour me another."

Maxwell placed his own back down and duly refilled the colonel's fluted glass until it swirled half full with a sweet aroma. He handed it over to Hopkins, who commented on a tingling sensation that had begun to spread through his mouth. He began to seem a little agitated.

"Are you all right, sir?"

"Get me that tankard of wild rocket!"

Maxwell became concerned. Wild rocket seed might be useful for body odour, but the colonel's demand for it, when a matter of minutes earlier he'd been praising the wine, didn't seem right at all. The man's breathing became noticeably edged with a rasp.

"I'll fetch someone," Maxwell said.

He left the room, hurried to the stairs and leaped down multiple steps at a time. His leather-soled shoes slid on the tiles and he knocked some pewter plates in a bid to steady himself as he went. When in the lime-washed kitchen, he urged Mary to call for the goodwife. She would know what best to do. But Maxwell didn't wait around for the woman to be roused, and instead rushed back upstairs to the room where Sir Richard was quartered and knocked on the door as calmly as he could. He tried to catch his breath. The resulting few seconds wait was enough to consider the notion that the colonel had been poisoned.

"What is it?" Sir Richard opened the door.

"The colonel, sir, I fear he's ill."

"What?"

Sir Richard's face paled the colour of his cambric linen nightshirt. Without a further word, he followed Maxwell towards the main bedroom and opened the door to find the colonel had collapsed on the floor. Maxwell dropped to his knees and called for Hopkins to respond, taking the man's head and then opening one of his eyes. Hopkins was not breathing.

"He's dead."

"He can't be," Sir Richard replied and then cursed several times.

Maxwell felt the colonel's chest. "There's no heartbeat. No movement."

"You said he was ill, not dead?"

"He drank some sack and then complained of a tingling mouth," Maxwell stuttered. "Lynch brought it."

"Gods wounds! This is all I need."

Maxwell looked at the glass he had very nearly supped himself and shivered. Infiltrating that pale, yellowy wine was poison. It had to be, for Colonel Hopkins had been fit and well. Maxwell had faced many a sword and gun – countered their threat and lived to tell the tale – but he'd never imagined that he might have been finished off in such a manner. "Lynch brought it in and poured two glasses. One for Hopkins and one for me."

"Lynch came to me yesterday asking where I kept the secret items."

Sir Richard went immediately to the fireplace. From behind the cast-iron fireback, which was emblazoned with the Halford arms, he took a small wire. Maxwell looked on as the man kneeled, hooked it between a small part of floorboard next to the hearth and then pulled it up. There he stopped, as if deep in prayer. Silent.

"They're gone. Lynch has them."

"Has what?" Maxwell hurried over and glanced down at the empty void.

"The King's seal and a cipher he left here."

"God damn that man!" Maxwell hissed.

"The fool."

"They will blame me! I was the last one with him," Maxwell replied and hurried out of the room.

His position at Wistow Hall was untenable, but what of Lynch? If the man intended to flee to the King with these items, that would also be dangerous for Maxwell. Lynch would surely report Maxwell's supposed betrayal of the King, and the turning in of the gold, details of which would be seen as nothing less than treason. How had it come to this? Murder on the one side, or traitor on the other. Maxwell faced the peril of being mistrusted by both sides and rapidly came to the conclusion that he must find Lynch and explain his actions to the man; to point out that betraying the gold coins had protected the cipher, as well as the intelligence he had gained for the King's benefit.

"Where's Lynch?" he shouted out to Mary, who held one hand to her chest.

She didn't reply. He ran on towards the exit of the house but noticed that the door of the study was open. Also gaping wide was the window. Without further delay, he rushed to the main entrance and opened it to speak to the sentries.

"I need to get some items from the forge."

A horse brayed. The sky was turning rose-red and the colour seeped down towards the treetops. A sharp breeze swept across them, growing louder as it rustled the branches like an incoming wave breaking upon the shore.

From the fields beyond the house the dull chatter of off-duty soldiers could be heard, most likely partaking of supper or playing dice. Then Maxwell heard the horse again and stepped outside. Looking towards the stables, he caught sight of a rider heading off, gathering speed so quickly that the sentries sprung to action and assumed it to be suspicious. They cried out for the man to stop and one of them took aim.

"That's the colonel, God damn you!" Maxwell cried and grabbed his arm.

"Aye, 'tis his horse, look," the other agreed. "But where's he headed?"

Maxwell remained silent and watched Lynch pick up speed and head off through the trees out of sight. "Said he had to meet some of Fairfax's envoys. Seemed quite urgent."

"He must have left by the other door?"

"I'll ask the captain whether someone should accompany him," one soldier ran across the lawns and towards the camp.

In the confusion that followed, Maxwell retrieved his hidden dagger from the forge, hurried off to the stables and then saddled up Sir Richard's stallion. If Halford's boasts about it being the fastest in the county were true, he'd be able to catch up to Lynch.

***

The damp earth did much to absorb the noise of Maxwell's horse as he rode west. He couldn't help thinking about the dead colonel back at Wistow, who had not even turned cold. Maxwell pictured Colonel Hopkins' face and his pale skin, which had been clammy to the touch; everything had changed in a heartbeat, or lack of one. Maxwell's undercover life at Wistow had come to a close just as he had thought that it was becoming ever more impossible to escape it. In the blink of an eye he was loose. Free.

REBELLION

The trees lining the route seemed animated by Maxwell's speed and their branches appeared to reach out in a bid to wave him on his way. The time at Wistow, however short, had offered him the opportunity to refocus his outlook on life. Though this premature escape meant that he travelled without gun, sword or armour, and was dressed plainly in a doublet and breeches, he at least knew the route well. He also knew the commander of the nearest royalist garrison.

The sky glowed a burnished orange, just like Wistow's furnace, and it was as though a new day was already in the process of being forged from the ashes of this one. While the heavens burned, the earth reflected the Almighty's glory by adopting the same glow. It highlighted fields and picked out the sheep dotting them, reflected in ponds and in the road he galloped along. Only the hedgerows and treelines resisted, and their darkened silhouettes provided a contrasting mid-point. Then from up ahead a rider briefly came into sight but vanished as he entered a copse. The chalky Leicestershire soil was scattered by Maxwell's horse as he approached the gathering of trees, and when he saw the rider again, he knew it was Lynch.

"John!"

The man looked over his shoulder and Maxwell held up a hand as he closed the gap.

"John, I have news!"

Lynch slowed, drew up and then turned his horse as Maxwell approached.

"What in God's name do you want?" Lynch asked and then drew his sword. The forty-inch blade echoed a steely warning. "Leading the chase after me, eh?"

"I am for the King as I always have been," Maxwell replied.

"Ha!" Lynch laughed. "You should have perished with your master back there."

"Why did you kill him?"

"To fulfil my orders!" Lynch's face contorted with anger that Maxwell had even posed such a question. "He was an enemy. There was no other way I could get the King's items and escape under the cover of nightfall."

"I have gained information that concerns the King's safety. Let me ride with you and we shall both return to our rightful places by his side."

"And let you betray me? I'd rather kill you," Lynch declared and pointed his sword.

"If I didn't reveal that gold, Hopkins would have torn the house apart."

"You betrayed the King and ingratiated yourself with that wretch," Lynch said.

Maxwell narrowly avoided being cut by a swipe of the blade. He seized the man's boot top, grabbed at his cloak and pulled with all his might. Lynch cursed and kicked his leg, but Maxwell jumped from his horse and toppled the man. Both fell to the ground and then scrambled to their feet. Maxwell backed away from the horses, led Lynch to the other side of the track, and made a decoy lunge to test his opponent's reflexes.

"This is madness." Maxwell continued to try and reason with him. "I have served the King for three years."

Maxwell circled Lynch warily. His shoes were far less impeding than Lynch's leather boots and seeing that there was to be no convincing the man, Maxwell pulled out the dagger from his belt. He insisted that it was self-defence. Holding it up in his left hand, which was protected by a curved triangular guard, he made ready with the nineteen-inch blade.

He had not imagined that the man would so stubbornly refuse to listen, less still that he would attempt to kill him for a second time, and he eyed Lynch's every movement and tried to read his every thought. Above them the sky ominously darkened.

REBELLION

"All I ask is that we ride together to the King!" Maxwell shouted.

Lynch's response came in the form of his rapier. The blade was double the length of Maxwell's dagger, but the attack was successfully blocked. The rapier met the dagger with a clang and when it slid down the steel edge, Maxwell forced his opponent's weapon aside and punched him in the face with his right hand. Now at close quarters, he grabbed Lynch's collar and kneed him in the groin, causing him to stumble. The pair collapsed to the ground again, whereupon Maxwell gained the upper hand and got Lynch onto his front. Maxwell kneeled astride him, one foot pinning down the man's sword arm, while he held his dagger to Lynch's neck.

"I have no wish to kill you," Maxwell said. "We will travel together and then present the King with both his items and the truth. Agreed?"

Lynch's face flushed. "Agreed."

Maxwell took the rapier, stood up and walked back to his horse with the sword in his right hand hanging by his side, and the dagger in his left. A deep sigh of relief escaped him; not just over the fact that the two men could return together, but also because he had kept control. Mercy over ruthlessness. Life instead of death. He hoped that by working alongside one another, Lynch would come to understand Maxwell's behaviour and actions over the past fifteen days.

"I will freely admit that I deserved that punch in the nose."

The silence following his comment made Maxwell stop. There was a faint scuffle of movement and as he turned, he saw Lynch coming right for him with a small blade of his own. Lynch cried out. He declared Maxwell a traitor. What followed blurred into streaks of silver and a frenzy of movement as Maxwell struck out. The briefest of moments left everything to instinct; an animal sixth sense. Maxwell was knocked off his feet and then saw blood on his hand, as if someone had spilled the finest red wine on it. Then Lynch coughed as the last vestiges of life departed his body.

"They know."

These two words seemed nothing more than a figment of Maxwell's imagination and as faint as if they had been put into his mind by some sort of spirit.

"Lord Jesus!" Maxwell cursed as he came to his senses.

John Lynch was lying beside him. The man's head was next to his and his linen collar was streaked with blood. Lynch's eyes were wide, and as cold as marble, with an expression moulded into a permanent one of horror. It was as if he'd died at the climax of pain whilst also realising what had just befallen him. Maxwell continued to grip his dagger, which was lodged in Lynch's neck.

"They know?" Maxwell repeated. These had been Lynch's last words, so hauntingly whispered; words that had escaped as blood had choked him.

Maxwell got up and made for Lynch's horse. He opened the leather saddlebags and rummaged around for the cipher and seal but could find neither. He hesitated and then quickly returned to Lynch's body. Kneeling down, he rolled the man onto his back, removed his buff coat and then put it on. Maxwell unfastened the man's belt pouch, opened the flap and found a small piece of parchment. Upon sight of a gold signet ring, he took the pouch and its contents.

With that, Maxwell dragged Lynch's body into the darkness of the trees, left the man's horse untethered, and then mounted up and made off. The daylight had all but trickled away. Where once there had been a glittering sunset, he now rode slowly along a track lined by trees that were permanently stooped. Bent so by the frequent winds that would relentlessly race across the adjacent meadow. Yet even now, without even a hint of a slightest breeze,

REBELLION

they stood poised for the inevitable – as did Maxwell, who also felt quite bowed by the gales that life threw at him. Just as he thought he'd turned a corner.

Chapter Seven

4th July 1645.

After four score miles, Worcester was now before Maxwell in all of its glory. The route towards the town took an easy slope downhill, making the last part of his journey that little bit easier, and took him past fields which were being tended. The sight of this cultivation offered reassurance that royalist roots were strong here. The archway of Saint Martin's Gate was where he was headed. Sitting like a crown atop its octagonal bastions were three gabled roofs. Certainly, Worcester had impeccable royal connections, having been in royalist hands for two-and-a-half years now. A pointed earthwork shielded the gate ahead – one of seven access points – while from beyond the red sandstone walls, the tops of twelve churches inquisitively poked out. The houses of the suburbs, which had once lined the route to Saint Martin's Gate, had been demolished and the remains of their contorted timber frames lay strewn like carcasses on a battlefield. The culling of buildings outside the walls prevented the enemy from using them as defensive positions, and like ants, the townsfolk were carrying the remains away to be reused elsewhere. It wasn't long before Maxwell and some other arrivals drew close to the gate and were met by the guards, whereupon he dismounted.

"What's your business?"

"I am headed to join the King and Sir Marmaduke Langdale of the Northern Horse," Maxwell replied.

"You have a pass?"

REBELLION

"I have the King's signet ring," he said, and showed the guard. "My name is Captain Maxwell Walker."

"Fetch the captain," the soldier asked his comrade and then ordered Maxwell to wait.

Maxwell remained silent and did as the soldier asked. A couple more civilians and some tradesmen filed past. It wasn't long before the officer of the guard approached with an expression like a distant, but perceptive, owl that had flown in to investigate.

"I understand you are en-route to His Majesty?"

"That's correct, sir," Maxwell nodded.

"If I may see the object."

Maxwell held the ring between his fingers and slowly tilted it left and right as if showcasing it to a prospective buyer at market, when in fact, he was selling his own credentials.

"I was instructed to return it to the King with the utmost urgency," Maxwell explained. "I am sure Prince Maurice will grant me a pass if he is still here."

"There is no need. I wish you well in your endeavours, sir," the captain replied and then turned to Maxwell's horse. "A mighty fine mount you have there."

After being allowed through, Maxwell entered the town and paused in the Corn Market in search of an inn. He looked past Saint Martin's Church, whose three eastern gables were matched by a further three on its southern side.

"A peculiar form of church building, eh?"

Maxwell turned to find a man looking right at Saint Martin's, as if he had not even uttered the words of observation and had no intention of carrying on conversation. As such, Maxwell resolved upon where to head next. He tried to block out the cries of the traders who passed by offering either oranges and lemons, to mend broken chairs, or clean chimneys.

"This building is much finer," the man held out a hand to stop Maxwell. "Home of the Berkeley's of Spetchley."

He pointed at a two-storied, half-timber house that did not much betray its two hundred years.

"If you insist on being my guide, then point me to a good inn," Maxwell said.

"I'd be most pleased to assist. My name is Thomas."

The man led Maxwell towards the Rose and Crown, avoiding a milch ass whose milk was at that moment being extracted for some young child or other. After seeing his horse taken by one of the establishment's stable boys, Maxwell, still accompanied by Thomas, now headed inside. Some playful dogs yapped and scurried past them. If Maxwell had thought to find it any quieter indoors, he was much mistaken; Wistow's sleepy haven seemed a long way from Worcester in many respects.

A serving girl winked at him. Thomas prattled on about how Worcester was preparing to become the next royalist capital after Oxford, whose location was apparently no longer safe. Though Maxwell could focus on little else but his hunger. As he walked through the building, he caught the familiar, rancid wisps of tallow candles, but the animal fat that they comprised of did not dampen his appetite one bit. An air of boisterous energy enthused the chatter of the customers and tankards clattered against tables as the clientele were refuelled with beer or ale. Maxwell took up a place on the end of a bench in the corner, next to a large stone fireplace and opposite Thomas, who ordered their drinks.

"Of course, the town is bursting because it's also Prince Maurice's headquarters."

"Forgive me, but who are you?" Maxwell asked.

"One of the King's scouts." The man strangely gave his role first. "Thomas Heskett is the name, and if I may enquire the same of you?"

"Captain Maxwell Walker."

"I was behind you when you spoke with the guards."

REBELLION

"Ah." Maxwell realised that there wasn't one corner of Worcester that was out of earshot. A lesson, if ever he needed one, about the benefits of restraint and caution.

"I couldn't help but overhear that you are making your way to the King?"

"On personal business."

"I understand." Thomas nodded. "I merely thought you might want to accompany me, as that's where I am also headed. I assume you know where he is quartered of late?"

"Well …"

"Raglan Castle," Thomas replied with a smile, "though it's heavily guarded."

"My thanks," Maxwell replied, having stopped at Worcester for many reasons, one of which was to discover the King's whereabouts.

"We could travel there together. I could do with some company."

"I would much rather go alone," Maxwell raised a hand.

A woman put their drinks down onto the table. Maxwell lifted his wooden tankard and supped the sweet ale, savouring the tang of the yarrow herb, which left a refreshing aftertaste. This taste of England soothed him; the same that generations of Englishmen had savoured, and one which he clung to in stubborn resistance of the foreign beer that was rapidly filling men's bellies.

"Did you know Shakespeare came here for his license to marry?" Thomas asked.

"I didn't." Maxwell wondered whether Thomas's knowledge of current affairs might actually prove useful, while his historical anecdotes were quite interesting. "So, he was married here?"

"It is alleged. But, if I may be plain with you, the only reason you were licensed to enter the town is because I spoke to the captain of the guard. I offered my own credentials and vouched for your identity."

"Whatever gave you the urge to do that?" Maxwell gave a frustrated laugh. "Prying on other people may be part of your role but let me tell you that I find it most unwelcome."

"I believe you don't possess a pass?" Thomas scratched his beard and then picked at it as if attempting to draw out his next words. "You rely on the goodwill of those who stop you by dazzling them with that ring … but it's a dangerous game to play. I humbly recommend that we continue on together."

Maxwell remembered his own calls to journey alongside John Lynch and just where Lynch's stubborn refusal had gotten him. "Then let us both travel to Raglan," he conceded.

Chapter Eight

It was two days before the rolling hills and Welsh wilderness gave way to a stunning castle that dominated the land thereabouts. It even seemed to tame Mother Nature by its very magnificence. Neat and flat terraces, knot gardens and a bowling green gave symmetrical greenery to the might of the gatehouses and octagonal towers, which rose from the walls of Raglan Castle. Within this grand edifice were two enclosed courtyards and in front of it the biggest tower that Maxwell had seen. Very much like a Welsh *Lighthouse of Alexandria*. It stood five stories high and was crowned with battlements, while its base was protectively skirted by an apron wall and six turrets, along with a moat. Carts trundled in and out of Raglan, full of provisions to supply the garrison and munitions to feed their weapons, while soldiers patrolled every corner, wall and gate.

As Maxwell and Thomas neared the outermost part of this fortress – a two-storied gatehouse, whose sharp brickwork signified its newness – they were approached by some red-coated soldiers.

"Thomas, you old dog!"

"Such a friendly greeting can mean only one thing; that you wish to remind me of my debts," Thomas replied with a chortle.

"Six shillings you owe me now," the officer said.

"Then we must play dice tonight, for I will receive a handsome payment soon."

"Then God bless Lord Digby, for his silver trickles through your palms and into mine!" The man grasped his hand and waved Thomas and Maxwell past.

"You're employed by Lord Digby?" Maxwell asked Thomas.

"Well ... I say the King, for Digby merely hands over my orders."

"I see," Maxwell replied, and wondered if Thomas had known John Lynch. "I must thank you for accompanying me here."

"It's my pleasure, Captain Walker. Come with me and I shall lead you inside."

Maxwell stopped a passing soldier. "Where may I find Sir Marmaduke Langdale and his Northern Cavalry?"

"I know not, sir." The man's melodic Welsh accent didn't soften the negative response. "For the King has brought so many with him."

Maxwell continued walking with Thomas across the arched stone bridge. It led to the main entrance of the castle; a three-storied gatehouse with half-hexagonal towers, narrow windows and gun loopholes dotting the base. To his left, the great tower loomed oppressively over him. Through the archway ahead, which bared the teeth of a portcullis, Maxwell could see a courtyard full of people.

"Look, you go on ahead and I will search out Sir Marmaduke," Maxwell extended one hand.

"With respect, captain, I have a responsibility for you at present and would prefer to escort you inside and see you achieve your task."

Once through the archway, the cobbles of the Pitched Stone Courtyard led into the heart of the castle. A well was at the far end, and behind that, the buttery, pantry and kitchen, which teemed with activity as much as any royal palace would have done. Servants and soldiers crisscrossed the yard and some stood around gossiping. Well-dressed civilians and officers came and went from the

Fountain Courtyard beyond. It was there, Thomas pointed out, that the family quarters of the Marquis of Worcester were located. Maxwell already knew of the Catholic magnate, and owner of Raglan, who was one of the richest men in the kingdom. They headed towards the hall, with its grand oriel window, and Maxwell prepared to surrender the King's possessions and also make his defence for all that had passed at Wistow. Stepping into the doorway was like entering a courtroom. He paused inside the sixty-four-foot chamber and waited as Thomas spoke with a footman. Above the Irish oak beams was a cupola, which lit up the wood-panelled hall and offered the Almighty a peephole into the splendorous realm of Raglan. Maxwell felt like he needed the watchful eye of God, in whom he placed his trust. He held firm to a belief that the truth always won out.

Thomas was now silent. Maxwell looked up at the carved stone arms of the Third Earl of Worcester which were stamped into the wall, for he had no wish to converse, nor anything left to say to him. It wasn't long before a well-dressed figure entered and drew the bows of those nearby, and it was to him that Thomas immediately gravitated. The two men conversed discreetly. Maxwell guessed that this had to be Lord Digby, one of the King's two Secretaries of State, and he bowed his head when the man glanced in his direction. Digby's attention remained with Maxwell.

"Captain Walker." Digby waved Maxwell closer, until he was barely six feet away and then introduced himself. "I believe you know of me already?"

"That's correct, My Lord."

"First of all, you have some items for me?"

"Yes, for the King."

"Then you will hand them over and I shall make sure he is reunited with them, for God knows, he has waited long enough."

"As you wish." Maxwell hesitated, before carefully taking the ring and cipher from his pouch. "If I may recount the nature of their rescue ..."

"Oh, I wish for you to do just that," Digby replied as Thomas passed the objects over. "But first I would know why it is you standing before me, and not my own man?"

"Unfortunately, sir, Master Lynch perished in the rescue." Maxwell stumbled over his words.

"Dead? Then how, pray tell, did he write to me of his impending escape from Wistow?" Digby asked. "I understood that some gold had been *lost* at Wistow, but did not believe that the retrieval of these items had cost the life of a loyal servant, too?"

"Alas, he would not listen to reason ..."

"Your reason, Walker? More likely he refused to listen to such a traitor as you."

"I prevented that cypher from falling into the hands of the rebels," Maxwell replied, "but had to sacrifice the gold, which I understand was worth far less."

"You prevented these possessions from falling into the hands of anyone but yourself, for you sought nothing less than the full glory of their return!"

"No, My Lord!"

"How did you get your hands on these? Hands, I might add, that must have the blood of John Lynch on them." Digby pointed a lily-white finger.

"I prevented the rebels from tearing Wistow apart, for if they had done so, then they would surely have discovered everything; gold, cypher and ring." Maxwell insisted. "Lynch refused to listen to my reasons. He killed the enemy colonel and fled."

"You betrayed the King." Digby's cold, blue eyes flashed with outrage. "You were in league with that colonel. John Lynch retrieved these items at great personal risk and has somehow ended up dead."

"He tried to kill me twice. Please, let me explain?"

REBELLION

"Where did Lynch die?" Digby asked.

"Allow me to speak with Sir Marmaduke Langdale."

"How did he die, captain?"

"He came at me with a blade and was killed in the scuffle that ensued. As God is my witness, I acted in my own defence." Maxwell could hear Lynch's last words in his head. 'They know'. Lynch had clearly written to Digby about all of his suspicions. It was almost useless to argue any further; Maxwell had been condemned before he had even arrived here. The tact and patience he had tried to espouse of late became ever more crucial and he thought about his sons, who were his all. He had battled the enemy to survive this war, but now he countered threats from his own side not with weapons of war, but with the truth.

"I fought for my King at Naseby," Maxwell replied. "I did all I could to protect what was his and return it to him. I am no traitor, but His Majesty's loyal officer."

"A traitor might explain his behaviour away with fine words," Digby's mouth creased with bitterness. "But a murderer is condemned in the eyes of God. Guards!"

"You cannot speak for God. He knows the truth."

"Arrest this murderer," Digby ordered.

"Allow me to speak with Langdale!" Maxwell persisted as two soldiers seized him.

"Take him to Hereford and imprison him until his trial can be arranged," Digby said and then looked at Maxwell with a scowl. "You will answer for the life of my servant."

Chapter Nine

Hereford. 12th August 1645.

Maxwell's grubby hands clung to the cold iron bars of the window. The small cell on which he'd turned his back was damp and miserable, making even the mizzle and mist outside a preferable sight. The only sight, in fact, that stopped him going mad. Hereford Castle may have been described as one of the fairest, largest and strongest castles in England, but John Leland who penned that observation had not been standing where he was. Despite the many grand buildings within its walls - even the remains of a vineyard – and having hosted King Henry IV, it was the bleakest place Maxwell had seen. There was nothing of beauty, nor anything of worth here. The gaoler had taken the last of Maxwell's coins in exchange for a coarse woollen blanket and some small cups of ale in the days after his arrival, but that had long since ended. After five weeks, Maxwell had also expended much of his positivity. His triple-unite, the golden coin that Colonel Hopkins had given him at Wistow, had offered a solitary ray of hope; he'd used it to pay for an urgent despatch to be sent to Peter Irwin, beseeching him to travel to Hereford and search out Sir Marmaduke Langdale on the way. Peter and his former commander were Maxwell's only recourse.

Within the ghostly vista the sun hung like a cloudy pearl. Beyond this shroud he wondered whether his sons were safe, where Peter Irwin might be and if he had ever received his letter, as well as how the King's cause fared beyond Hereford. Then the mist was lit up by an explosion that thundered across the town's mediaeval walls, enough to make Saint Ethelbert's Minster quake, or his well trickle with fear. The castle took yet another direct hit from a fifteen-pound roundshot, which punched into the wall and ground the stone of the high tower. In light of Maxwell's other worries, he had put the Scots out of his mind for a brief moment, but their artillery soon corrected that. Perhaps their dogged fire had become so regular that he was almost used to it. If being imprisoned by order of the King's Secretary of State wasn't enough to contend with, a Scottish army of twelve thousand had royalist Hereford surrounded and closely besieged. Although the Scots seemed determined to batter Maxwell's castle gaol, their victory would simply mean one captor being exchanged for another. For the past two weeks Hereford had been under siege and the castle's tower, standing tall on its motte, gave him a bird's eye view of proceedings.

"Night and day," Maxwell muttered. "They must have brought all of the gunpowder in Scotland with them."

A warning whistle had him hurry away from the window to stand at the barred door. He recognised the noise well enough. It heralded an incoming iron ball that struck near the window, and the stonework shuddered. Pieces of rubble fell away and some cracks appeared, whilst hundreds of years of dust and debris were shaken out of their nooks and crannies.

"Mother of God, that was close."

A key turned in the lock and the door clunked open. "Come with me," the gaoler instructed and bound Maxwell's hands with rope. "You're going to get a nice new place to live, courtesy of Colonel Scudamore."

"The governor?"

"Aye."

"Better than being blown apart by the Scots." Maxwell shrugged.

"Well, I can't say that won't remain a possibility."

"Where am I to go?"

"I'll let the governor tell you that."

A couple of other men were rounded up and led outside where a man on horseback waited to address them.

"Listen to me," Sir Barnabus Scudamore's voice was as gruff as his severe countenance. "You are all soldiers. Men who have fought for your King, but who have committed crimes for which you are being punished. This is your chance to redeem yourselves and prove that whatever you have done, you still retain loyalty to your sovereign, who is divinely ordained. Fight bravely for him and God will favour your service and perhaps forgive your sins. Are you with me?"

"Aye!" Maxwell cried with the others.

"By my command all clocks in the town have been stopped and church bells prevented from tolling. This shall leave the enemy without knowledge of time and hinder their efforts. When we defeat these rogues, the bells will peal once more. Meanwhile, let your hearts be filled with courage and loyalty."

The men cheered, evidently eager to gain some sort of freedom and the chance to redeem themselves. Maxwell, however, knew that the latter was not an option for him. Whether or not he was condemned in the eyes of God, as Digby had said, he was certain not to find any mercy while the peer remained so very influential.

"I do not need you to be soldiers, nor wield musket or sword," Scudamore added, "but to be moles and make dexterous use of spades and even your bare hands. We must tunnel out and counter mine the Scots before their sappers reach us and blow a breach in our walls."

Maxwell looked to the ground for a moment. No wonder they were being called upon, for such work was fraught with danger. By tunnelling in this manner, they could also be quite easily digging their own graves, but he had always believed that to confront danger offered a greater chance

REBELLION

of survival than to avoid it. Those who hesitated died. So, he voiced his agreement and added a huzzah. After that, they were led into the streets of town and one of their number, a lad from Birmingham, struck up a tune.

"I wish such shame come to all His Majesty's foes,
Let us drink to the thistle, the lilly and rose,
And royal Prince Rupert wherever he goes,
Which nobody can deny."

They were led to the north west of the town, through Castle Street, Cabbage Lane and onto High Causeway. The streets flowed with both soldiers and civilians who had clubbed together in the cause, hurrying here and there to repair any breach in the walls with wood and woolsacks. The ancient town walls had already been shored up with six feet of soil, as if they had died at the shock of facing a siege after all these years, and subsequently been half-buried. Such resistance gave an air of gritty determination. The bake ovens churned out food for the garrison and smoke spiralled heavenwards like it was Hereford's very breath. Every narrow alley, street and lane was more like a trenchwork line. Those who didn't join this defence, or worse still worked against it, had no place here. A body of a woman limply hung from the town gallows. Having betrayed secrets to the enemy, her lifeless body had been rendered forever silent, yet the creak of the rope in the breeze was enough to secure obedience.

A group of soldiers funnelled past Maxwell, heading for Saint Owen's Church, which had been struck once again and was in danger of collapse. The timber-framed houses of High Causeway were where Maxwell's group were headed, stretching right off to Eygne Gate. It was there that Maxwell and the others were directed to the royalist mine; one that seemed to lead down into the depths of hell.

"We have heard the enemy digging in the direction of this gate. If they mine under it and detonate their explosives, the town will be finished. I need not remind you of how ruthless these Scots are. They would plunder the entire place and take everything we have; coin, food, clothing and then finally your womenfolk." Scudamore bid them to get to work without delay.

Miners emerged with baskets of excavated earth which were then heaped against the town walls to double as extra defence. Their dirty faces and sweating brows betrayed their unseen struggles. Before Maxwell could think any more of it, he was given a pick and ushered towards the gaping hole which swallowed him up as he crawled inside. The tunnel got steadily deeper as he went. There was just enough room for two men to pass each other and it was around five feet high, though this varied in places, depending on how tough the earth had been. It especially got smaller towards the seam, due to the need for a speedy discovery of the Scottish tunnel. The backbone of the mine was the wooden planking and posts, which were all that prevented the snaking tunnel from collapsing in on itself. The humid atmosphere was oppressive and smothering, as if it had been near drained of oxygen by the men who came and went.

Occasionally Maxwell was granted respite from the claustrophobia. Where the sides had been hewn away to create a larger space, it proved enough room for a pause in proceedings, or for men to pass with baskets of earth. The sheer darkness of the route made it seem never ending, and though his hearing was dulled, he couldn't escape the muffled thuds of the surface cannons, whose firing reverberated through the tunnel. The impairment of his senses was unnerving. But feeling the earth on his hands, and every stone or rough lump along the way, offered reassurance that he was still of this world. The laboured breathing of other men came and went. He continued on,

REBELLION

which was all he could do, ready to do his duty and take his turn. To do whatever it took to survive.

When Maxwell's time came, he crawled forward into the most welcoming dull light of a lantern and began chipping away at the seam as quickly and effectively as he could. The point of the pick jerked stones out of their place and hacked earth away until there was enough for Maxwell to begin scooping into a basket. When full, he panted with relief at the prospect of getting out of this underworld and back to the surface. The ascent felt as if he was swimming against a tide, dragging the cargo of soil inch by inch until the shaft finally began to get lighter. Maxwell's desperation was matched only by an eagerness to escape. When free, he gasped the refreshing air. Never before had he been so thankful to breathe freely. It was a most basic act, and one that he had taken for granted every second of every day, until faced with these gruelling hours below ground. But daylight was fading fast.

As he stood and stretched, he heard the growls and barks of a dog who was having a length of match tied about it. The match was then lit. This fizzing, sparking animal was quickly turned out of the gate and the soldiers cheered as it ran for its life.

"What are they doing?" Maxwell asked one man.

"Keeping the Scots on the alert," the soldier replied. "These four-legged sorties send them into panic ... they squeal as much as the cats we released last night."

Maxwell's time above ground was short lived. He was soon herded back into the tunnel, where on his hands and knees at the face, he would more resemble an animal himself. Sweat rolled into his eyes as he gauged with his pick. But then the earth beneath him shifted. He let out a yell as it gave way and he dropped a few feet. He lay in the darkness, fearing that the mine had collapsed and that he was to be buried alive. His lantern had been lost in the fall. He dared not move. A voice called out; not from above where he had come from, but closer to where he was now. It was as though the world had been turned upside down and he'd been shaken around within its bowels.

"They're here!"

"A damned counter-mine."

The accents were Scottish.

"Hurry, send for brushwood and let us set theirs alight!" one of Maxwell's comrades barked with determination. "Walker, are you down there?"

Maxwell realised that they'd finally discovered the enemy mine and he listened as their scuffling and cursing receded as they withdrew along their earthen artery. He called back to his colleagues and reassured them. The cry continued for combustibles to set alight the Scottish mine, to choke those within it and burn the supports, which would result in its collapse. It didn't take long before some eager young boys brought the wood into the tunnel and it was passed down to Maxwell, who was carefully joined by another royalist.

With that, the rest of the royalists abandoned the underground earthworks in readiness. Maxwell and his colleague were left to carry out the most crucial act, the 'privilege' of which had fallen to them by being in the wrong place at the wrong time. They were the deepest placed miners. Together they crept further into the Scottish tunnel and dragged the bundles of lashed brushwood along with them. They laid a base first, then cut the ties on others and piled the loose sticks and twigs together, whilst laying other bundles up against the walls. When this was finished, and this web of wood was spun, Maxwell waited for his colleague to get back to the royalist mine.

Once the man called out that he was ready, Maxwell blew on the smouldering match cord, which gave it life and a resulting amber glow that lit up his hands, as well as the tunnel around him. He uttered a short plea for the Almighty's protection. Holding the end of the cord close to an old linen shirt that they had placed amongst the brushwood, he blew again and watched as the fabric browned and then a small flame caught hold. Soon enough the flicker grew at either side into a fiery smile, the centre of which blackened, and then the brushwood began to crackle. Like this war, which had engulfed the three kingdoms of England, Scotland and Ireland, the conflagration began to spread. Smoke slinked to the roof as if scouting out what else there was for the fire to consume, but by this time Maxwell had turned and left it. He rushed back to the royalist tunnel, and once there, the other man took his hand and helped him up. In the dim light of a lantern, the pair tipped earth from the baskets into the juncture of the tunnels to block off the path of the inferno. Wisps of deadly smoke slipped through the soil like a spirit rising from the grave, until finally the join was sealed, and the two men made their way back to Hereford. Every blackened support that charred and then crumbled within the Scottish mine – each one a milestone of the weeks that had passed in excavating it – also eroded the enemy's hopes of success.

***

When the first day of September had dawned, Maxwell, from the walls of Hereford, had watched as the Scots burned camp and made ready to leave. The sight had been a miracle. Twelve thousand troops had spent a fruitless four weeks trying to beat down Hereford's defences, amidst which one thousand five hundred royalists fought for their very lives – and David had emerged victorious over these northern Goliaths. Governor Scudamore had ridden through the streets on his white horse like he was floating on a divine cloud, basking in God's favour, while soldiers and civilians had given him their temporal affirmations. On one part of the walls the joyous royalists had even staged a mock fox hunt; a comparison to the wily

Scots being chased back out of England. That was three days ago.

It was a fine morning on 4th September 1645, when even those miraculous events were trumped. Despite having been incarcerated once again, now that Hereford's time of crisis had passed, Maxwell watched from a window as the royal procession slowly made its way through Hongery Street. Houses brimmed with jubilant people and rose petals were scattered in front of King Charles's horse. Maxwell could not help but feel proud that he had assisted with this victory, which had been aided by news that the monarch himself was leading a relief force. Though King Charles's presence inspired Maxwell, the sure knowledge that Digby would not be far away, lurking in the King's shadow, caused him dread. All it would take would be a brief court-martial and Maxwell could find himself on the end of a rope, even at this high point in proceedings. All because of John Lynch's stubborn refusal to see sense; the death penalty for striking out in the blink of an eye, and in absolute self-defence.

"Sir Marmaduke!" Maxwell shouted upon spotting his commander in the cavalcade that slowly trailed past. "Colonel Langdale."

Maxwell's voice had to compete with the acclamations that echoed out in support of the King. But Langdale met his eye long enough for Maxwell to know that he had been seen, even if the man could not say or do anything. He hoped and prayed. Everything that had happened to him of late had to be interlinked; Hereford's plight had brought the King and Langdale here, offering him the chance to plead his case. Like the passage of the sun in the sky, this glorious procession moved on, lighting up the rest of the town as it went. And then Peter Irwin appeared.

"Maxwell!"

"Praise God, you got my message?"

REBELLION

"Aye, and I have spoken to Langdale. I met the army on its way here. Thank the Lord you're alive, for I feared you might have been killed in the siege, if the authorities had not already proceeded against you."

"I am indebted to you for your help, Peter. But tell me, what did Langdale say?"

"Only that he was unaware of your captivity, as well as your actions in delivering the King's possessions. He said he would have someone find news of you when we arrived here."

"Surely he saw me as he passed."

"He will intercede on your behalf. He spoke highly of you."

"I pray that you're right. Did you bring the note I had hidden in the church?" Maxwell asked.

"I did, and Sir Richard Halford has penned a few lines that affirm your efforts to protect the cipher. Both of these I showed to Langdale."

"Truly, that is most kind of Sir Richard after all that has befallen him. I suppose I have you to thank for arranging it?"

"Not only me, but the maid, Goodwife Margaret and even Old George; people who recognised in you the qualities of a good man, though some took longer than others to see it."

"Then I am blessed to have such support."

"Make no mistake, you're also a difficult and complicated character, but I count myself lucky to have made your acquaintance … in fact, I hope to fight alongside you."

"Fight? You?"

"We all have backgrounds, Maxwell. You're not the only one who can hang up the tools of your trade and then take up the sword in defence of your beliefs. As a boy, I dreamed of being a soldier like my father, but I suppose I have always been too scared. He fought at the Siege of

Breda, you see. Was killed there. Yet, my yearning has always been for the army."

"You are most calm and collected; traits I don't always associate with a fighting man, but certainly ones that I wish I possessed more of."

"I've fought many battles without losing my head. Anyway, look!" Peter pointed out Sir Marmaduke Langdale, who was approaching on foot with an officer.

Langdale's voice had ordered Maxwell into many a battle. From Pontefract Castle to Naseby, his life had been put on the line through observance of Langdale's orders, yet now the voice of his commander was to be his only source of salvation.

"Open that door and let me speak with the prisoner," Langdale instructed the sentries.

The Yorkshire knight frowned, as if his eyebrows were weighed down by many concerns, not least this one. Certainly, no man in the elite Northern Horse which he commanded would ever disobey Sir Marmaduke, and it was testament to his force of character that they had ridden all over the kingdom in support of the King, despite their foremost loyalty being to their own county. The deep creases at the sides of his mouth defined his long face and added even more of a seriousness to his expression, which remained unchanged even when he entered the gaol and saw Maxwell.

"My sincere thanks, sir, for sparing me your time." Maxwell could not communicate his gratitude in any grander way. Langdale was not one for flamboyance and held up one hand.

"Captain Walker, this man has told me of your efforts in the King's service." Langdale pointed at Peter. "He also informs me that you found out some intelligence from the enemy?"

"Yes, sir. I discovered a note written by Colonel-General Poyntz, who reported that he was following the King."

REBELLION

"I have seen the evidence. Very interesting, and most timely, for we have, indeed, been pursued by Poyntz. He blocked our path through Yorkshire last month. But tell me, what of this man you killed?"

"He came at me with a dagger. He thought that I'd betrayed the King at Wistow," Maxwell replied. "He wouldn't listen to reason. Had I not reacted, then I would have been killed. It all happened in the blink of an eye."

Langdale paced back and forth while Maxwell explained the reasons behind Lynch's suspicions. "Unfortunate that he turned out to be one of Digby's men. I will crave a word with His Majesty and put the matter to him. That is as much as I can do."

Langdale turned to face Maxwell. Ever the meticulous commander, he reeled off a list of evidence like it was the units comprising a relief force. There was Halford's affidavit, the Poyntz note, the King's cipher which had been returned safely, and on top of Maxwell's past services was his courageous action during Hereford's siege. Langdale even spoke of mentioning the murder of Maxwell's wife as part of the argument that he would never favour the cause of her murderers; indeed, Langdale knew everything about Maxwell, as he did about all of his officers. The Northern Horse was like a brotherhood. Lastly, Langdale spoke of Maxwell's Catholicism. Nobody of that faith could ever support Parliament, led as they were by Puritans, who would sooner burn a Catholic than admit one to their cause.

"I am indebted to you, sir," Maxwell held up his hands.

"I will plead your case with much persuasion. But I will wait for a suitable opportunity to broach the matter, for the King is most distracted."

"Well, as I won't be leaving this place, at least you know where to find me at any hour of the day," Maxwell said, prompting a rare smile from Langdale.

"You may not leave, but the army might have to soon enough. Colonel-General Poyntz is at this moment delayed at Tewkesbury awaiting reinforcements, so while that is the case, we may take advantage and head north."

"If I might ask, what should happen if the army marches before you speak with the King?"

"Being on the move may actually offer me a better opportunity. Do not be perturbed. I need every one of my best officers with me and you are no exception," Langdale said, and then left without a further word.

"You are full of surprises, my friend," Peter exhaled sharply, as though he'd held his breath ever since he'd heard Maxwell's religion being spoken of. "A Catholic?"

"Well ..." Maxwell turned to the window, as if it offered a glimpse into a past existence. "A faith more hereditary, than from any devout belief, for my mother decided that I should share her faith."

From the confines of his gaol, Maxwell watched Langdale walk away. Clad in blackened armour, the man passed through the street like a dark shadow. He turned back to the room. The ceiling beams seemed to press down from above, while the timber frames of the walls contorted like old bones. The room was bare, and Maxwell was confined like a chastised dog locked in a kennel.

"Make no mistake, if I am condemned for carrying out orders, then before I am finished on this earth, I will have my day with Digby.

Chapter Ten

20th September 1645.

Colonel-General Sydenham Poyntz looked into the distance and towards Wales. A place forgotten by time. Penned behind King Edward I's mighty string of castles, the poor Welsh – so he had heard – still seemed dominated by folklore and legend. Most likely this was the cause of their misguided support for the King, who they followed as aimlessly as the sheep that wandered their hills and vales. Even now, King Charles and his army were amongst those people, herding new recruits, and heading north. Poyntz followed the monarch like a hunter; stalking him until he could get the King just where he wanted him, whereupon he could pounce and bring him down once and for all.

With the River Severn between Poyntz and Wales, he headed for Bridgenorth, where he could block the royalists from crossing into England. Poyntz could almost smell the royalists, they were so close. He stood in silence and weighed up the latest reports of his scouts. Indeed, he had a regiment of them to keep him fully informed.

The spring beneath his feet burbled along its course with cascades of pearl-like bubbles. The undertone whispered as if it could be the voices of Poyntz's second wife and their son, telling him exactly how French soldiers had murdered them in cold blood after plundering his estate at Schorndorf. The horrors of European warfare had left many a haunting whisper in Poyntz's subconscious mind, and these had not subsided after his return to a war-torn

England the previous year. The thirty-seven-year-old had been shaped by warfare and was now blinded to all else. He turned his back on the landscape and the stream.

"I bring news, sir." Gervase Harper strode towards him. "Our royal runaway seems to have plans for a second attempt to get to Scotland."

"And his strength, Harper?"

"Reports vary, but it's estimated at near four thousand. All horsemen," Harper replied.

"Then they outnumber us," Poyntz said, and clasped his gloved hands together. "We can make up the deficit by enlisting the support of our forces besieging Chester."

"Charles is as lacklustre a commander as he is as a King."

"I'm not naïve enough to think that the King commands that force. Mark my words, we face the likes of Langdale and Gerard, and the cavaliers move through friendly territory. Do not forget, Harper, that I have witnessed much more than England has ever seen. Or Wales for that matter."

"If Wales is friendly to the enemy, then let us show them the price of their loyalty." Harper spoke of crossing the Severn and striking the villages and towns across the border.

"We must save our wrath for the enemy's soldiers and maintain our cover. This will get bloody enough when we finally track down the King and his army and crush them."

"I will count the days until that moment," Harper replied.

"Take some horsemen and scout ahead of us. Let us not hold back on account of our infantry who bring up the rear. Speed and surprise are more essential to us."

Poyntz looked into the distance. The hills seemed to touch the sky itself and blocked out sight of anything beyond. It was as if his force was coming to the end of the world, but it was all merely an illusion. Further north and beyond those hills lay Chester, a town at the heart of the royalist cause. His spies had told him of reports that the King was heading to its relief. It made sense, for the port was one of the last remaining places where Irish reinforcements could land. Chester was a tap through which Irishmen could flow, and together with Welsh levies, they could replace royalist losses incurred at Naseby. But Poyntz was adept at conjuring up illusions of his own when it suited him. He had paid some travellers to report that his army had languished at Tewkesbury for days, when in fact he was marching north on a parallel course to the King.

"The element of surprise." Poyntz's two streaks of moustache were upturned by a smile. "Very soon, if it be God's will, I will end this war."

Chapter Eleven

Welsh Border
21st September 1645.

Silvery dewdrops had been strewn across the greenery of Wales. From the hills, which rose in worship of the Lord Almighty, and the trees crowning them like disciples, down to the grassy vales. The rising sun with its golden haze was locked in battle with the morning mist when Maxwell sat down on a large stone. Everything about this landscape belittled humans; the valleys looked as if they could swallow the entire population of London.

Maxwell had set out that morning as soon as it was light enough, thinking all the while of Langdale's letter, the words of which he had by now memorised. They had bounced around in his head during the furious ride and even as he stroked the mossy beard of the rock, waiting for Peter Irwin to catch him up, he could think of nothing else. He wouldn't, until he had found Langdale. The man had proved true to his word and engineered Maxwell's release, but the King and his army were heading to Chirk Castle, and Maxwell was desperate to join them. To be part of the royalist army once more.

The morning was chilled, but not particularly cold. The mist was somewhat refreshing on Maxwell's face. He stood upon hearing Peter's horse approach, the rhythmic pounding signalling that it would soon be time to get on his way again. He walked to his own horse, whose warm breath smoked in the air, replaced his felt hat and thought of how desperately he needed to shave before he met anyone of note. A whinnying broke the quiet. Peter Irwin drew up on the slope above Maxwell, his eyes wild and desperate, but before he could utter any word of warning, a more distant voice cried out.

"Stop, or I shoot!"

"Continue on, Maxwell," Peter insisted and then rode off to meet his pursuer.

Maxwell couldn't bring himself to untie his horse from the gnarled tree. Langdale might have orchestrated his release, but he had only succeeded through the evidence that Peter had risked everything to deliver. Maxwell would not give up his friend; his brother-in-arms. He removed his hat and then crawled up the small incline to peer over the bank and saw a man approach Peter.

"A wise decision to surrender, for a bullet in the back would not …"

"It's you," Peter interrupted.

Maxwell stared hard at the figure.

"Well, well, if it's not the groom from Wistow. Either you've got terribly lost, or you now serve a different master than Sir Richard Halford?"

"I could ask you the same thing," Peter replied.

"Oh, my loyalties have been clear from the beginning. My credentials lie not far from here in the form of three thousand cavalrymen."

Maxwell watched as Peter drew his sword. The opponent, who kept his pistol firmly trained, laughed sarcastically. Gervase Harper. To Maxwell that laughter was unmistakeable, rising as it did from the depths of Harper's evil soul.

"You are loyal only to yourself." Peter pointed his blade.

"You're a fool, but nevertheless a fool I'd prefer to take alive." Harper replaced his pistol and instead drew his own blade.

"A wise decision," Peter said mockingly, "for your powder would have been as damp as your breeches."

"I will cut the truth right out of you," Harper growled.

Peter and Harper dismounted, removed their buff coats and doublets, and held their blades outstretched. They circled each other like dogs ready to tear one another apart. Harper asked why Peter had left Wistow Hall. Peter remained silent. His only response was to lunge forward and take a swipe at his opponent. The two steel blades clashed with a rapid series of peals, ringing out in worship of Mars, and then Maxwell climbed over the lip and drew his own broadsword.

"My God, another one!" Harper took a series of backsteps. "Well, I'm sure I can handle a groom and a smithy."

"You're lucky I didn't crush your skull with my tongs at Wistow," Maxwell said, "for the temptation was there as you bent down to kiss your horse."

"I thought poison was your modus operandi? I'll wager you killed Colonel Hopkins." Harper's mouth turned up at one corner. "If the Lord interceded that day to spare me from your tongs, it was so that I could take revenge on you for the colonel's murder."

"Revenge?" Maxwell yelled, the veins standing out from his neck. "*You* accuse *me* of murder?"

"Maxwell ..." Peter raised a hand.

"I've always said you royalists can't handle the truth." Harper grinned.

"The truth?" Maxwell shouted and ran at Harper before he could make a dash for his horse. "You want the truth?"

"Aye, come on!" Harper blocked a barrage of cut and thrusts.

Both men fell silent and withdrew a few steps from each other. The look in their eyes and their posturing showed that this was but an interlude. Both words and swords would be employed to wound. Harper sliced his blade back and forth through the air with disdain and the whooshing noise seemed to taunt Maxwell.

REBELLION

"Our paths crossed before Wistow, Gervase."

"Now our swords must cross once more." Harper's glare seemed impenetrable, like that of a wolf. His unkempt beard, which grew from a high point on his cheeks, only emphasised such similarities.

"Since Sixteen Forty-Four I've waited for this moment." Maxwell's nose creased with hatred, his breathing shallow and fast.

"I must have made quite an impression."

Harper lunged forward, his sword strokes firm and almost arrogantly delivered, yet each potential death blow was parried. The men orbited each other as the upper hand passed between them. Maxwell kept moving and adjusting his footing. He locked his blade with Harper's to come to close quarters. Maxwell could feel his opponent's warm breath and roared with determination. The two sword hilts seemed fused together. Maxwell kept his eyes firmly on Harper's, sensing every minute change in pressure or resistance and anticipating his likely moves.

"What of our first meeting?" Harper asked.

"You killed my wife!"

Maxwell withdrew his blade, jumped back and cut up over, narrowly missing Harper's chest.

"I kill any royalists that get in my way," Harper replied, "or their whores."

Maxwell could not contain his rage. Streaks of the sun's rays skewered the remaining veneer of mist, and he was forced to sidestep to escape being blinded. His anger had already clouded his vision. It was only his skill with a sword that held Harper at bay.

"I'll have my revenge," Maxwell cried.

"Best I could do is to send you to join your wife," Harper said as he cut in from the left.

"Stop right there!" Peter yelled, aiming a pistol at Harper.

"For Christ's sake, did I kill your woman too?" Harper asked and then withdrew.

"The evil in you knows no bounds," Peter replied. "You've murdered so many that you cannot even recall them."

"Look, groom, if you shoot that gun, you'll alert thousands of my comrades. But if it misfires, I'll have your head off before your friend gets anywhere near me."

Harper made a run for his horse. Peter pulled the trigger and released the pistol's fury in a fiery flash. The ball caught Harper's forearm, tearing the flesh, and as droplets of crimson mixed with the dew, he let out a cry of pain. He dropped his sword and gripped his wound.

"Stop your squealing." Maxwell picked Harper's blade up and then punched him in the stomach, doubling the man up. He then slammed the pommel of his sword onto Harpers back, sending the man to his knees, whereupon he placed his blade to his neck.

"Kill me," Harper wheezed as he caught his breath, "and I'll have your wife in the afterlife."

"If I'd caught you at Naseby, you'd have had a bullet through your head. But I'm a different man now, Gervase, and you soon will be too. You're going to help the King." Maxwell grabbed Harper's black hair and pulled his head back. "I'm going to drag you all the way to His Majesty like the animal you are and you're going to tell him all about this army of yours that's nearby. All three thousand of them."

"Saint Smithy?"

"I never said anything about being good. I just said different." Maxwell knew that Lynch's shadow still hung over him despite his reprieve, therefore his word about the proximity of the enemy would be doubted. But bringing in the prisoner would be all the evidence he needed to forewarn the royalists as well as proving his loyalty. He grabbed Harper's wounded arm and squeezed it tight.

"Once I'm finished with you, I'll run my blade through your gut inch by inch. I'll make you feel all of the *pain* that you have inflicted upon others."

Harper cried out at the tormenting agony that paralysed him. Yet despite this, he kept a fixed glare upon Maxwell. Sweat appeared at his brow, his body began to tremble and when Maxwell finally let go, Harper fell forward and pushed his face into the earth.

"Good shot for a groom, don't you think, Harper?" Maxwell said. "Now, it's imperative that we find the King before Colonel-General Poyntz."

Chapter Twelve

Dawn. 24th September 1645.
4 miles south of Chester.

The morning sky had barely begun to stir when Maxwell and Peter, along with Harper, crossed the old bridge at Holt. The sunrise lit their way across the red sandstone arches. Sir Marmaduke Langdale and his royalist cavalrymen had not long passed over the same bridge, according to one of the locals Maxwell had just quizzed, and this was heartening news. He needed it.

Harper was between his two captors. Maxwell had ripped off one of the linen sleeves from Harper's shirt, using it as a gag to silence the man's arrogant outbursts and provocations. His hands were bound, securing him to the horse's neck. His legs tied to the girth strap. The proximity to Harper was suffocating. The man's presence raked up all of Maxwell's raw emotions and in echo of Matthew 18:6 it felt as if a millstone had been hung around his neck. Maxwell was slowly drowning amidst his darkened demons.

"Not long until your moment of glory, Gervase," Maxwell said, in an attempt to focus his mind on the ultimate goal; the only reason he had spared this vile dog. "When we warn the King of your army's proximity."

Harper's eyes narrowed. They were at odds with his mouth, the tight binding having pulled it into something of a wide smile. As Maxwell glared at his prisoner, he could not prevent his racing mind from going back over all the ways he could kill him; every one of them being slow and painful. The mere fact that this murderer was beside him tested every ounce of his restraint. Then the three men were shrouded as they passed beneath the tall gateway that stood almost halfway across the bridge. Maxwell seized the brief respite to try and suppress his anger. He thought of the lives he would save by not succumbing to his animal instincts, and instead delivering Harper up as evidence of the army that was stalking them. The hollow clip clop of the horses became a somewhat rhythmic and soothing focus.

Once on the English side of the River Dee, the men hastened away on the road north to Chester. A few pack horses trudged the route, but mostly it was devoid of traffic. It seemed nobody wanted to transport anything of any note while an army was in the vicinity, for goods were certain only to end up at the same destination; the purses and saddlebags of those very troops. But Langdale would, no doubt, be greatly interested in Maxwell's cargo and it wasn't too long before he heard horses in the distance. The braying was a most welcome noise; one of hope and relief. As they approached Millers Heath, an array of royalists swept down upon them with pistols drawn.

"Halt!"

"Langdale! We are here for Langdale," Maxwell yelled and stood in his stirrups.

The royalist troopers kept their fourteen-inch barrels trained. Upon realising that there were only three horsemen, they split in half and flanked the trio to escort them onto the heath, where not short of three thousand cavalrymen were drawn up in wait.

"Captain Walker?" Sir Marmaduke Langdale rode forward with a group of officers. "How good it is of you to join us."

"The pleasure is all mine, sir. Three months away from the army has felt like three years and aged me as much too," Maxwell replied.

"You come with a gift, Walker?" Langdale nodded his head at Harper.

"Not exactly."

"It matters not, we will soon gift the King a most noble victory." Langdale pointed north. "His Majesty is within Chester's walls and set to engage the rebels who besiege it, at which time we will also attack them in the rear."

"Alas, there is a surprise planned for us too. Poyntz is closing up fast. Even now he is approaching from the south with an army," Maxwell warned.

"How many?"

"Three thousand according to him." Maxwell pointed to Gervase. "He's one of their scouts. I'll remove the muzzle and let his loose tongue elaborate."

Gervase held his bearded jaw as if it had only been secured to his head by the linen binding. Even after it was untethered, he found it difficult to speak.

"Have your comrades any musketeers?" Langdale demanded.

"One hundred, Sir Marmaduke."

"That's one hundred barrels that will spit as much venom as their Puritan preachers." Langdale gripped his fist.

"Let me reassure you, sir, I am no idealist. I never did espouse their cause in my heart, so let me deal plainly ..." Harper said.

"I know that to be a lie!" Maxwell grabbed Harper's collar.

"Let him *deal plainly* with me," Langdale replied and bid Harper continue.

"Poyntz, as impetuous as ever, ordered his horsemen to race ahead of his foot," Harper replied. "He hopes the element of surprise will be of tenfold more worth than the musketeers."

"If you speak the truth, then we need to act fast, lest we get trapped between Poyntz and the rebels at Chester. Let us turn the tables on our approaching visitor," Langdale

REBELLION

said and ordered Maxwell and Peter to join Sir Philip Monckton's division. Maxwell handed Harper over to some guards. The action freed him of his shackles, but as soon as this battle was over, Maxwell would make sure he was free of Harper once and for all. He would seek justice.

As Maxwell rode away with Peter by his side, Harper stopped Langdale. This was God's will, he insisted. His conscience had been tormented ever since he had joined the parliamentarians, but after Captain Walker had arrested him, he had finally discovered himself. It was divine providence. He had been escorted to this army to serve the King.

***

It was merely twenty minutes later when a cry went up. Barely half past seven in the morning. Poyntz was closer than they had thought; his vanguard had been sighted and now these hunters were to become the hunted. Langdale marshalled his troops. The bulk formed two lines on Millers Heath with a small reserve, while a detachment was sent over to Hatton Heath directly opposite. The Chester road that led to this ambush was perfect for concealing it. The way was lined by hedgerows. Mother Nature had drawn up her grizzled, leafy troops in two lines to shield the two heaths from Poyntz's men, who now briskly funnelled into the lane like driven cattle. Then the hedges lit up with flashes of fire.

The parliamentarians cried out their surprise amidst the intermittent cracks of gunshot, which sent lead balls whizzing through the gorse and into rider and beast alike. But on top of the musketballs, the smoke from each four-and-a-half-foot barrel engulfed them in confusing plumes. Like a morning mist it hung in the lane. Spectral and malevolent.

"Charge!"

Maxwell and a line of cavalry advanced to the mouth of the lane with pistols drawn. Barely six feet from it, they discharged their weapons as the enemy emerged and tried to break out of their confined position. Poyntz, himself, led his lifeguard forward, yelling orders to form up on Miller's Heath. Two other regiments followed in support of the Colonel-General.

Maxwell drew his Irish-hilt broadsword and rode at the enemy. He closed up to a man with an eyepatch; an old foe, he now recognised, who came from Rise, in Yorkshire. Colonel Hugh Bethell had lost an eye the year before at Marston Moor. Maxwell cried out as he sliced his blade at the man once, twice and a third time, but each attack was blocked. Bethell parried from the left and right and then cut up with fast unpredictability.

The sweat had soaked into Maxwell's shirt, but this saturated linen now kept him cool. He lunged at Bethell, swiping his thirty-eight-inch blade in a desperate contest of speed and coordination. When they came to close quarters, he grabbed out at the man. Bethell's collar, or the two leather belts which crossed over his chest; one that held his carbine and the other his sword, but it was no good. Bethell turned his horse about and then came in again with a series of fresh blows. Then Maxwell smashed the fig-shaped pommel of his sword into the side of Bethell's face, between the face guards and his cheekpiece. Trickles of blood ran down his cheek. Just as Maxwell had managed to break the colonel's attack, a parliamentarian retrieved Bethell's taffeta standard while another closed in to assist the commander, who took the opportunity to escape. Maxwell managed a parting blow, which left only a silver scratch across Bethell's blackened iron gauntlet, before being set upon by this fresh foe.

It had only been fifteen minutes of sword blows, but the frenzy of desperate activity had taken its toll. The trumpets blared, calling the thin line of royalists back. Positively squealing for these tired horsemen to make way for

Langdale's full might, who had already begun to spill across the heath and towards Poyntz's vanguard.

Maxwell's arm felt heavy from the exertion. His buff gauntlet, with its fish-scale layers, had turned the double-edged blade of his opponent once already. No matter how much the trumpeters sounded their instruments, he could not shake off this persistent enemy trooper. Now in close, the man took hold of Maxwell's collar. But Maxwell tugged at the triple bars of his foe's helmet, pulling it off and then headbutting him. At that moment the enemy trooper fell backwards in his saddle with a pistol shot to his head.

"Harper?" Maxwell yelled with incredulity.

"Who would have thought it," Harper laughed. "Me, a royalist hero."

Harper drew his second pistol. Maxwell watched intently as the man pointed it in his direction. He felt betrayed by whoever had granted Harper's freedom; whoever had stupidly given this murderer a weapon in the belief that he would fight for the King. He yelled at Harper to shoot.

"Why would I do that? I've just saved your life," Harper shook his head, then aimed his pistol and shot a parliamentarian in the back. "We're on the same side now, Walker."

Harper grinned. His yellowy teeth were the same colour as his buff coat. Beneath the peak of a battered and crudely converted sallet helmet, his eyes seemed as dark as iron and as impenetrable. Langdale's cavalry thundered in around them, horses pounding and pistols thudding, followed by the clashes and clangs of steel that echoed the equal defiance. War had been the only thing that Captain Maxwell Walker had known in the last year and just being part of the King's army offered a strange sense of security. This loyalty had given him purpose and identity when he had lost everything. After Harper had taken everything.

Now the man had even taken this. Harper must die; whether friend or foe.

Historical Note

The Battle of Naseby was a key turning point in the civil wars. It destroyed the King's elite infantry, which had formed the backbone of his core army in England. For just over two months following Naseby, however, the King still had a chance of reversing his losses and pulling off a miraculous victory. His Scottish Lieutenant-General, the Marquis of Montrose, secured that kingdom by August 1645. Plans were made for the King and his cavalry to join Montrose's army and then restore royalist fortunes in England. But Montrose was defeated in September 1645, before the King could get to him. It's this crucial period after the Battle of Naseby, when the entire outcome of the war hung in the balance, that is the backdrop for this novella.

When writing, I adhere to the main historical narrative. This book accurately follows the events as they occurred; the Battle of Naseby, Siege of Hereford and the Battle of Rowton Moor. As Maxwell travels from place to place, what he witnesses is in strict keeping with the historical timeline. I have tracked the movements of the King and the armies of both sides so that Maxwell encounters them, or hears of them, in places that they would have been at that particular time.

Colonel-General Sydenham Poyntz was ordered to shadow the King after Naseby and bring him to battle. Lord Digby was the deluded, yet manipulative, Secretary of State who destroyed the King's cause from within. Sir Richard Halford owned Wistow and his descendent would become physician to the Prince Regent (later King George

IV). It was that particular Halford who would accompany the Prince Regent into St George's Chapel, Windsor, in 1813, after King Charles I's coffin had been discovered. Halford and the Prince Regent opened the lid and disrespectfully poked and prodded the royal remains and even took souvenirs of their visit. Colonel Barnabus Scudamore led Hereford's defence and I drew upon his letter to Lord Digby, which related the events of the siege – including a mock fox hunt on the town walls!

Historical locations covered in the story are also portrayed to the best of my research. John Speed's 1610 maps of Hereford and Worcester were very useful, as were descriptions of Wistow Hall prior to 19th century alterations. The conduct of the Battles of Naseby and Rowton Moor, as well as the units taking part in both (and their deployment) are factual. Rowton Moor features at the end of the book. That battle was in three parts, and this book only covers the first of these; the initial encounter which took place on Millers Heath, where Langdale successfully held up Poyntz. At that stage, both armies were evenly matched and brought to a stalemate. Poyntz received reinforcements first, and the two sides did battle again on Rowton Heath, where Poyntz scattered Langdale's troops. The final segment of the battle occurred when Langdale retreated to Chester and was engaged by the parliamentarian force that was besieging the town. These three parts are collectively known as the Battle of Rowton Heath (or Rowton Moor).

It was also quite common for ordinary soldiers to switch sides if they were captured, as was also the case for officers and even senior commanders. Sir John Urry is, perhaps, the most well-known turncoat, who transferred allegiance three times. Therefore, when Harper offers to fight alongside the royalists at Millers Heath, it would not have been unusual to have utilised him at that crucial moment. The motto on the standard I mention during the Battle of

REBELLION

Naseby 'Cuckold Wee Come' is thought to be a jibe at the parliamentarian Lord General, the Earl of Essex, who was forced to stand down after the Self-Denying Ordinance. Essex was said to have been cuckolded by each of his two wives.

I have listed below the named characters in the book who are entirely fictional. All other named characters are historical.

Captain Maxwell Walker & family
Gervase Harper
Peter Irwin
Colonel Hopkins
John Lynch
All servants & staff at Wistow Hall
Thomas Heskett

When I was ten years old, my parents took me to Helmsley Castle, North Yorkshire. In the gift shop I bought a pack of cards which featured portraits of the kings and queens of England all the way from 1066. On the reverse of each was a brief description of the monarch's reign. From the moment I first read about the civil wars and King Charles I, this period of history had me hooked, as it has done ever since. In 2019 the culmination of this fascination resulted in my first book being published; a novel set in 1642-43 called *'Allegiance of Blood'*. I also produce a podcast *'CavalierCast – The Civil War in Words'* that explores all aspects of the Wars of the Three Kingdoms.

Thank you for reading - I hope you enjoyed the story.

Mark Turnbull.

The King's Captain

Mark Turnbull

Chronology

14th June 1645
Battle of Naseby, Northamptonshire – decisive parliamentarian victory.

15th August 1645
Battle of Kilsyth, Scotland – royalist victory for the Marquis of Montrose, leaving him in control of Scotland.

10th September 1645
Prince Rupert surrenders Bristol, a key royalist city.

13th September 1645
Battle of Philiphaugh, Scottish Borders – royalist defeat.

14th September 1645
Prince Rupert dismissed from his military posts.

24th September 1645
Battle of Rowton Moor, near Chester – royalist defeat (Also where book one ends).

Chapter 1

4th October 1645.
Somewhere near Newark.

The sky was filled with plumes of dark clouds, as if giant muskets had fired in the heavens. Even the red breast of a robin stirred comparisons to a bloody gunshot wound. It seemed that wherever Captain Maxwell Walker turned, he could not escape this war. Maxwell's sandy locks were covered by a ribbed Flemish helmet; with dints and scratches, as battle-scarred as he was. He could not afford body armour. There was none to be had anyway. Instead, he relied on his old knee-length buff coat and its double-layered sleeves, which still sported a sword cut from his last battle. The breeches were of the same tough cowhide, and their ochre colouring was the nearest thing to a ray of sunshine on this dank and miserable day.

A cold breeze hurried past the cavalry pennants, though not enough to stir the two-foot taffeta to action. Clusters of dead leaves, which clung to the trees, rustled like old bones. The noise jeered Maxwell and the royalist horsemen who struggled on the track below. They were smeared and spattered with mud; symbols of the never-ending retreat from the battle at Rowton Moor, which had taken them on a journey of over one hundred miles. Ten long days. In fact, the troopers had something in common with the tussled leaves above, for these loyal remnants of the King's cavalry clung to his cause, despite doubts over whether they would make it to winter. All except one.

MARK TURNBULL

Lord George Digby. Maxwell likened him to persistent ivy, because of how the man's influence was reportedly spreading over King Charles I's affairs. As Secretary of State, his growth showed no signs of abating, nor did anyone seem to be in any position to cut it back. Despite recent military setbacks, the glorious Digby appeared in no way dulled. Not even by a backdrop of branches that clawed out at the October sky. Riding ahead of Maxwell, the man's golden curls peeped out from beneath a black helmet, as magnificent as the gilding that ran around the edges of his armour. The blue ribbon of the Order of the Garter crossed Digby's breastplate like a streak of summer sky, and certainly his outlook remained as bright. The Garter was a mark of favour; the highest and most chivalrous honour in the land. A mark of the King's undimmed trust. Maxwell, however, was not taken in by the peer.

The recent defeat at Rowton Moor had seen the death or capture of over one thousand royalist cavalrymen. The survivors had only gained one thing through that action; the dubious services of Gervase Harper. The turncoat had thus evaded Maxwell's many plans for retribution. Killing Harper would not have brought Maxwell's beloved wife back, but it would have been a sacrifice to the anger and vengeance that had eaten him away ever since Catherine's murder.

"Damn this mud!" Maxwell cursed as his horse slipped for the third time in as many minutes. The road had been worn away by yesterday's rainfall; droplets had eroded it like maggots at rotten meat and now it was a quagmire. Still, they were nearing Newark, which afforded a chance of some rest.

Vermilion sparks danced as delicately as tiny snowflakes near one of the trees ahead. They melted away almost as soon as Maxwell's eye had been caught, heralding a thudding explosion and a chorus of musketry. The horses whinnied as guns exploded at them. Burning cascades were vomited from the three-and-a-half foot barrels of the snaphaunces and shots flew at the ambushed royalists. Every lead ball, of one-and-a-half ounces, had the potential to tear through the flesh of man and beast with voracious appetite. One cavalryman fell to the ground with a cry of agony. As he writhed in a burgundy-brown pool, the royalist columns halted and returned fire, while others dismounted and ran forward to clear the enemy from their dens.

Maxwell's black leather boots splashed into the mud as he leapt from his horse. He advanced with a line of men, tightly gripping the walnut stock of his pistol and keeping the brass barrel level as he hurried along. Some parliamentarian dragoons sprang into the open, prompting Maxwell to squeeze the gun's trigger and then draw his Irish-hilt sword.

"Get them!" Maxwell yelled.

He lunged at one with his thirty-three-inch blade. It was parried. The second, third and fourth blows rang with steely resistance as they came together. Maxwell roared with determination as he cut across his foe and then followed with a *coup de main*, thrusting his sword into the man's chest. Most parliamentarians who were not yet engaged turned and fled through the trees and into the field beyond, mounting their cobs and riding off. Three others broke cover and made for Lord Digby. The peer dispatched the first with his pistol, but the others closed up to his black mare and brandished the curved blades of their hangers. Maxwell saw Digby's predicament. For a moment he hesitated, wondering whether it was best for everyone if the commander was slain, but then Gervase Harper struck.

"Swounds! Back to the bowels of hell with you," Harper shouted. While Digby fought one, Harper clashed blades with the other and grabbed hold of the belt that crossed the man's chest. He tugged so violently that the rebel lost his footing and fell to the ground. Now on all fours like an animal, with his helmet struck off, Harper brought his sword down upon the neck.

When Digby ran his remaining assailant through, there was no jubilation at seeing the enemy off; merely an uneasy silence. This was just another detachment of parliamentarians who were attempting to pick off the last of the cavaliers. Maxwell walked back to his horse and passed Harper, whose wolf eyes glared at him, fresh from his kill.

"By God, sir, I do believe you just robbed me of a rebel scalp," Digby said to Harper and made a point of sheathing his sword with an elaborate gesture.

"Humblest apologies, My Lord, but I would not risk them harming one so integral to His Majesty's cause."

"Oh, I fear it would take more than a few common hounds to bring me down," Digby replied with a smile. "But my thanks for your care."

"Well, sir, I can at least confirm that their *round heads* are as flimsy as their beliefs."

"Most humorous, indeed." Digby smiled.

"Enough, I pray, to forgive my poaching of your third quarry?"

Harper took off his helmet, wiping his brow and straggling black hair to allow Digby to get a good look at him, Maxwell assumed and looked on scornfully.

"Your name?"

"Gervase Harper, My Lord."

"Join my lifeguards, Harper. It is men like you who will see us through such troublesome times."

"It would be an honour."

"Mark my words, all of you," Digby called to those around him. "These may be dark days, but like the storm clouds above us, they will pass, and we shall soon bask in glory once again. The Lord will *not* allow traitors and rebels to prosper over our anointed sovereign."

REBELLION

Maxwell grunted with frustration. His chest was tight. He wondered why the Almighty seemed to favour Harper at every turn; having first saved him from Maxwell's vengeance, and now this. The only conclusion he could take from it was that God was steering Maxwell away from revenge. A true test of faith. So, perhaps it was actually for the best that Harper's promotion had united him with Digby – the peer would no doubt remain by the King's side in Newark where he could further ingratiate himself. Maxwell would be rid of them both.

Chapter 2

Three Weeks Earlier.

**13th September 1645.
Selkirk.**

The pearlescent moon shone benignly. Beneath it, mist rose from a tributary of the River Tweed and spread right across Selkirk, a town near the Scottish border. It was as if the ghosts of Scotland's past had risen up. Stirred from their very graves. James Graham, first Marquis of Montrose, stood at the open window where he'd been for half an hour, thinking and watching. Waiting. He felt as if he was between worlds, receiving the wisdom of his elders, men so famed as William Wallace, who had been appointed Guardian of Scotland nearly four hundred and fifty years ago at a nearby chapel. Montrose's ancestor had been Wallace's trusted friend. But something brought the great man even closer right now, as if he was entrusting Montrose with that very guardianship. Confirming him in position.

Certainly, the royalist Montrose had the whole of Scotland at his feet. Since he had unfurled the King's standard one year ago, with only a handful of men, he had gone on to vanquish every Covenanter army that had been sent against him. Time was all he needed to fight for now. He prayed for a few weeks more. His thoughts returned to the writs that he'd sent out in the King's name, summoning a Scottish Parliament to assemble at Glasgow next month.

REBELLION

The Covenanter opponents of King Charles had all fled, leaving Montrose as de-facto leader of the kingdom, but he knew the shadowy world of 1645 was ever-changing. It morphed and coalesced as much as the thick mist, and despite being at the peak of glory, with a string of seven victories to his name, Montrose felt somewhat uneasy. He expected an eighth test and this one would outweigh all others. The Covenanters had hurriedly recalled their army that was fighting against the King in England; the experienced cavalry arm of this force was reportedly at Berwick-upon-Tweed, thirty-six miles beyond this ghostly shroud, and rapidly closing in. They were to strike Montrose when he was most vulnerable. Six thousand of them, so scouts had reported.

The smell of his men's campfires enlivened Montrose. The smoky embers from Philiphaugh, one mile away, brought him back to the present, and this sweet-smelling reassurance offered a connection to his troops. He became acutely aware of their distance, being used to bivouacking amongst them. Perhaps this was one reason why he had not slept. That, together with working on endless despatches, the most important of all being an update for King Charles, which, as always, he took great care over. Some hours earlier, the scratch of his pen had been interrupted and a heartbeat of hooves had stirred him from his work. The duplicitous son of the Earl of Traquair had fled from Montrose's camp, taking with him one hundred horsemen. It was the man's father, and the other great border lords of Roxborough and Home, who had lured Montrose here with false promises of support. Lured him south, and far away from his highland den. But Montrose had lost more than these horsemen of late.

"Alasdair MacColla Chiotaich MacDhòmhnaill," he muttered in Gaelic and walked back towards the bed. If only his Irish ally could see beyond a sole desire to wreak vengeance on the Covenanter Clan Campbell.

"Put him out of your mind," Sir William Rollock counselled, his gruff voice wholly at odds with the calm of night.

"How can any one of us forget him?"

"Quite easily." Rollock shook his head. "The man has only ever been committed to his own cause."

"We'll unite with MacColla once more. We need him. Now isn't the right time to cross the border."

"Does he not understand he'll never reclaim his lands without a unified approach?"

"It's at the peak of success when men become most vulnerable," Montrose mused. "Every victory in this year of miracles has brought its own challenge, for they have bred apathy and overconfidence. These are God's victories, not mine or MacColla's. We are but His instruments."

"MacColla might burn Campbell lands like candles on an altar, but he has no reverence for God nor King."

"I fear such pillaging and destruction will consume us all. These actions make us little better than the Covenanters." Montrose sat down on the edge of the feather-filled mattress. He worried that everything he and MacColla had achieved together would also be cast into the flames. The men MacColla had taken west for yet more raids were some of his best Irishmen, veterans who had been at the forefront of the royalist victories.

"I know not how you remain so calm." Rollock's gruff tone betrayed his frustration.

"Because I must."

"Then you're a greater man than me."

"I do believe that was a compliment?" Montrose's chestnut moustache rose with a smile.

"Maybe," Rollock replied, "though don't fill your belly with pride. Our aim isn't to pull down Archie Campbell, only to replace him with Jamie Graham."

REBELLION

"For using my name in the same sentence as that arch-traitor, I do banish you to your bed. Go and rest, my friend."

Now alone in the flickering candlelight, Montrose took his pocket bible – barely one thumb-length wide – and opened it. He had bought it in France during the halcyon days of his youth, when aged twenty-one, he had toured Europe. Only nine years ago, the world seemed such a vastly different place. He had written on the tiny pages. Flicks of inky quotes that he wished to remember, words that were as inspirational as the biblical passages and which offered equal solace in times of need. Opening this bible was like opening a small portal to God, whereby he could personally communicate with the Almighty – as well as feel closer to his son, who had been called to the Lord's side last year.

"Non crescunt sine spinis," he read aloud, as if the words somehow imbued him with faith.

It was true – nobody could grow without thorns. He offered a prayer that God watch over his endeavours and guide his men on their retreat west, where he could recruit anew, as well as draw old allies back to his side. The yellow glow of the trembling flame sent both light and shadow across his bible. A sign, he judged, of his struggle to free Scotland from repression, as well as a reminder that even the smallest of flames could hold the darkest night at bay. But Montrose's grey eyes could no longer hold back the burden of responsibility. He lay down upon the mattress and was soon taken by a light and restless slumber.

"My Lord, the enemy are upon us!"

Montrose sprang up with a start. His dead boy, John, was nowhere to be seen. Yet he was sure he had felt the fourteen-year-old's presence, as if he had been standing by the bed, watching him sleep. Instead, there was a burly officer and a musty tang of sweat. The man's auburn beard seemed to stand on end from his chin as he caught his breath.

"The enemy, you say. Where?" Montrose leapt to his feet and grabbed his sword and belt.

"Less than a mile away and in good order," he exclaimed with a rasp. "The scouts last night were blind to it all and should be hung up by the neck."

"They have us, God damn them!" Sir William Rollock burst into the room.

"We face a test of endurance." Montrose clasped Rollock's shoulder and then hurried down the staircase.

Upon the first horse he could find, Montrose led the two hundred cavalrymen who had quartered with him at Selkirk. But the Covenanters had beaten him to his own army. The closer Montrose got to Philiphaugh, the more frequent the thuds of musket shot became, like the beginnings of a fire. The distant roar of orders became interspersed with cries of pain as battle took hold. No matter how hard and fast he rode, it felt as if Montrose was lost in the misty plane that he had observed during the early hours. The damp, cold air froze the frown of determination that crossed his face.

Chapter 3

12th October 1645.
Welbeck Abbey, Nottinghamshire.

Maxwell watched Cornet Anthony Durham intently. The young lad, like all of the company's officers and men, was relaxing on the grass. Durham, however, had taken a little too much ease and had fallen asleep, much to the ribaldry of the others. Maxwell felt a natural solace, as if he was amongst family. The men were not just comrades, many were neighbours and had been recruited from the same areas of Yorkshire. Their banter was amusing. A distraction too, which was good for morale.

"Naught but a loiter-sack," one said and pointed at young Durham.

"Deserves a rest after Newark, poor he."

"Poor he? I'd have given a week's rations for the chance to do battle with that girl every night."

Maxwell laughed along with the others. Having been hemmed into Newark's little haven for two weeks, with little else but patrolling the local area to occupy them, Cornet Durham had scouted out one particular girl in the tavern. Today's military rendezvous at Welbeck seemed well-placed to restore a sense of purpose.

"Someone feed him his bread and cheese," Maxwell called. "He must build up his strength once more!"

"For the love of God, how many forays did he make?" Peter Irwin smiled and sat up against a tree.

"Been on his back so much that he's unable to adopt any other position," Maxwell replied.

Durham's mouth dropped open, adding to the merriment. Even the swifts that flew overhead, as quick as their name suggested, squalled with apparent humour.

"Peter, throw him some bilberries." Maxwell pointed at the pile they had gathered from the bracken, which seemed to ensnare Welbeck.

"Upon your word of command, sir." Peter took one between his thumb and index finger and made ready to throw it.

"Give fire," Maxwell ordered.

It missed. The men poked fun at Peter's aim with as much good humour as if he had fought within their ranks from the very start. Maxwell then stood up with a grin and threw a particularly ripe berry. It squelched onto the cornet's forehead and made the lad spring up with a start.

"Nasty wound there." Peter's broad shoulders heaved with mirth as the purple juice ran down Durham's face. Laughter and cheering rang out.

"Don't worry, boy, you'll live to fight another day." Maxwell slapped Durham's back. "But let that be a lesson to you; always be on your guard."

"Sorry, sir."

"Seems like the mice may have been at your cheese." One of the soldiers pointed to the man's linen snapsack. "Damned big ones. Wearing buff coats and swords."

"To the Reformadoes!" Peter lifted his horn tankard and toasted the Northern Horsemen.

"Aye." Maxwell supped. "And to you too, Peter. May you always exchange your ale rations for my wine."

"Most happy to oblige." Peter's arched eyebrows rose in ready agreement.

The old Abbey of silver-grey limestone was behind them. Mullioned windows and gables gave it a look of haughty dismissal over the antics occurring in its grounds. A modern house had been attached to it, an array of square towers and symmetry that brought together the bygone world of the monks with that of the courtly Cavendish family.

"Captain Walker!"

Maxwell turned and observed Sir Marmaduke Langdale, commander of the twelve-hundred Northern Horsemen who had accompanied the King to Welbeck. Langdale's piercing eyes, appearing all the larger by way of the bags underneath them, had Maxwell on his feet in an instant. The commander's clean-shaven countenance betrayed every crease and wrinkle. In fact, the Catholic Langdale was more like a Puritan in his sobriety and appearance.

"Sir?" Maxwell stepped briskly forward.

"Have your men muster for an address by His Majesty."

"Yes, of course ..."

"Is something amiss?" Langdale frowned.

"Well, I merely wished to ask about Gervase Harper, sir. To point out my concerns about his newfound loyalty."

"He killed your wife. I do understand." Langdale's words felt as sharply dealt as any blade. "But were not you accused of murder after Naseby?"

"That was entirely different."

"You were given a second chance, Walker, therefore you are in no position to play the judge. We all have to live with decisions we do not agree with."

Langdale turned his black stallion, the coat of which glistened like his polished breastplate, and then left to spread the order.

"On your feet!" Maxwell returned to his company of sixty.

"What news, Maxwell?" Peter approached.

"Nothing worth mentioning, Lieutenant."

"Ah." Peter gave a knowing nod. "My apologies, I will pry no further."

"I did warn that if you served in my troop, you would be treated no differently."

"Which I respect entirely, you can count on my support as your friend, as well as your lieutenant."

Maxwell rubbed his forehead. The wounds of bereavement were worse than any incurred on a field of battle. They didn't heal. Whilst a sword edge, or a lead ball, could inflict physical damage, the loss of Catherine had dealt a blow to both his heart and mind. There were days when Maxwell simply couldn't cope. Days when he felt dead inside, the only sign of life being his continuous torment. But the army gave him the drive and determination to push himself through these dark times. And then there was Tom and Kit, his two boys.

"Get up, get dressed and follow me!" Maxwell called again. "The King will inspect us all."

*

Twelve hundred cavalrymen. They formed many long lines, overseen by the ever-dominating Welbeck. Maxwell's crimson sash was wrapped about his midriff; silk, edged with golden frill and tied in a grand knot at his back. His pale blue eyes remained focused on the Abbey, almost glazed beneath their heavy lids. He could not shake off Langdale's words. The very thought of them – of Catherine – caused his features to flush, emphasising his rather full, resolute lips and moustache, which in the sunlight took on a shade of flaxen. Catherine's glorious and golden curls had represented her rarity, so he had made a point of telling her many times. Yet she was gone. And Maxwell just had to accept it.

He'd passed the one-hundred-and-twenty-foot long riding house. The high windows prevented horses from being distracted by the outside world and Maxwell imagined how they must have longed for the expanse of an open field; tired of being manipulated by mankind for their own glory. But long gone was such courtly training. Gone too was the Marquis of Newcastle, owner of Welbeck and equestrian extraordinaire; he had given up on the King, having resigned his commission as Lieutenant-General North of the Trent, and left the country.

A flurry of movement attracted Maxwell's eye as officers mounted up in the distance. Langdale was bareheaded, as he would often be – even in torrential rain – so that his troopers could see him and the example he set. Next, a variety of grand men sporting plumes of red ostrich feathers, scarfs and ribbons. Iron armour, too, that was either burnished or blued and studded with golden rivets. Their buff coats were stitched with gold or silver thread, sparkling with their belt buckles, while frothy white lace draped their shoulders and flowed over boot tops.

"Make way for the King!"

The men moved aside, and King Charles emerged on a white steed, wearing a velvet cloak lined with plush ermine. The royal standard was carried before him, flashing gold, crimson and blue, as if energised by his presence. The horsemen cheered. Maxwell raised one hand and turned to his troop to encourage them.

"Huzzah!"

"God save the King!"

Energy abounded from man to man. The presence of the sovereign amongst them indicated trust and pride, while summing up their entire purpose. It gave hope. Maxwell knew that every man in war needed hope and he was no exception. Exclamations were added to by the jangling of bridle rings and spurs, and of horses braying and snorting. The King then held up his gold-tipped baton and the men quietened.

This was the closest Maxwell had been to King Charles. Etiquette usually dictated that nobody should look directly at the monarch, but the world had been turned upside down by this war, and now everything was different. He watched in awe, surprised that the King did not seem very tall and struck also by his regal countenance, which brought to life every shilling in Maxwell's pouch that was stamped with the same image.

"You, my loyal men of the famed Northern Horse, have proved yourselves numerous times," the King said with an occasional hesitation. "We came here with you on a venture north. Our aim is to join with the noble Marquis of Montrose. He has secured that kingdom and vanquished the core of traitors at its heart. By uniting with the marquis, our two forces can together defeat the rebels here in England."

Lord Digby now spoke. "We have today counselled His Majesty against personally undertaking this journey. We would, none of us, wish to give the rebels any opportunity of accusing the King of retreating north. Therefore, he shall remain at Newark. We will return to him at the head of a victorious army with the great marquis amongst us!" Digby's words drew the encouragement and approval of every senior officer. More cheers rang out through the ranks.

"I wish to show my faith in you all by appointing a new Lieutenant-General of my northern forces. One who will lead you on this crucial venture." The King looked along the lines of men. "Lord George Digby is a loyal officer worthy of such a position and enjoys our complete trust."

Maxwell cursed under his breath. Surely the King had taken leave of his senses? There came a momentary pause after this royal revelation. He observed some of the senior officers turn to each other, while others attempted to further incite the men's acclamations, though this time the responses were sporadic. Lord Digby moved his horse forward and called for quiet.

"I must profess to be as surprised as any of you by this mark of His Majesty's great favour." Digby turned to Langdale. "Though I accept the post wholeheartedly, I shall do so only with your approbation, Sir Marmaduke."

REBELLION

"I happily submit to the King's desire. It shall be an honour to have you lead us," Langdale replied.

"I will not fail with courageous men like you by my side." Digby smiled and turned to the cavalry masses before him.

Maxwell felt his heart sink. The only silver lining to this news was the fact that they were to head north; he would see his homeland of Yorkshire once more.

Chapter 4

King Charles moved aside a tapestry portraying Roman soldiers, which covered an open door, and then entered a small closet that adjoined the main bedroom. It was an intimate space and offered him somewhere to think and reflect. Though Welbeck Abbey was not his home, it was one of a dwindling number of havens that he could rely upon. He had not slept in his own bed for over three and a half years. Perhaps, he wondered, he had traversed more of England than any of his predecessors in the last two centuries; though given the circumstances, it was a dubious accomplishment.

He sat on a plush velvet chair, and upon thinking of Scotland, gave a deep sigh. How much he would have relished linking up with Montrose to personally thank him for his courageous service and the array of mighty victories he had secured. The King could have been part of a union of Scottish and English loyalists, Irish too, who formed the backbone of Montrose's force; all three of his kingdoms would be represented. Everything rested upon the marquis, for the man had secured Scotland, and this offered the only source of hope.

The king sighed again. Melancholy didn't suit him. He slid one of the books across the table's green velvet covering and brushed aside numerous quills, paper and sealing wax. The earthy scent of the leather binding reminded him of his own library. His joy of books was in no way dimmed by the fact that their smell had now become more heavily associated with warfare; of buff coats, cavalry boots and sword belts. This particular work,

REBELLION

embossed with a Cavendish stag's head, turned out to be about mathematics.

The King stood and stepped over to a painting that hung upon the green panelling. It was the Marquis of Newcastle's wife, by Daniel Mytens, whose style could not be missed. The lady had died two years ago. Perhaps this was the real reason why the peer had left England, and the royalist cause, amidst such an outburst of negativity. The world that the artist portrayed so well – that of King Charles's most glorious days – was long gone. Maybe it had been fitting that he had employed such talented men to capture those times.

"Your Majesty?" Digby waited at the doorway with a letter in his hands.

"What is it?"

"A despatch from the Marquis of Montrose."

King Charles took the folded parchment and broke the wax seal that affixed it. A crack split Montrose's coat of arms that was embossed upon it, and he opened the letter. Its greeting 'May it please your sacred majesty' was the same as ever but was hastily written. An inky dollop at the bottom of the page indicated so. The language, too, had an air of urgency. The King scanned the detail about the battle at Philiphaugh. Montrose's handwriting was tightly packed, like the lines of his infantry, which he described as having been hemmed in behind hedges, ditch and dike, and converged upon. The handwriting hampered the King's ability to scan the content, but then he came to the crucial part.

Montrose had been defeated. The commander's year of miracles had ended, and his despondency at barely reaching the battlefield before the rout was palpable. The King's heart raced; he could almost smell the cowardice of Montrose's few royalist horsemen, most of whom had apparently preferred to bait their horses than do battle with the Covenanters. Irony abounded. The Scot had often complained about a lack of cavalry, and delays in providing much needed reinforcements had proved to be his downfall – the King's downfall. A pang of regret filled the monarch.

"Montrose has suffered a reverse," King Charles said, handing the letter back to Digby. He walked into the bedroom, whereupon Sir Marmaduke Langdale bowed his head in silence.

"If I may venture, one defeat does not lose a kingdom," Digby reassured. "The marquis has, in the past, enquired after more cavalry. We will soon join him and reverse his loss."

"Then you must act swiftly," the King declared and turned to faced Digby. "Ride without delay and waste no time in your journey north."

"We are to continue with the plan and unite with Montrose?" Langdale's surprise was etched within the lines of his brow.

"Of course!" Digby snapped. "Why would we let a few rebels put us off?"

"Whilst I do admire your positivity, might I clarify that there are six thousand of them?" Langdale was unabashed. "I fear it may be perilous to take my men so far north and against such odds."

"I am Lieutenant-General; therefore, I shall be responsible for their success. Does that allay your concerns, Sir Marmaduke?" Digby asked, pointing with Montrose's letter as if it added extra authority to his argument.

"It doesn't change my opinion, nor shake my counsel against such a move."

"Montrose will recruit men and soon replace his losses. He has before called for a mere regiment of horse to complete his hold on Scotland, and we will provide him with one thousand two hundred, men of the famed

Northern Horse, at that. Veterans who lost their honour at Naseby, but who will fight like lions to get it back."

"A conquest to regain the north has been my main desire for a long time," Langdale said. "The North of England, however; to fight the enemy in Yorkshire and the Palatine of Durham. But, as you correctly point out, his majesty has invested you with command, and neither I, nor my men, will refuse an order."

"To join with Montrose is our express wish," King Charles added. "I command you both to put all debate aside and employ every endeavour to reach him."

Chapter 5

13th October 1645.
Sherburn in Elmet.
15 miles from York & 184 from London.

A dark mass of over one thousand parliamentarians stood together on the moor ahead. Maxwell had just fed his carbine a dose of gunpowder from a cow-horn flask. His thumb caressed the carving on the gun's butt. The forty-five-inch weapon would soon spout a fiery offering of lead at the enemy, who were of equal number to the royalist horsemen, though entirely comprised of infantry. Their moor was surrounded by ditches, like miniature dry moats, they gave the appearance that the country was physically fracturing beneath yet another encounter.

After covering forty miles since leaving Welbeck, this was the royalists' first test. Maxwell, along with Langdale's Northern Horsemen and Digby's lifeguards, advanced with a trot that was somewhat reassuring. One of unity and strength. They soon increased their pace to a canter, and Maxwell squeezed his calves to his horse's flanks to keep up; his heartbeat rose as the royalist lines neared the moor.

The standards that interspersed the enemy ranks opened up in the wind and slapped their colours upon the grey sky. The parliamentarians themselves also seemed affected by the cold front and some began to waver. Almost in dread of what was to come, one of their wings began to disintegrate and men ran for cover towards the trees behind them. Sight of this made Maxwell and many other royalists cry out with resolve. The enemy reeked of raw recruits.

"Come Reformadoes. Let us scatter them all!"

Trumpets blared. The royalists pounded onto the moor and briefly reformed, while those that had them readied firearms. They were no sooner on the move again, beating along the cold earth, when enemy musket fire rang out in a series of thudding echoes. The resulting smoke stalked the field. It dissipated long before reaching the attackers, leaving only the acrid smell of sulphur and charcoal. It was now the turn of every royalist carbine to answer, and as such, the horsemen drew up once again. Maxwell sent his own offering at the parliamentarians to further pepper their morale, and then drew his sword upon the order to charge. Now there was no going back. No more interruptions. The royalists hammered at the enemy, pointing their steel blades accusingly, and ready to deliver the judgement of God upon these rebels. Clods of earth flew like birds in their wake.

The wave of horsemen surged up to the lines of parliamentarian infantry. A few unlucky troopers were skewered on the ends of pikes and fell from their saddles. Maxwell and his men targeted the enemy musketeers; some reversed their muskets and swung them like clubs, though most dropped them and ran, only to be cut down before they had got very far.

Before long, the parliamentarian musketeers were as spent as their weapons and the pikemen so fractured that they could not lock together enough to stand firm. Too many of them had fled, leaving vulnerable gaps in their ranks. The royalists then split their attack; swinging around to fall upon the exposed flank of the enemy, whose eighteen-foot ash poles went down like trees felled by a storm. The rot spread fast. Even the surprise arrival of four hundred parliamentarian cavalry, filtering onto the moor from the north, could not stop the royalists now.

Upon his horse of fifteen hands, Maxwell had a good view of the oncoming riders and led his own men forward. The scent of victory imbued him with every rapid breath. The royalists met their opponents with a kinetic energy that seemed unstoppable; clashes and clangs, grunts and yells, all fed Maxwell's adrenaline. It wasn't long before the enemy horsemen broke.

They turned and hammered back towards Sherburn, unable to stop this royalist resurgence, spearheaded by the Northern Horsemen. Men who did not simply put their lives on the line for their King, but for their homes, families, and religion too. Maxwell drew up his mount and reined himself in from the temptation to give chase. He was consumed by relief and jubilation; sensations triggered not by the killing alone but by his own survival and the victory they had secured. He held his blade in the air. They were reclaiming their homeland after so long an absence.

*

Maxwell looked on as parliamentarian prisoners were rounded up, all of them being led through Sherburn's main street and into the fields to the north of town. Almost eight hundred of them passed under the shadow of All Saints Church; like penitent sinners, so Lord Digby scoffed as he oversaw proceedings. The enemy surrendered all of their weapons. Every musket, sword and pike were piled high in the street like bones that had been tipped out of a charnel house. Certainly, Lord Digby believed that the rebel cause in the north had just suffered a death blow.

"This is the Lord's work." Digby's eyes sparkled like sapphires. "I will reverse the rot that has festered in the north since Prince Rupert's defeat at York. We shall *reclaim* what the prince lost. Has not the Almighty repaid my faith with such a complete victory?"

"It does, indeed, seem so." Langdale's dour expression changed little as he turned to Digby.

REBELLION

"The north has been an open sore, which the rebels have fed upon for too long. They have bled all loyal subjects dry."

"I hasten to add that this is but the beginning," Langdale replied. "A lancing of one particular boil."

"A glorious beginning," Digby corrected. "And we chirurgeons who shall finally treat the ails of the north as we pass through it."

Maxwell's eyebrows dipped. His frown deepened and eyes narrowed, enhancing the shadows that encircled them. He watched as Digby, involving himself in every little detail, encouraged some men who carefully placed captured gunpowder. The politician-cum-commander laughed. Made jests. Looking down from his black stallion, as if the entire victory was his, he doled out encouragement and congratulations. Superficial words of praise. Digby's veneration of brave Sir William Blakiston, carried past in a litter with a shot to his leg, did no more than steal the man's glory.

Maxwell leaned against a wall; his manner resembled a restless spirit that had risen from the graveyard behind him. He picked at one of the swivel hooks on the shoulder straps of his armour. After judging Digby's arrogance and Langdale's intuition, he inhaled the familiar Yorkshire air. It smelled like home. Whether it was the smoke and livestock, imbued with the scent of fresh woodland, he felt a certain confidence at being on familiar soil. Home fed his instincts for survival but further rooted him to this county. He stepped forward and held out his hand, stopping a cavalryman from adding some pistols to the pile of weaponry. A second gun would do Maxwell nicely and he selected one.

"I am told that King Athelstan owned Sherburn – the first King of a unified England. A most poignant fact, considering that our victory will help steady that very crown." Digby looked around him. "The men must be ready for their next bout," he demanded, "because this success will *incense* the rebels and increase their determination to bring us down."

The captured weapons seemed more like medals in Digby's eyes. Maxwell could tell that he wanted them to demonstrate his prowess. As such, the commander was overly preoccupied with gathering them up; calling for wagons and issuing instructions to seize any that were available to carry this booty away.

Near to Digby, however, was something else that had come from the enemy, though in very different circumstances, and nearly one month ago, Gervase Harper. His hair was as black as jet, and the beard that crept up his high cheekbones gave him a deathly and gaunt appearance. Maxwell glared down the barrel of his new pistol and held Harper momentarily in its sights, before examining the brass wire decoration. Far from a mountain of weapons, he just needed one. Only one shot from it, too. Hate rose from his stomach, as if the recent battle had further fed it. Then Harper's thin mouth upturned with a smile.

"Sir, the rebels in the church refuse to surrender." Peter Irwin approached.

"Damn their foolish resolve." Maxwell shook his head. "I have had enough idling here. Let me try reasoning with them," he muttered and walked briskly towards the church.

"You seem distracted?" Peter asked.

"What brings you to that conclusion?"

"You appear so. In words, expression, and bearing."

"Every man who has fought for three years looks like this," Maxwell replied. "The disease of veterans; having survived so long, the experience leaves us looking more dead than alive."

"Then I pray this war doesn't last another three," Peter said, "otherwise no good lady shall ever marry me."

"Is every old soldier consigned to defeat in the affairs of the heart?" Maxwell smiled.

REBELLION

"There are many women who would enjoy being commanded by a strict veteran."

"It's a relief that I have no desire to marry again."

"Let's see you pay court to these lot." Peter pointed to the church.

The two men approached the door from where a loophole had been cut, though no musket barrel poked from it any longer. Royalist troops stood up against the church's walls in wait, with pistols or muskets held in close embrace. Maxwell called out to the commander inside. He gave his own name and rank.

"Be thou my stronghold, whereunto I may always resort. Thou hast promised to help me, for thou art my house of defence and my castle," came a defiant voice from within.

"This churchyard is full enough without more bodies to inter," Maxwell replied and rapped upon the door with his bare fist. "Surrender yourselves!"

"You a local man, Captain Walker?"

"Aye, Selby."

"Then you will know that a Yorkshireman's will is not to be taken for granted."

"I know that we always speak the truth," Maxwell said. "There are a thousand prisoners out here, none of whom are being mistreated. Surrender now and you will be granted honourable terms."

"We hold firm to our allegiance as well as our faith. Where better to seal this, than in the house of God?"

"Listen to me." Maxwell took a deep breath. "Your resistance is courageous. I admire it. But continuing this stance, risks you and your men being given no quarter. You know the rules of war as well as I. Now, accept favourable terms, and as God is my witness, I will see you all treated with respect."

"Respect?"

"Aye, like your comrades out here."

"The Northern Horsemen treat nobody with respect. You are Papists, all of you, ready to take up the sword like your Catholic brothers in Ireland."

"Enough ..."

"Like the horsemen of the apocalypse you wreak only conquest, war, famine, and death. We will go forth in the strength of the Lord."

"You face more than four of us, let me assure you of that," Maxwell said and joined the man in quoting from the Book of Common Prayer. "Take me out of the mire, that I sink not."

Silence ensued.

After further thought, Maxwell reached into his pouch to extract a small, lead medal and then dropped it through the hole. It landed on the stone floor of the church with a clunk and he waited pensively.

"Magdeburg?" The enemy commander asked.

"I fought there at the age of eighteen," Maxwell replied.

"You taunt us! This is a great horror. Most of the city torched and near twenty-thousand inhabitants burned alive by your co-religionists."

"The sole similarity we have with the devils who did this to Magdeburg is our religion. Nothing else. However, the bonds between your men and mine are vast. We share the same nationality, roots and heritage. The same Yorkshire will. Even, perchance, the same kinsmen."

With a cry to his troops, Maxwell ordered them to leave the churchyard and then suggested that the parliamentarians take time to confer about their situation. But whatever conclusion they came to, the medal must be returned to him. Maxwell watched his men cautiously depart, answering any doubts with a firm nod, the likes of which they had come to recognise and trust. Soon he was the only one left outside the church. When an eye and a sliver of face appeared at the loophole of the door,

REBELLION

Maxwell stepped back so that they could get a full look at him. But he kept his gaze on the hole.

"This is trickery!"

"I remain to give you clear reassurance of my intentions," Maxwell said. "My men cannot shoot without killing me."

As Maxwell stood in silence, his expression fixed and serious, he couldn't help but remember Magdeburg and how the river was full of charred bodies for four days afterwards. Unearthly memories from a foray into hell. Experiences he never wished to see repeated.

Iron bolts began to squeal as they were slowly withdrawn. The doors of All Saints tremored with apprehension. Maxwell stood straight, holding his hands behind his back, rather than resting them upon the sword by his side, or the carbine that hung limply from his belt. Beneath the armour his heart thumped fast.

The door opened, and a man appeared, much like Maxwell in appearance; breastplate and a grey buff coat beneath it, though with an orange sash wrapped about him. He stood framed by the doorway and met Maxwell's eyes before stepping out and removing his pot helmet. After exchanging respectful nods, the major approached and handed back the small medal. It took only a few seconds before he called on his soldiers to follow him out of the church.

"I have only one request," Maxwell said. "That you and your men leave your weapons inside, if you please."

Maxwell faced the one hundred and fifty parliamentarians who emerged into the daylight. He turned as they neared him and proceeded to lead them out of the churchyard, whereupon he selected some of his own men as an escort. The prisoners were summarily marched down to the street. As Maxwell watched them go, one after another, the anguish of Magdeburg was assuaged a little more by the avoidance of any repetition; every man who marched past – husband, father, son or brother – silenced the ghosts of the past.

Chapter 6

**Atop the tower of All Saint's.
Sherburn-in-Elmet.**

Maxwell looked down upon the main street, which led to the church and then veered off to the left, past the ruined remains of King Athelstan's palace. He wasn't good with heights. Cursing under his breath, he held onto the limestone battlements, whose four crocketed pinnacles pointed skyward like the jagged heads of partisan staffs. He had come not for the view, but for solace.

Up here it felt as though he was separated from the war. A distant observer. Yet, he was unable to cast off an agitation that consumed him. Even when the earlier fighting had petered out and the royalists had secured their victory, Maxwell still sensed a rush of adrenaline, as though he remained in danger. His head ached. He looked across to where the clouds seemed to scud, and the horizon of hazels and oaks that dotted it. His sons, Tom and Kit, could even now be amongst them, and he recalled teaching young Kit the names of the trees. Maxwell considered the boys' ages; eight and five years respectively. They were so close, yet so far. Selby was barely one day's march, but if he was to ride furiously ...

"Captain Walker." Peter approached, catching his breath from the climb. "We've found this hidden pouch."

"In the church?"

"Aye, someone clearly didn't want it to be discovered on their person."

Maxwell took it and carefully poured the contents onto his palm. Some silver shillings and a small letter, which crackled as he proceeded to unfold it.

"Will you still look upon Wistow as your home when this conflict is finally over?" Maxwell asked.

Peter sighed and removed his hat. "I'm not certain that the place truly felt like home to begin with."

"I see." The reply surprised Maxwell. He had assumed Peter to be one who valued stability above all else; a grounded individual affixed to Wistow Hall by way of his family roots, as well as the stable employment it offered. "I am far from as settled a character as you, yet I have no doubts about the innate pull my home has upon me."

"You mentioned Selby earlier. Is it far?"

"Seven miles distant." The words seemed to stick in Maxwell's throat. He longed to see his boys. To go home. "Warfare makes men forget they are fathers." His hands gripped one of the stone merlons.

"I once told you that my father was present at the first Siege of Breda." Peter seemed to avoid eye contact. Like one of the four gargoyles that jutted from the tower, he peered down at the graveyard. "He talked often of honour being infinitely more valuable than any amount of gold. I admired the way you encouraged those rebels to surrender."

"For what it's worth, I agree with thy father," Maxwell replied with a nod of thanks. "I have a mind that you might be much like him."

"Perhaps." Peter shrugged. "I hope so. There was no honour at Magdeburg?"

"Even the slightest discourse of it would feed such memories, and in turn they would consume me. I must leave them buried and take them to the grave."

Maxwell did not look up and instead began to read the paper in his hands. He cursed.

"What is it?"

REBELLION

"This note. It suggests we may be facing more than just the enemy's armies. Perhaps their assassins too."

"How so?"

"It's been transcribed. The King's last commander will be prevented from altering the course of the war – the author even suggests he may not live long enough to do so."

"Last commander? Digby, perchance?"

"Aye, it must be," Maxwell replied. "And the signatory is 'Protais' whoever that may be."

"What will you do – inform Digby?"

"It may be best if I hand this to Langdale."

A magpie edged along the tower, its black and white feathers bristling to reveal a shimmer of blue. For a moment the bird looked at the two men. Then, as if sensing their unease, it leaped from the limestone to glide effortlessly across the glinting pile of weapons in the street below. Maxwell watched for some seconds in silent contemplation. He decided that it was best to rid himself of this note forthwith and upon descending the steps of the tower, his resolve only strengthened. When he approached Lord Digby, Harper leaned in towards the commander and spoke.

"Ah, the Piper of Sherburn." Digby's smile was so false that it may as well have been painted on his face. The comment drew contrived mirth from others near the Lieutenant-General.

"I beg your pardon, My Lord?" Maxwell frowned, taken aback by his reception.

"Leading all of the roundheads out of the church, like the Piper of Hamlin." Digby shook his head slowly. "Though in your case, marching at their head as if you were in league with them, rather than entertaining any plan to dispose of them."

"An approach that saved both ammunition and time. And deaths."

"Preventing the enemy from being smoked out of their nests. Thus, saving their skins." Digby's expression turned to one of seriousness. "I do wonder whether your behaviour has revealed, once again, a hidden affinity with the rebels. Let us not forget the game you played at Wistow Hall, which saw the demise of one of my most loyal men."

"Should you insist on casting doubt and dishonour, sir, then I shall render up my commission."

"So that you may join the rebels?" Digby pointed to the prisoners. "Nay, Walker, you will stay close to me. I must keep an eye on you."

"These are unfounded slurs and I find them outrageous!"

"As is your untamed temper." Digby was quick to cut him off. "You will remain with my lifeguard until we are away from here and then you shall furnish me with the exact details of what occurred at the church." He turned to Langdale. "Have the men drawn up on Sherburn Common for a service of thanksgiving. Meanwhile, let us ride to Huddleston Hall, where I may procure further transport for our spoils."

Chapter 7

Huddleston Hall.
1.2 miles northwest of All Saint's.

Flames danced around the logs like yellow imps, causing a series of cracks that had no effect whatsoever upon the curled-up spaniel. The fire grew higher, as if outraged by the dog's sleepy indifference. Yet, it was a barely audible squeak from the door of Huddleston Hall that caused the spaniel's eyes to open. Its long ears, the bottoms of which lay on the floor, now twitched. Whilst an array of dull voices exchanged pleasantries in the distance, the dog's head rose and turned to its owner, Sir Philip Hungate.

Maxwell followed Lord Digby and his officers into the hall, where they were greeted by Sir Philip, a local magnate and royalist. The man looked more like a mere shadow. Dressed head to toe in black mourning, his embroidered sword-belt was all that animated him, for the firelight made its golden threads sparkle. Maxwell recognised the sorrow that lurked in the hollows of the man's gaunt cheeks.

"Sir Philip, how good it is to meet you." Lord Digby strode briskly up to the man.

"Allow me to congratulate you on your victory, My Lord."

"Most kind of you, sir. Despite the magnitude of our success, I remain saddened that it was accomplished *without* your dear son."

"Yes ..."

"I wish he had been alive to partake in our joy."

"As do I." Sir Philip closed his eyes and bowed his head.

"Francis was one of the Reformadoes' bravest officers. His courage last month at Rowton Moor will forever be his epitaph, despite our defeat that day," Digby said with a sigh that emphasised his words. "I wager his example spurred his comrades on to regain their honour."

Jesu! Maxwell gritted his teeth at Digby's implied criticism.

"When the King enjoys his own again, your loss shall not be forgotten." Digby gave a benign smile.

To Maxwell, the commander's speech rankled. The Northern Horsemen had not only been condemned over Rowton Moor; the insinuation was that even today's victory stemmed from some sort of guilt about it. Digby's words tarnished the very praise he doled out for brave Sir Francis Hungate.

"Forsooth, I do not desire to judge the past," Digby added, breaking the momentary silence. "Suffice to say that your late son deservedly basks in our glory."

"A most tender compliment." Sir Philip coughed.

"Your home is most distinctive. Its stone has an almost saintly glow," Lady Elizabeth Nithsdale remarked from the gathering behind.

"Ah, a local quarry, Milady." Sir Philip stumbled over his words in an eagerness to change the subject. "The same stone used to build King Henry the Seventh's chapel at Westminster."

"How fascinating." Digby's blond eyebrows rose in wonderment. "Now, I hope you will not take it ill, but I require use of your servants and their knowledge of these parts."

"Of course, I gladly extend my hospitality to you and your officers. Are you planning on remaining in Sherburn this evening?"

"Alas, no. We must resume our journey." Digby threw his hands in the air at the very thought of rest. "There is a mountain of weapons in your main street, which I shall retain for the King's service."

"I understand."

"I need waggons and then we shall be on our way. Might you know of any that can be requisitioned?"

"I own one, which I would happily give over to your service ..."

"Excellent, see to it." Digby seized the offer and turned to one of his subordinates.

The man's subsequent departure was followed by a rush of cold air that pervaded the room. The spaniel walked lazily towards the group. His claws clicked on the wooden floor and he glanced first at Digby, before quickly moving on to Langdale.

"A handsome little thing." Lady Nithsdale remarked.

"My apologies. In all of this haste, I have forgotten my manners," Digby said, and introduced the lady to Sir Philip. "She accompanies her husband, who rides in my ranks."

After sniffing Langdale's boot, the dog hurried over to Lady Nithsdale who kneeled down. Maxwell watched as she gently stroked its velvety ear and giggled as the dog tried to lick her hand. Her humour was kindly. A benign sound in the midst of such troublesome times, which had the power to change the atmosphere entirely. Indeed, Maxwell could almost hear Catherine, whose laughter had been the only accolade he had ever sought; more often than not elicited by some silly antic or his dry wit.

"Athelstan!"

Sir Philip called the excited spaniel as it scrabbled around Lady Nithsdale's silk dress; as if it should recognise the status of this lady, a cousin of the late Duke of Buckingham.

"Care to take him with you, My Lord?" Sir Philip apologised for the dog's antics. "A new recruit?"

"He could be your talisman, My Lord," Lady Nithsdale interjected. "Prince Rupert had his poodle, Boye. You could follow his example and carry dear Athelstan into battle."

"Judging by His Highness's current misfortunes, such a comparison does not endear itself to me." Digby's eyes widened. "Besides, I am a very different leader to the prince."

Never a truer word spoken, Maxwell thought.

The arrival of a newcomer, hurrying into the hall, distracted Maxwell from his disgruntled laugh of cynicism. The man's footsteps were firm and resolute but stopped abruptly when Athelstan began to bark. The messenger excused himself and gave an uneasy bow. Digby frowned at the dog with frustration and instructed the man to speak freely.

"The enemy have been sighted, My Lord."

"More? Where?"

"To the south. They are bypassing Milford and approaching Sherburn via the hedgerows."

"Evidently they fear our sharp shooters, who take aim from Milford's every window," Digby raised his head. "We must be ready for them. Let us draw our men up on Sherburn Common and await them!"

Turning on his heel, Lord Digby led his entourage out, looking as excitable as Athelstan over the very prospect of a second victory. Maxwell followed. If he was in command, he would be at the rebels before they'd even exited the lane, rather than waiting in the fields to the north of town. But Maxwell deigned to compare himself to Digby, for the two men were *very* different characters.

Chapter 8

Sherburn Common was slowly transformed. Clusters of shivering trees stood tormented by the cold wind, as if whispering to one another about the inevitable battle. Their branches flailed as one thousand five hundred royalist horsemen formed up on the dull expanse with its earthy brown undertone. Digby's entire force was here. But standing in one corner, hemmed in under guard, were the parliamentarian prisoners, a now cumbersome reminder of the encounter that had taken place earlier that day.

Gruff orders and trumpet blasts soon subsided. They gave way to an eerie echo of braying horses, intermingled with the occasional birdsong and tinkle of weapon or harness. Such delicate and hollow noises exacerbated a feeling of emptiness. The royalists waited for the enemy to come and do battle; waited as if they had the time to do so. It was four of the clock and daylight was itself engaged in a struggle with the onset of evening.

To Maxwell, it was somewhat surreal to be on the field of battle for a second time that day, as if morning had somehow lasted forever and the day was destined never to end. His hunger pangs had ceased after being ignored for so long. A tang of yarrow herb lingered from his ale; a reminder of all that had passed his lips that day.

"Well, this second encounter will be a blessing in one respect," Maxwell whispered to Peter Irwin. "I am now freed from his shackles." He nodded in Digby's direction.

Peter smiled. "'Let slip the dogs of war'," he quoted from the play, *Julius Caesar*.

"You call me a dog, my friend?" Maxwell grinned.

"Aye, and one whose bite is very much worse than his bark."

"Well, let us give these rebels as good a mauling as the last ones!" Maxwell called out in encouragement to his men.

Sir Marmaduke Langdale rode over to Lord Digby. Both men kept their eyes on the thatched rooves of Sherburn to the south and spoke with grave expressions – though Langdale's countenance was always serious. He proposed to lead a small party through Sherburn to assess the enemy's strength. Digby took out a spyglass and pondered the offer while examining the town and beyond. Finally, the Lieutenant-General gave a nod. This was all Langdale needed. His recognisable figure – clad in polished black armour – was at the head of his horsemen in an instant, readying them for their task.

"Colonel Christopher Copley is approaching us. Our scouts report his numbers to be insignificant. Six hundred at most," Langdale said, and proceeded to select those that would accompany him. Maxwell's troop were named. "Copley's motto is *'For Reformation'*. Let him feel the might of the Reformadoes!"

Huzzahs rang out. Hundreds of royalists rode off, clattering through Sherburn's main street and past the stash of weapons that stood like a monument to this morning's accomplishment. The church peered down at them from its high ground.

Maxwell was energised by the motion of the ride, as he and his men spilled through Sherburn and into the fields beyond, he soon noticed the rebels deploying to the southeast; four bodies of them, each numbering approximately two hundred, and behind them more still. Langdale had his men form up. Maxwell's grip went instinctively to his carbine, for the enemy were close enough to be in range, and their fluid ranks rippled with movement. He could sense the inevitable magnetism that had already taken hold of both sides.

It was immediately apparent that the royalist detachment was outnumbered, perhaps two-to-one. Maxwell put the enemy at one thousand four hundred in all. If the royalists turned back to Sherburn now, they would be pursued and annihilated; cut up like meat on a butcher's slab. Langdale was quick to face up to facts.

"Gentlemen! You are all gallant men," his deep voice was full of gravitas, "but there are some that seek to scandal your gallantry for the loss of Naseby field. I hope you will *redeem* your reputation and still maintain that gallant report which you have ever had."

The troopers did not cheer. The commander's words were heard with respectful silence until his pause became obvious. Only then did the men roar. Deep-rooted roars of determination to avenge their honour. Roars that fed upon their shock at the enemy's strength, as well as the apprehension that this caused. Maxwell was no exception. He cheered as if the royalists had already secured the second victory they so desired.

"I am sure you have achieved such business that never was done in any war with such a number." Langdale went on to list their past successes, and in particular the relief of Pontefract Castle. 'Sherburn' was then repeatedly chanted as the men eagerly added it. "I will not have you go anyplace, but where I will lead you."

Soon enough shrill trumpets sounded, and the royalists were off, with Langdale –

true to his word – at their head. The horses seemed to nod in agreement with the commander's resolution as they carried lines of royalists forward in tight formation relatively slowly at first. A speed that enhanced their gritty resolve, until further blasts had them pick up pace; whereupon each cavalryman pointed their blade at the enemy.

As Maxwell's horse pounded along, the reverberations of every hoof fall passed right through his body. They became his very heartbeat, sealing him as one with his steed. Adrenaline blurred sight of all but the immediate opponents coming at him, and with an iron grip upon his sword, his mind was entirely focussed on the attack.

A barrage of gunshots enveloped Maxwell and a lead ball pinged against his breastplate with a glancing blow. Both sides scudded across the fields like storm clouds until every royalist and parliamentarian were brought face to face. Flashes of pistol fire sparked like lightening. Smoke wound its way through the tangle of cavalrymen and then dispersed as fast as the spirits of those killed in this initial onslaught.

Maxwell slashed with his Irish-hilt sword and the piercing din of swordplay rang in his ears. One rebel went down with a blood-red hole in his coat, like a deathly sunset. Another with a cut from Maxwell's double-edged blade. At every turn there was a blinding flurry of movement that was almost hypnotic. Maxwell's veins stood out as he yelled with determination and the muscles in his arm burned like the fires of his old blacksmith's forge.

"Reformadoes!" He raised his thirty-eight-inch blade.

Against the odds, Maxwell's troop, and those about them, slowly began to penetrate the enemy ranks. Langdale's nickname 'The Ghost' seemed especially apt after he proved impervious to four different pistol shots, all discharged at close range.

Colonel Copley's standard hung above the enemy centre; the blue taffeta displayed a hand gripping a sword, which came alive with every ripple. Soon, Maxwell could glimpse the darkening landscape through gaps that began to appear in the rebel lines. But just as the day was waning, so was Maxwell's energy, though the very desire to live, as well as the adrenaline that coursed through his veins, kept him going.

During a brief respite, he caught his breath. His sword hung by his side, pointing to the ground, which was fresh with the imprints of hundreds of horses. The dead lay scattered; sown across the field – some so well-trodden that they scarcely resembled bodies any longer. Amidst it all a man was on his knees. The royalist officer, Colonel Sir Francis Carnaby, seemed to be praying for the souls of those around him. He gazed to the sky and stretched up his arms in a most haunting manner. Though Carnaby's figure stood out amidst the horror, he was well and truly part of it, proven by a ruby-red trickle that wound its way down his buff coat.

"Lord have mercy upon me. Bless and prosper His Majesty!"

With that utterance, the colonel was dead. He collapsed to the ground as if being dragged down into his grave, leaving Maxwell struck by the sight. So much so, that it took some moments for the trumpets to stir him with their tune, the sharp signals impelling the royalists onward and pulling their minds back to their duties.

The parliamentarian reserves were almost all committed, and the last ones galloped up in a bid to stabilise their struggling, depleted left wing. The royalists, however, had none to plug any of their gaps. Maxwell glanced across to the opposite side of the field, only to see – by stark comparison – the royalists being chased off. It was abundantly clear that the left wings of both sides were breaking, but weight of numbers was rapidly taking its toll on the Reformadoes.

"One last bout!" It didn't matter if most of Maxwell's men couldn't hear. His own words impelled him forward and it was his personal example and energy that mattered.

Maxwell wouldn't give up. The fortunes of war were far too fickle. He raised his blade; the nicked edges stood out against the sky as he made for his next foe.

*

Lord George Digby's wary eye fell upon Sherburn as fleeing cavalrymen emerged from the town. The steady stream of routed troops was fast, and they made desperate noises. Friend or Foe? He had little time to spare to find out and no desire to do battle while eight hundred prisoners remained in his rear. Should any of those escape, or be freed, then they would be re-armed from the pile in Sherburn's street; like dead men brought back to life.

Digby could not discern enough to be sure of anything at this point, save the need to ready the remaining troops about him – those as yet uncommitted. He was forced to watch and wait for the crucial details he so required.

"They are our cavalry yonder!" the Earl of Carnwath's bulbous nose screwed up. "Langdale is defeated. He has let us down again."

"God damn him!" Digby cursed. "He assured me the rebels had but six hundred men."

"Either he was gravely mistaken, or his men are more hapless than we suspected."

"Hapless and cowardly. Double dyed with both faults."

"The damned Reformadoes have left us in an untenable position." Carnwath's bushy red beard hid an angry grimace. "Henceforth, I shall look upon them with a jaundiced eye."

Digby hesitated. His gauntleted bridle hand made no move with the reins, despite the October air taking on a chill of finality. His face felt its bite. The watery-blue ribbon of the Garter, which hung across his chest, now more resembled a dressing that covered his wounded pride. If this was to be defeat, then Digby would preserve his half of the army and lead them, at least, to Scotland. He would not suffer the humiliation of having his entire force dispersed in Yorkshire.

"God's teeth, I'll not presume to direct you." Carnwath's gruff tone was compelling. "But decide now whether we stand and fight these dogs. You must entertain no regrets."

"Sound the retreat!"

The trumpeter raised his instrument. The long sleeves of his ceremonial garb hung from his elbow in a trail of red and blue. No sooner had the noise echoed across the field than Digby's cavalry streamed north, leaving Sherburn Common behind them, along with the Lieutenant-General, who remained to oversee their departure. A messenger soon confirmed that Langdale's troops had been routed, though only after a desperate fight. The enemy had deployed on such uneven ground that half of them had initially been out of sight; they were also far from being inexperienced recruits, like this morning's offering.

"A pox on you, Christopher Copley!" Digby hissed of the rebel commander. He recalled that Copley had once been prosecuted for claiming to be better born than the Earl of Kingston. "Will you now assert your dominance of me?"

He spoke as if Copley was before him and resolved to defend the Digby name. The family motto was apt; Through God and not Chance. The calculating Digby would leave nothing to chance.

*

Maxwell heard the ghostly trumpet call from behind. Ignoble retreat. He grunted with every sword blow and was now made vulnerable by this interminable rasp. Drawing a pistol, he fired it at point blank range. It kicked back and a flash spewed from the eighteen-inch barrel; smoke cocooned him, and the smell of gunpowder hung in his nostrils, while speckles of warm blood dappled his face. His opponent recoiled.

Maxwell circled his horse. The motion betrayed the tormented uncertainty that withdrawal brought; of shifting for himself and forgoing everything that he had just been venturing his life for. The once unified royalists were now transformed into hundreds of retreating individuals, unable to see the pursuers at their backs, and each one making for Sherburn.

Sherburn's street, however, offered neither protection nor reassurance; through it flowed not just an exodus of royalists, but broken parliamentarians too. The designated battle cries of each side were bawled back and forth in a bid to identify friend from foe. Isolated fighting played out. It even took place within the wooden skeleton of a building that was under construction. Thatched houses and their dank timbers were stained with blood, or pock-marked by pistol balls, while small fires flickered here and there in an attempt to feed off this frenzy. Dead men lay in the grass. Guns spewed flame and smoke with bewildering rapidity and amidst it all was the array of captured weapons that was now worthless, fool's gold.

"Head north to Skipton," a royalist colonel yelled.

"You go on." Maxwell slapped Peter on the back.

"What?"

"Go!" Maxwell pointed, and then squeezed the flanks of his horse. He had already decided upon his route; east to Selby. Death and destruction had galvanised him. This could be his last chance to see his sons again.

Chapter 9

It felt as if Peter Irwin had been torn asunder. The heavens were streaked a shade of Flanders red, as if to emphasise the killer blow that was being dealt to the King's cause. For Peter, the outcome struck him doubly. As Captain Walker rode off, enveloped by his own fog-like demons, Peter couldn't help but worry that his commander was making a very grave error of judgement. He thought of pursuing but the intransigent Maxwell wasn't a man to be reasoned with, especially when he had made his mind up.

The truth was, Peter felt equally honour-bound to the Reformadoes – the troop that had welcomed him so heartily to their unit, no matter his Protestantism, nor his lack of martial experience. He could not abandon them as their captain had done. Instead, he anticipated the part he might play by remaining here and healing whatever breach Captain Walker's absence might provoke.

"God's blood, Maxwell. You damned fool." It was unlike Peter to swear, but he looked upon Maxwell as a great friend; almost a brother.

The routed royalists fled all ways, some north to the common, where Digby might still be, and others south, on the road to Ferrybridge. Peter did not know where to go for the best. From both victors and victims came roars of aggressive determination and howls of acute pain. Acrid smoke, malevolent and edged with black, billowed from a burning house, cutting them all off from the sight of God.

Peter drew his mount aside as a carriage came closer. The four horses pulling it were wide-eyed, yet they continued with blind unity – none willing to deviate from the road ahead, nor lose the secure presence of the others. The large back wheels, iron-shod and as tall as any man, rumbled past. Peter watched it disappear south and then caught sight of Marmaduke Langdale's two-foot standard, which he made for without hesitation, in the hope of finding his colleagues. Now a second coach passed alongside. This one struck him, for he glimpsed a lady within, whose terrified face was framed by the window as she peered out. The square cab tremored, suspended as it was from the chassis with leather straps.

When the rider grasping Langdale's standard threw the pennant on top of a number of others, Peter's heart sank. He realised it had been captured. The once-proud symbol lay dead on the ground; no breath of wind could stir it, nor could it incite those who had once followed it. Beyond the banner, he watched the last coach veer off into a ditch, whereupon it came to lie precariously at a forty-five-degree angle.

He headed towards it. The horses gave high-pitched whinnies and desperately writhed around in a bid to get to their feet. The carriage was tugged this way and that as they refused to give up their struggle, and as it slipped onto its side, the wheels gave one last spin. When the coachman cut the horses free, Peter leapt from his own and clambered onto the side of the cab. The leather-clad frame creaked. Emblazoned on the door was a two-headed eagle holding a shield that displayed a black saltire, a coat of arms that Peter did not recognise.

With gritted teeth, and lying across the body of the carriage, Peter opened the door with difficulty and peered inside. He saw the passenger – the lady – and extended a hand down towards her. A twinkle of jewels betrayed movement and when she stood, Peter seized the woman and lifted her until she was able to gain some leverage.

"Do not let go!"

REBELLION

"Hold onto the frame, Milady."

Peter wrapped his arm around her and pulled. She eased her passage by way of her feet and only after she came to lie on the cab did Peter jump to the ground and then encourage her to follow. She was, however, already doing so.

"Are you hurt?"

"Merely superficial," she said, whilst catching her breath.

With the back of one hand, Lady Nithsdale quickly wiped tears away from her strong cheekbones. Her blue eyes were already looking into the distance and past Peter.

"Be you for the King?"

"Aye, Milady."

"Might you know of my husband's whereabouts – The Earl of Nithsdale?"

"Alas not."

"Then pray leave me," she insisted and pointed at the other carriage. "I implore you to protect that one."

"Will you permit me to take you back to Sherburn?"

"No. The rebels must not have the contents of that coach."

"Is it so important?"

"It is imperative, sir. I insist you do as I say."

"Then I shall do my best," Peter replied and drew his blade. "But you must leave now. Have your coachman protect you."

Ahead, an armoured horseman with a closed helmet had forced the driver of the first coach to dismount. Peter, after treading slowly closer, now stopped in his tracks. Enemy foot soldiers began to swarm around it like rats. One of them climbed inside and called out that he had found a small cabinet. Another threatened the coachman and demanded the key.

Peter shook his head. There were too many of them and he would not engage himself in such a hopeless task, even if it was at the behest of a rather haughty noblewoman.

"Lieutenant! Enough prattling," the horseman called and pointed at the cabinet. "That must be delivered to Colonel Copley."

"Aye, sir."

"Inform him it is with the compliments of Monsieur Protais."

Chapter 10

Maxwell had left his horse tethered in woodland with his armour and pistols hidden nearby. He was now on foot amidst soft undergrowth; a route that would lead him to the southwest of Selby. The moon shone like a new silver shilling and the branches of the trees extended in worship, as though holding it up to light the way. But Maxwell could navigate this familiar track without any assistance. Everything about it stirred memories of life before the war – right down to the horsetail he had gathered here for Catherine, so that she might polish their prized pewter.

Home. It seemed as if this was all but a dream, and Maxwell merely returning within the confines of a deep slumber. He had prayed for this moment for over a year, and when the opportunity had presented itself, he felt as if it was meant to be. He was finished with the war anyway; exhausted by it. He *needed* home.

When the covering of trees began to thin out, he squinted at the two roads that led off towards town. Two of four routes into Selby; a place without defensive walls of any sort, but almost moated by bogs, rivers and brooks. He stood still and listened; faint swishes from the canopy of trees overhead, the gurgle of flowing water, scuttle of a rabbit or some other creature. He identified each one and stripped it away. A scattering of leaves in the breeze. A bird taking flight. Nothing he could determine as human, and that was his prime concern.

These two roads would eventually join as they approached Selby - however, Maxwell had no intention of setting foot onto either. He did not exit the woodland, but instead continued under its cover. Contradictory waves of concern and excitement filled him, with most local parliamentarians now at Sherburn, pursuing royalists that fled north and south, the ever-unpredictable Maxwell had hammered east.

The silhouette of Selby Abbey loomed large. Maxwell recalled being told that Lord Fairfax had ordered a trench to be dug, linking the two roads for defence, but poor old Fairfax had not grown up here. He wouldn't know much about the Mill Dam that flowed to the west of Selby. Certainly not how it silted in one place, reducing depth to only a few feet. With boots folded above his thigh, Maxwell waded across the water and soon came face to face with the oak door of his home, studded with square nail heads.

"Thank ye Lord," he muttered. This humble building housed not just his precious sons, but all of his worldly goods and happiest memories. He paused. The shutters were closed over the windows, as if the house was cocooned from the war, as well as from time itself. He tapped on the door.

"Mistress Russell?"

"Have you no consideration of the time?"

"Pray open the door, 'tis urgent," Maxwell whispered.

"What's your business?"

"It concerns your nephews."

"Be off with you, lest I call the constable."

"Grace, do not make a scene."

She did not respond, but the lock clunked, and a sliver of faint light appeared as the door opened. Grace Russell, with features as pale as her linen smock, held a shawl over her head and shoulders, gripping it at the neck.

"By all that's holy," she hissed. "Come inside."

Maxwell hurried over to the fireplace. He complained matter-of-factly about the October chill, and as he pulled off his boots, cursed the water that had soaked his breeches. He glanced up to see Grace standing against the closed door, watching him with wide eyes and pursed lips - rather like an owl, he thought.

"Speechless?" Maxwell asked with a strained laugh. He began warming his hands. "That will be a first."

"Oh, I could say much, Brother. Though you would not harken to me if I did."

"How about enquiring whether I have eaten of late? I have a mighty hunger."

"Eaten?" Her mouth dropped open. "I am not an innkeeper, nor one of your men to command as you please!"

"Perhaps you could fetch me a change of clothes instead, if that's not too much to ask?"

Grace gave a sigh of frustration. Maxwell began fumbling at his doublet in a bid to unfasten it. But, losing his patience, he tugged at it, such that some knitted buttons squeezed through the eyelets, while others tore free altogether. He then flung the garment to the rush mat on the stone floor.

"Ever the hothead."

Maxwell ignored her. He feared looking around the room – apprehensive of the emotions it would provoke. Frustrated too, that after all the risks he had gone through to get here, he should be cowed by such fears. He kept his gaze on the discarded doublet. The scent of drying herbs hanging above the fireplace failed to soothe him, and then he caught sight of the boys' small breeches, which had evidently just been repaired. His eyes welled up. He turned his back on Grace.

"What are you doing here?" She held up her hands.

"I've had my fill of the army," he mumbled. "I want my boys. Where the devil are they?"

"They are in bed, Maxwell, where they should be at this hour."

"I'll change my clothes and then go to them."

"Is that wise? I do not wish to see them upset. After all, you cannot stay."

"This is my home!"

"Your very presence endangers those boys. It is madness to have even considered coming here."

"Then a lunatic I must be, sister."

"If you have been seen, then we are all undone."

"I am unrecognisable even to myself of late." Maxwell rubbed his forehead. "Look, I cannot continue another day without holding my sons. Surely, you can understand such a desire?"

Maxwell proceeded to unbutton his breeches, and as he went to pull them off, Grace uttered some religious sentiments and hurried past him.

"Have a care! You are in the presence of a woman!" She hissed without looking back. "You've been in that cursed army too long."

Maxwell grimaced.

"Wait until I am out of sight," Grace instructed and then began to climb the stairs. "Mother of God, save us from such foolhardy men."

Maxwell laid his breeches in front of the fire and stood in his thigh-length linen shirt. The warm flames rejuvenated his cold body, though his broad shoulders began to tremble. At over six-feet-tall, and no matter his physical strength, he was powerless against this grip of anxiety. Shadows danced around the room as if taunting him. Concerns over what his sons might think of his long absence fostered doubts about whether it had been selfish to come here, no matter how genuine his desire.

He turned to the spinning wheel – Catherine's spinning wheel – the faint, but reassuring, creak of which he had frequently listened to whilst laying in front of the fire. She used to sing as she worked, her voice sweet and calming. Every item he beheld triggered memories of her – of their life together – which at the time he hadn't realised would be some of their last. The house felt alive with her presence once more, as if the very walls had retained something of her spirit.

"God bless thee, my own sweetheart."

A pile of old clothes, thrown from above, landed with a swoosh nearby. Immediately after dressing, he was ascending the staircase, heading for the bedchamber door that Grace stood ready to open. She warned that Kit had been experiencing bad dreams of late. Thomas, on the other hand, never spoke of Maxwell or Catherine. At this most important of moments, Maxwell felt dejected, and he defensively brushed Grace aside, along with what he deemed to be her innate negativity.

He took the proffered light and held it out into the small room; the dried rush stalk, fixed in its holder at a forty-five-degree angle, burned dimly. The mutton-fat coating emitted its familiar smell. It did the trick and Maxwell could just make out his sons tucked up on their chaff bed. He placed the light onto a small wooden form. Tom looked serene, cuddled into a ball. Kit lay at an angle, arms stretched out and his mouth slightly open, giving off an occasional rasp. The very sight of their innocence caused tears to roll down Maxwell's cheeks and he held a fist to his mouth in a bid to silence this emotion. He kneeled on the wooden floor and wiped his eyes; nothing – not even tears – should obscure sight of his sons. As he reached over and gave them his blessing, Kit's eyes suddenly opened.

"Father?"

The word made Maxwell's heart explode with joy. Kit's voice was tender. His tone hopeful.

"My son," he whispered.

The lad sprang off the mattress. He flung his arms around Maxwell's neck, and legs about his body. The boy's sobs, sniffles and gasps of joy enveloped Maxwell. He held him tight, so tightly that they might never again be separated. From Maxwell's chest emanated a soothing warmth of unconditional love, which spread into every nerve and sinew. He had questioned life after Catherine's murder and whether he had the strength to carry on – if life was worth it. Indeed, it was. Wholeheartedly. Catherine lived on in their boys.

"Father?"

This time the question was subdued. Tom was sitting up in bed, hugging his knees to his chest.

"Tom, 'tis I, returned to see you both."

"Has the King won the war?"

"Alas, not yet …"

"Then he will want you back?"

Maxwell had not even faced up to this question himself. He had not dared to out of concern that it might have put him off making this journey. Once again, as was often the case, Tom was able to get to the crux of the matter in an instant, despite his young age. The boy laid his forehead upon his knees. Maxwell couldn't bring himself to respond, he and Tom knew the answer anyway.

"God took Mother to his side, but I have prayed every night for your return." Kit's lip trembled. His eyes looked up to the thatched roof in an attempt to hold back his emotion. "He has listened and answered me."

"It's thy prayers that got me here safely." Maxwell kissed Kit's head. "Come, let the three of us talk in the hall. There is so much I want you both to tell me." Maxwell reached out to Tom as the spluttering rush began to give up its struggle.

Chapter 11

Maxwell sat at the small table with Kit on his knee and an arm around Tom, who was perched rather awkwardly next to him. The youngest reminded him of Catherine in both looks and nature. Tom, however, possessed more of the Walker traits. Behind them, the fire attempted to warm the atmosphere, casting its golden glow upon the few pieces of wooden furniture. Every time Maxwell's words faltered, the relentless flames encouraged him to continue.

"Do you both still swing on the tree in the woods?"

Kit nodded. Tom looked away.

"Not a day passes without me thinking of you both. And you, Tom, have you finished making yourself a staff from that old branch?"

The cracks of the fire were Maxwell's only answer.

Grace fussed around the perimeter, collecting up wet clothes and placing a reassuring hand on Tom's shoulder. At this intimate moment, Maxwell was split by both irritation and sadness, his eldest was brooding, but, even worse, the boy was unforgiving.

"Here, Brother, some potage," Grace placed a wooden bowl with a pitiful look. "I was lately forced to sell your saw-horse, some rope and tackles."

"No matter. Take that purse." Maxwell pointed.

Grace opened it and poured out a number of shillings, which landed in a heap on the table. They may have had clipped and uneven edges, worn imagery and dull patinas, but she stared at them as if they had been pure gold.

"God be praised," she exclaimed, and clasped her hands together.

"The money I get from the army is all that keeps us."

"Don't the people of Selby have need of a blacksmith anymore?" Tom asked.

"Not a royalist one," Maxwell replied.

"Perhaps if you hadn't chosen the King, you could have stayed."

"I had good reason to join the army ..." Maxwell could not elaborate without revealing his thirst for vengeance against Catherine's killer.

Grace, meanwhile, began picking at a small paper that she found in the purse and unfolded it.

"What's this? Army news?" she asked.

"Aye." Maxwell barely gave the note a cursory glance. The one that had been found in Sherburn church, and which alluded to the fate of a royalist leader.

"Surely, it's perilous to retain such things?" Grace sighed and shook her head. "Must I get rid of it?"

"It is no longer of consequence."

Maxwell began sharing his potage with Kit. Grace threw the small paper into the fire; barely making it onto the burning log before combusting into a bright golden-orange ball. It was gone in an instant.

"Are the cavaliers here with you?" Kit asked.

"No, son, just me. But neither of you must tell a soul that I have been here, otherwise the rebels may make life hard for you."

"It's hard already," Tom said.

"You're right, Tom. We have all suffered in this war, and you and Kit most especially. You have both experienced enough heartache to last a lifetime. The loss of thy precious Mother is a great grief to every one of us." Maxwell paused and turned to Grace.

"This past year we have lost you, too," Tom replied. "What hurts most is that you chose to go."

"Let me assure you, I do not willingly leave you both, do you hear? I fight for you; for a stable country where the

REBELLION

laws of the land are upheld, but also for money to put food in your bellies and clothes on your backs. There was no other way."

"You fight for him." Tom's small, thin fingers held up a coin with the profile of King Charles struck upon it. The features were worn, leaving the King with a blank expression, impartial to the judgement of the eight-year-old.

"He is the king." Maxwell felt the stinging words. "Soldiering is the only option I have."

"You once told me that without the weapons that smithies forge, no soldier could conquer their enemies. Without horseshoes, no scout could explore new lands," Tom replied, repeatedly scratching his finger across the wooden surface of the table, as if searching for the true reason behind his father's behaviour.

"And I stand by what I said." Maxwell sighed. "Let me deal plainly with you. The fact is that my broken heart had filled with anger and vengeance. No amount of pounding out horseshoes or blades could satisfy it …"

A succession of firm knocks came at the door. Maxwell quickly put his finger to his lips.

"Open up."

Kit's grip became tighter. He buried his head into his father's chest. Maxwell carried him and led Tom into the small pantry and there waited for Grace to open the door. It gave a knowing squeak. From outside, the whispering wind toyed with the signpost that hung on the house, which had once advertised Maxwell's trade.

"I know he's here. Do not deny it."

"Please," Grace said as the parish constable forced his way inside, looking around as if he could sniff Maxwell out. "The boys are in bed."

"Show yourself, Walker."

"Henry Naylor, constable now, eh?" Maxwell stepped forward and gently placed Kit onto the floor.

"Aye, for my sins, I might add." He nodded firmly and removed his hat. "Though you make it no easier for me."

"I was never an easy man, though was I, Henry?"

One side of the constable's mouth rose, and he shook his head. "Where are the rest of your men?"

"At Sherburn."

"You are here alone, you swear it? No trickery or subterfuge?"

"Alone. Upon my honour."

"For all your damned stubborn nature, I know you to be an honourable man, Maxwell," Henry replied and placed his hands on his hips in a quandary. "I heartily wish we had not met again in circumstances such as these …"

"I came to see my boys," Maxwell explained, in answer to what he assumed would be the next question. "You understand my situation more than most." He recalled the bonds of friendship that had once existed between both of their wives.

"You know I cannot allow this to pass?" Henry got straight to the point.

"Nor would I expect you to." Maxwell began to roll up his sleeves. "Let us have a fair fight. If you manage to fell me, then you can hand me over."

"Fight?" Henry shook his head. "By God, you have not changed one bit, have you? I will take my leave of you without need for any fisticuffs, but I shall return in thirty minutes. If you have not gone from here by that time, then I shall summon the soldiers. That's as fair as I can be. Remember, I have my own family to protect."

Maxwell remained silent, but fixed Henry with a nod of thanks. A nod that saw Maxwell bowing to the inevitable; that as much as he could feel done with the war, it was never going to be done with him until one side had bludgeoned the other. This was a war of attrition.

Chapter 12

16th October 1645.
Skipton.

A rope was thrown over the signpost of the White Hart Inn, one of the buildings that graced the incline of Skipton's main street. One end was tied into a noose and then lowered slightly. All eyes were upon it. Pursing his thin lips, Gervase Harper gauged its height from the ground.

The wind played with the sign and made it squeal to and fro. It portrayed a white hart, which looked down with haunting majesty as a man was led towards the building by two soldiers. He was to be hanged by the neck until dead. A deserter no less, now recaptured, and to be made an example of; for God knows, the royalists had been decimated enough by defeat at Sherburn, without being further eroded by runaways.

The ring of rope had drawn a number of townsfolk. Like an all-seeing eye, it appeared to watch everyone as it turned idly, threatening them all and making ready to squeeze the soul out of its victim. As some soldiers took the end of the rope from Harper, he noticed Peter Irwin in the crowd.

"Behold a coward!" Harper cried, every line on his face deepening in judgement. "A deserter who ran away from his colours, betraying his King, cause, and every one of his comrades."

The prisoner, hands bound behind his back, was led to a barrel and made to climb onto it. He was a member of Lord

Digby's guardsmen, tasked with protecting the peer's life, but now he was to pay for his crime by forfeiting his own.

"God spared him in the late fight, while many brave men fell. Yet, he repaid such grace by abandoning his duty. Justice must be done. God cries out for it."

Once the noose was in place, Harper signalled for the soldiers to make ready. The barrel was shoved aside, the man's legs kicking beneath him. His face flushed and eyes bulged. As his windpipe was crushed, the rope twisted him from side to side, showing him off to the assembled spectators.

"Keep it tight!" Harper barked.

The crowd remained silent. From below, the brims of their hats, heads almost cowed, the inhabitants of Skipton watched the man's feet jerk. It crossed Harper's mind that some may see this as symbolising the end of the royalist cause in the north; for Skipton, the last royalist garrison in Yorkshire, was squeezed into a similar death-grip, encircled by swathes of enemy territory. They must have pondered their own fates.

He turned to Digby, who sat bolt upright on horseback watching proceedings; even the commander had a rather glazed expression. As the deserter slowly gave up his struggle, Harper addressed Irwin.

"Perhaps your captain will be next – when he's discovered?"

"May you choke on such a base accusation."

"Is that a curse, Lieutenant Irwin?"

"Do you intend to hang every remaining royalist?"

"Only cowards must don the deathly necklace," Harper smiled. "It is a mercy to them. After all, who could live with such dishonour?"

"I recall that you absented yourself from the rebel's ranks barely one month ago. Does that make you a deserter? In fact, having fought for them, are you not guilty of both treason and cowardice?"

REBELLION

"Your outrage would suggest that there may be some truth in my *base accusation* about your precious captain," Harper replied.

"Perhaps you fear Captain Walker?" Peter asked, his voice rising and falling as if pondering the question himself. "You will not be safe from his retribution as long as he lives."

Harper laughed. He eyed Irwin, who turned to the hanged man and bowed his head out of misguided respect. Digby then readied his braying steed; a hollow clatter of hooves echoed as he and his officers slowly made their way up the street and towards the gatehouse of Skipton Castle.

*

The rotund drum towers of Skipton Castle dominated the town from the crest of the street. Despite being over five hundred years old, it appeared as much of a stronghold as ever, standing resolute in the King's cause. Pinned to the edge of a precipice that dropped down to Eller Beck, it was seemingly as precariously balanced as Lord Digby and his royalist remnants. As he entered the courtyard at the heart of the original keep, the King's Lieutenant-General was deeply troubled. With the watery sun throwing a shadow across him, Digby began to climb the steps that led to the banqueting hall, having been starved of the victory he so craved.

After initial success at Sherburn, his army had spiralled spectacularly. Let down again by Langdale's Northern Horsemen, who he felt had so often proved unwilling, or unable, to repel the enemy. But Digby remained determined to succeed, determined to have his troops pull off a magnificent victory that would restore King Charles's fortunes and forever mark him out as the architect, if not a maker of kings, then their saviour. An officer hurried up to him, interrupting his thoughts.

"You carry news from the Governor?" Digby asked.

"Alas, Sir John's health is no better, My Lord."

"My enquiry is regarding the orders I sent to him, not of his condition."

"Of course, my apologies. He sends his compliments and is willing to turn over the required horsemen from the garrison."

"Excellent." Digby waved the man away. One hundred of Sir John Mallory's troopers would be a much-needed boost to numbers.

Digby passed through the withdrawing room and into the Lord's chamber, most recently occupied by the late Earl of Cumberland. He felt the emptiness of the castle. It was no longer a home; no fire burned in the large fireplace. With the departure of Digby and his army planned for the following day, Skipton's time was nigh, and no doubt it would soon be the enemy striding through these very rooms. He gave instructions to gather the senior officers together immediately.

"Sir Marmaduke," he greeted his second-in-command, who was waiting for him. The door was then closed, leaving the two men alone.

"My Lord."

They stood for a few seconds in silence, the atmosphere as cold as the thick stone walls. Digby paced to the window and looked through the diamond panes. Each one was held in place by strips of lead, which segmented his view of the outside world. As political Secretary of State and military commander, he often, by necessity, saw things very differently to others. A sigh escaped him. The courtyard below was as busy as his overwrought mind.

"Let us speak plainly." He turned to address Langdale. "I have one hundred reinforcements from the Governor of Skipton and another two hundred who have arrived from Castle Bolton. That takes us to nine hundred, or thereabouts. I propose we continue and find Montrose."

"That would be folly," Langdale retorted. "You mean to take us deeper into enemy territory, with no certainty of joining Montrose, who, might I remind you, has suffered a major defeat?"

"I am His Majesty's Lieutenant-General, North of the Trent."

"I'm well aware of your commission, sir, but I have led these men for the past four years. I speak as one well acquainted with them and extremely familiar with the territory hereabouts. This is, after all, our home county."

"Let me reassure you." Digby smiled. "I have seen quite enough of your troopers to come to know them well enough, and what's more, recognise their limitations."

"With the greatest of respect, they cannot be made scapegoats for this godforsaken mission, or our late defeat."

"Tread carefully, Sir Marmaduke." Digby held up one finger. "This is the King's mission. His orders. If I cast my mind back to Sherburn, I believe it was *you* who thought the enemy numbered but six hundred …"

"That was the intelligence I received."

"Yet *you* took your men forward and found there was three times as many. You led them onwards, Sir Marmaduke. If you wish to deflect any blame from your men, then think wisely upon where that would fall."

Langdale did not reply; his features were pale and drawn. A knock echoed from the door and upon Digby's permission, the senior officers filed into the room. It wasn't long before the bustle settled, and they waited to hear what their commander had to say.

"Gentlemen, we find ourselves at a crossroads. I am informed that we did lose near four hundred men at Sherburn, the vast majority taken prisoner. Yet today, we have three hundred reinforcements. The Marquis of Montrose remains in need of our support, and despite his late defeat, still holds Scotland. Therefore, I propose we continue to him. We join our forces together and retake the north – your homeland – from the rebels."

Langdale, hands behind his back, looked into the empty grate, the fire within him seemed as equally extinguished.

"Would it not be wiser to return to His Majesty at Newark? Our absence leaves that town and the King quite vulnerable," Sir William Blakiston suggested.

"A fair concern." Digby nodded. "But we have two regiments of enemy horsemen pursuing us even as we speak. I am also informed that the Scots have despatched one thousand from Northallerton to join the chase; therefore, we have drawn the enemy away from the King. In short, I believe we have come too far to turn back. The enemy fear what we might achieve."

"Are we confident of the King's safety?" Blakiston replied.

"Pray tell me how turning back in the face of two enemy forces shall help? The noble marquis in Scotland cries out for cavalry. With a token force, he has conquered that entire kingdom in less than one year. Do any of you wish to abandon him at such a crucial point?" Digby looked at each man in turn. "Together, we could secure Scotland and then take England – in short, restore His Majesty to his just rights. Gentlemen, victory lies within our grasp."

"I also entertain concerns," Langdale said with a calm, but firm, voice. He did not turn around. "Yet, if that is your command, we will obey it, for my Northern Horsemen have always been champions of the King. They have achieved spectacular feats."

"Aye, nothing ventured, nothing gained, as they say." Blakiston followed Langdale's lead.

"Come, gentlemen!" Digby sighed and paced the floor. "How in God's name can we hope to restore the King with such flimsy statements? I say let us *wipe* these rebels from this island. Let us drive them into the seas and let your

REBELLION

families congratulate you for playing such a crucial part in bringing peace. Are you for it?"

"Aye! Aye!"

"That's more like it! I hear the passion in your voices and that heartens me. When you go back to your men, I wish you to impart that very same energy unto them." Digby pointed to the window behind him. "We ride tomorrow."

As the men filed out of the chamber, Digby called after Langdale and asked him to remain.

"Have you suitable men to replace the officers we have lost? Sir Francis Carnaby and Sir Richard Hutton are both dead, along with three other colonels captured."

"I have and will see to it," Langdale replied.

"Hutton," Digby pondered, "of Goldsborough Hall and High Steward of Knaresborough?"

"That's correct. A brave and loyal man."

"Then by royal decree, seeing as he died in the King's service, the son will inherit his father's offices. Might you inform young Hutton for me?"

"Of course."

"One last question, what news of your man, Captain Walker?"

"None as yet. I believe he is missing."

"He was the topic of a discussion I overheard earlier. The men whisper about his cowardice and claim that he has absconded." Digby's nostrils flared with disgust.

"Mere rumours, I might add, for it is most unlike Walker to flee from anything. You greatly underestimate him, and besides, we have five captains in all who are unaccounted for."

"I do not care for the man. Mark my words, he is far too friendly with the enemy and of a most rebellious nature."

"Wherever he might be, if there is still breath in his lungs, I can assure you that Maxwell Walker will be using every last bit of it in the King's service."

Chapter 13

Maxwell lifted his leather tankard, gradually tipping it back and gulping down the ale. Peter Irwin watched in silence. The hint of liquorice root was refreshing, both as a thirst quencher, and because of its familiar and reassuring taste. He placed it back onto the table and then let out a sigh of relief. It felt good.

"Have I grown horns?" Maxwell frowned. "Engage your tongue if you have something to say."

"I do." Peter nodded candidly.

"We smithies are used to toiling in hot forges all day. I have quite a thirst!"

"I speak not of that, nor do I cast any aspersions." Peter folded his arms, leaned closer and whispered, "Maxwell, I think I saw the man named *Protais*, who wrote the note we discovered."

"Who is it?"

"I only saw him briefly and he wore a closed helmet. Yet, he used that very name and seemed to direct the rebels to Digby's coach."

Maxwell paused. The physical presence of this man, however fleeting, made the prospect of a traitor in their ranks much more real than a scrap of paper. Then he recalled that Grace had burned the note. He cursed.

"What is it?"

"I no longer have the writing," Maxwell admitted.

"Did you hand it to Langdale?"

"No." Maxwell closed his eyes momentarily. "Why do you suppose this man directed the rebels to the coach; could he have assumed that Digby was inside?"

"That I do not know. I hear that Digby's letters were in the coach, along with the King's own surgeon. Both were subsequently captured."

"What were you doing so close to all of this?"

"Assisting the Countess of Nithsdale, whose coach had gone off the road. Though she hasn't arrived in Skipton, so I assume she, too, was taken at Sherburn," Peter replied. "She charged me with saving the contents of Digby's carriage from the rebels."

"There seems a strong possibility that this man was hoping to catch Digby."

"To kill him?"

"Perhaps. After all, the note did refer to eliminating a royalist leader," Maxwell said, keeping his voice extremely low. "Protais, I assume, is but a code name. It may, perchance, have even been translated incorrectly?"

"What should we do?"

"What *can* we do without evidence?" Maxwell shook his head.

There lingered in Maxwell an unwillingness to be further embroiled in this whole affair, especially having such little regard for Digby. He glanced up to see Peter watching him again. The man held his large chin apprehensively and his broad shoulders sank as he leaned forward once more.

"Maxwell …"

"Peter?" He sighed at his friend's hesitancy. "Come out with it, man."

"Earlier this afternoon, a deserter was hanged outside this building. One of Digby's guardsmen, I believe. Harper was overseeing it, having been promoted to captain …"

"What!"

"That is not my point," Peter held up a hand and continued. "Harper called out some slanders about you. He accused you of the same crime."

Maxwell felt his face flush. From outrage. From guilt. It felt as if Harper might somehow have guessed his intentions; his most private inner feelings, concerns and desires.

"A pox upon that whoremonger."

Maxwell called for another tankard of ale. He realised how close he had come to forfeiting his own life over such a headstrong act as returning to his home. How could he have thought it possible to walk away from both the army and the war? The usually pragmatic Maxwell wondered what in God's name had come over him of late.

"I felt it best you knew of his accusation."

"If only *Captain* Harper spent more time focussing on his own men, and less upon me, then he may not have lost one of them."

"I am relieved to see you here alive," Peter took a deep breath. "Though 'tis a shame that the paper did not survive. How, if I might ask …"

"It would be a long tale to tell, Peter," Maxwell coughed and sat up straight on the stool. "Besides, I am not a good storyteller."

"You're no deserter either, that I am sure of."

"I will ever be the King's Captain."

Chapter 14

21st October 1645.
Near Dumfries, Scotland.

A biting wind raced across the rugged landscape of southwest Scotland. It ushered away the bleak clouds that had shielded sunrise, as well as the mist that had settled into the valleys. Mist, which made each successive hilltop seem ever more distant, like a forebear of the last.

Maxwell scoured these slopes for signs of life. The dramatic contours of the highest were patched brown and yellow, as if rusted by the interminable mizzle. These stark slopes seemed to hide nothing; as honest as every Scot that Maxwell had so far encountered. All that could be heard was the constant trickle of water that filtered through rock and vegetation, or birds singing in praise of such natural beauty.

Yet, somewhere beyond these never-ending peaks was the Marquis of Montrose. It was said he was even now travelling south to meet Lord Digby and finally procure the union of their two armies. Seven days after setting out from Welbeck, Maxwell had orders to act upon these rumours, to find the Highland Fox and escort him to Digby.

"Do you see anything at all?" Maxwell asked Peter with a sigh.

"No. Only the strongest can survive such a climate as this," Peter replied and pulled his long, grey riding coat about him.

"Are you insinuating that the great marquis does not fall into such a category?" Harper asked as he rode up to the two men.

"On the contrary, I am the one who is struggling." Peter continued to scan the horizon. "I have heard that the marquis and his men are in no way cowed by it."

"Relatively straightforward terrain, I'll wager, for such a token force as his," Harper said.

"Before doing battle at Inverlochy, they covered thirty miles in thirty-six hours," Maxwell added. "Across snowy mountains, at that."

"He could become a Scottish Hannibal." Peter smiled.

"If only he was riding an elephant. You both would have no difficulty in sighting him, and thus cease your complaining." Harper's eyes narrowed as he let out a sarcastic laugh.

"I'll smash every one of your teeth if you make another remark like that!" Maxwell growled.

"Is that a horseman?" Peter pointed into the distance.

"Aye, I believe it is, but now I can't see him because of those trees," Harper replied and moved ahead of the group to try and get a better look.

"I understand the need for sending us ahead to discover news of Montrose, but I can't help feeling that Digby's playing for time," Maxwell said as he craned his neck.

"Heaven forbid he might wish us to cross any mountains."

"If it allowed me to escape him, I might be tempted." Maxwell replied.

Harper resolved to head the man off. He had barely finished speaking before he clicked his tongue and impelled his horse forward, leaving Maxwell and the group of twenty-five troopers behind. Maxwell looked on with some relief, having struggled to hold back his anger towards the man.

REBELLION

"In all seriousness, do you think this a fool's errand?" Peter asked.

"I know not. Maybe it's merely my dislike of Digby …"

"Sir!" Peter interrupted.

"What is it?"

"Harper's backplate, it bears a strange mark on the upper right. Do you see?" Peter pointed.

"Do you mean scratches or dints?"

"No, more deliberate than that. The sun picked it out just now."

"I didn't see." Maxwell shook his head as Harper rounded a clump of trees and vanished. "Is it of any significance?"

"Yes – or at least, I think it could be."

"Most of our armour is damaged in some way." Maxwell frowned. "Exactly what concerns you?"

"The man at Sherburn. The one who called himself Protais. His armour was stamped with a cross in the same place." Peter turned to Maxwell. "It had slipped my mind in the chaos, but now I recall it."

"You think that was Harper?"

"Alas, I cannot be certain. As I said before, the man wore a closed helmet." Peter shook his head. "But those marks do strike me."

"That damned note. The plot we assumed was to kill Digby …" Maxwell hissed. "It may be Montrose, instead!"

"Montrose?"

"Think about it. If any royalist commander can bring the King victory at this point, 'tis he. To kill the man who has secured all of Scotland, and who is now on the brink of being reinforced; that would be to end the King's cause north of the border, if not completely."

"You have a fair point. Though we cannot let him know of our suspicions."

"Come on!" Maxwell entertained no doubts. He headed off at pace in pursuit of Harper.

MARK TURNBULL

*

That Same Morning.
Annan.

The stallion's body rippled; skin momentarily streaked by lines. Langdale gave a reassuring pat of his horse's velvety neck. It brayed, picking up on the scent of the thousands of horses that had brought the enemy to this corner of Scotland. The mount was unnerved. Just as Langdale's fellow royalists were too, no doubt, as they watched their opponents in the morning light. Yet, the lines of cavalry on both sides remained absolutely still.

The enemy had already scored an early victory. They were drawn up opposite, on Annan Moor, amidst a scattering of dead and wounded royalists. Men and horses. These corpses – part of the one hundred reinforcements from Skipton – had been surprised and routed. Those broken royalists who had survived this initial clash were even now vanishing into the landscape; swallowed up by it in their retreat towards Gretna. But before they had fled, a messenger had been sent pounding back to Annan, where the main royalist force was quartered, to alert them to the danger. Langdale had responded without hesitation. He had led his detachment across the hill, but despite his eagerness to attack the enemy, he now found himself reduced merely to watching them. Langdale's pale face was flushed with frustration. He was powerless and it was infuriating.

Both forces were held in check by Mother Nature, which wielded supreme control. The high tide of the River Annan had, as normal, flooded the lanes and fields, settling into the contours of the land and separating the armies. Like animals in a baiting ring, Langdale and his opponent, Sir James Brown, were left waiting for the moment when they would be unleashed upon one another. Langdale knew fine well that it was such inactivity that gave his troops time to think – a dangerous distraction.

"Montrose, our Highland Fox, might just be over yonder hills," Sir William Blakiston said.

"As you know, Sir William, I never consider matters that *might* be," Langdale replied.

"Well, according to Digby, our union with Montrose is imminent."

"I consider what comes out of his mouth even less," the ever-honest Langdale muttered.

"True. Though I wouldn't underestimate him, sir."

"Ah, I never said I did." Langdale raised his eyebrows. "Though he was once a competent officer, he is first and foremost a politician, and his character is better suited to the latter. The rebels passed a Self-Denying Ordinance to prevent their politicians from holding military rank. We have taken the opposite approach."

"Our leader, I fear, would never deny himself anything."

"Nor would the King let him. Now, what of our enemy?" Langdale pointed across the moor. "Sir James Brown of Fordel. A wily Scot if ever there was one."

"Approached from a lane to the south, past Dornock Church. Then managed to cut the Skipton men off."

"Promoted to colonel but five months ago," Langdale recalled of Brown.

"Anxious to make his mark."

"Well, let us hope that our scouts do find Montrose – and soon," Langdale grunted.

'Fordel has forded the Solway!' Lord Digby had exclaimed upon hearing of Brown's sudden appearance. But this had been far from another of Digby's sardonic and irritating remarks – of which Langdale had had his fill. Even Digby was ruffled by Brown's initial success. The Lieutenant-General had kept the bulk of the royalists by his side at Annan, in reserve, holding onto them like a miser hoarding his money. Langdale had been sent forward to confront the enemy with a detachment, just like Sherburn.

In his mind, Langdale cursed numerous times. What he observed didn't help one bit. The enemy looked like one giant body of horsemen; their appearance was unbroken by any colourful cavalry pennants. United and determined. A dark and brooding mass. All of Brown's standards and their bearers had been withdrawn, fluttering away and departing from their ranks. This had left Langdale suitably perturbed; Brown clearly felt he didn't need the flags to unify or rally his men. All of his troops were summarily forged together as one, with a single goal in mind. But Langdale had an iron will, and nothing would lessen his resolve. The men of his Northern Horse, too, had the same grit, hardened by years of campaigning.

Water crossed the earth like streaks of mirror glass. It was as though the Almighty was pressing both sides to reflect upon the coming clash and the futility of war – most especially civil war. Instead, Langdale pondered nothing but sight of the muddy earth, tantalisingly revealed as the water was slowly drawn back to the river.

The lowering of the levels prompted the royalist advance. Hooves splashed through the water, causing cascades of tear-like droplets, while others slipped and struggled on the sodden ground. They closed up to Brown's men, who glowed with pistol and carbine fire. The precursory noise of ringing steel pierced the morning as both sides began hacking and slashing. Some were skewered from their horses and others blasted off by gunshots. Puddles were contaminated by swirls of bloody crimson, and the clouds reflected in them made it appear as if the world had truly been turned upside down.

The dead mounted up as Brown's troops regrouped and came on again and again in waves. So, the desperate action continued, until gradually, Langdale's royalists were pushed back towards their original position. Over fifty of his men would never follow him again, the majority of casualties being officers. Sweat, dirt, and blood ran down Langdale's face. As this skirmish rapidly turned into another royalist defeat, he glimpsed Brown himself slump with a shot to his side. Small consolation – and too late. Langdale's men and horses were already in headlong flight back towards Annan's single street.

Annan itself was surrounded by peat stacks, which rose like burial mounds, ready for the royalists and their cause. The dung heaps stank; as did Digby's incompetence, for he had sent no support during this entire action. Even now, as Langdale thundered towards Annan, he could see the main royalist body in full retreat. Then he caught sight of the Lieutenant-General himself.

"Why do you flee?" Langdale cried.

"I will not end my days in such a dismal place as this," Digby retorted.

"Had these men been led in the opposite direction and brought up in support of me, the outcome may have been very different."

"We ride for Dumfries!"

"What of Montrose? Where is he?" Langdale asked. "You told us he was nearby."

"God knows. I lied. I thought the prospect might make your men fight like beasts, yet instead they drown in their haste to escape."

Digby pointed at the river, in which dead royalists lay submerged. Despite being devoid of life, they still moved, though only with the lazy ebb and flow of the receding tide. Langdale spat on the ground. He bellowed at his men to follow him to Dumfries, holding his sword aloft to mark his presence; his personal pennant having been captured and its bearer killed. Barely six hundred royalists remained. Montrose was now all that stood between them and utter ruin.

*

Harper's horse sped downhill. The blurred landscape enveloped him. The speed matched his desire to be at the lone horseman, whether it was Montrose, or a mere messenger of his. This was Harper's chance to complete the confidential orders he'd been given from his masters; a task made all the easier by his defection to the King's side. He let out a roar of excitement – premature, maybe, but the ever-confident Harper didn't let that stop him. He pounded past a cluster of trees that seemed to huddle together in the valley and rounded them to see the horseman in highland attire. Draped in a colourful pattern, it seemed as if clan allegiance alone was the man's armour and his only defence. Every royalist – no matter their nationality – was a misguided fool in Harper's eyes, blinded by the aura of majesty and oblivious to the faults of the man who wore the crown.

"Halt!"

Harper yelled the order again and pulled out his pistol. He rode directly towards the Scot, who drew a blade, much to his amusement, or was it his disdain. Like many of the Scottish royalists, the man was poorly armed, indicative of the defective cause they served.

"Are you sent from Montrose?" Harper shouted.

"An' who might you be?" The Scot countered.

"I'm here by order of Lord Digby."

Harper kept his pistol trained. All men spoke freer when faced with the mouth of a gun.

"I bear a message from the marquis."

"Verbal or written?"

"Both." The rider patted his saddle bag. "Where is Digby?"

"Riding south. The decision has been taken to fall back to England. It's no longer possible to join up with Montrose," Harper explained, in a bid to scupper any plans. "Take that news back to him."

"We are in agreement, in that case."

REBELLION

The man's affirmation took Harper aback. "I will deliver your letter to Lord Digby," he said, and held out a hand.

"You must tell him that the marquis is at Braemar."

"Where?" Harper frowned.

"Braemar, near Aberdeen."

"What distance is that from here?"

The man laughed. "Too far for you English to ride, even in one week."

"I see the Marquis has trusted his message to a jester?" Harper growled and grabbed the letter. "Do you want to get back to Aberdeen alive?"

"Kill me, whoreson, and you prevent your reply from being delivered."

"I'll blast you all the way back to your godforsaken master."

"Captain Harper!" Maxwell cried. "Are you in trouble?"

Harper cursed. Walker was a proverbial thorn in the side. "By this fool? Nothing of the sort."

"Then why do you threaten him?" Maxwell demanded.

"Precautionary. I couldn't deduce from his apparel which side he was for."

"Well?" Maxwell closed up and challenged the Scot. "State your business."

"I carry a message from Montrose," the man replied, idly pointing at Harper. "He now has it on his person. The marquis is at Braemar. There is a significant body of enemy cavalry between you and he, near Glasgow."

"I see," Maxwell replied. "I think we'd better take that letter, Harper, and convey it to Digby with all speed, don't you?"

Harper looked at Maxwell and then produced the missive, which displayed Montrose's handwriting – this seemed to be the closest they would ever get to the enigmatic commander.

Chapter 15

25th October 1645.
Four miles south of Workington, Lancashire.

Four days after defeat at Annan, Lord Digby's royalists had streamed across the border and back into England. Their wild journey had proved entirely fruitless and Montrose was nowhere to be seen. The ranks of royalist cavalrymen were unravelling with every passing day, and they were pursued not just by numerous enemy forces, but also by a growing anxiety that picked them off one by one. It was contagious, and induced them to desert, spreading faster than a dreaded summer plague. Even a trumpet rasp, which came from the rear ranks, was enough to cause a rumour that the enemy was about to fall upon them. No word of command could now counter the panic that ensued, nor any amount of cajoling convince the fraught men that it was a false alarm. Only one truth mattered; time was, indeed, running out.

Maxwell's stomach churned at the sight of royalists riding off in all manner of directions. Seeing his comrades abandoning their colours en-masse, leaving their colleagues and looking to their own salvation, utterly sickened him. It was shocking. Men he had known and fought alongside were hurrying for the hills, seeking to hide in the terrain that had earlier been referenced as their greatest security. If Maxwell was the self-delusional type, it would be easier to go along with the belief that an enemy attack had, in fact, scattered these men. To accept this pretence as a way of masking the implosion of the King's remaining cavalry. But Maxwell was ever honest with himself. The intention to join Montrose had been full of risks from the very start, and though this moment had gradually become inevitable, he could never have imagined how such devastating finality might feel. He wondered if this was the war's end.

The royalists had been proceeding down the Lancashire coast, with the intention of escaping the parliamentarians at their heels via Furnace and Cartmel. Mountains hugged one side of the route, and the sea the other. Along with sands and tides, it combined to offer some sort of protection from the enemy, psychological at least. Across the water, they could see the outline of the Isle of Man in the distance. But as they funnelled south, hemmed in, they all knew the enemy was still tracking them. Digby's hope for assistance from Ireland, and his dogged suggestion that Montrose, even now, might still come south to their aid, was a mere rambling that few believed. Not that Maxwell had ever believed the man.

Troops galloped away in droves. They swarmed into this mighty landscape like erratic and disorientated moths; attempting to escape the darkness of their fears. Maxwell wondered just how many would remain.

"Stand firm, I beseech you all!" Langdale rode down the lines.

For the first time, Maxwell wondered what would happen to him if the King's cause was entirely defeated. He remained motionless, watching and waiting to see how this moment would end. His knuckles were white from his tense grip upon the reins. Peter was nearby. Harper too, up ahead with Digby. All but a dozen of Maxwell's own troop had vanished, and those that stayed refrained from looking at one another; they simply gazed into the distance as if fearing what they might see in each other's eyes.

"Listen to me," Digby called out. "I give you all free liberty to dispose of yourselves as you so wish. Run if you like. Flee with all of them." He flicked his hand in the direction of the deserters, as if he was abandoning them and not vice-versa. "But if your heart remains full of courage and conviction, then stay with me. Let us fight our way back to the King."

Digby's words simply added to the exodus. If Maxwell had not gone to his children after Sherburn, he would have hammered west at this very moment. Yet, he knew that he could not return home again, nor could his sons be safe, until this war was officially over. Within the hour, barely two hundred cavalrymen were left. A visually shocking number. So small that they now appeared rather insignificant amidst the desolate and dramatic environment, and Digby was forced to address them once more.

"You have displayed to me your single-minded loyalty and devotion." Digby's lone voice seemed to echo in the void that was left. "Loyalty and courage in the face of great adversity."

Maxwell looked across the shattered remains. Langdale was bolt upright, his gaze fixed and proud; Maxwell's only reassurance came from his presence.

"We are reduced to such numbers that I fear we have no alternative. We must look to our own salvation – each and every one of us – but not as they do," Digby said. "Take yourselves to safety. Whether it be Skipton, Newark, or any other such garrison that still holds firm for the King. Wait for further orders. Continue our fight."

Maxwell was presented, along with a handful of other officers, with instructions to accompany Digby and Langdale further south. It was a relatively silent journey. The small party eventually arrived at Ravensglass; a place haunted by jagged Roman remains. A dank and ruined castle too. The once-glorious supply town of the Empire was as reduced to extremities as this small royalist band. The rain clouds swirled overhead as a dozen men headed towards the shoreline where two ship's boats, attended by a handful of sailors, awaited them. Further out was a shadowy rigged vessel, and beyond that, the vague, watery outline of an island.

The Isle of Man had been a constant presence during Maxwell's ride to Ravensglass; a symbol that offered a solitary vestige of hope, for it was to that royalist haven where they were headed. Relegated to an island thirty miles long and ten miles wide. He watched as Digby stepped into the larger pinnace. The oarsmen nodded respectfully. The golden threads that decorated the Lieutenant-General's buff coat were dulled by mud, and his blond locks, no longer flourishing into curls, now damp and limp.

Maxwell dismounted onto the shale and watched as Langdale joined Digby. Lord Nithsdale was next. Harper entered the second boat.

Maxwell looked at Peter. "What's your intention?"

"I am but a lieutenant, so there will be no room for me," Peter replied. "Though perhaps it would be best if someone kept an eye on him." His eyes glanced at Harper.

Maxwell sighed. "Good idea, I'll drown the bastard."

Peter laughed. "I'll go to Skipton and thence to Newark."

"Or Tutbury Castle, where Blakiston and some others are headed."

"Wheresoever I end up, I shall no doubt see you there," Peter said.

"God willing."

Maxwell began to walk towards the second boat but paused and turned. "My boys live in Selby. If you have the chance, pray write to them for me. Tell them I will return home when this war is over."

Peter nodded. Maxwell got into the boat and then a grating noise heralded Digby and Langdale's being pushed off. It bobbed in the sea as the oars took control and stirred up ripples in the calm water.

"Make haste and be seated!" A sailor called.

Maxwell looked at the coastline and hills behind him. England began to slip away; his boys were slipping away. When he turned back, he was left facing Harper.

"It seems our destinies are intertwined," Harper muttered with a grin.

In a moment the second craft was also pushed into the water, ready to follow in the wake of the other.

"When this war is over, I will finish our conflict," Maxwell vowed.

He stood, much to the protests of the sailors, and then stepped out of the craft. With the water to his boot tops, he waded slowly back to the shore and ignored the cries from behind, relieved to have broken free. He smiled. Then he began laughing to himself. As he trudged up the pebbles, he turned and waved to Harper.

"God save the King!" Maxwell cried, and thrust one fist into the air. He would rather take his chances with the enemy.

Chapter 16

Five Months Later.

March 1646.
The Palais Royal, Paris.

Cardinal Jules Mazarin took hold of the neck of a Gallica rose. It seemed to blush a deeper shade of crimson within the grip of his immaculate white glove. He selected a pruning knife and with its hooked end, caught the stem and sliced through it, like a chirurgeon amputating a battlefield wound. Holding the rose for a moment, he observed the clusters of velvet petals, from where a bright yellow centre beamed like a summer sun. Mazarin smiled. He handed the rose to a small lady next to him.

"*Votre Majesté.*"

"*Merci beaucoup, Cousin,*" Queen Henrietta-Maria replied with a distracted smile that lent more to etiquette than pleasure. Her husband, King Charles I, and his royal cause was never far from her thoughts every moment of every day. Today, however, she was more distracted than ever. The neat and sweet-smelling gardens of the Palais Royal did little to soothe her anxiety.

Mazarin craned his neck and proceeded to sever more of the roses, looking at them like a sculptor overseeing his work and making final adjustments. Henrietta, standing slightly to the side of him, rolled her eyes but she politely held her tongue.

"I believe the English named it the Lancaster Rose, a symbol from another of their civil wars."

"An unhappy link." Henrietta sighed and began toying with the ring upon her finger. "Though France, I am certain, will give more succour to my husband than a flower." She phrased it as a statement, rather than a question. If Henrietta had anything to do with it, then it would be so. She had the support of her sister-in-law, who ruled as regent for the seven-year-old King Louis XIV, but the opinion of their chief minister, Mazarin, mattered enormously.

The Cardinal continued with his work. "We must cut them quite ruthlessly." His words were delivered in a slow, staccato manner as he concentrated. "Only then can they bloom greater and more vibrantly."

"If only a few of those English rebels had been cut down, then this unhappy rebellion might have been avoided. But with support, we may still achieve a happy settlement of affairs, which will be much to the benefit of all kings and princes." She watched him from the corner of her eye. "The Dutch, for example, have promised soldiers."

"I pray for a successful conclusion."

"*My* prayers are that France might provide similar aid." Henrietta noted his reticence and moved the subject along. "If I might enquire, have you heard from Monsieur Montreuil about his delicate task?"

"I understand your concerns, Madame. Truly. Allow me to offer you some reassurance. I am informed that hopes for a union between King Charles and the Scots are high. With Montreuil's cultivation, I am certain that such an alliance shall come to fruition. Together, they can secure a treaty with the English Parliament and an honourable peace that would much favour the King."

"We must endeavour to win the Scots over without the King having to take their Covenant, nor concede anything else that would be as dishonourable. Is Montreuil certain that he can secure their full cooperation?"

REBELLION

"He is much encouraged thus far. The Scot's have vowed that if the King were to go to their army, he would be welcomed as their natural sovereign with freedom of conscience." Mazarin glanced at her. His rather pronounced mouth held back a smile. "I am sure someone as astute as Your Majesty knows, as well as I, that the Scot's have their own interests at heart. They stand little chance of introducing their beloved Presbyterianism to England without the King's support. Montreuil will use that as leverage."

"It is that which concerns me. The King is proving intransigent on the topic of religion and sees it as his duty to protect the church as it is established."

"An unbending stance would prove most challenging. Pray exhort him to show consideration of the Scots' desires and not to refuse them outright."

She frowned. "He remains committed to the church hierarchy and stands by his bishops. At best, he will only countenance Presbyterianism for a fixed period."

"The King and the Scots have no alternative but to stand with one another. Should they fail to unite, then the English Parliament will destroy them both."

"A result that would benefit nobody, is that not so?" She squeezed the tips of her thumb and index finger, both red from the innumerable letters she had penned of late. "Let us hope that your envoy works his charm well. The Scots began all of these unhappy wars; therefore, they have an obligation to end them."

Mazarin sniffed. His long, slender nose enhanced a regal air, while his eyes remained almost glazed, preventing the indomitable queen from penetrating his thoughts. The wind played with his plain lace collar and red robes, though personally, he seemed little ruffled by the outcome of the rebellion across the Channel.

"There is also the question of my eldest son and his marriage, which would offer another alliance," she ventured. "If, God forbid, the English rebels and their Puritan leaders were allowed to prosper, then they would no doubt come to blows with France."

"*Tres Vrai*. Though in the eyes of some here, King Charles's religious policies are just as heretical as those of the Puritans. Not my own opinion, I hasten to add."

"It makes me sick to hear the King compared to such rogues." Henrietta placed a hand to her chest, feeling the whalebone stays beneath. "He is God's anointed sovereign and we must prevent the spread of this rebellion. Puritanism is a scourge."

"Let Monsieur Montreuil continue his work, Madame. In the meantime, I implore you to use all means at your disposal to persuade the King to reconsider his stance on the church; or appear to do so, at the very least. His categorical defence of episcopacy may undo all of our hopes."

"There is not a day that goes by when I do not counsel him on that very subject!" Henrietta shook her head. "He must save himself over the bishops. If *his* cause is lost, then by default *theirs* shall be too."

"An understanding between the King and the Scots will leave London trembling," Mazarin cupped a particularly attractive flower and then spared it.

London. Henrietta feared London. Rumours reached her that the King was contemplating a very different plan altogether; a foolish notion that he could travel to the capital and address Parliament in person. A bid to seize the initiative, so it was proposed, and shock the rebels into a favourable peace by his sudden royal presence.

Of course, it was pure folly. He must not go there; she had insisted in many a letter that he stand firm and not venture anywhere near the dreaded city, otherwise the rebels would have him in their clutches. His cause – and their family – would be finished in one fell swoop. She felt as if she may go insane, entirely mad. Henrietta fought endlessly against the rebels, like any royalist commander, and continued fighting even now, when there was barely an army left in the King's service. She dealt with the French and Dutch like any good ambassador. But, like a good wife, she also struggled to bolster her husband's resolve and constancy. Her greatest joy in the world would be to behold him once more, a king with his lawful prerogative restored to him.

Chapter 17

13th April 1646.
Leicestershire.

Maxwell rubbed his stubbly jaw. His finger idled over a raised scar from Sherburn, a reminder of the tumultuous last ten months. Unkempt sandy hair hid his sweating forehead, while the musty smell of his old doublet just about kept hunger pangs at bay.

Walking through the countryside, it was easy to forget all that had happened in this short time, not least because he was treading upon familiar ground. Wistow Hall, where he'd been sent after the battle at Naseby, was not far to the west. But there was one big difference between then and now; this time, Maxwell was alone. He marched with no army. His nearest companions were the deer who roamed – ghost-like and distant – with the occasional high-pitched whistle of one who had lost its mother. Or the geese, who sounded more like drunkards in a tavern, laughing along to a good tale. He much preferred such company to that of humans. The track rose up an incline, and once at the top, he saw a coach with two men standing by it.

"*Excusez-moi, Monsieur?*"

Maxwell looked up but kept walking. One man – small and stocky – was smartly dressed in blue silk. The other was a trumpeter, with long elaborate sleeves that fell loose from the elbow, both embroidered with fleur-de-lis.

"A moment, if you please?" The trumpeter called.

"What is it?" Maxwell frowned. "I have a long journey."

"We are lost. Might you assist us?"

REBELLION

"This kingdom is unrecognisable to many these days," Maxwell replied.

Nevertheless, he headed towards the coach. He froze when one of them pulled back a flap that covered the window, immediately suspecting some sort of trick. An ambush. A pistol. But instead, it was a woman who looked out, and though Maxwell didn't glance long at her, he resolved to assist the party.

"We'll soon be on our way, Louisa," the well-dressed man reassured her.

"Where are you headed?" Maxwell asked.

"Do I speak with a soldier, perchance?" The man looked intently. "The reason for my question will become apparent."

"I came to offer directions, and not to discuss my business."

"*C'est vrai*," the man held up one hand and nodded. "Let me be equally plain. I am a French diplomat. There is much prejudice towards my country and I merely wish to ensure you will not make mischief for us."

"I have no time for mischief!"

"I see you're an honest man, God be thanked. Are we on the Newark road?"

"Aye. Newark is that way," Maxwell replied, casually pointing a finger.

"Ah, I see. And Harborough this way?" the Frenchman asked.

Maxwell gave a nod. "'Tis where I am headed."

"As are we, *mon ami*. Perhaps you would like to travel with us by way of thanks for your assistance?"

"No." Maxwell held up one hand. "You would not find me much company," he added and resumed his journey.

Barely minutes later, the birdsong from above ended. As a multitude fled from the branches, it gave the appearance that the trees themselves were dissolving away. A pounding grew louder, and Maxwell glanced over his shoulder. The dry, dusty earth left a trail behind three horsemen who were fast approaching, and Maxwell stepped back from the road and into the shade of the oaks. He stood ready to pull out the safe conduct pass that authorised his journey to royalist headquarters at Oxford. But the cavalrymen drew up at the coach and leaped from their horses.

"What have we here?"

"Fancy looking gentleman. A rebel by any chance?"

"I care not, because all rich men are rebels!"

Maxwell listened to the soldiers and their bravado. The coachman looked down at them with a deep sniff and then spat out a globule of phlegm.

"This is Jean de Montreuil," the trumpeter announced, as if the trio should recognise the name.

"I'm a French diplomat and travel with the protection of both King Charles and his Parliament," Jean added and produced a document.

"Parliament? Those mighty men have provided you with a mere sheet of paper to defend yourself? These are dangerous times. Too dangerous to sit on the roadside like this," one of the horsemen replied and then looked to his comrades. "I think we can help safeguard their valuables, can't we?"

"I am sent by King Louis and Cardinal Mazarin! You insult them both with such base threats," Jean warned. "Everything here belongs to France. There would be a grave diplomatic incident if any of my possessions were removed."

"We don't need poxy Frenchmen, swooping in like scavenging gulls."

"You are men of King Charles's army?" Jean asked. "Listen to me, lest you hang for your folly."

"You won't reason with those three!" Maxwell called out and began walking slowly back towards the coach, discreetly holding a stone behind his back.

REBELLION

"Who are you to judge us?"

"Captain Maxwell Walker, of Langdale's Northern Horse."

"Then why aren't you in the north – be you lost?" One of the trio retorted with a smirk.

"Oh, you'll wish I was soon enough," Maxwell laughed. "I suggest you three men get on your way."

"Is that an order, Captain?"

The leading cavalrymen stepped forward to square up to Maxwell.

"The rebels have just released me after four months of captivity. I would relish the chance of taking my frustration out on you, who behave more like thieves by the highway than soldiers."

"Thieves?"

"Aye, I judge you no comrades of mine, nor fit to serve the King. Therefore, I do not command you. Call it a warning, instead."

"A fine speech, Captain!"

Maxwell's single-minded determination left a deep crease in his brow and wrinkled up his nose. He stood glaring at the men. Then, as anticipated, the leader acted, swinging a punch with his large fist. Maxwell evaded the blow. Without hesitation, he brought the stone against his opponent's head, so quickly and with such effect, that it seemed as if he had an iron fist. The crunch of the impact produced a howl of pain. The coachman drew a two-foot dagger and jumped from the carriage to join the fray, stabbing another of the trio. The uninjured soldier raced back to his horse, with the others following in his wake, amidst cries of outrage and anger.

"Mon Dieu! Should I be offended that you proffered your identity so readily to those rogues, and not to me?" Jean said. "You are an officer with as much courage and skill as ever I did see."

"A child can swing a stone well enough." Maxwell cast the object into the trees and then wiped the blood from his hand.

"*Très modeste*. Though I've never seen a child do it quite like that," Jean said, lifting his palms. "You and my coachman could have been cut down. Like martyred brothers; Saints Gervais and Protais."

"Protais?" Maxwell frowned.

"Saints invoked for the discovery of thieves, ironically enough."

"An interesting comparison." Maxwell was reminded once more of the coded letter from Sherburn. Not that he had ever forgotten it. Protais and Gervais – could this be mere coincidence?

"You are troubled by something I have said?" Jean observed.

"I suggest you resume your journey, Monsieur," Maxwell replied, his mind now entirely distracted.

"And I insist you accompany us. For your own benefit as much as ours. You see, the Scots have refused to provide me with any scouts, so I find myself little better than a blind man in these parts."

Jean de Montreuil opened the coach door and got inside. Maxwell relented. Partly out of a desire to reach Oxford as quickly as possible, but also because he had next to no money left. When he placed one foot on the step, he glimpsed the lady within. The twinkle of her large blue eyes left her pearl necklace dull by comparison. Her every feature was enthralling; small, exquisite lips that seemed poised upon a smile, down to the small, lone freckle on her cheek. Maxwell's heart began to race. In nearly two years, the only other cause of this had been battles, skirmishes and each and every fight for his life. Yet, now it felt as if life was being pumped back into him.

"I shall sit atop with the coachman."

"As you wish." Jean shrugged his shoulders.

REBELLION

"I am in no condition for a lady's presence."

"On the contrary." Louisa gave a slight shake of her head, movement that made her curls caress her neck. "The scent of a real man is not to be found in bottles of perfume."

"Madame." Maxwell coughed and then stepped away. He felt his face flush. Her forwardness was quite captivating, but at the same time it was the very cause of his retreat. A push and pull of emotions that fostered both desire and guilt, excitement and anguish.

He climbed up to the seat next to the coachman and listened as the iron-shod wheels turned, slowly crunching over the chalky ground as they embarked upon their next journey. The clinking harness played a tune as the coach began to speed up and the warm spring air flowed past Maxwell's face. The world around him was soon a blur.

Chapter 18

The fields along the route had been torn open with a plough and the earth churned up into rich, brown waves. These patterned streaks were soon obscured by thatched buildings that sprouted up around Harborough, and the coach passed the crowded butchers' stalls to draw up in the main square. The Grammar School, which stood on ten wooden posts, and Saint Dionysius's Church, seemed to be waiting in welcome of Maxwell, who took hold of the side of the coach and jumped down from the seat.

"You're bleeding," Louisa said upon stepping outside.

Maxwell glanced at the side of his hand.

"To the Swan Inn, my dear." Jean pointed at the timber-framed building just north of the church. He strode neatly ahead with walking cane in hand, his Roman nose somewhat raised, it seemed, out of inquisitiveness over his surroundings.

"Allow me," Louisa said and took Maxwell's hand, dabbing it with a fine linen handkerchief. It left red spots on the embroidered motif; a scourge, club and sword.

"I think you should catch up to your husband." Maxwell nodded towards Jean.

"Husband?" Louisa laughed. Delicate dimples appeared at either side of her mouth. "Jean courts Kings, Princes and Ambassadors rather than any woman, least of all me."

"And you prefer it that way?" Maxwell turned to Louisa. Her humour was infectious, and a spontaneous smile crossed his own features.

"Of course. I am happy to assist him with his duties."

"Happy to woo these Kings, Princes and Ambassadors?"

"What are you suggesting, Captain?" She gave a wry smile and looked him up and down.

"Nothing, save your noble desire to serve France."

"Quite." She nodded. "Though I desire no personal alliance with any man bedecked in jewels or doused in perfume."

"Apologies if my words were too familiar."

"Captain …"

"Due to a lack of female company." Maxwell turned away and began walking.

"Oh, Captain!" Louisa followed and linked his arm. "Do not look so concerned. I much prefer you with your handsome smile."

"Well … thank you." Maxwell, who had been momentarily frozen by her very touch, was now uncomfortably warm, as if the sun was focussing its rays upon him and melting his icy core of mourning. A rather awkward silence arose. One that Maxwell felt utterly ill-equipped to break as each step took them closer to The Swan Inn.

"Tell me, you said you had been captured by the rebels?"

"Yes, at Newark. I had recently joined the garrison." Maxwell recounted with an eagerness to focus on all things martial. It was the war that offered him shelter from the stark reality of his emotions, as if they were his true enemies. "We made a sortie."

"Sortie?"

"Erm, an assault. Charging out of town to attack the besiegers."

"Ah," she pursed her lips and nodded.

"Well, the Scots captured me. Newark is being besieged by over fifteen thousand troops, you see. Both rebels and Scots."

"Why do you not class the Scots as rebels? I do not understand you English and your three kingdoms. They resemble a multi-headed beast that continuously butts its own heads together."

"A fair comparison!" Maxwell laughed. "In reality, both are rebels. But the parliamentarians are much more deserving of the mantle."

"Jean is currently engaged in discussions with the Scots. They certainly seem open to an honourable peace."

"Is that so? Then this war could soon be over?"

"You are a hasty man." Louisa playfully wagged one finger. "I said only that Jean was talking to them."

"Well, you certainly have given me some hope, Madame."

"Hope that may bring a smile to your face once more?"

Maxwell looked up at the archway of The Swan Inn. During the short walk to the building, he had been struck by so many differing emotions. He didn't want the conversation to end. Nor, if he was honest with himself, did he wish to relinquish her arm but as she slipped it out of his, he felt its loss keenly. Surprisingly so. With this came a sense of guilt, too, at the waves of delight that had coursed through him during their conversation. Though he barely knew this woman, he sensed there was more to her and desired to discover it for himself.

"Let us march to that table and occupy it, Captain." Louisa pointed. "You move in from the west, and I from the south."

"Allies?" Maxwell raised his head.

"Perhaps," she pondered and then gave a firm nod. "I think you are worthy."

"A grand victory." Maxwell sat down opposite her.

"And hopefully not my last."

"I am certain it shall not be so."

"Only, I require a suitable title, like the Queen. Her-She-Majesty-Generalissima, as some rakes of her own side style her."

REBELLION

The drinks reached the table before Jean, who broke open a letter he had just been handed. The man's dark eyebrows dipped as he read it. Maxwell supped his beer, for once unconcerned that it was not ale, for he had many other matters on his mind. He placed the tankard down onto the table, whose cracked surface resembled the dry earth outside.

"Your thirst is quenched?" Louisa asked.

"Aye, though not fully," Maxwell took another gulp. "A Northern Horseman is rarely satisfied."

"Oh yes, you're a northerner. So, how did you come to be at Newark?"

"After our defeat in Scotland. There was not a great choice of places to go."

"Scotland? You were attempting to join Montrose?" Louisa's eyebrows rose.

"That's right. Though, alas, it was too late."

"Such a shame. Had Montrose been vanquished?"

"He was in the highlands. Hundreds of miles from us," Maxwell replied.

"I see. He has suffered a reverse in his fortunes, has he not?"

"Yes, that's correct. He wasn't of sufficient strength to strike south."

Jean joined the pair at the table. "I have a request of you, my dear. You must travel poste-haste to Oxford."

"As does our errant knight," Louisa replied.

"Captain, I would be obliged if you could travel with Mademoiselle Laurant and keep her safe. It is imperative she reaches Oxford unmolested."

Louisa smiled at Maxwell.

"I will make sure of it, sir."

Jean, seemingly relieved by the answer, handed Louisa the letter he had just received and then took another from a leather satchel. He grasped each side and held it in front of him, the red seal standing out like a setting sun, and then proceeded to tear it in half. Next, into quarters. As if that wasn't enough, he ripped it again, though this proved much more difficult. Maxwell's curiosity was piqued. He watched as Jean carefully threw it into the flames of the fire, piece by piece, meticulously waiting for each part to combust, before adding yet another.

Chapter 19

**22nd April 1646.
Merton College Library, Oxford.**

The book was attached to the desk by a chain, like a shackled prisoner, and was so old that the goatskin binding looked mummified. Gervase Harper opened its dull, thick cover. He was only mildly interested in the theology contained within the pages and screwed his nose up at the musty smell. Whilst absent-mindedly tracing his long fingers over it, he studied a different matter altogether; what he would do if he was in King Charles's position.

The glorious sunshine gave the oak of the wagon roof a golden hue. It lit up the leopards, Tudor roses and dolphins that were painted onto the metal badges. Yet Harper's mind remained as dark as ever. The King was check-mated and now a very different game had begun. Would the monarch flee Oxford and surrender to the Scottish army at Newark, or to the English Parliament in London? Or might he make yet another attempt to join the Marquis of Montrose and fight on?

The click of leather soles upon the stone tiles stirred Harper from all thoughts of the vital task before him. His fellow French agent had arrived. Francois Duval would surely have some answers that would assist with the endeavour.

"When did *you* arrive in Oxford?"

"Only this very morrow," Harper replied. "Since Digby's defeat in the north, I have had to trail from one godforsaken place to the next with him."

"Why choose to meet in a library of all places?" Francois chortled. His features were naturally ruddy, but his humour brought an ever more carmine blush to his cheeks, which contrasted acutely with his silver hair.

"It's better here. Quieter."

"But drier though. No wine."

"I won't risk exposing my connections for the sake of a glass of *Bourgogne*."

"True, you risk nothing here. It seems nobody has any interest in reading anymore," Francois said and glanced about the empty library. "Or maybe King Charles has all of the students holed up in his last few garrisons?"

Harper gave a knowing shake of his head. "I purchased such solitude for us. A golden crown in the warden's palm."

"You – paid money so that we could be alone?" Francois chortled. "My friend, I knew not your depth of feeling."

"Not in that sense, Duval!" Harper grimaced. "I want you to advise me of everything that has occurred here in the last month or so."

"I fear there is little I can say."

"When did Montreuil leave for Newark?"

"The second day of April. But I have heard nothing of him, nor how he has fared with the Scots."

"Then the Scots must surely have shunned Montreuil's proposal that they welcome the King into their army. Either that, or the misguided monarch has changed his feeble mind again." Harper frowned.

"Well, whatever way this turns out, I won't be here to see it. I leave for Paris tomorrow."

"Am I the only one left to carry out our orders to safeguard France's interests?"

"You don't need me. You're now seen as a trusted royalist captain, and in Oxford you find yourself at the epicentre of this end game."

REBELLION

Harper sighed and slammed his hand against the old book. An array of dust particles cascaded through the shafts of sunlight.

"I must savour this pretty library that you have bought for me. Who knows whether it will survive the parliamentarians when they take the town? Their New Model Army cannot be far away."

"You speak as though a siege will prove necessary, and that the King will not surrender?" Harper's small eyes narrowed.

"He may cling on like a barnacle, but one way or another this will be over."

"Let it be soon, please God," Harper replied.

"Can you not give matters a nudge in the right direction? Don't you have the ear of Lord Digby?"

"The fool is in Ireland."

"All you need do is prevent any juncture between King Charles and Montrose."

"I have been doing that for six months! Working from within against such an outcome."

"It is not in France's interests to have the King win this war outright, and Montrose is his last hope of doing so."

"You sound like Mazarin."

"Just make sure it doesn't happen, for both our sakes."

"Mon Dieu! I stood ready to kill Montrose if I came across him in Scotland."

"I admire your ruthlessness, Gervase. It's no wonder you were entrusted with such a mission. You are on the cusp of success. Your tenacity will soon be rewarded, of that I am sure."

"Don't you have *any* news about Montreuil's efforts?"

"I've heard naught, I tell you. The contact has gone quiet."

"Then I must sit and wait," Harper replied with a growl of frustration.

"Be patient. Try prayer," Francois smiled. "Or read some of these books."

"I am not a patient man. Many have come to realise that all too late."

"Watch the King. Observe his every move, who he talks to and his routine. You will notice when he is ready to act."

"Your parting insight is most useful."

"Such sarcasm is beneath you, Gervase."

"There will only be one thing beneath me tonight …"

"Oh, I pity her, whoever she might be."

"I need something to brighten this enforced idleness. I shall ride as hard as if I was on the road to Dover, ready to leave this damned country."

"Might I remind you that your time needs to be spent near the King and not in a whore's chamber."

"Away with you."

"I shall reassure Mazarin of your efforts when I reach Paris," Francois replied, and went to give a kiss on both cheeks.

Harper stopped him. "People who get so close end up with my dagger in their bellies. Now, safe journey, Francois."

"*Adieu. Bon chance.*"

Francois had barely left when Harper paced towards a window at the opposite end of the library. As he went, he fumbled in his purse and took out a silver Half-Franc, rubbing it between forefinger and thumb for luck. He leaned against the window frame and observed the coin, which was so worn that only King Louis XIII's ruff remained visible on one side. It had been minted in 1616, the year of Harper's birth, and had been given to him, aged eight, by his French mother on her death bed. Perhaps it was through her influence that he identified himself as French, wholly overlooking his English father.

He stared idly out of the window and looked across the gardens of Merton, beyond Turnbull's Stream, and towards Christchurch Walks. Many well-dressed gentlemen and their ladies were taking the air. With a sigh, he resolved to go and search out the King.

He stood straight and was about to leave when a woman standing in the gardens below caught his eye. Harper recognised her immediately and a grin crossed his face. The absent agent he and Francois had just spoken about was right here; she had seemingly blossomed like the apple trees under which she stood, surely ripe with details regarding the activities of Jean de Montreuil.

Chapter 20

9am. 26th April 1646.
Oxford.

Maxwell smiled. His features felt naturally inclined to do so of late. As both pupils dilated, the pale blue irises receded, leaving an opening that led straight to his soul. Louisa leaned closer to him as she spoke. He watched her lips, as if he could see the very words that came from them and relished the soft tone that rose and fell with her humour. She laughed with a hint of abandon. Confident in her manner, yet delicately so. She linked his arm without hesitation as they walked – at one point during their discussion, turning to face him – and those dimples in her cheeks …

"Tell me again, where were you born, Captain?" she asked.

"Selby."

After the briefest of frowns, she giggled. "I repeat, *where* were you born?"

"Yorkshire," Maxwell clarified. "In the north."

"And what did you do in the north before you became a soldier?"

"I was a blacksmith, like my father before me."

"Aha." She raised her eyebrows as if it matched her assumption. "Your family seem to have been rooted to Selby – settled – until this war plucked you. What made you turn to the army?"

"Necessity. I shall say no more, lest I tire you."

REBELLION

"My, you have a mysterious side, Captain! The people of Selby must miss their skilled smithy?"

"I wouldn't say that." Maxwell paused. "My mother was a Catholic, you see. So, most of the town shunned my father's services and that somewhat passed down to me."

"They feared the smithy might bend them all to his wife's religious will?" She shook her head. "Just as absurd as the claims they make about Queen Henrietta."

"Some people could be quite cruel to my mother, but my father stood by her always."

Maxwell's broad shoulders tensed. The noise of the people around them seeped into his subconscious mind; he had overlooked his surroundings until now. They hadn't mattered.

"What about you, where in France are you from?" Maxwell asked.

"I was born in Fontaine Belleau."

"*Where?*" Maxwell smiled and playfully mimicked her questioning.

"A hamlet south of Paris," she replied and jerked his arm with hers. "But my home is now in the capital."

Maxwell considered what more he wanted to know about Louisa. He imagined her life in Paris, fine houses, palaces, and the world of etiquette that must exist there. She would suit such a place, and it her. Verbalising a compliment about her appealing accent, he glanced aside as he tried to find the right words, but then suddenly lost his trail of thought. His eyes narrowed.

"Are you unwell? You have turned pale ..." Louisa's words petered off.

"A ghost from my past, you might say."

"Then let us leave and take some air," she suggested.

Across the room was Gervase Harper, his long face seemed even gaunter when he was concentrating, and symmetrical lips betrayed none of his thoughts. A black moustache hung above them, while a beard wisped its way from his chin, up his jawline and encroached onto his cheeks. Harper was in conversation with a woman at the opposite side of the room. He was an anchor to every emotion that had scarred Maxwell in the past two years; an anchor that needed to be cut loose if he wished to live again.

"My apologies, but if you care to go on without me. I shall join you shortly."

Maxwell left Louisa and made his way past people and crossed the chamber. The woman Harper was talking to quietly slipped away with something in her grasp. Maxwell had no idea what it was, nor did he care. He merely noted her features for future reference.

"We meet again," Maxwell said.

"Did I not tell you that our destinies were interlinked," Harper replied.

"Is that your destiny, or that of your alter ego, Protais?"

"What?" Harper's nose screwed up as a scornful smile crossed him.

"That is your other name, if I am not mistaken?"

"Has your grief become so burdensome that you now forget who I am?"

"Be you Protais or Gervase? Certainly, you're no saint."

"Of course not – all saints are dead. This world is not a habitable one for them."

"And you think you're the one to judge who lives or dies. I have a mind that you once hoped to sacrifice Montrose, but for what? For who?"

"What a fanciful idea. I'll wager you have not a shred of evidence to substantiate it."

Maxwell glared at Harper. That was a fact, a most sickening one.

"On the contrary," Maxwell inhaled deeply. "Just imagine if I happened to chance upon a letter at Sherburn; writing that incriminates you?"

Harper leaned in close. "Go and resume your dalliance. It pleases me that you have found yourself a new woman."

"Did not Saint Gervase succumb to a lashing from a scourge and Protais the blade of a sword?"

"Bravo. You, sir, should have become a priest. If you had been celibate, you would not have had a wife to lose at my hands," Harper retorted under his breath.

"When I take my revenge, Harper, I shall not give you the choice of how you die."

Maxwell turned and left. He felt overwhelmed. The very talk of Catherine stoked fires of guilt within him, which he had felt so acutely since meeting Louisa. He was overcome by a sense of betrayal towards his beloved wife as if any new memories might displace such tender ones forever.

Forgetting Catherine terrified Maxwell more than the sights and sounds of war itself. But to be thus tormented by guilt, as well as the heartache and anger, was just too much to bear. Harper must die. Perhaps then, the scarring memories of Catherine's demise could also be laid to rest, memories that were beginning to overshadow all others and turning Maxwell's deepest fears into a reality.

Chapter 21

**Midday. 26th April 1646.
Christ Church College.**

The white wine had only just begun to trickle from the lip of the silver jug when King Charles raised the fingers of his right hand. A gesture at which the servant withdrew. The King took his glass, gently swirled the crisp looking contents, and then took a sip. The sweet taste was enlivening following a delicious dish of salmon. After a little more, he was quite finished with it and turned to William Dobson, who stood a little distance away. As Dobson sketched, the gentle application of the man's charcoal to the paper at his easel was all that could be heard, a noise that was most calming and understated, yet a wonderful piece of artwork was taking form with every stroke.

The King stood and hooked his thumb around the blue ribbon of the Garter that hung around his neck. He walked slowly towards Dobson, stopping a short distance from him to glance at the drawing. The nod of the King's head was barely noticeable. Dobson was a most impressive artist.

"Very good."

"Thank you, Your Majesty."

After some moments, the King now turned to face his counsellors, who waited at the other side of the room and waved them forward. Like the changing of a stage setting, the artist began packing up his equipment and these newcomers made ready to play their parts in the events of the day. Dobson's squirrel-hair brushes tinkled into a case and he wiped his hands on a cloth. After he had left, the King gave a great sigh.

"What news of the Queen – have we received any letters by today's post?"

"None, Your Majesty," the Duke of Richmond replied.

"And nothing from Montreuil, either?"

"No, sir, I'm afraid not."

"Then I must despatch a letter to my wife, Richmond, for I cannot wait any longer. I make my move this evening."

Aside from a bond of blood, Richmond being his cousin, the peer's benign eyes and level-headed manner appealed to the King, especially at this crucial point. For weeks, King Charles had been ready to leave Oxford at an hour's notice. Through prayer and meditation, he had prepared himself mentally for the dangers and uncertainty that would surely accompany such a decision. One final act was to pen a letter to his wife, and in the absence of her advice, declare his intention. As such, he took a quill, dipped it and began to write.

"Might I counsel against leaving Oxford?"

"The time has come." The King shook his head without looking up from his work. "Were it not for Rupert's backwardness over the matter, I would have left weeks ago. I am impatient with the delay and can suffer it no longer."

"Would it be advisable to make the entire council aware of this decision?"

"Only those closest to me are privy to it, my son, nephews, Ashburnham and Hudson. Some of my council have been privately informed, though not all, for that would give warning to the rebels. I eschew all kind of captivity. If I stay here, that would surely be the result, for we face a siege any day."

"What of your destination?"

"First to Kings Lynn. If I cannot procure honourable and safe conditions from the rebels, then I will leave for Scotland. If Montrose is in no fit state to receive me, then Ireland it shall be."

"It is a journey full of perils. Is the King's route to Lynn secure?" Richmond asked of Jack Ashburnham, a Groom of the Bedchamber.

"There are one or two trusted riders who have been sent ahead to procure fresh horses and assess the route," Ashburnham replied. "Captain Harper of Digby's lifeguard will await us in Wheathampstead. Major Hopper is scouting the countryside around Lynn. Both men left Oxford this morning."

"What of the Scots, can their intentions be trusted?" Richmond asked, his voice even and steady, despite his apparent concern. "How certain are we of Montreuil's claims that they will support the King in securing a favourable settlement with Parliament?"

It was a question that greatly affected the usually self-controlled monarch. Frustration caused him to apply slightly too much pressure to the delicately balanced quill, which subsequently leaked a blot of ink onto the paper. He crumpled the letter and threw it aside, before selecting a fresh sheet of paper, though his hand was left stained by the words that had not yet dried.

"M-my condition is made worse than ever because of the relapsed perfidiousness of the Scots! Admittedly, they do not give Montreuil the same reassurances they once did about how they might deal with me."

"We will send messengers to the Scots at Southwell and verify their intentions. At the moment, we rule out no options," Ashburnham said, reassuring Richmond, and by default, the King also.

The monarch wrote his customary salutation to his beloved wife and poured out his inner-most thoughts, those which he would share with none other than Henrietta. If he should miscarry in his plans, he instructed her to continue the same endeavours for their son, Prince Charles. Above all, the King urged her not to whine over any misfortunes that might befall him, but to behave like a true and worthy daughter of King Henry IV of France – Henry the Great. Her namesake.

Chapter 22

Evening. 26th April 1646.

Maxwell strode along a corridor watched by an array of portraits that lined its entire length. They were interspersed with landscapes, which upon the wooden panelling, were like gilded windows onto another world - far removed from the one he inhabited. But Maxwell had eyes only for the way ahead, which led to the rooms where Louisa was staying. He could not stop ruminating over his conversation that morning with Harper, and the unanswered questions about this unravelling treason. There was one particular thought that had come to him, which needed to be addressed without delay.

A clunk echoed from his right and a silver ball rolled erratically along the floor towards him. A pomander. Maxwell looked down at it and went to pick it up, but before he did so, a woman stepped forward.

"Excuse me, sir, I must speak with you."

"Do I know you?" Maxwell replied and then rolled his eyes upon recognising her. "Oh, you were conversing with Gervase Harper earlier."

"I shall not trouble you long. What I have to say …"

"Please, I do not have the time," Maxwell interrupted.

"I am informed that you are a loyal officer of His Majesty."

"What has that to do with you?"

"I beg of you, sir, this is of grave concern to us all."

REBELLION

Maxwell laughed sarcastically. "No, you and your master do *not* concern me. Let me give you some advice; stay clear of Harper and do no more of his bidding."

"Will you not give me the courtesy of listening to what I have to say? Do you hold me in such disdain?"

Maxwell continued walking. He wondered whether there was anybody he could trust.

"Then be on your way, sir. I will do this alone."

No sooner had he arrived at the door than he knocked upon it. The raps were firmer than he intended. There was silence. The seconds felt like minutes and still there was no movement. Granted, Louisa was not expecting him, and nor had he been to her rooms before for her to guess it might be him, but he needed to speak with her at once. He could not keep this to himself any longer. There was nobody else to whom he would – or could – turn.

"Louisa."

The door opened slightly. "Captain Walker?" She seemed surprised. It was the first occasion since the day they had met that she had addressed him so formally.

"I must talk to you. It is of the utmost importance."

"It cannot wait until the morrow?"

"No." Maxwell shook his head with exasperation.

"Pray give me a moment to make myself presentable."

The door closed and Maxwell waited. A sigh of frustration escaped him; that she seemed somewhat cooler than normal, but also because he was not one to suffer delays. He possessed little patience and had no regard for the formalities of Oxford. Here, he felt bridled. By comparison, most of the last few years had been spent on horseback – free. He had not had to spare any thoughts of manners or etiquette when hacking at the enemy and defending his own life, as well as those of his men. He was the King's Captain, and not the King's courtier.

Finally, Louisa let him inside. He walked into the centre of the room and then turned around to look at her. She held a cloak around her that reached down to her feet – silent at first, but then she laughed.

"You force your way into a lady's chamber, yet have nothing to say for yourself?"

"I have plenty to say, but I know not how to begin!" Maxwell sat on the chair at the foot of the four-poster bed and held his head.

"Well, whatever it is, you have deemed it important enough to pay me this visit. And I know you are not a man who struggles to speak his mind."

"You are as perceptive as ever." Maxwell smiled.

"Then talk to me, Captain. Did we not become allies at Harborough?"

"Strangely enough, it is of Harborough that I wish to speak." He looked up. "I noticed Monsieur Montreuil burn a letter at The Swan Inn. Do you have any knowledge as to what it might have contained?"

"I do, as it happens," she nodded, and then tilted her head in expectation.

"Would you care to share it with your ally? It could be of vital importance in a plot I have uncovered. It is serious Louisa."

"A plot?" She turned away and sighed. "You ask me to betray Jean."

"Betray is a strong word. I seek clarification. There is something afoot."

"It was an order from the King. For the surrender of Newark." She hesitated and then held up her hands. "Jean feared it might fall into rebel hands and be used in a malicious attempt to gain the town."

"The King wishes the garrison to surrender?" Maxwell was taken aback.

"No - well, at least not yet, which is why it was destroyed. It was written to prove his desire for peace; that he would be willing to order Newark's surrender to the

Scots if they would join with him in calls for a peaceable settlement."

"I see." Maxwell nodded slowly. Louisa was privy to much, it seemed. "Does its destruction bode ill for all hopes of peace?"

"I wouldn't know that. Please, must you ask me such questions?"

"Forgive me," Maxwell replied.

"I have already imparted too much."

They remained silent. Maxwell couldn't help but feel he had compromised her; his stomach churned over one final question. This was, by far, the most important, not only relating to this whole business, but more personally to them both. He hesitated.

Louisa's expression was the most serious he had ever seen. Gone were the giggling, playful remarks that both had enjoyed, and along with these, the physical closeness that Maxwell had relished. On many occasions they had walked and talked with intimacy, but he was acutely aware of the gap that politics had opened up between them. Yet, in spite of this, as Maxwell looked her in the eye, he felt the pair being drawn closer on an emotional level.

His breathing quickened. She pulled at the ties of her cloak and it dropped instantly to the floor. It was easy to imagine her smock of cambric linen similarly falling from her shoulders and something in her eyes suggested she could sense his very desire. She bit her lip. He longed to place his own to them.

"You would have me reveal more?"

Louisa's voice was almost a whisper as she stepped closer and flicked off her velvet heeled slippers. Her very movement was arousing, so sensual and delicate. Every curve of her alluring figure acted in unison. Then she was before him. Maxwell held her waist and she lowered herself to sit astride him on his thighs. There was only one doubt in his mind.

"Louisa, I need to know. Are you aware of anyone by the name of Protais?"

"Enough questions."

Their lips were almost touching. Hanging on a kiss.

"Are *you* Protais?"

"I'll be whoever you want me to be," she replied with a wry smile.

Her words – her voice – were captivating. There was nothing between them but the excitement of their warm breath. Maxwell slowly eased her closer.

REBELLION

Chapter 23

The tailored smock hugged Louisa's figure. It seemed almost translucent, and unable to hide the glow of her body beneath. Curls of hair lay across her chest, settling into the linen pleats – until Maxwell moved them gently aside. He toyed with the cords of the smock, prompting a smile that revealed her mischievous dimples. One kiss of her soft lips and then his tongue caressed hers. She began unfastening his doublet, effortlessly easing the buttons out of their openings, but the concern deep within him would not budge.

"Your handkerchief …"

The words slipped out. That one memory would not leave him, of the small piece of linen she had used to dab at his cut back in Harborough. After his encounter with Harper, Louisa's simple act had come flooding back. All of the sensations that coursed through his body were, even now, beholden to the doubt it fostered. He went to speak again.

"Pray do not spoil this moment. I know you have desired it as much as I."

She ran her fingers along his stubbled jaw.

"The embroidered pattern." Maxwell took her hand.

He got to his feet, and as he did so, lifted her up too. She struggled and stood before him; barely up to his chin and glaring with disbelief.

"You spurn me?"

"No …"

"You have used me all along?"

"No. If that was the case, I'd not have stopped."

"Why do you humiliate me so? Was your desire nought but pretence?"

"Jesu, I desire you more than ever. You may see that for yourself." His gaze fell to his breeches. "But I need the truth."

"You run from the truth!"

"What I feel for you is much greater that lust alone."

"Yet, you cast me away?"

"I need to speak of that which remains unsaid. Of something that you seem to be avoiding. One answer is all I need, Louisa."

"This damned plot; your mind is full of it."

"When you wiped my hand at Harborough, I saw embroidery. A scourge and a sword; I've since found out that they are the symbols of Gervais and Protais. There are some that work against the King …"

She slapped him. His cheek stung like the burning outrage she exhibited. Her eyes welled up, but by stark contrast, her features were full of anger; so much so, that every bit of what had so nearly occurred was swept aside in an instant. Still she stared hard at him, as if expecting an answer. An apology.

"I fear you might be linked in some way to what I have unearthed. Foolish, I know, but these doubts torment me all the same."

"You have had this in your mind since Harborough? Entertained me and led me on a merry dance, yet all the while suspecting me of treachery to your beloved King?"

"No, 'tis not like that. I only realised the significance when I spoke with Harper today, a man I should have killed long ago."

"Gervase Harper?" She frowned.

"Aye, that's him. Hold – you know the man?"

"You have ruined what may have blossomed between us."

"Me?"

"Get out!" She cried and pointed to the door.

"I see. Then you are involved with that evil whoremonger and his plans?"

"Whatever I might say, you have me condemned already."

"You, who played the victim. Imploring me not to ask you this question or that. Feigning loyalty to Montreuil. Do you have any loyalty to anyone?"

"My family, I am loyal to my family," she hissed. "And France. I care not a whit about King Charles!"

"God only knows what you and Harper are aiming at. But I offer my congratulations on hooking me with your flirtatious manner. A most cunning way of controlling me, the one who has begun to unravel your treasonous game."

"Captain Walker, you are pig-headed and have a nasty streak about you," she replied in a low voice. "I shall give your regards to my dear cousin when next I see him."

"Your cousin?"

"Much has come to light this evening, so let me deal plainly with you. I knew nothing of your suspicions, nor could I ever have imagined that you might have had dealings with my cousin, Gervase. My feelings towards you were entirely without artifice. Mon Dieu, you could say I had been falling in love." She laughed at the last word. False laughter that rang in Maxwell's ears and made him feel more vulnerable than ever.

"Harper is your cousin?"

Maxwell could barely get the question out. Indeed, the very words left a bitter taste in his mouth. She didn't need to grace it with a single word of verification, for her unreserved and lofty expression said it all. This shocking revelation twisted his insides, robbing his barren heart of all that had begun to flourish there of late. Harper had humiliated him.

"Your *cousin* ... murdered my wife!" Maxwell yelled until he was red in the face.

A tear began to run down Louisa's cheek, hanging onto her chin like a tiny glass bead that had captured this terrible moment within it. If only it could have retained all of the sorrow and heartache that pained the pair. But in an instant, it was washed away by a steady stream that followed and Louisa ran to the bed and threw herself upon it. She sobbed.

"I suggest you find your cousin before me, otherwise you will not behold him again."

Maxwell stormed out of the room with a roar of anger escaping him as he left - or was it sorrow. His head thumped and mind raced with wild and uncontrollable thoughts. Nothing seemed real anymore, nor could he even trust his own judgement again. He prayed for an end to all of the lies, betrayal and suffering, and then noticed the woman he had encountered earlier, standing right in his path.

"It sounds as if you treat all women with contempt!"

For the second time, he felt the stinging rebuke of a hand across his cheek. Maxwell cursed. Then she thrust a paper at him.

"Who the devil are you?"

"That matters not. I am employed by the governor to keep watch upon certain men whose loyalty is dubious, including Gervase Harper."

"The Governor of Oxford?"

"Yes," she replied firmly. "Now, read this."

Maxwell snatched the letter, causing the pearls at her ears to tremble and her ruby lips to arc in a manner of detestation.

"God knows, if the King's cause was not in such peril, I would never have given you another second of my time," she said under her breath. "The high praise that the governor received about you is the only reason I stand before you now."

"Begone. Leave me!"

"Gervase Harper implored me to deliver that letter to Mademoiselle Laurant." She pointed to the paper in Maxwell's hand several times. "He lodged at my father's inn, but left Oxford this morning after speaking with me. I chose to read it, and most glad I am to have done so."

"Where has he gone?"

"Read it and see." She demanded. "When you come to your senses, you shall find me in the house next to the sign of The White Bear. Ask for Maria."

She left without a further word. Maxwell crushed the letter within his grasp. He moved to the open window casement and held the top of it to steady himself. The missing beats of his erratic heart caused him to hunch at their loss. Through the swirls of grey-tinted glass, nocturnal Oxford made for a confusing and eerie sight. He felt dizzy, as if he'd drowned his grief in ale, then looked at the letter and saw Harper's signature.

*

Cousin,

I am mighty glad to see you once more and your arrival in Oxford <u>cannot</u> have been better timed. I am without contacts here, therefore I send this one letter via the daughter of my landlord, for I cannot be seen with you. Do not acknowledge me if we should meet.

This great business has finally progressed, and the grand fox will soon be leaving his lair. I stand ready to give chase. Once again, the objective will be to prevent any juncture with MM – at all costs. I shall reside tomorrow night at Wheathampstead. Pray write to me there.

MARK TURNBULL

I see that you have a new admirer, though I give fair warning to avoid becoming too entangled with this one, for I know first-hand of his meddlesome nature. <u>He has discovered too much already</u>. Therefore, I charge you to tell him nothing, but by the same token, keep him close. His distraction may work in my favour.

Gervase

Chapter 24

3am. 27th April 1646.

A nocturnal curtain brought privacy to one who spent his days in a blaze of public scrutiny. It offered peace and time for reflection. Solitude. Nightfall had always appealed to King Charles I.

The church bells tolled three times. He was abroad in the crisp night air, riding through Oxford's East Gate with only two men ahead of him. It could have been a dream, had the King not been anticipating this moment for weeks – and had his heart not been thumping so much now that it was finally upon him. This evening was unlike any other that had passed before.

"Farewell Harry!"

The Governor of Oxford's words seemed to dissipate into the darkness. The King didn't respond, nor did he look back as the gate was locked behind him. He headed across East Bridge. For the present, he was no longer King of England, Scotland and Ireland, but a mere servant called Harry. He shivered. Not from any chill, for the breeze was refreshing, but from the emotions that ran through his body; worry and apprehension, as well as relief and a sheer thrill to have escaped the confines of the town. The New Model Army was closing in on Oxford and the place had started to feel more like a prison than his headquarters. After weeks of excruciating silence from the French envoy, Jean de Montreuil, who had been negotiating with the Scots at Newark, King Charles had finally made his move.

Ahead of him rode Jack Ashburnham, his Groom of the Bedchamber. There was also Michael Hudson, a former scoutmaster-general, but now a royal chaplain – and a plain-speaking one at that. The darkness that shrouded the King accentuated the adoption of his new persona. He certainly didn't feel like he was the same man he had been before the war – not least because of the physical changes that had taken place in the last few hours. He was unaccustomed to feeling the breeze tussle his hair quite so easily, but Ashburnham had cut it at midnight. Gone was his fashionable lovelock. Neither had his immaculate beard been spared; a characteristic feature that he had sported for over twenty years – half of his life. Rather than a crown, tonight he wore a simple Montero cap.

The towers of the gatehouse behind him rose like shadowy horns on some sleeping beast. When Oxford woke on the morrow, only a select few would know of his disappearance. Fewer still that he was headed for Kings Lynn, where he could take ship for Scotland. Ashburnham had a travel pass, signed by General Thomas Fairfax, which had been taken from a captive parliamentarian; they could use it if challenged along the way.

Sleepy Marsh Baldon was the first point on the route that had been agreed. As the three riders sped up, Hudson's red cloak seemed to reach out to the King in a bid to keep them together. The thrill of being loose on horseback was exhilarating, as if he was once more indulging his passion for hunting. Banished to the corners of his mind was the certainty that once his departure was discovered, then he would be the fox, ruthlessly pursued by Parliament's hounds.

"Lord be my guide," he whispered. "Make me a glorious king, or a patient martyr."

Chapter 25

**Early Hours. 2nd May 1646.
Little Gidding, near Huntingdon.**

Somewhere in the inky night was the King and his two companions. Harper too. For several days, Maxwell had been in search of them after riding hard from Oxford. Then at Wheathampstead – on London's outskirts – he had veered north after discovering that strangers had been seen heading in that direction. It was a gamble, but there was nothing to lose.

Ahead was a little church. The windows were alive with the dancing glow of candles, each one vying to outdo the others. The sight drew Maxwell; a warmth that piqued his exhausted senses and gave him something to focus upon other than Harper. As he diverted towards it, the grey outline of a tower emerged from a backdrop of trees, and he tethered his horse at the entrance, near a table tomb spotted with moss. The place was strangely quiet considering the light from within. No singing, nor any voices.

Maxwell pushed open the door. The brass eagle of the lectern was all that looked back when, after a moment's hesitation, he set foot inside. The wooden floor was immaculate, as was the wainscot panelling on the walls. The polished brass font sparkled. Ironically, the cover that sat atop the font was a crown, complete with fleurs-de-lis, crosses and trefoils. It cast a regal shadow across the nearby wall; a crown at the mercy of every flickering candle, forced to jump one way and then the other as the flames saw fit. Somewhere in these enemy heartlands was King Charles, in an equally precarious position.

As Maxwell walked up the nave, a sense of unease filled him and goosebumps raised his skin, accentuated with each footstep. The hiss of a candle made him turn around with a start. The past continuously haunted him, while the present kept him in a state of perpetual anxiety, and there was no escape. No respite. Every time he tried to sleep, his racing mind could think only of revenge. Or more specifically, that fateful night in Selby two years ago, which was gradually smothering him.

"God give me peace."

Maxwell's voice sounded lonelier than ever. He dropped to his knees. The Lord's Prayer, Creed and Ten Commandments stood out from a brass plaque on the wall, burning its words onto his stinging eyes so that he could see nothing else. The entire church began to dissolve into a golden haze. He closed his eyes to shut it all out. Prayed fervently. These whispered words were given alongside the drumming beat of his constricted heart.

"State your business, sir!"

Maxwell drew his sword before he'd even fully stood. The piercing ring responded to the question, for he could not. Instead, he glared at the man and tensed in readiness to leap across the pews and sink his blade into him.

"The war does not extend to the haven of Saint John's. Pray leave it."

"Nor do I bring it here. I wish to escape it!" Maxwell cried.

"As do we all. Now, please leave."

"Who are you?"

"John Ferrar. My family founded this religious community."

"Well, Mister Ferrar, why burn so many candles at this late hour?"

REBELLION

"God never sleeps, sir. His flock need him at every hour of the day – and night."

"Might I ask who required him tonight?" Maxwell probed and sheathed his sword.

Ferrar began to blow out the candles. "Good evening."

"Tell me, damn you!" Maxwell yelled. It was as if something from deep inside was speaking for him. He was overcome by desperation. "Was it the King?"

"He who disturbs us is a burden whilst he stays and shall bear the Lord's judgement."

"Tell me!"

Ferrar continued extinguishing the candles one by one and shutting out the light. Maxwell gave a third demand, though his voice broke. He staggered forward. "For the love of God, I beg you."

"What is it that ails thee?"

Maxwell collapsed against the pews and they subsequently screeched across the floor. It was the last noise he heard. The final sight being Ferrar's face looking down at him.

Maxwell's broken mind and exhausted body had barely two hour's rest. Then the nightmares returned to haunt him; images of Catherine's bloodstained face. His teardrops had dappled the blood. He had held his hands over her wound in a reflex action – helplessly – as if the bleeding could somehow have been stemmed. It had been impossible to do anything more than cup her head in his hands and pull her limp and lifeless body close.

"No!" Maxwell's eyes opened.

He curled into a ball. The memories had dragged him from slumber and his stomach knotted when reality confirmed the truth of them.

"Soldier?"

He opened his eyes to see John Ferrar. "Where am I?"

"Little Gidding."

"The King?" Maxwell asked.

"Who are you?"

"Captain Walker, of His Majesty's cavalry."

"Do you possess anything that may prove your claim?"

Ferrar's red hair was stark. A serene man of sixty years, Maxwell guessed, whose small mouth seemed unsuited to any utterance but that of peace and prayer. All of his experiences seemed to be stored in the saggy skin under his eyes; and he had clearly seen much in his time.

"I have a pass from the rebels that allowed me to return to Oxford." Maxwell fumbled with his satchel. "It's from there that I came."

Ferrar nodded. "Do not trouble yourself. I checked that not long since."

"I was captured at Newark."

"What is the reason for your journey?"

"I am …" Maxwell remembered that he could trust nobody. "I am unable to say."

"Then perhaps you may furnish this gentleman with the details." Ferrar stepped back.

"What are you doing here, Captain Walker?"

Maxwell turned to the other man who had a thick head of brown hair. Within seconds he recognised the fresh-faced Jack Ashburnham, a Groom of the King's Bedchamber, even in the absence of the man's thin moustache. His mouth was downturned at either side, as if permanently displeased, but seeming even more so at the lack of response.

"I repeat. What business do you profess to have with the King?"

"I fight for him today the same as I have done these years past, Treasurer."

"You recognise me?" Ashburnham asked, following the reference to his position as paymaster of the army.

"Aye, John Ashburnham. I saw you in Oxford up until Friday last."

"What made you leave Oxford?"

"A plot, sir. I must warn you. There is a man who is set to betray the King and prevent any union with Montrose."

"Hold your tongue!"

Ashburnham paced the nave in contemplation. Outside, the birds had begun to sing in welcome of dawn. The contorted candles wept trickles of wax as their glow was stolen by the morning light. Maxwell retrieved Harper's letter as evidence and explained how he came by it. Ashburnham took it and read intently. Then he groaned.

"Are you injured?"

"My wounds are not physical. The man I seek is not just a traitor, but a murderer too. He killed my wife," Maxwell explained.

"Then you will come with me. I must warn my companions."

As the daylight broke, Maxwell was back in the saddle and following close behind Ashburnham. He assumed the man knew of Harper, for he asked no questions. Equally, Maxwell made no enquiry over where they were headed.

Chapter 26

**3rd May 1646.
White Swan Inn, Stamford.**

Gervase Harper slowly climbed the rickety staircase once again. The noise of the customers below seemed to follow behind him, rising with the smoke and smells of the inn. However, he didn't look back. Wearing a blue doublet that had faded to grey, along with a sleeveless buff coat, and holding a tankard of ale in one hand, he certainly didn't look conspicuous. Only he knew of the knife that was hidden discreetly beneath his woollen sleeve.

Walking resolutely along the corridor, Harper's gaze remained on the door at the opposite end. The floorboards creaked at one another as he passed over them. He ignored the voices emanating from one room, as well as the rhythmic thumping from another. The King had the chamber at the very end of the timber-framed building. It provided more privacy, but also meant that every other room had to be passed to reach it, increasing the chances of being seen. Harper's arm hung by his side with the knife resting at his cuff, though he felt the need to twist his hand to check that it remained securely in place. Now, finally at the door, he knocked sharp and fast, two times as he had done earlier. The door opened almost immediately with a clunk.

"Ah, my drink?" Doctor Michael Hudson asked.
"Aye, sir," Harper replied.
"As I like it; buttered ale?"
"With extra nutmeg and sugar."

REBELLION

Following this pretence, Hudson waved Harper inside. He entered the room and saw the King, whose back was to him, sitting on a stool and looking at the fire. The flames wisped lazily in the grate as Harper placed the wooden tankard onto the table. He fumbled with his sleeve, then stepped closer to the King and Hudson, who conversed between themselves. Harper extracted the knife.

"Ah, my thanks for procuring it," Hudson said and took the small blade.

"My hair is short enough." The King sighed. "Is this entirely necessary?"

"It doth risk you being recognised. The captain's news means we must take more care than ever," Hudson whispered and then turned to Harper. "Did you happen to discover why the militia have mustered in Kings Lynn?"

"No, but they were described as patrolling thereabouts like dogs upon the scent of rabbits."

"And you heard this yesterday?" Hudson grunted.

"Aye, sir."

"The devil take them all."

"It matters not, for going to the Scots is the only option." The King held up one hand. "I had already come to realise that some days ago."

"Whilst I agree, they remain two day's ride away," Hudson replied, and urged the King to allow him to trim his hair.

"Then make haste."

Hudson carefully adjusted the King's head and put the blade to a handful of curls, whereupon it became lost in the silver flecks that streaked them. And then Hudson drew the knife back and forth, painstakingly cutting at the strands bit by bit. Harper watched as sweat broke out on Hudson's forehead.

"Was I not to take on the guise of a parson?" The King asked under his breath.

"Aye, but whoever heard of one with locks as glorious as these?"

"Well, do not make a full *roundhead* of me!" The King gave a half-smile.

"Never! Let the Lord guide my endeavours." Hudson laughed. A nervous one – though he did not seem the nervous type. "Give me that ale," he ordered of Harper.

Harper had no sooner handed it over – and Hudson taken a mouthful – than the floorboards groaned at a fresh burden upon them. The wide-eyed Hudson gulped the contents of his mouth and stood listening. He pointed at Harper, gesturing for him to move aside. Two raps came and then Hudson opened the door.

"What is it?" Hudson's face changed, evidently recognising the man, though Harper did not.

"You must both come with me," Ashburnham warned and then approached the King. "We have to leave this place immediately."

"As you wish."

King Charles stood up, looked around, and then slipped on a plain russet doublet. Harper beheld the features of the forty-five-year-old, and in these fleeting moments, the world seemed to shrink to these four walls; an unlikely host for the key moment that was playing out within them. The monarch's very appearance echoed the fragility of these turbulent times; his eyes were sunken, and eyelids hooded, but nevertheless, he moved with the quick step of one who remained agile and alert.

"Your information has been most valuable. Pray wait here until we have gone and then ride in the opposite direction," Hudson said to Harper and pointed at the few severed curls on the floor. "And dispose of those."

"Of course."

King Charles walked past Harper without looking at him or offering any acknowledgement of his presence. It only took a moment for the three men to go. Harper was then left alone to entertain a fleeting fancy of doubt over all that he had witnessed, less still that he had just been in the presence of the divinely appointed ruler of these three kingdoms. He had recently heard young King Louis of France being described as the 'Sun King', after the golden age it was hoped his accession would herald. Charles, however, was a king eclipsed, and his three kingdoms mere moons orbiting glorious France.

Harper walked towards the spluttering fire. He stooped, pinched at the hairs that lay upon the floor, and then cast them into the grate. They sizzled. The heat contorted them, and the silver turned to black, before vanishing with a hiss. It was as if he had just cast some sort of spell; resurrected a spirit even, for at that moment more footsteps could be heard. The floorboards called out their now familiar warning. This time slower. A drawn-out creak seemed to signal that Harper's time was nigh.

Chapter 27

Jack Ashburnham gave Maxwell a discreet nod as he, the King, and Hudson left the inn. Maxwell then followed Ashburnham's earlier directions and made his way to the room they had rented, slowly closing the door behind him without saying a word. Harper's eyebrows lifted in surprise and a smirk crossed his face.

"I wondered if you'd chase me. Well, you're too late."

"For what?"

"The King has left."

"And if you've had a hand in it, I'll wager he won't be heading to Montrose?"

"I cannot possibly say." Harper shook his head dismissively.

"Why does all of this matter so much to you?"

"It matters to France. My country."

"Ah." Maxwell shook his head.. "I should have guessed. France wishes to keep us neutered even after this war is done, hence the number of your countrymen now crawling out from under every stone."

"Not that you minded one of them in particular?" Harper asked.

"Damn you and your family!"

"My father helped build the Church of Saints Gervais and Protais in Paris. Now, do you understand my choice of code name, Walker?"

"A traitor needs no name. Ashburnham knows of your plot; I handed him your letter that proves it."

"Ever the loyal soldier, eh? Is that because it is the only purpose left in your life?"

"You misjudge me. My reason for being here is not to save the King. It is to save myself."

"Poor Walker." Harper grimaced. "I seem to have broken your heart for a second time, have I not? My cousin has written to me of all that passed between you both. How unfortunate. Now you tell me that you have abandoned your King. And you have lost *so* much in his service, too."

"I promised that when the war had come to a close, I would end our conflict." A wave of revulsion welled up within Maxwell; the blood felt as if it had drained from his face and every muscle burned. His fingers curled around the brass-wired hilt of his sword. "I believe it's over now."

Both men drew their swords.

"Yes, my work here is done. I *shall* bring you peace, Walker; I will reunite you with your wife."

"You bastard," Maxwell hissed.

"No, no, I am Saint Protais." Harper laughed.

Their blades flashed. The clash brought them together for a few fleeting seconds. Then they circled one another. Maxwell kicked a stool aside sending it, and a tankard of ale, rolling to the corner. Harper lunged at him, cutting in close. Maxwell evaded the strike adeptly and followed his foe's every move, to take the measure of him.

"Let me bring you peace," Harper whispered.

Maxwell didn't respond. The provocation barely entered his mind, so intently did he watch the man. Harper sidestepped. Maxwell anticipated it. He cast his blade against Harper's and blocked it, before withdrawing and then cutting across the man's torso.

Harper backstepped in a bid to escape, but contact was made. Maxwell felt it. Harper brushed his hand along his stomach; there was no blood, for his buff coat had turned the blade.

"There'll be no more lucky strikes." Harper's jaw was set, teeth gritted with determination.

The two men came at one another again, dancing with death. Their fast steps moved with every hollow ring, grunt, or intake of breath and then Harper had his hand at Maxwell's throat. The man's breath stunk of oysters. What happened next was a blur; a series of frenzied blows that culminated in Maxwell being knocked backwards. He fell against the wall and saw Harper's scuffed boot come at him but moved aside just in time to lessen the impact. Then he leapt to his feet, striking out in defence.

"Damn you!" Harper hissed.

In close combat once more, their blades locked together. Sweat beads ran down Maxwell's forehead and Harper's black hair hung across his face like a shadow. When the swords slipped aside, a succession of cut and thrust continued until one of the swords found its mark. First it was clothing and skin that slowed the blade's passage, followed by fat and muscle. Harper cried out in tormented agony.

The exhausted Maxwell could do little more than hold onto the protruding weapon. Harper froze. Like a puppet, he was now entirely powerless, and Maxwell seized the man's hair, pulling his head close.

"May you rot in hell."

The men were left face to face; two wounded souls glaring at one another. Harper's eyes bulged, no longer narrow and wolf-like. A pitiful groan escaped from his throat. Blood seeped from his clothes and the dry boards at his feet absorbed every drop that fell upon them; however, a pool soon began to form. The dripping counted down the seconds that remained of Harper's life.

"Your wife … 'twas but a stray shot."

Maxwell's face screwed up. His grip tightened on the hilt of his sword. Pulling it back in one almighty movement, he extracted it with such speed that Harper was left clutching at his abdomen. As soon as the man collapsed, it was with the muffled thump of a corpse, a noise that sickened Maxwell, for it reminded him of Catherine's last moments.

In all of the battles he had fought, men had fallen to the dense earth in their last moments; they had slumped onto fields or splashed into puddles. Never again did he wish to hear such a hollow thump. It echoed with a chilling and unnatural finality; born not of battlefields, it therefore carried no mask of duty. Instead, it was the sound of murder.

Crimson droplets ran down Maxwell's blade and gathered within the engraved lettering upon it. Harper's pale face contrasted with the blackness of his hair and gave him a malevolent appearance. Maxwell shivered – a numbness gripped him. He stumbled for the door, making his way downstairs and through the din of customers. The bone dice rattled as they decided the victor of a game of main, dogs barked, conversations merged together into one mass of drowning chatter - while upstairs, in the far room, silence reigned.

Harper was dead. But Maxwell did not experience the relief, nor the respite, that he had so craved. Outside, he mounted his horse and then realised he had no idea where to go, or what he must do. North, he resolved without further thought. Towards the Scottish army, where, God willing, he could catch up with the King's party and secure further orders.

Chapter 28

**5th May 1646.
Southwell.**

The distant bells of Southwell Minster tolled seven o'clock. For over one week, the various morning chimes of many a church had been the point when the King would retire to bed, in some wretched inn, or tavern, somewhere or other, on his route to nowhere. Nowhere, being because his destination had remained uncertain for so long, but now it was firmly Southwell and the Scots.

They had travelled by night; King Charles, Michael Hudson and John Ashburnham. Maxwell had of late, with their approbation, ridden ahead to scout their destinations. But today, with fine cobwebs floating on the balmy morning air and bees animating the flowers nearby, Maxwell waited for them for the last time. The King nodded his head as he and Hudson slowly passed; the first acknowledgement that Maxwell had received, and a mighty honour, though he had not needed or expected anything of the sort. Ashburnham, however, stopped.

"Well, Walker, 'tis time for you to depart."

He handed Maxwell a small document with the King's signature at the foot; the grand loops of 'Charles R' did not reflect the rather tired and bedraggled signatory. No man smiled. Even Ashburnham's voice was hollow with dread. None of them, it seemed to Maxwell, looked particularly hopeful, considering their destination was in sight.

"Thank you, sir."

"I wish you luck."

REBELLION

Maxwell quickly bowed his head. He felt somewhat nervous, as if being cast adrift, but that was more than matched by a sense of relief - of freedom. He had his travel pass and was discharged.

As the gentle rhythm of the three men's horses faded into obscurity, Maxwell began to ride on a journey of his own. His path was through a golden field of wheat. As it swayed softly around him, the wheat heads gently caressed one another and seemed to whisper with encouragement. Maxwell Walker was returning home.

Historical Note

Much focus is frequently given to how the Wars of the Three Kingdoms started, whereas the eclipse of the royalist cause, and in particular the two battles at Sherburn-in-Elmet, are often overshadowed. I haven't heard of any work of fiction that incorporates these two quite crucial encounters. In fact, most non-fiction books do not contain much detail about them either. The more I researched, the more they appealed as a setting for Maxwell Walker's continuing story.

The movement of the armies in *The King's Captain* are accurately listed and battles described true to sources. Following their initial defeat, some parliamentarians did, for a short time, doggedly hold out in All Saints church at Sherburn. The pile of captured weapons in the street is well-attested to. There was also an undercurrent of bitterness towards Digby, who had regularly criticised the Northern Horse both before and after he took command of them. Following the Battle of Rowton Moor, Digby had written that 'the reserve of the Northern Horse (just as they did at Naseby) took a fright before any enemy was near them, and ran." Around the same time, he also described Sir Marmaduke Langdale as a 'creature' of Prince Rupert's – the prince being Digby's chief rival.

All Saints Church and the Elizabethan Huddleston Hall still exist to this day and helped orientate the events of 1645 in my mind. Sherburn also has its own Local History Society, whose website is very interesting. One of the sources I drew upon was Christopher Copley's letter to the commissioners for war, in which he described the second

REBELLION

battle at Sherburn. The (sometimes unreliable) narrative of Lord Digby gives a royalist account. Additionally, there is Sydenham Poyntz's letter to William Lenthall, the Speaker of the House of Commons, dated, 18th October 1645. '*A Rabble of Gentility*' by John Barratt provided great detail regarding the background of Langdale's Northern Horsemen, as well as their movements and combat history.

In describing the King's escape from Oxford, and the tense circumstances surrounding it, I drew upon letters of the time. His route to Southwell, including a nocturnal visit to Saint John's Church at Little Gidding, was revealed by Dr Michael Hudson when he was later interrogated about these movements. It seems that King Charles remained open to his ultimate destination right until the very end, much to his wife's anguish; either to go to London and address his enemies in Parliament, to surrender to the Scots, or to attempt once more to join the Marquis of Montrose. At one point, the undercover King was nearly discovered at an inn, when his companions attempted to cut their hair with a knife.

The intrigue and espionage double as the King's last garrisons were defeated and his few remaining forces dispersed. The involvement of the French in the end game is also a crucial factor. The many letters that went between Jean de Montreuil, Cardinal Mazarin and the King and Queen, are fascinating and reveal the hopes, fears, plots and intrigues of all parties. Though the military battles in England, Scotland and Wales came to an end (albeit temporarily) in 1646, the King's surrender saw the start of a very different struggle; peace offered the chance to turn the military outcome on its head. Many feared the emergence of any one strong and outright faction, leading the King's Scottish and English opponents to divide amongst themselves.

Regarding the French, the King saw fit to warn the Queen in 1645 that 'Lenthall [Speaker of the House of

Commons] brags that Cardinal Mazarin keeps a strict intelligence with him; though I will not swear that Lenthall says true, I am sure it is fit for thee to know'. The French were acutely aware that brokering peace would offer innumerable benefits to them and their young agent, Montreuil, negotiated with all parties. To have an eternally grateful King and Queen back at the helm would have best suited France. Henrietta wrote to Mazarin in 1646 'I shall only beg you to believe that I can never fail in the obligations which I am under to you, nor in the gratitude which I owe you, and that all my actions will show you better than my words, how truly I am, and will be all my life'. Montreuil himself reported to Cardinal Mazarin, 'You have in him a king who will be eternally obliged to you', though Mazarin certainly didn't need to be told so!

Thank you for reading. I hope you enjoyed Maxwell's story in this second novella in the ***Rebellion*** series. For more details about my civil war articles, podcasts and other publications, you can visit **www.1642author.com** or follow me on Twitter and Facebook.

Fictional Characters

Maxwell and family
Gervase Harper
Peter Irwin
Henry Naylor, Constable of Selby
Francois Duval
Louisa Laurent

The King's Cavalier

Mark Turnbull

Chapter 1

**Near Selby. Yorkshire.
4 November 1647.**

It was a bitterly cold morning. So cold that borders of frost crossed the ground, marking where the wintery sun had failed to penetrate. It made for a stark scene; one that picked out every sign of life. For the birds perched in the barren branches, down to the mice that scurried across the decayed undergrowth, there was little cover. Maxwell's breath hung in the air. He walked alongside his horse, which carried his two sons. 'Diamond', so called by Kit, due to the white shape on the animal's forehead, was part of the family.

"I want to ride at the front."

Maxwell ignored the plea. Instead, he led them towards a cluster of trees, mind entirely focussed on finding the fruits of last night's storm.

"Let me ..." Kit persisted with a drawn-out whine.

"No," Tom replied.

"Dismount, both of you," Maxwell instructed. He removed his linen snapsack. "Gather up sticks while I chop these broken branches."

He took an axe that had been sharpened in readiness the day before. Maxwell was a man that prepared himself for every opportunity. Even in the absence of the army, it was a principle he lived by – one which well-suited his determined and resolute character. He brought the glinting edge against a mauled branch. It hung from the trunk like a severed limb, and after several well-aimed blows it fell away. The toil was enough to occupy his mind. He warmed up quickly. Off came his red Montero Cap, the band of which had been unfolded to protect his neck and cheeks from the cold.

Despite it being eighteen months since he had left the king's service, wielding a weapon still gave him a familiar adrenaline rush. This had never quite left him. It was as though his mind remained scarred and ever on the alert. Waiting. But for what, he did not know. He had already taken vengeance on his wife's murderer, Gervase Harper, and killed him. Both King Charles and Parliament were also negotiating a peaceable settlement to the late war. Any agreement would surely bring the security so craved by all; the king's restoration might even lead to a settlement of Maxwell's arrears, though ever the realist, he didn't hold his breath. As well as money, he was in need of friends. Many in Selby had turned their backs on him because of his past.

"Can Tom sit behind me on the way home?" Kit asked with a frown.

"Help thy brother." Maxwell pointed.

"But 'tis too cold to toil so long."

"If you worked as much as you talked, you *would* be warm. Now do not argue with me, boy."

Maxwell took his cap and slipped it over Kit's head, leaving only the boy's dejected face visible within the opening. He watched him turn and trudge away, and then nodded at Tom, who was making a particularly good job of it. His eldest had come on well and was always willing to work hard. This morning they had been up before sunrise. Dawn had only just broken when they had set out, with the aim of gathering enough wood to warm their house and fuel the fire in Maxwell's forge. The task was frustratingly mundane. But after so many long years of war, he had come to accept the safety of such monotony. Maxwell had barely resumed his own work when a noise attracted his attention. Gruff voices. Next, the crunch of breaking wood and movement in the trees at the other side of the forest.

"Come, lads," Maxwell called to his sons and retrieved his snapsack. He felt an unease. Perhaps the crisp air simply heightened his senses.

Their sticks were tied together in two bundles and secured across the horse's back, where they hung at either flank. Then some men emerged from the trees opposite. Maxwell scanned the woodland; there were no more, but the trio were approaching in a menacing manner. He quickly lifted Kit onto the horse and instructed the boys to make their way home if fighting broke out. They asked no questions. Maxwell had received a second anonymous threat of late and taking no chances he walked forward to meet the newcomers. His sister-in-law's pleas to leave Selby came to mind. As reluctant as he was, he recognised that it was becoming inevitable.

"You have some business with me?" Maxwell walked forward with his axe in his belt.

"Aye, you think papists can take the best wood?"

The men all wore masks and stuck together.

"I am no papist. God has scattered plenty for us all."

"Ha!" One of the men mocked. "The Almighty has blown down more than this. Your king, for example, who isn't as divinely ordained as he claims."

"What do you want of me?" Maxwell maintained eye contact.

"This is a new age where all men might have a say in government. We say that you should leave. Selby is no place for you!"

"A pox on all cavaliers," another shouted in a Scottish accent.

"Ah," Maxwell said with a mocking laugh. "John Douglas, I do believe?"

"What if it is?"

"Barely been in Selby two years. Plundered your way south with the Scots and didn't leave again."

"The war might be ended, Walker, but have a care, for you lost."

"I can assure you that I will win any battle you pick with me."

"Fighting talk?"

"Well, I believe that is what you three are looking for, is it not? Fighting over a few sticks. Perchance, because there's no wood in those breeches of yours?"

"You whoreson!"

Douglas pulled his covering away. Like a snarling dog, with his nose screwed up, he ran at Maxwell with a dagger. The attack was adeptly blocked by Maxwell's axe, giving him enough of a break to grab Douglas's forearm and pull him into a headlock. He twisted the man's hand and forced him to drop his weapon.

"Make no move," Maxwell warned them all.

"To hell with you and your kind."

"I seek only to protect my family," Maxwell replied.

"As do we."

Maxwell released Douglas from his grip and retrieved the dagger. "When next you threaten me, I will not be so lenient."

"Next time we will come prepared with pistols."

"Aye, not even the *Walker the Devil* can survive a lead ball to the head … in the same manner as his wife," Douglas growled as he went to re-join the others.

The words had barely been uttered. With a deep roar of anger, Maxwell struck out immediately. He brought the butt of the axe down against Douglas's back, knocking him to the ground. One of the other men brandished his own dagger, but Maxwell was unstoppable. He swung the axe left and right, forcing the man onto the defensive, and then found his mark, judging by the piercing cry.

REBELLION

Two of the men fled. Douglas squirmed and tried to rise. Maxwell was left panting from rage more than exertion. It had his insides mauled and knotted. A bitterness lingered in his soul; of heartache and resentment that he usually channelled into driving himself onwards. To raise his sons and give them his all. But Catherine's memory was sacrosanct.

He turned and walked back towards the boys. Douglas got to his feet, edging away like a wounded sparrow as the black-clad Maxwell passed him.

"Call me what you will, but never mock my wife's memory."

"Please …" Douglas held up his hands.

"Tell them to keep their distance. *Walker the Devil* says so!"

Chapter 2

Putney.
5 November 1647.

The Church of Saint Mary the Virgin sat alongside the meandering River Thames at Putney. This modest building now found itself at the epicentre of English politics and the war of words that would decide the peace of the kingdom. It was surrounded by canvass tents. From these, officers of the New Model Army came forth to preach their views – or those of the regiments they represented. On the opposite bank was Fulham Palace, home of the Bishop of London. Its red bricks seemed to flush with rage at the very nature of the irreverent discussions across the water. Debate centred on the king, constitution and how government might be settled for a lasting peace. The old world was keeping a beady eye on the fast emerging new one.

Inside Saint Mary's, Colonel Thomas Rainsborough sat alongside numerous other officers around a large table. Despite being close in proximity, many were distanced in their opinions and ideologies, and this grew with each passing day. Nearly one week of debating had elapsed. The church interior was cold; as icy as the reception Thomas's fellow Levellers received from the army high command, represented by Lieutenant-General Oliver Cromwell. General Thomas Fairfax was absent on grounds of health – predictably so, for there wasn't a radical bone in his body. Apart from being Fairfax's second-in-command, Cromwell was also his enforcer, and no friend of the Leveller manifesto.

REBELLION

It was therefore left to Thomas, as the Leveller's highest-ranking supporter, to fight for that cause; one of extending suffrage to every man, with a biennial Parliament and the abolition of the House of Lords. His struggle was two-fold, for his own survival was also threatened. Fairfax and Cromwell, he was ever more certain, were itching to remove him from his command in a bid to side-line the movement.

Before the war, Thomas had been a navy man like his father, but he was also a Member of Parliament for Droitwich. If forced, he would rather give up that Parliamentary seat than his military post. The cawing seagulls outside laughed at the never-ending to and fro. Thomas – bolt-upright – followed every word of the heated discussions.

"Might a purged Parliament satisfy our desires and declare the king guilty of the bloodshed and ruin of the war?"

Thomas nodded in agreement with the speaker. Although there were some enthusiastic echoes, these gradually gave way to a mere hum of voices. The insignificant chatter prevented any awkward silence but didn't lead to anything more than a suggestion for prayers. To understand God's will on the matter. But the Leveller position was already clear to Thomas. The outcome of the war was not only about the king's fate, but that of his people. Whatever government was settled upon, it had to be fair and just for the common man.

"It is a vain thing to seek God if we do not listen to his answer. During our discussions this morning, the lieutenant-general remarked that what was being suggested was not the mind of God," William Goffe ventured.

Thomas turned to Cromwell. The delegates quietened at the insinuation that not even this influential leader could dictate the judgement of the Almighty. The scratching quills, which assiduously recorded all that was said, gradually came to a halt. Cromwell's ruddy features appeared to flush.

"There was a lying spirit in the mouth of Ahab's prophets. '*He speaks falsely to us in the name of the Lord*'. Let us not be hasty in abandoning points so quickly," Goffe followed up. "Truly, if we wait for God and then do not hearken to him, then we shall bring much evil upon ourselves."

"Your words appear as a reproof to me, sir," Cromwell said. His gaze remained firmly on Goffe. "It is for me to decide my own satisfaction. I do not judge conclusively, or negatively."

"Pray accept my humble apologies, sir, for I intended no ill or malice," Goffe replied. "It is merely best that we are all clear on the matter."

The pause was rapidly taken up by another officer, who held out his hand with frustration. "We are all distracted. Yet this kingdom is in a dying condition. The reason is the apparent desire to preserve that *Man of Blood*, and his principles of tyranny, which God has manifestly declared against."

Thomas followed the back and forth. It more resembled a courtroom with every man being judged on his opinions. The parliamentarians looked in upon themselves and reassessed what each of them had truly fought for over the years. Deeply held principles had brought these men together, yet in the hour of victory the interpretations of these principles had begun to blur.

Cromwell's son-in-law, Henry Ireton, kept the speakers in line. Debate centred on the role and power of the king and House of Lords. Ireton declared a firm view that the monarch could continue to sanction laws but could be overruled in the event of his refusal. Upon the question of the frequency of Parliaments, Thomas judged it fit to intercede.

REBELLION

"I take exception that only those men with incomes of more than twenty pounds a year can have a say in who sits in Parliament. This shall bar the common man from any involvement in their own government."

The point was not answered. The topic gravitated back to the king and the peers of the realm and whether they were above the law.

"If a petty constable or sheriff was to apprehend a peer, how would the matter proceed in that case?" Thomas questioned.

Ireton pointed at Thomas. The very motion held the other speakers at bay. "The king and lords are not individually bound by the law. But if they are ministers of state - and the king is – then they are to be subject to the judgement of the House of Commons."

"How can the Commons hold the king to account but not all lords?" Thomas frowned at such contradiction.

"It is the privilege of a Lord to be tried by his fellow peers."

"I think that the poorest he that is in England hath a life to live, as the greatest he. If a man has no voice in electing a government, then neither is he bound to it."

"I would have an eye to property, Colonel Rainsborough," Ireton replied. "No person has a right to share in the affairs of this kingdom unless through his holdings he has a permanent interest in it."

"Truly, I wish you would not make the world believe that Levellers are for anarchy," Thomas retorted.

"The consequence of what you propose tends to anarchy and must end in anarchy if men with no interest, other than the fact that they do draw breath, shall have a voice in elections," Cromwell interjected.

"But what shall become of those many soldiers who fought for Parliament? They have no estate to their name. Was it not their breaths that called out our battle cries? It looks to me as if they shall be betrayed."

Thomas continued recording Ireton and Cromwell's responses. He excused himself on the grounds of a poor memory. His goose quill sped across the paper before him. Notes such as these allowed him to formulate his arguments, whilst also holding his colleagues to account.

Conversation was picked up by other officers in the meantime, leaving Thomas wholly unsatisfied with what he heard. He was no less dismayed by all that had passed since the beginning of these extraordinary sessions.

The army leaders were swimming against the tide. After fighting a war against the king, even Cromwell and Ireton – but minor gentry – were willing to uphold the entire status quo as a means of preserving themselves. Such behaviour left a bitter taste for Thomas; that of betrayal at the highest level. This disgust emboldened him to speak ever more freely. If he was to be transferred back to a naval role – as was the rumour – where his arguments might be blown aside and drowned out by winds, then so be it. No ship remained at sea forever. He would navigate the storms that looked to beset the parliamentarian cause and fight for the Levellers against any king, lord, or general who stood against them.

If a pilot should run his ship upon a rock, or a general mount his cannon against his army, should he not be resisted? Thomas pondered his next argument.

Chapter 3

London.
6 November 1647.

Gone was Charing Cross, which had been the most marvellous of the twelve Eleanor Crosses. After standing proud for over three hundred and fifty years, the Purbeck Marble monument had been pulled down by the parliamentarians. Gone too was the iconic one-hundred-foot maypole, which they had deemed nothing more than a heathenish vanity.

With the sites of these vanquished landmarks behind her, Jane Whorwood walked briskly east along The Strand as a wintry sunrise broke. This was beauty that no miserable Puritan could destroy. As if captured by a multitude of artists, its pink hues were everywhere; replicated in the diamond panes of many a window, as well as in every puddle. It danced in Jane's ever-perceptive eyes. Morning offered less chance of her being discovered, and she knew this city well, having been born in Westminster.

Poking out from between a row of run-down tenements was the gateway of Denmark House, the queen's residence. The Romanesque pedestals and pediments of its entrance resembled a mouth, as if the illustrious house was gasping for breath within this rebel capital. She continued past a small alleyway that led right down to the Thames. Past Saint Clement Danes, where The Strand was divided in two by a row of houses. The timber-framed buildings on either side leaned towards each other as if whispering about the striking redhead who traversed the city on secret business. Jane had been careful to arrange a linen coif to cover her locks. A large-brimmed felt hat offered further discretion.

It wasn't long before her destination was in sight; Corner House, home to William Lilly, the famed astrologer. It seemed to be in deep slumber. The shutters were closed, but this didn't stop Jane Whorwood. She rapped on the door. Nobody stirred from within and she gave a second knock.

"Do you seek answers?"

"Mister Lilly?" Jane asked with a frown.

"Pray slip your question under the door with your name upon it."

"Will you not permit me to enter?"

"I have just buried a maidservant of the plague."

"I fear only the pox, sir," she replied and entreated him to open up.

"You are a most wilful lady," Lilly replied.

"Indeed, and particularly so when it comes to furthering my master's cause."

"Very well, I shall speak with you, but you have been warned."

When the door opened, Jane beheld the astrologer. One of the man's eyes seemed to squint. His small mouth – almost hidden beneath a sandy moustache – looked permanently poised on the verge of a smile. She stepped inside.

"I come for your urgent advice," she said, getting straight to the point.

"*De Rege?*" He raised one eyebrow.

"That is correct."

Jane closed the door with a clunk. From the wooden panelling several fixed candles danced imp-like in front of small mirror glass. Their glow was reflected back into the hallway.

REBELLION

"Why should his majesty desire my services above all others?" Lilly's squint was accentuated, as if even he was struggling to divine this answer.

"You mean why should he trust one whose sympathies lie with the rebels?"

"I do not judge my customers, madam, nor do their politics influence my work." Lilly gave a sniff from his Roman nose. "I am but a conduit to God and merely deliver his advice."

"Then there is your answer, Mister Lilly. In addition, I have also heard many positive remarks about you. You are far from a mere piss prophet," she replied with a smile. It animated her round and pretty face.

"You are refreshingly honest."

"They are pock marks," she said in response to his gaze. "Hence my earlier remark. Now, may we discuss business?"

"But of course." Lilly cast up both hands. "So, I assume you recommended me to your master?"

"He makes his own choices. As for his question, that is to know where …"

"Pray hold thy tongue!" Lilly led her towards his consulting chamber. "I must be ready to record the particulars. The precise time they are given is of great importance."

The astrologer took a clean sheet of paper. With a flourish of his hand, he plucked a cut quill from a small pot and dipped it into some ink – clearly passionate about his profession. The coated nib was poised for action as he turned expectantly.

"In what quarter of this kingdom might the king be safest, and remain undiscovered until he pleases it otherwise?"

Lilly did not reply. Instead, he wrote the date and time onto the paper.

"He remains, as I lately read, confined to his palace at Hampton Court?"

"At present, yes," she confirmed.

"Held by the New Model Army?"

"That is correct. He grows ever more concerned about the nature of their discussions at Putney."

"Give me half an hour to prepare a horary. Then I shall answer."

Lilly rested on the astrological chart before him. His fingers were spread, hands like two stars upon the paper. It was divided into twelve sections. He began making notes, scribbling like a man possessed, and consulted some books lying open to the side. Jane recalled that the second box on the chart represented money. The twelfth was that of secret enemies. As to the rest, she was not at all sure, only that each one was called a 'house of heaven' which signified a particular facet of life. Lilly pored over the chart, working in an anti-clockwise manner.

"What planet rules his zodiac sign?"

"You require the date upon which he was born?"

"Just so." Lilly didn't look up.

"Nineteenth of November, in the year Sixteen Hundred."

"Mars!" Lilly gave a grunt of irony.

As the man continued his work, Jane sat on a chair beside the fireplace. The astrologer removed his embroidered nightcap and scratched at his head. After some further scribblings, he replaced the cap and began pointing at each section of the horary chart. When eventually Lilly took a deep inhalation of breath and stood up straight, she knew he had finished.

"The planetary positions symbolise the desired outcomes," he told her. "They must align favourably with the person's birth chart."

"Where would the king be safest?"

"My advice is around twenty miles from London. Essex, if I had to name a county."

"Aha." Jane's eyebrows rose. "I recall a place of that distance. An excellent house that possesses all conveniences that may be necessary for this business."

"It is in Essex?" Lilly queried.

"Yes."

"Then I think you have your answer. It has been an honour assisting you, madam," he said as he took the proffered twenty pieces of gold. "Certainly, a more interesting question than those I normally receive."

"Tell me, what is most asked of you?" Jane replaced her hat.

"Whether a proposed marriage should be accepted."

"Really? If only I knew of your abilities thirteen years prior," she replied with a sigh.

Lilly remained silent. Only as she turned to take her leave did he speak again. "One last point, Mistress Whorwood. A man shall descend from the north who will assist with your endeavours."

"Interesting. My thanks, Mister Lilly." She stepped onto the street once more. "I shall search this man out, for we are in need of friends."

Chapter 4

Selby.
6 November 1647.

The linen blindfold wasn't as tight as it could have been. Maxwell could just about see underneath it, though not very well. Evening had drawn in. When facing the fire in the hearth he saw fleeting movement, interspersed with juvenile mirth. He rushed forward and tried to catch Kit but missed him and accidentally knocked some plates from the table. They rattled to the floor, scattering cheese and bread. Some oysters too.

"You poltroon!" Grace snapped.

Maxwell pulled the blindfold from his eyes and held up one hand as if to brush the issue aside. As if they had enough food to go around and were not beholden to the charity of Henry Naylor, perhaps his only remaining friend. Their pewter had been sold and some of Maxwell's tools pawned. Even his good dagger had gone to pay the rent.

"It matters not. I don't like oysters." Kit shrugged his shoulders.

Maxwell laughed. The boys were similarly amused. Although times were hard, it was moments like this that kept him sane. He put an arm around Kit.

"Dislike them? There's nothing else." The ever-honest Grace did not see the funny side and got back to combing the lice out of Tom's hair.

"There's enough left for the three of you." Maxwell pointed. "My ale will fill me up until the morrow."

REBELLION

"Father!" Kit pointed at the door.

A note slipped underneath and the boy retrieved it. Maxwell hurried to the door and pulled it open. He stepped onto the street and looked left and right, but there was nobody to be seen. The muddy ground was littered with footprints. Whoever it was had moved quickly – assuming this to be another threatening message. Maxwell recalled the last, which had accused him of behaving as if he was the 'King of Selby' and warned that all kings were to be called to account. A hiss of frustration escaped his lips. Such ridiculous words did not cause him any fear, for he would roast the author on the fires of his forge. It was the hatred that was of concern, which could easily be aimed at his young sons. He returned inside.

"Give it to me." Maxwell held his hand out.

"What is it that concerns you, Father?" Tom asked.

"I was anxious to see who delivered it."

"It wasn't the same person as before."

"How in God's name do you know that?" Maxwell shook his head.

"This one was a woman."

"What?" Maxwell coughed. "You saw her?"

"No …"

"Then what a ridiculous claim to make!"

"I glimpsed her passing the window. The way she moved was unmistakable."

Tom's remark about a mysterious female resurrected some of the ghosts from Maxwell's past. Could it have been Gervase Harper's cousin, Louisa Laurent, who might very well carry a grudge? Maxwell glanced down at the latest letter. But the writing, neat and meticulous, was instantly recognisable as that of Peter Irwin. He recalled how his friend had written out a commission at the behest of Sir Marmaduke Langdale during the war. That all seemed so long ago – almost another life. Word from Peter would prove a welcome distraction.

"A good observation, Thomas." Grace finished up with the lad's hair. "I am sure your father thinks so too. Now, go fetch me the last of the bread. Kit, you go too."

"He is more aware of his surroundings than you are," Grace whispered to Maxwell as the boys left. "Can you not see he desires your favour? You are as equally blind to our predicament."

"I praise when he rides well, Sister. That is much more worthwhile than entertaining such silly assumptions."

"We cannot continue here like this!"

Maxwell opened the letter. The fold marks divided it into sections. He wondered if a small stain came from any of the horses, for Peter, a dedicated groom, almost lived in the stables at Wistow Hall.

"I pray this is good news?" Grace asked from behind him.

"Have patience."

"You are insufferable."

"It's about the smithy at Wistow. A simple man, he must be at least three score years of age … oh, at least he was."

Maxwell read on. The old man had died, and Peter was writing to say that he had begged leave of Sir Richard Halford to venture Maxwell as a replacement. Over two years ago, Maxwell had been tasked with collecting some royal ciphers from Wistow and had put his skills to work by posing as a blacksmith to avoid detection by the rebels. Sir Richard hopefully remembered both Maxwell's expertise and his loyalty to the king.

"Then I pray they need a replacement." Grace's eyes widened and she clasped her hands together.

"My good friend, Peter Irwin, has put in a word for me."

"A generous act and a fortuitous turn of events."

"Not for old George," Maxwell replied.

He held the letter closer and read the last line with some astonishment. Sir Richard had agreed to offer the post. Maxwell's past stepped out from the shadows once more,

REBELLION

but this time in a positive way. God did, indeed, move in mysterious ways.

Chapter 5

**Wistow Hall. Leicestershire.
9 November 1647.**

Grace and the children were captivated. Wistow Hall, barely quarter of a century old, stood magnificent and grand on high ground. They spent some time admiring it, even from a distance. Its crisp, neat bricks were almost without blemish.

A nearby windmill waved in greeting and the grass bowed before them in the blustery winds. Kit excitedly asked many questions about the place, while Tom imagined learning to ride in such surroundings. Grace whispered a prayer that the house might need a cook. She also spared praise for 'blessed' Master Irwin. As for Maxwell, he noted the church. The vicar had surely saved his life two and a half years ago, when he had been sent here in the aftermath of the Battle of Naseby. Their final approach to the red-bricked hall, however, was in silence. Seven large windows looked back.

Near the stables, Maxwell caught sight of Peter Irwin's slim frame. The man leaned against a gnarled tree trunk watching a mare and her offspring. Maxwell hesitated. He felt unsure of how to express his gratitude. There was sadness at leaving Yorkshire. The feeling that he'd been driven out made it worse, but there was no doubt that this opportunity was providential. He looked on as the foal cavorted and hurried ahead of its mother, who upon sensing a presence, turned in Maxwell's direction. So, she remained, motionless and fixated - watching warily. With a bray, the excited foal was called back. Peter then span around.

"Captain Walker!"

"Maxwell will do just fine," he replied. It jarred to hear his military title used after all this time.

"Once a soldier, always a soldier. In fact, I think you might have told me that."

"Perhaps."

"Greetings aside, 'tis good to see you, my friend." Peter smiled.

They embraced. It felt strange that Maxwell could have such enduring affinity and respect for someone who was not family. A man he had only known for a short period. It was born out of a shared experience of the hell that was war; of putting their lives in one another's hands without so much as a second thought, nor feeling any need to acknowledge it. Such instinctive trust could never be broken. Neither of their families were privy to the sights and sounds these two men had endured. The very fact that there was someone else who had also survived it stirred Maxwell's emotions. He hastily pointed at the horses.

"Did I disturb your work?"

"No, I knew you were there." Peter's arched eyebrows rose. "They told me."

"Had I known of your skill, we could have ascertained many an enemy secret through their mounts." Maxwell laughed.

"It's all observation, my friend. They convey much by their manner and movements alone."

The mare had returned her attention to the young one, nudging it as if they were entirely alone. Both tugged and munched at the grass. The way she looked after her offspring was a heart-warming sight.

"Our own intuition is easily lost," Maxwell observed.

"The problem is that life has a habit of pushing us forward. Especially soldiers – we look for the next battle, meal, or place to rest. Always thinking ahead to outwit the enemy. We rarely reflect."

"By God, Peter Irwin, you have a way with words."

"A compliment, I take it?"

"Aye, it most certainly it is. I heartily wish I could express myself as eloquently."

"I've seen you do it, sir. With both your tongue and your sword."

"I have little time to reflect, even when I wish to. And of late, that desire has been strong."

"I know your love of Yorkshire," Peter said. "I'll wager that has a lot to do with it?"

"Aye, and Catherine too …" Maxwell stopped. The house in Selby had been privy to so many happy times. It felt as though he had left those, and his wife's memory, behind.

"Forgive my honesty, but you're a level-headed man. Practical and brave. You wouldn't have come here if you didn't feel it was the right course."

"Aye, you're right." Maxwell nodded.

"There is a chance that you might even miss the army."

"Alas, you're wrong on that point though," Maxwell replied. "I have no desire for it."

Peter rubbed his chin. Maxwell recognised this sign and pointed a finger at his friend.

"What is it?" Peter was taken aback.

"My *intuition* suggests you have a mind to convince me otherwise, but I am not one to be cajoled."

"You have found me out." Peter smiled. "I admit that was my design. There have been whispers that Langdale has need of us once more. That the king might require his old horsemen to free him from the grasp of the New Model Army."

"Have we not had enough of fighting? Surely the matter is settled once and for all," Maxwell replied. "Even the king must realise the war is over."

REBELLION

Peter stepped closer. "He was held barely twenty-five miles away from here until recently. I helped in the stables there ... amongst other things."

"I see."

"He is held hostage by men who wish to crush the lawful church and unleash anarchy."

"Peter, I came here for a new life. To secure employment and raise my sons without fearing for their safety."

"I thought you might join me?"

"You may think you know my mind, but you don't. I sincerely hope that this wasn't your sole objective for inviting me here."

"Of course not, Maxwell, what do you take me for? Forgive me for pushing you on the matter."

"The army has left many scars," Maxwell said with a sigh. "But it also forged a bond between us that I will value to the end of my days." They began walking towards Grace and the boys. "Come, let me introduce you."

"I will not be here much longer. Langdale has asked me to go north to Berwick and send him reports of all that passes there. The Scots look set to declare for the king. That town will be crucial if they are to cross the border."

Peter's words left Maxwell guessing at the future. If war was to erupt again, then nowhere was safe, whether it be Selby, Wistow or any other place in this troubled kingdom. Then Peter begged a favour; that Maxwell might deliver an urgent letter to Hampton Court. Nothing more than a request for settlement of his fees. Peter promised not to impose any further, explaining that he simply needed a courier; if he was seen anywhere near the king, then it might jeopardise his northern venture. Maxwell could not refuse. Delivering a letter for his friend was one thing, whereas renewed military service was quite another.

Chapter 6

**Hampton Court Palace.
11 November 1647.**

Thursday. A day in which King Charles always retired to his bedchamber to write. But this one was significant. Taking a gold watch, which had belonged to his father, he glanced at the time. Four o'clock. He'd been writing for two hours, and there had been much to commit to paper. Some red sealing wax was cooling on the last of three letters and he gave it a gentle blow. A diamond seal hung from his watch. He pressed it into the wax, whereupon the engraved coat-of-arms left a perfect imprint. Now complete, he stood and stretched.

The bedchamber was his inner sanctum. Perhaps the only haven left in his kingdoms that offered privacy, even in his captivity. The New Model Army guards respected this. Outside of the one-thousand-five-hundred rooms of Hampton Court, England remained troubled. He had heard much about the dangerous debates taking place at Putney. It seemed as if the army's commanders might soon need his support, judging by the radicals who were taking an increasingly militant stand. They were, by all accounts, out of control.

Quite a turn of events, he thought, and walked to the door. His loyal greyhound, Gipsy, followed him.

The lock in the large mechanism gave a clunk as he turned the key. The door opened and he proceeded to Patrick Maule, one of the Grooms of the Bedchamber.

"Bring me candles and snuffers, if you please."

"Yes, Your Majesty."

"See to it that I am not disturbed."

Maule bowed his head.

"On any account, that is. I have some important despatches to write to the Princess of Orange."

"As you wish."

The king returned to his bedchamber, securing the door behind him once more, and then kneeled beside Gipsy. The dog's ears folded back across its thin head. Her eyes looked up adoringly.

"These *Levellers* would have thy master murdered," he whispered whilst giving her a gentle stroke. "Parliament, the Scots and even the army's commanders fear them. They all approach me to secure their own salvation. They use me. Yet, I am described as a '*dead dog*'. If that is the case, then I wonder why these people bother courting such a cursed canine?"

The king smiled. The officer in charge of him, Colonel Whalley, was a cousin of Cromwell – yet another man linked to the lieutenant-general. He recalled the letter that Whalley had shown him this morning. It had been sent by Cromwell himself. There were rumours of an attempt on the king's life and Cromwell had asked for the guard to be doubled. The king no longer knew who to believe. Was this an elaborate hoax aimed to increase his confinement, or could it be an attempt to pin his subsequent murder on another party? He had refused to sanction a plan laid by the Scots some months ago, who had offered fifty horsemen to take him to Berwick. The refusal stemmed from his having given Whalley his word not to escape. He had, however, withdrawn this promise in light of recent events.

"Master Lilburne has even made approaches to me," he told the ever-obedient greyhound and shook his head at the overtures of the Leveller leader. "I will not suffer an inglorious end. Nor am I foolish enough to trust any of these factions. Every one of them would fall to ruin without me."

He sighed and looked around his gilded cage. There were silk pillowcases embroidered with gold, on which he could lay his troubled head for a few hours' respite. Ermine bedsheets, carved oak, as well as gold, silver and jewels dotted the room. The men who clamoured beyond his door day after day aimed to hide their true machinations, just as the array of tapestries concealed the bare walls. But at least the tapestries added a certain beauty and held back some of the chill of winter. Whalley had shown a second letter of late in which the king was described as an 'obstacle'. The anonymous author had described speeches excusing the monarch's murder as essential for the good of the kingdom. King Charles would outwit them all. In around one hour's time, he would be free.

***

Just after four o'clock.

Dusk fell. The array of lights within Hampton Court twinkled benignly and beautifully in the distance. The irregular line of turrets, cupolas and crenelations gave an odd appearance, as if built in numerous sections with each one vying for prominence. It was a veritable rabbit-warren of stone. Burrowed somewhere within it was the ever-hunted King Charles.

Maxwell had deliberately arrived at this late hour to avoid as many people as he could, both on his journey and within the palace. As he neared the place, with swirling gulls overhead, he kept the name of the addressee in mind. Peter's letter had to be given to Nicholas Oudart. A strange name. At the east front of the palace, a walkway led across a small moat and up to an arched entrance. He was met by an advancing guardsman in a red coat.

"State your business?"

REBELLION

"My name is Peter Irwin with a letter for Secretary Ou .. Nicholas Oudart."

Upon sight of the letter, the soldier bid Maxwell follow him. He was escorted through several grand passages, some studded with paintings and adorned with sculptures. Turning one way, and then the next, they finally stopped in a gallery that was over two hundred feet long. Here, he was ordered to wait. A second soldier was duly despatched to fetch the secretary. Watched closely by the other guards, Maxwell continued to sweat. The linen shirt underneath his doublet was already stuck to his body.

He turned and looked at one of a series of nine immense paintings, all much taller than him at eight feet high and nine feet wide. They were astounding. There was everything from a triumphal chariot and procession, with soldiers, standard-bearers, vase bearers and musicians. Even animals, prisoners and booty galore. This was some sort of grand Roman victory. It struck him as ironic, for the king who owned them had met with an equally spectacular defeat. Maxwell stepped back to admire the works, but at the same time a lady turned the corner and almost bumped into him.

"My apologies, madam." He bowed his head.

Her face struck him. It was another ghost from the past. He recognised her, though could not place her name.

"Move aside if you please," she breezily replied.

Maxwell was drawn to her. Try as he might, he could not remember any further details. A soldier approached the pair, his shoes echoing on the wooden floor like Maxwell's increasing heartrate.

"You've ogled her for long enough. Let her pass."

Maxwell flushed. It was not like that at all, but he could not counter it. "Pardon my hesitation."

She did not respond or acknowledge his words. Instead, as she haughtily went on her way, he turned his back and gazed up at another of the paintings. He had felt the coldness of her expression. She was feisty and demonstrated an innate negativity towards him that was plain to see. But why?

"You'll have to fight a few of us to get to her," the soldier said. The tone of his voice was more like a warning, in spite of his grin.

"I'm no soldier. And I'm honest enough to admit you'd have a swift victory. But tell me, what's her name?"

"Mistress Maria. I know no more. Turned up yesterday with a red-haired woman. Pock-marked she was though."

At that, the second soldier returned and advised Maxwell that Oudart was engaged on another matter. He called for the letter to be handed over and then Maxwell was dismissed. He didn't need to be informed twice. The sooner he was away from Hampton Court, and back in Leicestershire, the better.

Chapter 7

**Antechamber of the King's Apartments.
Six o'clock.**

Despite being a woollen-draper by trade, Colonel Edward Whalley was the son of a High Sheriff. As a result, he had some insight into protocol and officialdom. Yet despite this, he couldn't help letting out a frustrated groan at the king's servants.

"The king always emerges at five o'clock for prayers," Whalley insisted, as if they didn't know this already; as if he himself wasn't already certain of it. He accompanied the monarch on every occasion.

"His Majesty was adamant he was not to be disturbed. There must be some extraordinary occasion that makes him late," Patrick Maule replied.

The Groom of the Bedchamber's expression was blank. All of these servants shared that same look and bearing. Whalley was no fool. He had fought at Naseby, that decisive royalist defeat. He was part of the same game that these men were playing.

"I wonder how he can be so long writing?" Whalley sighed. He looked at the clock, with its tortoiseshell and brass-inlaid ebony. It chimed six times.

After another hour, Whalley saw the guards who had arrived to take their places outside the royal bedchamber. Because the antechamber door was locked, they could not pass through the necessary rooms to get to their posts. The king was now two hours late.

"Might he be ill?" Whalley enquired.

No real answer was given. Just a nonplussed shake of the head.

"Will you knock?"

"I dare not disobey an express royal command, Colonel," Maule replied. His colleague Harry Firebrace nodded agreement.

"You have no way of entering that door?" Whalley asked.

"No. His Majesty bolts it from the inside."

"It is most unlike him. This is proving to be very concerning, indeed," Whalley sighed.

A further hour passed. The clock struck eight o'clock. Whalley felt it was now the right time to act. As a result, he stooped and peered through the keyhole several times. Behind him, the servants muttered in disgust at such behaviour. He could see nothing of note. Nor could anything be heard, for the distance to the bedchamber was simply too far. Three hours late. That would be quite enough, he decided, and turned to the soldiers.

"Fetch me Master Smithsby," he instructed.

In no time at all the Keeper of the Privy Lodgings arrived.

"I must gain entry to the king's apartment. Can you assist?"

"I'm afraid not, sir, for the door is bolted on the inside."

"Is there no other way of getting inside?"

"There are the backstairs," Smithsby replied.

"Then lead the way!"

The men walked through the garden. Rain blew in Whalley's face. The wind whistled intermittently as they entered a spiral staircase and made their way to the top.

REBELLION

The door was unlocked and Whalley pushed his way forward, stepping into the Privy Chamber to see a black cloak strewn across the floor. The colour drained from his face. He rushed over and retrieved the item, which was embroidered with a silver star of the Order of the Garter. It was the same cloak that the king frequently wore. He searched for other signs, but there were none.

"Listen?" He called to one of the guards.

Pathetic whimpering could be heard. He turned on his heel and stepped closer to the bedchamber door. A dog's cries.

"Bring Maule here!"

Whalley waited. His mind raced, even though this situation was not unexpected; he had harboured an inkling for several weeks that the king was planning to abscond. Showing cousin Cromwell's letter had most likely accelerated it. He thought about the Putney Debates, which were tearing the army apart, and anticipated the renewed unity that this timely escape would surely bring. Right now, there was also his own position to consider, and the need for witnesses to be present as he penetrated these rooms.

"See to it that all doors are guarded," he instructed as Maule arrived. "Open this door."

"I cannot, sir."

"Open it, I say," Whalley barked, "in the name of Parliament!"

He stood behind Maule as the man fumbled with the lock and pushed him aside when the efforts finally met with success. It was thirty minutes after eight o'clock. Three-and-a-half hours since the monarch had gone missing. He strode into the bedchamber to find the greyhound whimpering in the corner, but no other sign of life. His eyes darted from one side of the room to the other. There were four letters placed on the table. One was noted as being a declaration to the king's subjects of England and

Scotland. Another was addressed to Lord Montague, one of Parliament's Peace Commissioners, along with the anonymous letter that had warned of an assassination attempt. The fourth, Whalley snatched up, was for him.

He tugged it open, breaking the red seal. The pieces dropped to the floor like hardened tears of blood. He read the exquisite handwriting and shook his head at the words of this 'parting farewell'. It desired the colonel to protect the royal household items and moveables, in particular, Van Dyck's painting of the queen. Gipsy, the king commanded, should be sent to the Duke of Richmond.

"The devil take him," Whalley hissed. "Does he have no sense of his predicament?"

Chapter 8

Near Hampton Court.
Three Hours Prior to Whalley's Discovery.

Maxwell headed towards the River Thames, the silvery ripples of which he could see in the distance. Masses of trees stood like sentries, ushering on the approach of night. The solitude of this shadow kingdom was healing, and those of all ranks were equally relegated to its darkness. When clouds permitted, the moon highlighted the way ahead, as well as numerous pools of rainwater that looked like scattered diamonds. He could feel Catherine's presence.

He had resolved to cut across a wooded area, rather than follow the route; it seemed necessary. Admittedly, he did feel somewhat vulnerable after visiting the palace. But he reminded himself that in no time at all he would be sitting in a wherry, skimming across the glistening water towards a warm inn. There he would enjoy a well-earned tankard of ale. The very thought of it was tantalising to his dry throat. But this fleeting thought vanished when he noticed two figures up ahead and he quickly withdrew behind a large tree.

"Forgive me, sir, I am not as fit as you," one man excused himself.

"No trouble, Legge."

The rain pitter-pattered onto the branches above Maxwell and dripped to the undergrowth at the base of the tree. It played a similar tune on his felt hat and an array of glassy droplets clung to the brim. These repetitive trickles contrasted with the hum of the men's voices, though he could make out few words. His hand gripped the silver bandages of bark that wrapped the birch tree whilst he peered at the cloaked figures. One was smaller in stature. It was impossible to make out any detail of their features, for the shadows twisted about them as the branches moved in the moonlight. They seemed to coalesce like spirits, their outlines shifting from one moment to the next.

"It's the damp air that does me mischief. I am ready now."

Maxwell watched with some relief as they resumed their journey. He adjusted his footing, but a twig snapped beneath his feet. *Damn it!* The smaller man stopped. The taller one turned and slowly drew a sword. Maxwell knew he'd been seen even before this stocky man headed for him. It was no good.

"Wait!" Maxwell held up his hands.

"How long have you been there?"

The man stopped. His monotone voice was gruff but not raised. It was clear that he was also anxious to avoid undue attention.

"Just this moment."

Soft illumination struck the smaller man's face, picking out a moustache and beard. The features appeared much like the king's. Maxwell would have dismissed this fleeting thought as the workings of a tired mind but for the way it had instantly come to him.

"Who are you?" Legge asked.

"Captain Maxwell Walker."

He kept his eyes on the man's thirty-three-inch blade, which pointed menacingly, and grasped at the only option that presented itself. He quickly bowed his head to the stranger in the distance.

"Why such a gesture?" Legge closed up. "Tell me?"

Maxwell's hunch was correct. He was sure of it.

REBELLION

"I am a former horseman of his majesty's service. I served in the famed Northern Horse."

"You expect me to believe such a thing?" Legge asked.

"Aye." Maxwell focussed on the fellow. "I remain a loyal subject. I came here to deliver a letter to Nicholas Oudart."

"We cannot delay," the smaller man warned. "Who is he?"

"Says he was in the Northern Horse."

It was clear from Legge's set jaw, and the way he held his sword, that he was contemplating a deathly strike. Maxwell could recognise it. The man's eyes had turned to opaque circles, devoid of emotion and clouded by the desire to kill. To protect.

"His name?"

"Captain Walker," Legge replied.

"I do not recognise it."

"By your favour," Maxwell interceded, "I accompanied you to Southwell in forty-six. I have no blade," he assured, and held out both hands.

"Prove you were in the palace. Did you see Oudart? Describe him."

"He did not meet me …"

Legge grunted and thrust his blade forward. The double-edged steel whooshed as Maxwell leaped aside. He struck again, though Maxwell anticipated it, as if these moves were ingrained into him.

"I saw nine large paintings," Maxwell said with desperation. "Roman, they were."

"Mantegna's *Triumphs of Caesar*," the other man replied. Maxwell saw the faint sheen of his teeth, as though he had given a smile.

"I killed a French spy when last I accompanied you, sir," Maxwell insisted.

"Spare him, Legge," came the instruction.

"If I do, then he must come with us. We cannot risk betrayal."

"The man speaks the truth. I recall his services," the king replied.

"As you wish." Legge sheathed his sword, grabbed Maxwell, and checked him for weapons.

"My humble thanks." Maxwell hesitated before the figure of the sovereign. It was just as well that he could not see clearly, for royal scrutiny would have been too much. His head already thumped, and he felt short of breath.

"It's providential for me that you are not armed. You move with skill," Legge acknowledged.

"We have no time to lose," the king insisted.

With Maxwell walking in the centre and Legge leading, the trio made their way to the water and found a designated rowing boat. They climbed in and sat hunched on the wet seats. Maxwell was ordered to row. He soon got into a regular motion. The oars dipped and rose as he pulled them closer to Ditton, the location that he had been given. He kept them on course, shaking the rainwater from his face and single-mindedly focussing on each stroke. His whole mind and body slipped easily into such toil, as if he was entirely suited to achieving this set mission. Entirely suited to being a soldier.

***

The journey did not stop at Ditton. It was there that King Charles, Colonel William Legge and Maxwell were joined by two others: Jack Ashburnham and Sir John Berkeley. Maxwell had foolishly assumed that Ditton would be the point where he could have left them. It was not to be. Not privy to any details, least of all where he would end up, Maxwell had no choice but to accompany them further south.

They got lost in Windsor Park. At Bishops Hutton, in Hampshire, where the men were scheduled to rest, they found a parliamentarian committee in session. A quick change of horses was all that was possible. After that, things took a further turn for the worse. An alarming debate ensued; the king favoured Jersey as the destination, while Berkeley opted for the West Country and Ashburnham the Isle of Wight. It became quite clear there had been no prior agreement and no boats organised. In the end, the Isle of Wight carried sway; Berkeley and Ashburnham proposed to sound out the island's governor while the others waited at Titchfield Abbey, near Southampton.

Maxwell was thankful to reach the relatively modest walls of Titchfield, which had almost as many chimneys as turrets. He had soon changed his clothes, leaving his wet doublet steaming in front of a roaring fire. He turned to Colonel Legge, who pulled a dry linen shirt over his head.

"If I might ask, sir, was this venture sufficiently planned?"

"Do you ever plan your questions, Walker, or are they always as blunt?"

"It was not intended to be so."

Legge sat down on a wooden form. Taking a clay pipe and lighting it with a taper, he put it to his lips and began to draw the tobacco. As it caught hold, smoke was expelled from the corner of his mouth and he sat back, resting his broad shoulders against the wall. His eyes closed momentarily. The Irishman did not have particularly warm features, but after taking a deep breath, his expression eased.

"Now I have a good pipe, I may give you a better answer," Legge said. "Suffice to say, that this plan was put into operation rather quicker than we expected."

"I see," Maxwell replied.

"Let us hope that you prove to be a talisman and bring us luck."

"Amen."

Maxwell lay down in front of the fire, hands behind his head. His body was cold to the core and ached even more so because of it. The dancing flames were mesmerising, and were it not for a desperate thirst, he could have fallen into a deep slumber there and then.

"By God, shall I fetch you a bone? The rebels call us cavalier dogs, and you most certainly lie like one!" Legge's cheeks reddened as he laughed heartily.

"I care not what you call me, sir," Maxwell smiled. "The only thing that shall stir me is if the king himself was to enter."

"Where is your home?"

"Yorkshire. Though I had just taken up a post at Wistow Hall, in Leicestershire." Maxwell sighed and sat up. He took a poker from the fire and dipped it into his ale. With a satisfying hiss it warmed the drink.

"Family?"

"Two boys. And an imperious sister-in-law."

"Well, at least you'll not be seeing her for some time."

"But what if the king goes to the Isle of Wight – might I not return to Wistow at that point?"

"Of course not," Legge replied as one of the servant boys pulled off his leather boots. He gave a groan of relief. "A loyal soldier and adept swordsman is precisely what the king has need of. One that is not known to the authorities is even better."

"Lord have mercy …"

"If we head for France, or Jersey, then perhaps you may take your leave. But otherwise not."

"I have little money and will surely lose my post as smithy."

"Your sister can find employment." Legge held up one hand. "Wistow is owned by Sir Richard Halford, a good royalist."

"My sons need me."

REBELLION

"They need a father who inspires them with loyalty and honour. Such qualities cannot be bought."

Maxwell didn't reply – there was no point. Instead, he took his leave and went for some much-needed rest on a small truckle bed in the room next door. It seemed like little time had passed when he was awoken by the noise of raised voices. Berkeley and Ashburnham had clearly returned. Maxwell listened in silence.

"What on God's earth possessed you to bring Hammond here?" Legge asked.

"He will help us. Remember, he is related to the royal chaplain," Ashburnham replied.

"As well as being Cromwell's cousin!" Legge retorted.

"Oh, Jack, you have undone me," the king lamented.

"We can kill him?"

"Murder? I will not countenance such a thing," the king retorted. "There is nothing to be done. I must go to Wight."

Maxwell cursed under his breath. The decision, by default, also dictated his own destination. He had never even heard of the cursed Isle of Wight. Ironically, this royal bid for freedom looked set to lead to Maxwell's confinement. He tried to convince himself that it was God's will, though the purpose of this divine intervention, on the eve of a new life at Wistow Hall, remained unclear. He should have enough time to pen a quick letter to Grace. This might be his only chance to inform them that he was safe and currently engaged in the king's service - as well as send humble apologies to Sir Richard Halford.

Chapter 9

**Corkbush Fields, Hertfordshire.
15 November 1647.**

A blue sky was interspersed with fine, white clouds. Their soft forms blended seamlessly like spreading watercolours. The day was brisk, but not cold. Beneath this canvass, what was occurring brought a chill of its own, so Colonel Thomas Rainsborough judged. Seven regiments of the New Model Army had been marched up, pennants hanging limply from their poles. The soldiers' expressions were haunted and sullen.

Facing them in the near distance was the army's high command, in the persons of General Fairfax and Lieutenant-General Cromwell. They were drawn up opposite as if ready to do battle over the Leveller's radical ideologies. Thomas's eyes narrowed. The troops were lined up like animals to the slaughterhouse and herded forward to add their names to a protestation: one of loyalty to Fairfax and the army council, but also to the army's watered-down proposals for a settlement. By opposing key Leveller desires, this protestation was designed to neuter them.

Soldier by soldier the Leveller cause ebbed away with each mark made. After each man advanced to pledge agreement, they stepped back into line in more ways than one. Thomas's heart raced; the entire proceeding was a disgrace. They had taken up arms to oppose royal tyranny, yet this manipulative act risked keeping the common people in chains, despite the war having been fought for freedom.

Thomas extracted a folded copy of *The Agreement of the People* – the Leveller manifesto. He rubbed his thumb across its surface, as if attempting to resurrect the principles; those that he would continue to espouse, even if it meant opposing his own commanders.

"Damn their blood," he muttered.

This was to be the first of three meetings, designed by Fairfax and Cromwell to divide and conquer. They did not dare tackle the entire army in one go. It seemed as if all was lost, but then Thomas noted movement on the horizon. Beyond the dull expanse of fields, with the sunlight behind them, masses of silhouetted horsemen came closer. They more resembled the dead of the wars, risen to protest that their lives had been spent in vain. Orders were barked around the regiments. These newcomers were unauthorised; Colonel Thomas Harrison's men who were designated to attend a different session. Thomas knew exactly who it was and that other regiments were also willing to make a similar protest. This was, indeed, the moment to strike. He rode towards Lord Fairfax.

"General!"

Fairfax turned. He gave a dark expression, as if he could guess at the reasons for this bold interruption. As Harrison's horsemen rode up to the main gathering, calling out in protest, some of the General's attendants moved to block Thomas from getting closer.

"Do not betray our cause, I beg you," Thomas exhorted and held his document aloft.

Like a battle cry, it was instantly recognisable. Barely one month old, the black words of the printing press expounded the desire for a '*firme and present peace upon grounds of common-right and freedom*'. However, its very presence at this moment was more threatening than if Thomas had drawn his sword. Mutters of discontent spread like a musket volley. Harrison's cavalrymen cried 'England's Freedom' and 'Soldier's Rights'. Piecemeal cheers erupted from the ranks as they threatened to dissolve.

Thomas extended his arm and proffered the Agreement. The General ignored him and made ready to move, his horse braying with equal disdain. Thomas shook the paper indignantly, but it was of no use.

"Those men must be contained." Fairfax pointed at the intruders.

"You tried to present a petition to the king on the eve of the late troubles, General," Thomas called. "I recall he refused to receive it, and almost rode you down."

"This is mutiny," Fairfax cried.

"I beg you do not treat us with the same disregard."

The General and his officers hammered off towards the troops. Amidst the growing chaos, some of the common soldiers urged their comrades to support Thomas. Their angry voices carried on the crisp air like the birds that swooped above. Fairfax's lifeguards, however, were already in amongst the dissenters like hounds, sniffing out and arresting anyone who dared speak up in favour of Thomas or the accursed *Agreement of the People*. Harrison's men even had the printed papers folded into their hat bands, like a sign of their core allegiance. Now a second regiment was marching onto the scene – Robert Lilburne's infantrymen – who had also come to make a stand.

It was there, in that sea of men, that Thomas's presence was needed. He rode quickly to the side of these courageous soldiers, ready to add his voice to theirs and hold fast. His principles were solid, no matter how torn his heart might be over this dissention. The bloody king had escaped his confinement days ago and was even now on the loose. The army leaders must not be allowed to use that fact as a means of imposing a tyranny of their own, for by doing so they were behaving little better than Charles Stuart and were most certainly playing into his scheming hands in the process. Thomas kept his sword purposefully sheathed. Leveller's, he believed, should fight their cause with reason and common belief, rather than violence. When some of the soldiers threw stones at Fairfax's cavalrymen, Thomas immediately condemned it and called out the principal desires that every Leveller instinctively knew.

"Enough I say!"

Cromwell drew up in front of the disorderly troops, reaching out and tearing a paper from one of their hatbands. He threw it away as though discarding dirt from his hands. There followed an order that every soldier should remove them.

"All men are equal!"

"Do as I command," Cromwell yelled, and waved his officers on.

"England's freedom!"

"This is mutiny," Cromwell declared. "God has delivered us a glorious victory. Let us stand united and enjoy the fruits of it."

"So that you might gorge upon those fruits?"

"We fought for a better life."

Cromwell drew his sword with a defiant ring. Chants quickly mixed with hoots and jeers as the lieutenant-general and his retainers seized some of the men and manhandled them. Individuals were dragged away whilst commanding officers bawled orders that eventually led to the return of order. The main body of troops were then formed into a square. A court martial was set up. Thomas's long face paled against his red woollen coat. Two drums, twenty inches in diameter, were laid on the ground and paper was called for. A scribe began to damningly record all that had just occurred.

Some of the most vociferous soldiers were marched up to Cromwell and Fairfax, held by the arms and scruffs of their necks like animals. Names were called for, and no sooner were they confirmed than a charge of mutiny was presented. Three were found guilty. Their crime was clear for all to see, it was averred. A sentence of death pronounced, much to Thomas's astonishment. He considered protesting, but matters had progressed too far.

"Mutiny is a heinous crime. To betray your cause by moving against your comrades is the most base of actions. God, however, is all merciful, and because we fight in his cause, it is right that restraint be shown," Fairfax called to the assembled men.

"As the good general commands, only one shall perish. You must cast for it," Cromwell stepped forward.

The guilty trio were ushered forward. Small bone dice were thrown from their sweaty palms one by one. They danced on the stretched calfskin. The hollow beat was like the footsteps of the Grim Reaper, creeping up in readiness to take the designated victim. Private Richard Arnold, the last of the trio, looked to the sky as the bones turned up a measly total of three. His lot in life had been meagre, and now his body was to be riven apart by musket shot from his own side. The man held his hands in the air, as if to embrace his maker. It had come to this.

Chapter 10

**Carisbrooke Castle. Isle of Wight.
27 December 1647.**

Six weeks later, Maxwell stood in the makeshift royal presence chamber. His back was to the stone wall, which was dappled fawn, grey, and white. The floor slabs were worn and uneven. He could imagine the cause to be the numerous sentries that were forever patrolling around King Charles. Though the castle was a prison, grand furniture dotted the monarch's rooms, all brought over from Hampton Court. It looked as out of place as Maxwell felt himself to be. Despite the unexpected turn of events, however, he was adapting. He played a new role of a royal servant; one that made him almost invisible. He was quite content with this, being a man of few words.

Today, the king was talking discreetly to three Scottish Commissioners. The Earls of Lauderdale, Lanark and Loudoun were arrayed before him, standing like ravens in their black attire. They had swooped down upon the island almost as soon as the king had arrived, in the hope that he would make a deal with them - one which would favour their Presbyterian religion. The representatives of the English Parliament were also here with rival terms, though they were conspicuously absent today. These two factions hoped to put the other to flight. Between them both, the king scattered hopeful words and played for time in the anticipation that something better might come along. He attempted to clip their wings by using one against the other. Maxwell knew this because his purpose was more than simply holding the king's gloves, running messages, or helping prepare the royal carriage. He was also to watch and listen. To facilitate the monarch's secret communication with the outside world.

"In past centuries, Countess Isabella, a previous resident, displayed fish in this place for her amusement." The king glanced around the room. "It feels very much like the army use me in the same manner."

"We desire an end to your captivity as soon as may be," one of the Scotsmen replied.

Maxwell noticed a redhead quietly enter the room and give a brief curtsey – Mistress Jane Whorwood – who had become a frequent visitor. The king's brown eyes momentarily flicked in her direction. She, however, remained focussed on the basket in front of her, which was piled with laundry.

A linen nightcap, decorated with whitework embroidery fell to the floor. Maxwell stooped and retrieved it, handing it back to Jane. Her hand brushed his as she took it back, pressing a note into his palm in the process. With that, he withdrew and stepped back into place. The exchange lasted barely a few seconds.

"Will you walk?" The king enquired of the three Scotsmen.

"Most certainly, sir, the air will do us good."

In Maxwell's left hand, he held the royal's doeskin leather gloves, trimmed with silver lace. Quite seamlessly, he pushed the small piece of paper Jane had given him into one of the gloves. When the king approached and took them, Maxwell bowed his head. The transfer was complete. King Charles would be at liberty to read the insert whenever he was alone and discover whatever news it conveyed. The soldier on the opposite side of the room remained oblivious, which gave a certain satisfaction.

"It appears to be cold. Fetch my cloak."

REBELLION

Maxwell acknowledged the instruction and left the presence chamber. He climbed a small stone staircase to the upper floor and entered the bedchamber. By the four-post bed, Jane was brushing a carpet back into place with her foot.

"I have the latest papers." she patted her chest.

"I will inform the Groom of the Bedchamber," Maxwell replied. He knew nothing more, other than the king regularly retired for hours on end to write. "Excuse my forwardness, madam, but might I ask something?"

"Yes." She barely looked up and handed over the cloak. "Be quick."

"More a favour. I do not know you well …"

"There's no time for niceties."

"Ah," Maxwell replied with relief at her plain approach. "Might you need another washerwoman? My sister-in-law offers her services, and it would mean my family could join me here."

"You have children?"

"Two young sons."

"Is she discreet?"

"Yes, she will do anything."

"Leave it with me. Now, go."

***

The steps opened up onto the castle walls – a perimeter of a mile and a quarter – where the king took a deep breath. It imbued him with renewed energy and optimism. He waited for the commissioners to catch him up and looked across the fields beyond. Carisbrooke crowned a chalk plateau almost at the centre of the Isle of Wight. Newport, the island's principal town, was one-and-a-half miles away in the distance, and between it and the castle, there was barely anything but fields and the occasion copse. Walking this curtain wall offered time to ponder and plan, as well as provide insight into the comings and goings of the small garrison. It kept his body and mind in good health; enough to hold at bay any bleak mood that might overshadow his positivity.

The Earl of Lanark arrived on the wall first. Loudoun, the oldest, was next, followed by a flushed Lauderdale. The king lifted his walking cane of blue feldspar and pointed at the stone keep to the northeast of the courtyard. The morning light made the pearlescent feldspar shimmer like a clear ocean.

"From there, you may see the Solent and even the coast of England. I can keep watch on my Puritan opponents in the New Model Army – extremists who are as much your enemy as mine."

"The treaty we have agreed this day shall lead to their confinement in your place, sir," Loudoun discreetly replied.

"Indeed, God will not allow such traitors to prosper," the king said.

He considered the Scots to be the lesser of two evils. Rather, he preferred, the imposition of Presbyterianism on England for three years than let the devilish Puritans loose. Especially since the Scots were willing to leave control of the militia to him, along with the choice of officers of state, and a veto over legislation. By comparison, the English Parliament wished to secure all of these for themselves and have him as a mere puppet.

"We will return to Edinburgh and muster support for our engagement, as well as the necessary troops to support your restoration," Loudoun added.

The men began to walk with him.

"When might your enterprise be ready?" The king enquired.

"Perhaps by Lady Day next year, if all comes smoothly to pass," Lanark replied.

"Very good." The king gave a firm nod. "I will seek my liberty in readiness for when your troops cross the border."

Chapter 11

**Carisbrooke Castle.
20 March 1648.**

The interminable rain rattled against the small window of the king's bedchamber. It dampened all thoughts of escape. This was proving to be the wettest few months in living memory. The tip-tap counted the ongoing seconds of this demoralising imprisonment, for that was what it had become after his refusal of Parliament's terms for a settlement.

His closest staff had been dismissed and he was confined to the castle. None were permitted to approach him unless authorised by Parliament. But a select few of his personal attendants remained, and were it not for their efforts, he would have been wholly isolated.

Carisbrooke reeked of fusty stone, saturated by the torrential downpours. This emphasised the fact that it was a gaol and no royal palace, despite the furniture and books his captors had shipped over. The fire hissed as rain infiltrated the chimney. As off-putting and monotonous as the weather was, the king managed to draw a positive from it; the noise meant that he could barely hear the guards who slept outside the two doors of his chamber each night. Nor would they be able to discern any of his movements.

He walked to the narrow window, barely fifteen inches wide, and carefully opened the latch to look out. There was nothing to see. The night was one of the blackest he had known. Gripping the iron bar that split the window in two, he considered once again the seven inches that he would have to squeeze himself through. He had successfully tried his head, so was certain his body would pose no problem. Besides, there was no time to ponder this any further. The time had come. Tonight, he was to escape, and on the ground somewhere beneath the window his servant, Harry Firebrace, would be waiting.

After a further glance towards the door, he began to climb out of the window, suppressing the reluctance that gnawed at him. The pressure of the bar against his breast soon began to tell. It felt tight, but he stubbornly persisted, desperately trying to complete his exit. Claustrophobia took hold, convincing him to end this attempt almost as soon as it had started. His intentions were reversed; now he wished to get back into his room at all costs, but he was stuck fast.

With a groan, he attempted in vain to free himself. Rain gradually permeated his clothes. Panic spread. Being wedged in the window hampered his increasingly anxious breaths and left him struggling for air. He pulled with all his might. Finally, after the slightest movement, his body eased free and he managed to get back into the bedchamber.

After recovering for some moments, he closed the window casement and then looked at the doors once more. No movement could be heard. The attempt had failed, but surprisingly, he did not feel as dismayed as he might expect. It could have gone infinitely worse. Upon noting the time on his gold watch, he retained some hope; an attempt had been made that his captors knew nothing of. Had he fitted through the window, then the plan would have come to fruition. Liberty had been within his grasp. Perhaps this outcome was even for the best, because the Scots had still not mustered their army to come to his aid. His faith in God was in no way shaken.

Following a few deep breaths to settle his pulse, he took a candle from the table and set it on the sill of the window.

REBELLION

Somewhere in the murky night, Firebrace would now know that all had not proceeded as planned. The king sat down at a small desk and opened a leather-bound book entitled *The Faerie Queene* by Edmund Spenser. It was an enjoyable read that filled his days alongside the plays of Shakespeare. He dipped a quill and proceeded to write 'Dum Spiro Spero' onto one of the pages. This very act helped restore order to his troubled mind.

"Whilst I breathe, I hope."

He looked at the window. The bar would need to be removed. He couldn't file it due to the noise this would inevitably cause. But there did remain one other option.

***

The small room was covered in linen of all shapes and sizes. Shirts, smocks, nightcaps and sheets. They hung from every corner and were even draped across a wooden form. The next batch stood soaking in the buck tub, dirtiest at the bottom. The solution of lye in which they were immersed comprised of urine and wood ashes, the smell of which pervaded the place. It lingered wherever Maxwell went. Even the food seemed to taste of it; or maybe it was simply blander than ever, due to their shortage of money. But were it not for these garments, and Grace's sore hands that scrubbed them, who knows what they would do?

"Have a care of those wet clothes," Grace called. "I don't want them falling onto this filthy floor."

"Worry not." Maxwell craned his neck but kicked over a pot of urine.

"Maxwell!"

"Must it be hung all over like flags of truce?" Maxwell gestured at the washing.

"Well, you surrendered us up to this existence," Grace replied. "Wistow Hall would have been perfect."

"I had no choice."

"Kind Master Irwin had secured all that we needed there."

"Might I remind you that he charged me to deliver that letter to Hampton Court?"

"He is also your friend. Pray do not speak ill of him."

"Then you return to Wistow and leave me and the boys here."

"And let you look after them?" Grace gave a dismissive laugh. "They would be left to fend for themselves. Little better than scavenging dogs."

"I did not have a choice," Maxwell retorted, emphasising each word.

"Life is full of choices."

"Are you suggesting I should have refused the king?"

"Surely he should realise how much you have already sacrificed for him?"

"Once the kingdom's affairs are settled, we shall return to Wistow," Maxwell said with a sigh.

"Agreed upon? I toil like this so that other *washerwomen* can spend their days intriguing for King Charles. It seems that he will never treat with the roundheads."

"Enough, Grace. You will compromise us with such talk."

"I speak it how it is."

"Hold thy tongue."

A knock came at the door. Maxwell opened it to find one of the royal servants from Carisbrooke and invited him inside. So wet was the man's felt hat and black cloak that they glistened in the glow of the fire and wan light of the tapers.

"Master Walker, I have a message from his majesty."

Maxwell took the proffered note – a small scrap of paper. Surprised, and somewhat confused, he unfolded it to see the king's cypher 'CR'. There was an order to follow the command given by the bearer. Maxwell glanced again at the man, who took his cue.

"You are required to travel to London. Someone will meet you at Bow Lane in four days. Together you must collect important items for the king's use and fetch them to the castle."

Maxwell glanced again at the note. It was a sad sign of the desperation that had consumed the monarch and those surrounding him. A tiny message that emphasised the pressing confinement of its author. Despite the reluctance Maxwell felt about this journey, he couldn't fail to be honoured by the sovereign's trust and felt a certain pride that he had written directly. Things had come a long way since 1645, when the king had addressed thousands of horsemen at Welbeck Abbey, including Maxwell.

"Well?"

"I will do as his majesty bids. I will be loyal and discreet."

"For this enterprise, you will be known as *Eglamour*."

"*Eglamour*?"

"You have not read *The Two Gentlemen of Verona*? It is *Eglamour* who aids the escape of *Silvia*."

Maxwell shook his head. "I am unfamiliar, but so be it. I assume the king is *Silvia*?"

"No, his code name is *Fleance*."

Maxwell nodded. It had all turned somewhat bewildering.

"You have committed those names to memory?"

After one last repetition, Maxwell agreed. It was just as well he had a good memory. For some moments after the servant had departed, Maxwell stood in silence and watched the little waterfalls that cascaded from the top of the doorframe. An array of ferns nearby wilted under the continuous downpour. An unanswered question, in hindsight, was money; he would have to secure more credit to undertake this trip.

Chapter 12

London.
27 March 1647.

The sign above Maxwell squeaked intermittently with the breeze. The image it bore – a row of coffins to advertise the carpenter that hammered within – made him roll his eyes. He hoped it was not a divine warning of impending failure. On the adjacent building, a second sign displayed a bag of nails and swung with an alternate noise. This was, however, only a fraction of the many distractions around him. At one end of the narrow street two coaches had stopped and the coachmen argued over precedence. A woman approached, carrying a basket on her head. Her grubby face looked up at Maxwell with hope.

"Cherries, sir?"

Maxwell declined. She was about to persist but must have noted his expression. He continued to look about Bow Lane. A barking dog sped past in pursuit of another. Men and women called out, selling all manner of things from oysters to rags. Another offered to sharpen knives. Maxwell could barely think as he waited for the chimes of one of the many churches nearby. The stone steeple of Saint Mary-le-Bow, which the street was likely named after, was a landmark that many referred to. Because of its looming presence, he was confident he was in the right place. From one of the houses opposite, a woman poured the contents of a chamber pot into the street. The smell of excrement had hit his nostrils upon entering the city, but he was all but used to it now. The capital was a far cry from

REBELLION

the isolated Isle of Wight, where most of the noise came only from the wind and sea, or the ever-present gulls.

"Tuppence chapbook?" A man extolled the quality of the humorous stories within.

"No."

"Might put a smile on thy face."

"Move on, lest you feel a taste of my humour."

Maxwell rubbed his eyes. He knew nothing about the contact he was meant to meet here. The Shakespearean code-names were more suited to elaborate play-acting. He wondered if the king had personally chosen all of these inane details, and if that was the case, whether he had become detached from reality. Maxwell had been granted a pass for his journey from General Hammond, the island's governor, after claiming that he had to collect some books for the king. A futile royalist uprising on the island months earlier had been suppressed with the execution of the instigator – a man who called for support to free the monarch. Maxwell was engaged in serious business. He did not overlook that fact.

"Sir?"

"I do not want any cherries, books, nor anything else!" Maxwell retorted.

Silence ensued. He turned to the woman and recognised her almond-shaped eyes, which were as blue as ice, and unperturbed. Her jaw had a certain delicate firmness about it. He gave a sigh of regret.

"Eglamour?"

"Maria, I do believe," he replied. "We met at Hampton Court last year did we not?"

"Avoid using my name. Come, follow me," she instructed.

"I have a mind we had met before that too? Certainly, you seemed to display a coldness towards me, though I know not why."

Still, she did not answer.

"Do you live in the city?"

"Must you ask so many questions?"

They halted as a Sedan Chair passed them by. Its window closed like the blink of an eye when the covering was pulled down over it. The pair continued to traverse the street. He hoped that as well as fulfil the king's orders, he might finally have the chance to talk to Maria about the crossing of their paths.

***

The motion of a Sedan Chair had always appealed to Louisa Laurent - far easier than rattling around England in a carriage with iron-shod wheels. An equally attractive feature was that it could only hold one passenger, thus debarring undesirables in a way that a public Hackney might not. There was also something about having two strong men carrying her. But as she was borne along Bow Lane, she was entirely focussed upon a passer-by, the very sight of whom made her flush. She sat back and thought of Maxwell Walker; the courageous, handsome, but rather awkward captain. He had captured her attention from their very first meeting. Despite not seeing him in over two years, she knew she was not mistaken. She had just been carried past him like a gift in a wooden box, though he remained oblivious to her fleeting presence.

Her thoughts went fleetingly to her late cousin, Gervase Harper. He had killed Maxwell's wife. The likelihood was that Maxwell had then killed Gervase in the end – though all Louisa knew for sure was that Gervase had been stabbed at an inn. If Maxwell was his killer, she did not entirely blame him. The truth was, she missed Maxwell and was filled with a wish to see if the feelings they had once shared could be revived, in spite of her connections to Harper.

She considered ordering the men to retrace their steps and take her back to Bow Lane. But Walker was with a woman. Though she could only guess at their relationship, she knew from her time attached to the French envoy that Maria Wilkins was a royalist agent. It was something that the Derby House Committee would be most interested in. Perhaps such a course would also provide an opportunity for Louisa to make Maxwell's acquaintance once again.

She smiled. Men usually chased her like hounds did a fox, yet Walker was different. She would have to hunt him and was most willing and ready to do so. Her hair would need some attention – a mixture of sugar and water to maintain her curls. Also, some Spanish paper as rouge for her cheeks, though a growing excitement seemed to do the trick. After serving France's envoy for so long, Louisa knew what it was to fawn and pay court to men of importance. This had left her in no doubt that what she felt for Maxwell Walker was genuine. To sense it still, after two years had passed, simply strengthened her certainty.

She knocked on the wooden frame. It wasn't long before the bearers stopped and gently rested the chair on the ground. She opened the door that was directly in front of her and addressed the lead man.

"Derby House, if you please. Cannon Row."

Chapter 13

Maxwell followed Maria to the upper chamber of a house that overlooked the busy street. He glanced out of the leaded window to orientate himself with Saint Mary-le-Bow in the distance. Maria instructed him to wait and then disappeared into another room. For hours he had traversed London's streets with her, picking up two mysterious packages from different places. Now alone, he turned and looked around the room with unease.

Cream tiles surrounding the fireplace contrasted with orange embers in the grate. The lazy glow reminded him of his smithy's forge and gave him an instinctive desire to ignite them with some bellows. Right now, he could quite easily succumb to the rhythmic hammering of hot iron. To mould and shape it with satisfaction and have some control over his work.

He ran his hand across the wall's impressive leather panels, embossed with patterns of fruit that were covered by silver leaf. The background was painted cerulean blue. On the table was a loosely folded paper and he headed over to it. Perhaps he might discover more about this woman. Addressed to 'Sweet 390' he was immediately intrigued, assuming it to be from one of Maria's admirers, though he could not imagine her paying court to anyone.

Yet I imagine that there is one way possible that you may get 26:23:66:50:12:3:222 from me (you must excuse my plain expressions) which is to get acquaintance with the new woman (who conveys all my letters) and by her means you may be conveyed into the stool room.

REBELLION

The difficulty of removing the window bar hath made my thoughts run much upon the later design and the aqua fortis. So far one officer of the guard has been brought into my service to assist me. I know that nothing will come amiss when it comes to your hand.

Your most loving 391.

The handwriting looked remarkably like that of King Charles. Notwithstanding the code that disguised a particular word, it was affectionate to say the least. He wondered if Maria was a royal mistress? Before he could give it any further thought, he heard her footsteps and hastily folded and replaced the letter.

"Sir Eglamour, you are to take these items of prime importance to our master. I shall explain."

"Please, enough of the names. I would know who you really are?" Maxwell asked.

"We first met in Oxford …" Maria's gaze went to the letter for a few moments. She took it and then cast it into the fire but did not turn around again. Instead, she continued facing the fireplace. Her slim figure was highlighted by a warm glow as the paper combusted.

"I knew we had met before Hampton Court. I recall it now," Maxwell replied in the hope of rekindling conversation. "On that occasion in Oxford I was not in a good frame of mind. I recall you asked me to assist the king with his escape from the city."

"And now I am required to trust you once more."

"Trust me with what?"

"As I said, there are two items you must convey back to the island."

"You speak as if you doubt me?"

"I am wholly loyal to this cause and give it my life. Unfortunately, there are many I see who appear rather more intent on self-interest."

"Pray explain that accusation."

"You do not command me, Captain Walker."

"I know that all too well," Maxwell replied. "You were abrupt with me at Oxford and have been ever since."

"And do you blame me? You are an imperious and arrogant man who does not give women respect."

"I have not travelled here to be insulted! Tell me what I must take and let us go our separate ways."

"I suspect that you know already?"

"Aqua Fortis?"

She nodded. "You read the letter then."

"If it was of any secrecy you should have burned it long ago. Lucky it was me and not an enemy of the king."

"Must you be so indiscreet as to name our master?"

"For the love of God. Can you not see we have a shared loyalty? I am no rogue and it insults me that you treat me like one."

"Here is an iron file, too. Take great care of them."

Maxwell took the packages. From the street outside the noise of a scuffle fast footfalls silenced him. Maria hurried to the window, gasped and then recoiled. She fixed him with a glare.

"Troops!"

He peered through the uneven glass. It was clear the soldiers were in a hurry. There was no doubt in Maxwell's mind that this house was their destination and he could tell Maria held the same opinion.

"A pox upon them," Maria hissed.

"We must leave. Quickly," he urged.

"Go out of the back door and through the alley. That will take you into Cheapside Street, from where you can escape," she explained.

"You are not coming?"

REBELLION

"No." Her reply was quick and firm. "You shall carry the objects; therefore, I will have nothing of incrimination here. Unless, of course, I have been betrayed, either deliberately, or through indiscretion."

"What are you insinuating?" Maxwell noted her suspicion.

"Just go!"

With a leather satchel tight in his grip, Maxwell hurried down the stairs and into the narrow way that led to Cheapside Street. The dung-laden cobbles were slippery. A chimney sweep and his boy passed, and then a carriage. Its rear wheels were almost the same height as him and gave off a thunderous noise. A child clung to the back, laughing at his impromptu ride, until falling off. Whether this or physical admonishment of his mother caused most pain, the resulting cries were a good diversion.

Amidst all of this Maxwell wondered about Maria. Her suspicions of him aside, someone had clearly tipped off the authorities, and the cutthroat nature of espionage became all too apparent. Such service was perhaps more deadly than the battlefield. At least there he knew his enemies and could see their intent.

Chapter 14

Carisbrooke Castle.
28 May 1648.

King Charles was impeccably dressed in a black satin suit and cloak. Gold and silver buttons sparkled in the candlelight. But the same glow accentuated the shadows around his sunken eyes, the creases at his brow and silvery flecks in his hair. Nevertheless, he still cut a majestic figure; perhaps more so. As Maxwell looked on, he couldn't quite believe this was the king he'd fought for during the war, now reduced to such circumstances. Less still, that he might be so close to him during these dark days. The group were halfway through their sixteen courses, but the monarch appeared hungry for news.

"Has any word arrived about my son's whereabouts?"

The king sat bolt upright. He glanced around the officers at the table and began eating some tender-looking beef. It seemed that this approach worked well – it left an awkward silence over the topic of the fourteen-year-old Duke of York, who had just escaped from captivity.

"I'm afraid not, sir," Hammond eventually answered.

"He escaped under the guise of a game of hide and seek, so a news sheet claimed," the king noted.

"Perhaps."

Maxwell was sure he saw a wry smile as the king continued to eat.

"Is that, perchance, the reason you have moved me to new lodgings within the castle?" The king enquired.

"It is not linked in any way."

REBELLION

"Rest assured, sir, I will not begin any such games. There are precious little places to hide in this unforgiving place." The royal's eyes twinkled like those of a mischievous schoolboy. The same look that Maxwell's son, Kit, gave when he was attempting to goad.

"It relieves me to hear that." Hammond's reply had a tone of sarcasm.

"Let us change the topic. Tell me, is this weather normal for the island?" The king asked.

"No, sir, it is a long time since we had such persistent rain," Major Rolph replied.

"It might be enough to fill your dry moat, Governor," the king said. "Now, that would please the army commanders, would it not?"

"Yes, if it assisted us with maintaining your safety."

"Is that how you all view the matter? You *safeguard* me with this imprisonment. Do you also contend that attempts to break my will are for my own benefit?"

"Nobody wishes to break your will, sir," Hammond replied. "The army have long since presented most generous terms to you."

"The army have no legal authority to negotiate a treaty of their own making. They attempt to side-line Parliament's terms." The monarch fixed Hammond with a look. Heightened frustration accentuated his stammer. "If I agree to the army's proposals, it would submit us all to the power of the sword. I stand fast, sir, in defence of my people and the laws of this kingdom."

Hammond did not reply. The company continued to partake of their meal for some time with only the occasional chink of glasses or plates.

"Have you ever tasted an artichoke, colonel?" The king asked.

The very word 'artichoke' triggered Maxwell's immediate attention. He kept his eyes focussed on a tapestry ahead so as not to betray any recognition. The signal had been given; the word meant that the bribed guard was on sentry outside the royal bedchamber.

"I have not, nor do I have any desire."

"The Spanish are very keen on them," the king said, recalling his visit to the country as a young man. "I, on the other hand, was not particularly enamoured. At least on this subject we find ourselves in agreement."

The monarch turned to a page and asked for a fire to be lit in his room. The man approached Maxwell and conveyed the order. A chain was set in motion and Maxwell now left to carry out this instruction. Outside the bedroom he saw Floyd, a soldier who was sympathetic to the royal cause. Maxwell entered and closed the door behind him.

The fire was already laid. He kneeled before a basket of wood that he had arranged to be brought up and took a particular piece. With a small knife that had been concealed in his shoe, he picked out the cover of an opening in the hollowed-out log. From inside, he withdrew a small phial of Aqua Fortis from London. At the window, he eased out the lead filling from around the bottom of the iron bar to leave an encircling void. Into it, he carefully poured some of the acid and watched intently.

To work, damn you, he silently urged.

Bubbles began to form around the base of the bar. Soon it was obscured by the reaction and the acid took on a green hue. Faint wisps of brown-red were sucked out of the casement, which was ajar, and dispersed into the night. When necessary, Maxwell added more droplets of acid in order to further the process. A gentle shake of the bar was encouraging and the small groove that had been filed into it seemed to help the erosion.

Next, Maxwell took out a small note from his shoe, which had been given to him by the clerk of the kitchen. A tapestry on the other wall displayed scenes from the life of Abraham. The lush green hills and blue sky, complete with angels, was lifted aside to reveal a small hole between the irregular stonework behind. It was into this crevice that Maxwell pushed the note and then took another that had been left there. He replaced the covering and brushed it flat. Now the fire had to be lit, which would take on the guise of all his efforts here. While waiting for it to take hold, he noticed some freshly written documents on the king's table.

I have cause more than enough, to meditate upon, and prepare for My Death: for I know, there are but few steps between the Prisons and Graves of Princes.

It shocked Maxwell. The forlorn and desperate words were at odds with the king's seemingly endless optimism. Maxwell wondered just how many layers there were to the man. A genuine pang of sadness came over him, as if this message had somehow touched on the most sacred of all events – the death of an anointed sovereign. It gave a shocking finality to everything that was occurring on this remote island. Maxwell realised in that instant how deeply committed he had become to the monarch and how his own existence had been similarly reduced. This bleak forecast left him with a feeling of desolation.

He thought fleetingly of Peter Irwin and where he might be. Of Maria, too, and his old comrades. Even Selby and Wistow entered his mind, as if they were far-off places. Then a particularly loud crack from the fire stirred him.

The acid would be done. It was the last of numerous applications, most of which had been added by other people. Maxwell took hold of the bar and gave it another tug. There was good movement. A linen cloth was used to wipe the acid away and then disposed of in the fire. Lastly, some wax was dripped into the area around the bottom of the bar and the lead insert placed back into it. The setting wax would hold it in place. With that, he opened the door and departed without giving Floyd a second glance.

Chapter 15

A sentry made ready to prepare his bed outside of King Charles's door. The monarch was about to take his leave of Governor Hammond, who had escorted him to his bedchamber. Hammond stood uneasily. There was something awkward about his gait, betraying a discomfort with his role as gaoler.

"Why do you use me thus?"

"I beg Your Majesty's pardon, but I know not what you mean?"

"You continue to remove loyal servants from my presence. Mister Ashburnham and Mister Legge have gone. When I resolved to come here, did you not engage your honour that you would take no advantage against me?"

"I said nothing of that."

"You are an equivocating gentleman. Will you at least allow me my chaplains?"

"Alas, I cannot permit it."

"You use me neither as a gentleman nor a Christian."

"I shall speak with you, sir, when you are in a better mood."

"I slept well last night. My mood is as fair as ever."

"I have used you very civilly," Hammond replied, his frown not one of anger, but of hurt.

"You do not do so now," the king persisted, sensing the Governor's divided loyalties.

"Sir, you are too high with me." Hammond sighed and went to leave.

"My shoemakers fault then, if I stand too high." The king smiled, as if this jest could lessen the growing frustration – and allow him one last request before they parted company. "Might I have liberty to go about and take the air?"

"No, I cannot grant it."

The king acknowledged the Governor's parting bow and entered his bedchamber. He drew back the tapestry, took a small slip of paper and opened it. Sweet Jane Whorwood – codenamed Hellen, or 390 – was reportedly still at Queensborough, waiting with a ship for him. Tonight, a man would be poised just beyond the castle's outworks with two saddled horses. Another servant would be standing below the window waiting to assist the monarch when he lowered himself via a rope. Two sentries, as well as the guard outside his door, had been bribed.

His gold watch showed eleven o'clock. Beside it, in a silver bowl, a lump of wax floated in some water as a nightlight. It would remain lit after his departure and flicker in the room with benign regularity as if moved by his royal breath. Soon he would be free like his son – blessed be to God – and ready to join the Scots, whose army would cross the border. Like a phoenix his cause would rise from the ashes.

He took some grey stockings and pulled them over his boots. They would muffle the sound of his footsteps. He pondered the password by which he would identify his supporters in the darkness; 'Phideas' after the Greek sculptor. Then picking up Hookers *'Laws of Ecclesiastical Polity'* and sitting in a chair beside the fire, he flicked through it as a way of remaining calm and collected until the appointed hour.

"We measure not our cause by our success, but our success by our cause," he whispered to himself.

***

REBELLION

The drum towers of Carisbrooke Castle's gatehouse blended into the backdrop of the night sky. Candlelight at some of the upper windows made it appear as if these were casements that opened out from the heavens - that the Almighty was keeping watch over them at all hours. A sliver of moon peeked out from the darkness like a reluctant and half-closed eye.

"Who goes there?"

Maxwell stopped and gave his name. The soldier was Floyd, who had pledged his support to the king and who was engaged in tonight's plot. He had come to know the man reasonably well; he was serious-minded, but affable, and always spoke of his young daughter with tender regard.

"I heartily wish I was, like you, about to leave for home," Floyd said.

"Weren't you at the king's door earlier?"

"Yes, but our duties have been changed again at the last moment."

"Does that worry you in any way?" Maxwell whispered.

"I think not, for there have been a number of such alterations these past weeks."

Maxwell made his way outside of the castle and beyond its curtain wall. His movements were in keeping with that of every other evening; he would always leave after King Charles retired to his bedchamber for the night. But once at a sufficient distance, he turned and followed the line of the castle's immense outer defences, which circumvented it. They were so extensive that it proved difficult for the small garrison to man them in their entirety. This perimeter – a ditch with stone wall beyond it – acted as a second skin to the inner fortress he had just left. The royal bowling green lay to the north-east extremity. It was there that he was headed.

Despite nightfall, Maxwell was relatively confident of his location, having traversed the walls and passed between the inner and outer wards many times. The king bowled as much as possible of late to increase familiarity with the layout. At the designated point, Maxwell found a designated ladder. He ascended it, climbed over the top of the wall and then made his way down the earthwork slope behind it. Before long he was on the sunken green and approaching a gilded shed in one corner. Here the king often took shelter from the rain.

Tonight, it was merely a mizzle. He peered into the darkness and discerned the outline of the vast castle keep. The distant sea and hills were hidden by the night, which kept much more than this obscure. He was not comfortable at all. The expanse of the bowling green made him feel conspicuous and far from alone. Especially so with the hooting of an owl who marked its territory. Trees creaked in the breeze and birds flew past, their wing strokes easily mistaken for the noise of sentries swooping in to make an arrest.

It must be midnight by now, he thought.

The plan was for the king to make his escape across the green, whereupon Maxwell would conduct him to a man who had two horses at the ready. Perhaps it was the darkness that heightened his senses and accelerated concerns? Whatever it was, he thought back to Floyd and the change of duties. There had also been fewer people than normal in the inner courtyard tonight. As a result, Maxwell left the small shelter in that instant. He clambered back over the wall and stood on the ladder, from where he watched and waited.

The minutes passed slowly by. He became ever more certain that the escape had been foiled. Then a flickering light appeared from the direction of the inner ward and shadowy soldiers rushed across the grass, their presence was unmistakable, such was their energy and haste.

Maxwell quickly descended the ladder and traversed the ditch, heading back towards the road that led to Newport.

REBELLION

He ran as fast as he could. Mud splashed up his breeches as he cursed the failure and then a musket shot rang out into the night. This unmistakeable noise brought him to a halt. It also scattered an army of birds, who took to the sky from all around. Maxwell had already resumed his own flight when a second shot erupted, followed by the noise of horses.

He raced towards the edge of the wood, where his small lodgings proved a welcome sight. All of this persistent subterfuge had turned his mind into a place as dark and remote as the Isle of Wight. It made him question whether he should, in fact, have joined Peter Irwin and once more taken up arms and fought for the royalist cause.

Chapter 16

**Preston, Lancashire.
17 August 1648.**

Watery-red trickles streamed down Peter Irwin's face and dripped from his pronounced chin. Rain attempted to wash away the blood that seeped from a cut to his cheek, as well as the crimson spatters of his commanding officer's. The man had been shot through the neck and lay dead in the mud. This weather could not, however, cleanse any of the battlefield horror. Splashing through the fields, Peter took refuge behind a bristling hedgerow and peered over the top at the advancing enemy. He caught his breath. Opening his mouth and tipping his head back, rain droplets began to dissipate on his dry throat.

Oliver Cromwell's soldiers – over eight thousand men of Parliament's New Model Army – came on relentlessly. The red coats of the infantrymen were soddened with blood of the retreating royalists. Red like the devil that was Cromwell. The man himself was with his cavalry; their horses drawn up on the lane behind, watching and waiting. Poised to deliver a coup de grace.

It felt like some sort of trick to Peter. Reports barely days old had placed Cromwell in South Wales, yet this malevolent spirit had nevertheless appeared here. Peter and the English royalists were outnumbered two-to-one. Their allies, the Scots, could have more than made up the difference, but they were nowhere to be seen. Only a handful of Scottish lancers had appeared in support of the

REBELLION

English, who had been battling it out for hours in a fighting withdrawal through the hedgerows.

"Bloody knaves," Peter growled.

The English contingent was commanded by Sir Marmaduke Langdale, and to their rear was the town of Preston. On high ground, the church stood out as a cold witness to the scenes of desperation in the valley below. It rapidly doubled as a stone marker to the fallen, who were trampled into the mire by the wall of redcoats. Muskets misfired in the rain. Flashes of gunpowder fizzled into nothing but a lame hiss. Instead, clashes of steel chimed in men's ears until blades sank into bodies or sliced through limbs.

With Eaves Brook on the royalist left wing, the River Ribble and some woodland on their right, it would have been a strong position had they been supported by the Scots. Peter poked his eighteen-inch pistol barrel through the clawing bushes and curled his finger around the trigger. A flash of fiery gold lit up this dank day; as fleeting as the life just taken by the resulting lead ball. The thud echoed through Peter's numb body. Sulphury smoke plumes enveloped him.

Cromwell's men advanced with their pikes held vertically in front. Beneath this array of poles some of their troops clambered on all fours, like dogs. Approaching the hawthorn bushes, they stabbed at the royalists behind them. Peter twisted and turned as he struck out with his blade. As the downpour grew worse, the splattering noise entirely drowned out the whimpers of the dying. Bleak clouds darkened. The moorland seemed to crawl with bodies and the flow of water across the dead looked like it had reanimated them.

Peter slashed at one rebel who came at him. They engaged in a rapid to and fro before momentarily locking swords. The man's eyes burned with hatred. But Peter had the upper hand and ran him through. Around him, a few of

Cromwell's troops were taken prisoner and sent under guard to Preston, as living proof of their commander's presence. It was hoped that they would stir the Scots to action. But it was all in vain.

Royalist drums conveyed the order to retreat. The steady beat was monotonous enough to stand out amidst the din of the battlefield. As Peter's comrades melted away, slipping back towards Preston, he quickly followed. The streets offered a chance of survival – that the enemy would sate their bloodlust on Preston Moor, so that by the time they reached the town, they might be exhausted enough to grant mercy.

He ran until his legs burned, and as if they might come away from his body. There was no looking back. Nor did he need to, for the noise of death remained in his ears, impelling him on. Running for all that his life was worth.

Chapter 17

**Newport.
20 August 1648.**

The rain was relentless. For months there had been no break – a divine message, some said, which dampened the spirits of even the most faithful. God's tears over the fact that no peace settlement was yet agreed upon, in spite of the lives lost in the late war. Maxwell turned into Saint Thomas's Square in Newport. He pulled his long cloak about him, not only against the weather, but also to help conceal his identity. This journey was prompted by a message that had been delivered not long ago.

Turning onto Saint James's Street, he headed for the Three Cranes Inn. Typically, just as he neared his destination the rain eased. The inn was alive with chatter and laughter. A fire was screened by newcomers who aimed to dry their outer clothes whilst soaking their insides with alcohol. Maxwell didn't have any desire to be here long enough to do the same and sought out the keeper.

"I am to meet one by the name of Smith."

"Pray follow me, sir."

The man led Maxwell past tables that teemed with customers and towards the opposite side of the room. An old grey cloth had been drawn across a small alcove and the keeper pointed to it.

"Many thanks."

"I'll wager you'll warm up in there," he chuckled.

Maxwell drew the curtain aside and was somewhat surprised to see a lady looking out of the window with her back to him. Her hood remained up. He stepped inside and let the covering fall back into place behind him.

"Maria?"

She turned; he was wrong. The hood was removed to reveal an array of damp curls that framed Louisa Laurent's face and hung about her neck. The ends of some seemed snared by the lace collar of her dress. Louisa's pale blue eyes sparked like a cloudless summer sky; a rarity of weather that was in keeping with her unique beauty. All that he had once felt for Louisa had been put aside when it transpired that her cousin had been Gervase Harper. He was struck by her presence.

"Are you disappointed, Captain Walker?"

"Surprised."

"In a good way, I hope?"

"That depends on the nature of your visit, *Master Smith*," Maxwell replied, quoting the name used on the note he had received.

"Ah, that was a play on your former occupation."

"You remembered?"

"Yes, but I had quite forgotten how you are prone to blush," she replied with a smile that left dimples in her cheeks.

"Blush?" Maxwell repeated. "Why are you here, Louisa?"

"I do not mock." Louisa gestured for him to sit beside her. "You are a man of few words, but all are honest. A woman knows exactly where she stands. You are a contradiction; a courageous soldier who nevertheless has a gentle streak."

Maxwell shook his head and sat down. "A soldier *cannot* be gentle."

"Is that so?" She looked at him intently.

"Louisa." He couldn't help but smile. "Tell me, what has brought you all the way to Newport?"

"I sense suspicion in your tone?"

REBELLION

"Well, I doubt that you just happened to pass by."

"I came to speak with you about an urgent matter."

She slid a tankard towards him, also professing to recall his love of ale – the 'taste of England' as he so called it. Maxwell took a swig and gathered his thoughts.

"How in God's name did you know where I was?"

"All of those who serve the king are known about. Let us be clear, the authorities are aware of everything that goes on here."

"Are you part of these authorities?"

"No." She shook her head. "I simply know people."

"Ah, the intrigues of the French. Paying court to the victors?"

"They are most certainly not who I seek to court. Now, tell me about Maria, who you thought I might have been."

"Just a strange woman I came across in Oxford."

"And does she *remain* a stranger to you?"

"Why do you ask?"

"My errant knight, I am to depart England at last." She lowered her head and whispered. "Events are escalating since the Scots were defeated. Do not get too deeply involved with your king."

Louisa's rose scent was uplifting, as was her proximity and the way she spoke so softly. His heart pulsed faster. He drew back.

"The Scots are vanquished?"

"At Preston. The uprisings in Kent and Wales have been crushed and those of your master's party who hold out in Colchester face ruin any day."

Maxwell's thoughts turned to Peter Irwin. "What of the English royalists who fought at Preston?"

"Cromwell took thousands of prisoners," she replied and placed her hand on his. "There will be moves against the king's person because of this second war. It has doomed him. Please come with me."

"Where to?"

"France."

"You surely jest?"

"I have never been more serious." She looked into his eyes. "Maxwell, I'm truly sorry for the actions of my cousin and if I could change the past, then I would. My hope, however, is that I can influence the future. Our future."

Maxwell looked at her, his eyes widening.

"My heart is yours. Bring your sons with you. Let us leave this kingdom."

"I do not know what to say," he replied. "It is easier for you to leave than it is for me."

"Did you not hear what I said? When I saw you in London …"

"You saw me?"

"Yes, and I heard about the arrest of the woman that you were with. It was Maria, I assume?"

"Yes, you know of her? Is she safe?" Maxwell asked.

"As safe as you can be in Newgate gaol. Is she of any consequence to you?"

"No."

"You answered rather quickly?" Louisa averted her eyes.

"I don't even know her full name. Our paths have simply crossed a number of times."

Louisa breathed a sigh of relief. Her head tilted slightly as she looked at him. "In that case, come with me. You will love Paris."

"I cannot."

"What is it that holds you back?"

"Many things, Louisa. I do care for you …"

"You are a good man." She took both of his hands. "I have something that might soothe your worries."

From her pocket she extracted a small sheet of paper and opened it. The neat writing was official, and Maxwell read the order.

"It grants Maria's release?"

REBELLION

"I was unsure how much this woman's incarceration might have affected you. If it is her fate that holds you back, then let this allay your concern. She may walk free, whilst you and I fly from here."

"You interceded for her?" Maxwell's thumb stroked her hand. "Louisa, you are the one who possesses a gentle streak. You hide it behind a mask of confidence."

"Admittedly, I did it more for you than her," Louisa replied with a reluctant smile. "I can arrange passes for you and your boys to travel with me. Listen to your heart, I beg you."

"I must first obtain leave from the king."

"Then go to him. I will return to London and procure the paperwork. If you are willing to embark on our adventure, meet me there in a few days."

Louisa kissed him on the cheek. This warm touch lingered on his cold skin. Her features portrayed hope and happiness – emotions he had not initiated in any woman for many years – and then she embraced him. He placed his arms around her.

He felt the rise and fall of Louisa's chest. It was as if they were united in that moment; perhaps he did love her. If he accepted her offer, then it would truly be a fresh start for his family. There were certain things, however, that remained unresolved, such as Peter's fate, and Maria Wilkins – he would first clear his name with the woman over her allegations of treachery.

Chapter 18

**London.
29 August 1648.**

Newgate Gaol was a notorious prison. It incorporated a gatehouse that was set into the city walls, with the teeth of a portcullis poking from the archway. Cries and desperate moans came from the windows, which were barred with iron. Arms hung through, as if the inmates found satisfaction that one limb, at least, could be free. Even three statues on the frontage, located in niches, seemed consigned there against their wills. Maxwell had not imagined that it could be as grim as this. He resolved immediately to get inside and reassure Maria that she would soon be at liberty, as well as stress his innocence over her capture.

"Gaoler?" Maxwell pushed his way past several bystanders.

Numerous people congregated about the entrance, as if bound to this miserable place. It clung to them like a debilitating disease. Many looked bereft of sanity. One woman tugged pitifully at Maxwell's clothes, begging him for money to free her starving husband; a debtor, who was perpetually kept so by the prison fees and destined never to leave. Then two officials latched onto Maxwell.

"What's your business?"

"I want to speak to a prisoner."

"We got plenty of them." One of the men laughed. "What do you want them for? Price depends on that, see."

"To speak with her."

"That it?"

"Aye," Maxwell replied and gave Maria's name.

"Hold a moment." The man held out a grubby hand. His fingers had already begun to curl, poised to clamp shut over whatever was proffered. "A shilling, at least."

Maxwell handed over a silver coin from his pouch. He had been careful to ensure that it contained only a token amount – not that he had much. As a result, he was escorted through the dingy female ward, which held an array of women in various stages of undress. Their eyes glared like those of wild beasts. Some held babies that wailed with hunger, while others babbled incoherently. Hacking coughs echoed from every corner. But it was to a cell that he was conducted, where he found Maria and a few other women. Although it was not much better, it did at least isolate them from what he had just witnessed, and a tiny window gave recognition of night and day.

"You!"

"I'm sorry to learn of your arrest." Maxwell glanced awkwardly at the other women, before sitting on the floor near Maria.

"Have you come here just to tell me that?"

"On what grounds do they proceed against you?"

"Do they need any? Perhaps you can enlighten me?"

Maria's serious expression was accentuated by her round eyes and piercing glare. Her head was raised slightly in some defiance. The features of her pretty face were as sharp as her nature; she possessed a straight nose, with a defined groove in her upper lip.

"I know nothing of why you are here," Maxwell assured her. "Though you will be freed soon enough."

"By your authority?"

"No, but trust me on this," Maxwell replied.

"You of all people speak of trust? I *need* no-one."

"I can see you are stubborn, but please …"

"Why is it that men cannot bear a strong woman who refuses to be cowed?" Maria asked with a shake of her head. "You try to compare me to a wilful child."

"Maria, what can I do to assure you I had no part in this? I would swear it on the bible itself."

"Whoever is responsible has paid for my food and lodging."

"I don't know who it could be."

"Do not patronise me." Maria shook her head. "If you are so confident of my release, then you must know who ordered it?"

"A French lady has procured your freedom."

"And why might this woman put herself to my cause?" Maria asked, raising her eyebrows. "At your special behest?"

"In a manner, yes," Maxwell replied. "You have heard of Louisa Laurent?"

Maria considered the name with a frown. "She was once attached to the French envoy?"

"That's right," Maxwell said.

"I saw you leaving her rooms in Oxford some years ago."

"Yes, on the first occasion I met you," he confirmed.

"You must know Madame Laurent quite well ..." One side of Maria's lips rose. "I assume you put yourself to great exertion to secure this."

"We have never been *occupied together*, if that's what you mean," Maxwell said. His words initiated a snigger from another prisoner close by.

Maria turned away. "She withheld such favours? Then that does not surprise me, after all, you yelled at her so terribly in Oxford. I recall your anger very well."

"On that occasion, I discovered that she was related to the man who murdered my wife."

Silence. Maria looked to the small window, as if the light that cascaded through it had illuminated another perspective.

REBELLION

"That was the reason for your outburst?"

"It has all scarred me."

"I had taken you to be nothing more than a ... whoremonger." She hugged her knees. The word seemed to leave a distaste and her gaze fell to the grimy floor. "One who used and mistreated women."

"Hence your dislike of me ever since?"

"I dislike whoremongers. My father had a different woman in his bed most nights, much to my poor mother's sorrow. It seems we are both shaped by our pasts."

"Though I refuse to be dominated by it any longer."

"You will forgive me if I don't express any gratitude to our French friend. I seem to recall she was as untrustworthy as she was beautiful. Besides, I cannot but question how she came to know of my predicament in the first place."

"I know not, but do not spurn her gesture."

"Oh, I will happily walk free from here. I merely question her motives, for we barely know each other."

Maxwell didn't answer. He wished not to reveal the fact that he was to leave with Louisa, bound for a new life in France. The cynical Maria would only cast aspersions on that too. Or accuse him of yet more falseness.

As if on cue, the gaoler banged the door with a metal rod. Maria began making patterns in the dirt with her finger. Her tight brown curls were tucked under a stained coif. Maxwell considered their shared loyalty to the king's service; something more had to be said, considering all that had passed. He could not leave like this.

"God speed, Maria. Our cause needs you now more than ever."

"Had I not been deposited here, then I would have been with our master."

"Really?"

"I have a post as a maidservant."

A second set of raps prevented Maxwell from responding. Perhaps it was for the best. He glanced back at her one last time as he was escorted out, and she briefly nodded her head. As the two men's footsteps echoed along a barren passageway, Maxwell considered whether this visit had presented him with more questions than answers.

"Tell me, who pays for her?"

The man turned to Maxwell and grinned, prompting the exchange of one last shilling.

"I don't know names."

Maxwell grabbed his collar, swung him against the wall, and held his throat.

"Do you take me for a god-damned fool?"

"Let me go," he gasped. "It's a woman. A Frenchy. I never saw her because she was inside a closed chair."

"French, you say?"

"Aye. I heard her. She spoke to the officer that brought your woman here."

"She's not my woman," Maxwell barked. "Did this French woman arrive with the soldiers?"

"No ... but she wasn't long after them."

Maxwell discarded him like an old rag. The gaoler froze for a moment. He brushed down his coat and then hurried away to the main door. Maxwell was about to follow when a voice whispered his name. A prisoner was up against the grate of a door, fingers squeezing through in a desperate bid to be seen. The place was dark. A beard also obscured the man's features.

"Help me, Maxwell."

"Peter?"

"Get me out."

"Jesu! Aye, you have my word."

The gaoler pounded on the main door three times. There followed an elongated creak as it opened, as if expressing doubt that Maxwell Walker could possibly keep such a promise.

Chapter 19

Maxwell arrived at the house where Louisa Laurent lodged. A small alleyway led to it, setting it back from the main street and shielding it from the sights, sounds and smells of the city. He was shown into the garden. The briar rose hedges gave a sweet scent. Gravel crunched beneath his feet, every step freeing it from a stone roller's enforced neatness. Louisa was standing at the far side of the flower beds. They were interspersed with small statues, each one painted with lifelike colouring. She was queen of all she surveyed, and these stone courtiers were as frozen by her charm as Maxwell.

"My handsome captain."

He took the elegant fingers of her hand and placed a kiss upon them. "This is a secluded haven."

"I thought it fit to take advantage of the break in the weather."

"A good idea. The cursed rain is sickening."

"Perhaps this dry spell is a good omen. I am pleased you came."

"You didn't think I would?"

"I feared my proposal might have frightened you off. But you are a brave officer."

"Not anymore. I chose my sons over the army."

"Modest to the last." She gave a brisk nod. "You still serve the king, only in a different manner. Speaking of your boys, have you told them of our plans?"

"Not yet. I thought best to make sure you could obtain our passes."

"I have them all."

She gave a reassuring smile as they began to walk together and then linked his arm. Memories of their very first meeting came flooding back; of the way she had done the same thing, quite unexpectedly, and how he had been disappointed when she had let go again. It felt so natural. A contentedness had overtaken him back then. It would have done so now, were it not for his visit to Newgate.

"I sense there is something troubling you?" Louisa asked.

"Perhaps. A question if I may?"

"Of course."

Her lips were the shade of a blushing rose and complexion as smooth as velvety petals. Tight ringlets hung beside her ear, into which he could easily whisper his innermost desires.

"I visited Newgate earlier to find Maria. To reassure her that she would soon be free. But she was convinced I am responsible for her imprisonment."

"Why you of all people?"

"It seems she has never had a good opinion of me. When I spoke with the gaoler, he told me that a certain *French lady* had been paying for her upkeep."

"Ah, yes ... my secret is discovered. If not me, then who would have done so?"

"But why are you so engaged in her welfare?"

"For you," Louisa replied. She stopped and turned to face him. "Has cannon fire rendered you deaf over the years? Did you not hear me when I came to Newport? I love you."

"If I have ever been distracted, then it is only by your beauty."

"I think that Maria Wilkins is a source of distraction?"

"I wished to clear my name with her."

"Is that all you wish for?" Louisa asked.

"You are refreshingly honest, Louisa. I like that about you."

REBELLION

"A characteristic we both share."

"Then let me be clear. I have no designs upon Maria Wilkins. In fact, I had no wish to be close to any other woman after Catherine. I have lost much; my wife, home and employment. You, on the other hand, have no hesitation about our venture."

"I know what my heart tells me, Maxwell. It was God's will that we stumbled across each other once more."

"But why go to the trouble of covering the fees and arranging Maria's release?"

"I concluded, rather hastily, that you might have been close to the girl," Louisa sighed. "Upon hearing of her arrest, I wished to help you."

Maxwell looked away. Was it the sentiment that stirred him, or the fact that he might love again? He could not find the words to express himself, but Louisa seemed to understand his silence. She took his hand in hers.

"Do you know why she was arrested?"

"I am not privy to the reason," Louisa replied.

"Can you find out?"

"I think not, Maxwell. But she is free to go. Let me fetch all the documents. I have travel passes for you, your sons and sister-in-law. Is that correct?"

"Aye," he replied. "But perhaps you should keep them until we are ready?"

"No, you take them. That way you may see we have the means to leave as soon as you are ready."

"I am not sure I am."

She remained in silent disbelief at first, and then attempted to persuade him; to warn of the storm that was breaking over these kingdoms. But her arguments, however impassioned, could not clear the doubt that remained with him. It was not only doubt about moving to a different country, but over the incarceration of Maria Wilkins too. Doubt about Louisa herself. He wished it was not so. He would not lie to others, nor himself, no matter how much he might have wanted to.

The grey clouds shifted above them like the rolling smoke of a battlefield. Each plume was a differing density and these layers held back the sun's golden light. It struggled to burn through and show itself. Maxwell's heart was just as shrouded. He saw disappointment in Louisa's eyes and felt guilty for it.

***

Newgate.

The gaoler yelled at a screaming prisoner and threatened a beating from 'Old Ironside' – the trusty metal bar that he brandished. It had the desired effect. With a smirk, he compared the rod to the mighty Cromwell, Lieutenant-General of the New Model Army, who had battered the royalists into submission. Maxwell handed over a document. The man held it towards a lighted taper and squinted as he studied it.

Within Newgate, daytime came and went unnoticed. The fellow's mouth remained open as he struggled with the writing, his breaths shallow and fast. As Maxwell waited, his thoughts were interrupted by varying yells and screams, or moans and groans. There were also echoes of dragging leg irons and the clink of chains. Then, with a shake of his head, the gaoler passed the paperwork back.

"You can't have her."

"This grants her release. Will you defy the Derby House Committee?" Maxwell demanded.

"I have no time to fetch her today."

"No time to turn a key in a lock?"

"You speak of one woman, yet I have an army of prisoners to attend to."

"Then ease your burden and release her," Maxwell insisted.

"Lest you threaten me again?"

REBELLION

"Not I, but you might listen to the real Ironside."

"Cromwell?" The man's nose screwed up in surprise.

"Aye. Must I return to the army and obtain a warrant from *Old Noll* himself?"

"You know him?"

"I am one of his captains. He will provide suitable reward for your good service – if I furnish him with a positive report on the matter. How else would I have a pass from the Derby House Committee?"

"I had not realised …"

"Let me write you a promissory note. A sum equal to one week's worth of accommodation here. Would that help?"

"That would be very agreeable …"

"I'm pleased we have an understanding." Maxwell took up a cut pen that lay next to the metal bar. "If you provide me with paper, I can write it while you fetch her?"

"Aye, I will so," he replied, and tore a blank strip from one of the many strewn letters.

After the man had gone, Maxwell took the metal bar and hurried to the door where he had seen Peter. Almost immediately, he appeared at the grate, as if he had been listening to the conversation that had just taken place.

"Thank God."

"When the gaoler comes back, you must tell him someone is dead of the plague in there," Maxwell instructed. "You have found buboes on his body."

"Whatever you say."

"When he enters, then you strike him," he said, and eased the bar through the grate.

Maxwell returned to the desk and scratched out a promise to pay. On the instruction for Maria's release, in the gap where her name had been inserted by the committee, he added that of Peter Irwin underneath. Then he waited. When the gaoler returned with Maria, the man barely had time to take a glance at the promissory note before a cry went up. Plague! The very word made him hurry to the door to peer inside.

"There's one dead in here!" Peter shouted.

"Dead? You sure?"

"Swellings at his neck. As black as devil's barnacles."

"Where is he?"

"In the corner," Peter replied.

"I can't see," the gaoler said, and craned his neck.

He took a dirty piece of linen, covered his mouth and nose, and slid back the iron bolt. Then with a jangle of keys, he unlocked the door and entered. Maxwell held his breath and listened. Then came the anticipated thump. As soon as Peter emerged, they closed the door and bolted it once more.

"Maimed?" Maxwell asked.

"I am termed a delinquent for serving the king, but I am no murderer."

"What in God's name have you just done?" Maria eyed them both with disbelief.

"This is my good friend and comrade," Maxwell replied and then grabbed the promissory note. "I will explain once we are out of here."

"Comrade?" Peter questioned.

"All right, I didn't fight with you this time. But if I had done so, who would have freed you?" Maxwell gave a playful shove of Peter's arm.

"One day I hope to possess your gift of foresight," Peter said.

"If only I had such powers. That would help ease my decision about France."

"France?" Peter frowned.

"Never mind. Now, we all leave together. I will say that you have both been released for interrogation."

Maxwell led them to the door and recalled how the gaoler had banged on it earlier that day. He quickly did the same – three distinct raps. The bolt screeched aside, and the door creaked open. Maxwell handed over the release order to an guard and briefly stated his purpose and authority. The wax seal on the document drew the man's eye and he gave a nod.

"Where be John?" He peered behind the trio.

"Quieting a prisoner with *Old Ironside*," Maxwell replied and pointed back with his thumb.

The man laughed. They were waved through. Maxwell shielded his eyes as he stepped outside; even the bleak sky was bright in comparison to Newgate. Maria and Peter struggled, but he led them away towards a hackney carriage.

"Did your French lady help with his release, too?" Maria pointed at Peter.

"No, that was my own doing," Maxwell replied.

"Where will we go?" Peter asked.

"Back to Wight."

"We cannot travel there with you," Maria retorted. "I will take Peter to a safe house for some rest and food. After that, he may go wherever he pleases."

"And you, Maria?" Maxwell asked.

"I'll take up my post with the king as soon as the situation permits."

Chapter 20

Doncaster, Yorkshire.
30 October 1648.

Several starlings chirped their birdsong outside the window casement, their speckled feathers ruffled by the morning breeze. The joyful trills prompted a sleepy sigh of contentment from Colonel Thomas Rainsborough. It was as if the kingdom was settled and Pontefract Castle, a royalist thorn in the side, had finally surrendered. He squinted to find the room still dark, and the furniture in it took on an almost velvety form.

Thomas turned over on an upper mattress of feathers. He stretched and let out a groan as he did so, hoping to return to sleep for perhaps another hour. His foot idly stroked the wooden bed stave, a wedge that held the blankets in place. Just as he was beginning to drift back off, he heard thuds that sounded like a knocking at the door. It was far too early for visitors - surely, nobody required him at this hour. The floorboards outside his room began to creak and a tap echoed from the door.

"What is it?"

"Three gentlemen, sir. They have a message from the lieutenant-general," the secretary replied and then upon permission, he entered the room. "I would have sent them away, but I recall you are expecting a letter."

"Send them up in five minutes."

"Let me light a candle for you, sir."

A shifting orange glow illuminated the bedchamber. The small flame danced in celebration of morning as Thomas

REBELLION

rubbed his eyes and sat up. He stood no chance of returning to bed after receiving Cromwell's message. His day had begun. In his mind, he went over all the tasks that lay ahead. The room continued to jerk in the candlelight as he got to his feet.

Taking his black woollen breeches, he pulled them on and tucked his shirt into them. Next, came his doublet, though he left it unfastened. Once his stockings were on and his boots folded below the knees, he ran his fingers through his hair. A felt hat proudly sported the Levellers' green ribbon. It was as much a badge of allegiance as his tawny parliamentarian scarf, which was left draped across the chair.

Ever since his time in the navy he had relished sunrise. He resolved to ride out and watch as God painted the land in shades of gold; signifying the treasure that a new day could offer. But first, he had to deal with his visitors, who opened the door and entered.

"Good morrow, gentlemen."

"We have something for you, Colonel Rainsborough."

"Yes, I am expecting it."

One of the men drew a blade. The steel scratched as it slid from its scabbard. Thomas bolted towards the table in a bid to grab his own, but it was no good. The men were upon him in an instant. One of the strangers thrust his sword right into Thomas's chest. A knife was then stuck into his neck. The assassins left quickly, knocking the candle from its holder and splashing wax across the floor. The flame was snuffed out in an instant. Silence ensued.

One of the little starlings hopped onto the windowsill with a caterpillar in its mouth, showing off the bounty that the morning had brought him. With the bedchamber pitched into darkness once more, it was as if time had somehow backtracked. Thomas was dead before his body had even hit the floor. His was now an eternal sleep. The Levellers had lost their most influential supporter and it remained to be seen whether their cause had suffered a blow as deathly.

Chapter 21

**Newport, Isle of Wight.
2 November 1648.**

The king sat at the head of a table on a red chair of state. A cloth canopy was above him. Royal footmen sported new suits laced with sparkling silver, along with various courtiers that had been permitted to attend the monarch during these treaty negotiations. There were old faces, such as the Duke of Richmond, Marquis of Hertford and the Earls of Southampton and Lindsey. There was also an array of clergymen, led by the Bishop of London. But this micro-court was mere show. The king's grand position appeared much more splendid than his fortunes. There was to be no shelter from the relentless parliamentary commissioners that faced him.

Day after day, for over three weeks, they had gathered like this to scrutinise royal responses to the strict peace terms that Parliament proposed. Proceedings were as dogged as the driving rain that rattled against the windows. The one positive for the king was that the building was a welcome change to the gloom of Carisbrooke. It was here that he would lodge throughout the allotted forty days that had been granted; yet there was very little talking. All negotiations were done in writing, passed to and fro during the sessions, with many responses drafted overnight.

"Your Majesty, we humbly require further clarification," the Earl of Northumberland ventured, as spokesman for the parliamentarians. "It concerns your reply regarding the settlement of religion and the church."

"Have I not been clear enough, My Lord?"

"We aim to avoid unnecessary delays and resolve all doubts. If we submitted your answer as it stands, then Parliament would raise the same questions."

A secretary approached, bowed, and then handed over a note to the king. He opened it and scanned the contents. These men persisted in requiring explicit answers over what he would, and would not, agree to. On the utter abolition of archbishops and bishops, he had not, apparently, given a clear consent. The king shook his head.

"Let me adjourn and discuss this with my counsel."

"Of course, Sire, as you wish."

The king's chair was eased out for him as he stood. Parliament's representatives also got to their feet as a mark of respect and left. He withdrew into a curtained vestibule and passed the letter to his cousin, the Duke of Richmond.

"They treat me little better than a schoolboy. My answers are scrutinised and assessed by their masters in Westminster. Nothing I say is good enough."

"Though you have sanctioned Presbyterianism for three years, sir, they wish you to agree to an act that abolishes episcopacy," Richmond summarised for the benefit of the other counsellors.

"His majesty agreed to suspend the power of the bishops for those three years, with an assembly of divines to a settle the matter," the Earl of Southampton replied.

"We are informed that this is not enough." Richmond shook his head.

"I grant concessions yet receive nothing in return." The king walked to the window and looked out. "In conscience I cannot abandon episcopacy. I made an oath at my coronation to uphold the church, which, may I remind them, is lawfully established."

"There is also the Book of Common Prayer," Richmond added, moving discussion on. "They will not permit you or your household to use it."

REBELLION

"For pities sake." The king sighed. "Have I not already agreed that the Presbyterian directory could replace it."

Richmond confirmed that there were to be no exemptions, even for the sovereign himself. Alongside this was a ban on the hearing of Mass – again, the king had not specified the inclusion of the royal household within his agreement.

The monarch had consented to the speedy apprehension of all Catholic recusants. Their children were to be educated in the Protestant faith. But to forbid his wife the right to hear Mass was another step too far, and he felt certain Parliament were bent on goading him. There was no time for such games. The New Model Army continued to watch from Windsor, expressing opposition to these very negotiations, even threatening to move against Parliament to prevent a treaty.

"They take aim at the queen over Mass! My wife is entitled to exercise her faith by the terms of our marriage. I have consented to all other aspects, but she must be exempted."

"There is also the proposal touching on the militia. They call for control of the kingdom's forces for a period of twenty years."

The king remained standing at the window but felt detached. Raindrops formed on the panes, some clinging on longer than others. They merged, became too large, and then slid down the glass to disperse. And so it continued, relentlessly obscuring his view. All buildings and people were distorted. Their forms were irregular and unrecognisable. King Charles could not comprehend what had become of his kingdoms, nor his own position. He closed his eyes as tears gathered and trickled down his cheeks.

"I consent to the militia," he said, before sarcastically repeating the entirety of their demands; all the forces of England, Ireland, Wales, Guernsey, Jersey and Berwick-upon-Tweed. "Let there be no ambivalence. The world may see how far I go to secure peace."

A scratching was heard at the door. Perhaps the commissioners itched to be at him for another round, the king thought. But when one of his attendants went to investigate, they found his greyhound, who ran to her master and sat at his feet.

"Gipsy," a smile broke the king's melancholy. "Sweet Gipsy. If only I enjoyed such loyalty from those dogs at Westminster."

There was a tense silence and no man knew quite what to say. Then one enquired whether the king preferred greyhounds over spaniels. They love their masters equally – he replied – though greyhounds do not flatter them so much. The affectionate caress of Gipsy's smooth, grey coat was reassuring to both king and canine.

***

When the day's proceedings were finally over, the king withdrew to his bedchamber. It was well that the negotiations were time-bound. He could not survive much more than forty days' perpetual attack upon his principles and beliefs. Gipsy curled up on the bed. As the king slumped onto a chair and took a deep breath, a knock disturbed any respite he might have hoped for.

"Your Majesty, might you permit entry to one who requires your touch?"

The king reluctantly nodded. This was his divine duty. He felt powerless in his kingdoms, unable to heal the breach with Parliament and seemingly punished by God. Therefore, the opportunity to soothe a suffering individual was rewarding. It gave a sense of purpose. If he could continue to apply the healing powers vested in him by the Almighty, then God must not have abandoned him.

A young girl was shown in and guided towards King Charles. One of her eyes was swollen. Her pale features much resembled his youngest daughter, Elizabeth, who had been under house arrest in London since the start of the unhappy wars.

"Your Majesty," she whispered in a trembling voice, which was barely audible.

"Tell me your name."

"Elizabeth Stevens, from Winchester."

"And what is it that ails thee, my child?"

"My sight. I have been blind in one eye these sixteen days past."

"Close thy other eye, if you please."

The king placed both hands upon the linen that covered her head. He gently stroked his thumbs over both eyelids and looked to the ceiling. The decorative plasterwork swirled like heavenly clouds. He prayed quietly, calling for the Lord's blessing upon the girl. Next, he spoke some words from the Book of Common Prayer; words that were usually read by a chaplain, but with which the king was well-versed.

"May the good Lord bring you ease."

She began to cry; stifled sobs of relief. If he was not wholly exhausted, he would have succumbed to such emotion himself. With some hesitation she lifted her head.

"Let the Almighty fill your heart with hope and love."

"I can see! God bless you, sir ... thank you."

His body tingled as if he, by default, was also benefitting from the divine energy that channelled through him. Her relief imbued him with a wave of euphoria. At the conclusion, he stroked her cheek and nodded.

"Pray for me at Winchester."

As she was escorted out, he turned and sat at his desk. The ceremony had enlivened him; he was a lawful king, ordained by God and answerable to him alone. A renewed determination overcame him. Almost as soon as the Duke of Richmond entered, he insisted on countering Parliament's terms with some of his own.

"Tomorrow, I will put to them that a general pardon must be offered to my most loyal supporters. My lands and revenues should be restored to me, and I expect to be dealt with in a condition of honour, freedom, and safety."

"They are most reasonable proposals, which Parliament surely cannot dismiss." Richmond gave a nod.

"I am lost if I do not escape here," the king whispered.

He took a quill and began to write. The strokes of the nib were fast and determined. He called upon one of his loyal servants to go ahead with a last-ditch escape plan – one that had been spoken of for a week or more. It was based on the fact that these lodgings provided an ideal location and opportunity. Was it not God's will that he had been moved here?

The proposal put forward was for a betrothal; a *futuro* union of a man and woman from within his attendants. It would offer a suitable distraction. Many would relish an opportunity to make merry, and whilst they did so, he could climb down a ladder from his window and travel to a waiting boat. His mind was set. Now just to choose the central players.

Chapter 22

**Newport. Isle of Wight.
16 November 1648.**

The George Inn was as rowdy as ever. The proprietors made no secret of their loyalty to the king, hosting frequent gatherings that both celebrated royalist successes. A fight between a royal footman and one of the island's soldiers made great entertainment and emphasised the chasm that split the kingdom. The place had become so notorious that Governor Hammond's musketeers were often deployed to restore order. Both alcohol and the febrile atmosphere of this small town served to loosen many a tongue. Clientele daily debated the progress of the ongoing peace negotiations.

This evening, every bench, table, and corner was full. Men stood chatting around the fire while the mud that was caked to their boots dried and cracked. Children and animals were left to their own devices amidst the crowds. A game of piquet took place, which occasioned a host of separate wagers on the outcome. Arrivals to the island brought news of failed crops drowned by the rain and whispers that the New Model Army wished to try the king for his life. Even the rumoured birth of a two-headed baby in Southampton was given as an ill portent for the kingdom. But there was an additional reason that augmented the numbers in The George; a betrothal of two who served King Charles.

Maxwell glanced at Maria through the clouds of tobacco smoke. Despite the dingy atmosphere, he could see her unease and felt it too. She had barely spoken to him. Ever since he had signed an 'M' on the document that listed their future intent to marry, Maria had been withdrawn. Luckily, nobody else seemed to notice. Tankards clashed and well wishes were given alongside all manner of advice until, as the night wore on, it was deemed acceptable for her to leave. Maxwell remained, as per his separate orders. The more focus that could be drawn to the inn, the better – thus giving maximum benefit to the king's design to escape.

"Why not marry in the present?" One of the castle guardsmen asked.

"Ah, I have not spoken to her father," Maxwell replied.

"A man of honour, eh?" He nodded. "Then tame your codpiece. Good luck to thee, for she is a pretty one!"

Maxwell feigned a smile and took another swig of ale.

"To hell with honour," Charles Mordue chortled in response to the soldier. "I'll entertain her if he isn't willing."

"You wouldn't get near her." Maxwell pointed. "Your gut safeguards all women against your vile intentions by acting as a barrier. Aye, I'll wager it keeps your powder dry."

A chorus of laughter broke out. It rang in Maxwell's ears; deep roars, accompanied by the banging of tables and one or two choking on their drinks. Maxwell stared resolutely at this man, who had pestered Maria ever since she had come to the island. His small chin drowned amidst a neck that bulged with outrage.

"Do you often think about my manly musket?"

"You will leave her be," Maxwell commanded in a menacing tone.

The two men eyed each other.

"Refuse to plough her if you will. In the meantime, she may graze upon my crop."

REBELLION

The voices around Maxwell became dull noise. The drone of laughter was lost as a haze of anger overcame him. He lunged at Mordue. It was only after the impact of his fist against the man's face that Maxwell's vision returned. Mordue tumbled backwards. Those surrounding the pair chanted raucously and then deep cheers broke out. Hoots of excitement. Mordue was flat on his back amidst the mud and straw while Maxwell stood over him.

"Let this cool your lust," Maxwell said, taking Mordue's horn tankard and pouring the contents onto him. "This man treats women as though they are animals yet squirms on the floor like a pig. I warn thee never to approach Maria again."

Maxwell took his hat and cloak and left. His head thumped from anger and the copious amounts of ale he'd supped. Outside, however, the fresh air was bracing. He stood for a moment to savour it. When he continued walking, he looked up at the night sky and the stars that blurred into silver streaks within it. Passing the king's house, he noted the golden glow from the bedchamber and hoped that the monarch had made his escape. As he left Newport behind him and headed back to his lodgings, Maxwell wondered how bound he was to the intention to marry Maria. To make it legal, they would have to consummate the agreement. Being so close to the brink of a second marriage, however artificial, was somewhat alarming. Never would he have imagined that the king's service would have led to this. He stumbled across the contours of the muddy track, cursing between deep breaths of sea air.

When he opened the door of the small dwelling, he was surprised to see Maria. She sat wrapped in a blanket with young Kit smiling up at her. Her laughter was a glorious sound of innocent amusement. It lit up her features. This moment lingered with Maxwell. Maria's hair was loose – damp from the rain – and her clothes hung from a drier that was suspended from the ceiling. Tom supped from a tankard like he was the man of the house. Grace also appeared more animated than usual, busying herself with preparing potage, which gave a wholesome smell. It was a homely and welcoming sight that basked in the glow of the fire. Maxwell felt as though he was peering across the threshold into a different world; a family scene that stirred memories of the past, but also hinted at what might be. But when Maria turned to him, the smile left her face.

"Maxwell." Grace hurried over and took his arm. "Come in."

"I didn't expect you, Maria," he said.

"The weather is foul. It is best she stays with us," Grace replied and brushed her hands on her apron. "What a day it has become!"

"You know that what occurred was for the king's benefit?" Maxwell whispered.

Grace didn't seem to hear, or care. Instead, she pointed to the doorway that led to the bedroom. Peter Irwin stood looking back. Maxwell laughed heartily at the sight of his old friend. He then extended his arms and embraced him, slapping Peter on the back many times.

"Thanks be to God! When did you arrive?"

"This evening," Grace interjected, "is it not marvellous?"

Now it became clear why his sister-in-law was so visibly carefree; why she had not said a word about Maxwell's breath and the alcohol he had quite obviously consumed.

"How did you get here?" Maxwell asked.

"Good Mistress Wilkins," Peter replied. "She not only arranged somewhere for me to hide these past months but also had a false travel pass drawn up."

"I am grateful for what you have done." Maxwell turned to Maria and nodded.

"The weather also helped facilitate my passage. Even the most officious sentries have little desire to examine a new arrival in this rain," Peter added.

"I shall enquire after a boat to convey you to France, but in the meantime, you mustn't leave this house," Maxwell warned.

"Then I am at your sister's mercy, who I hope will look after me well enough," Peter replied, securing Grace's ready agreement.

"Come, you must tell me all about the battle with the Scots," Maxwell said, and then embraced both of his sons.

Tom expressed a desire to be a soldier and fight for the king, standing proud and straight. It came as a surprise to Maxwell. The very declaration seemed to add extra years to the lad. The concept of time seemed as upside down as the state of the world. Yet despite everything; dangers, isolation, and uncertainty, the threads of life were knitting together to lead them through these turbulent times. Maxwell turned to Maria and after a moment's hesitation, asked about the king. She shook her head with disappointment.

"It wasn't safe enough for him to depart. He remains on the island."

Chapter 23

Carisbrooke Castle.
24 November 1648.

"Might you assist me?"

From behind a door, Maxwell listened carefully. It was ajar, so he could see the young soldier that was on duty outside the Governor's room. Not a wrinkle of doubt creased the man's fresh face as Jane Whorwood requested his help. His lips had been pursed with concentration until she had spoken.

"This chest is too heavy, but you look strong enough to budge it."

Thick eyebrows enhanced his serious nature, and an upturned nose gave the appearance of a youthful haughtiness – a certainty that he could succeed in anything he put his hand to. Proving his strength to a pretty woman of mature years was too good to pass up. He stepped away to follow Jane.

Maxwell emerged and hurried to the door that the soldier had abandoned. He entered and then closed it gently behind him. A desk stood in front, made of oak that had darkened with age. The furniture gave the impression that an unseen presence was sitting at it, even though he knew the Governor had left to walk the battlements. There were rumours that the New Model Army was preparing to move against both King Charles and Parliament; it was telling that the monarch was in the ramshackle Carisbrooke, whilst the commanders of the army were holding court at Windsor Castle. A letter had been delivered to the governor that morning. It was imperative that the king was kept informed of all new developments.

Maxwell soon found the small packet and snatched it from the desk. It was a brief missive from General Fairfax, summoning Hammond to New Model Army headquarters. Notifying him, too, that a colonel had been despatched to take care of the island in his absence. There was no doubt that this would place control of Wight – and the king – firmly in the army's hands. This was all Maxwell needed to know. He replaced the letter and hurried out of the room, whereupon Maria appeared from a staircase and gave an enquiring look. He nodded. They had barely crossed the corridor when Governor Hammond turned the corner.

"Sentry?"

The governor repeated his cry and ordered Maxwell and Maria to stay where they were. A scuffle heralded the soldier's panicked return. He quickly replaced his doublet with profuse apologies.

"I was helping Mistress Whorwood."

"And leaving others to help themselves?"

"I could not budge the chest, sir, it is true," Jane said in an attempt to pacify Hammond.

"Enough!" Hammond barked and called for more troops. "Everyone must be searched."

Maxwell and Maria moved to the wall and stood with their backs to it. The Governor strode towards the pair when further guards arrived.

"Unbutton your doublet," Hammond demanded of Maxwell.

The Governor briskly stroked and patted the sides of Maxwell's body and arms, before ordering him to turn out any pockets. A small letter was then extracted from the pouch at Maxwell's belt, which made Hammond's lip curl with satisfaction. After he unfolded it, all smugness left the Governor's round face.

"This is nothing of mine, at least. Who wrote it?"

"A friend."

"She is clearly much more than that." The governor turned to Maria and raised an eyebrow. "I counsel you to keep a close eye on your betrothed. I am taxed by the intrigues of the King's servants, yet it seems this one has a secret of his own."

"What?" Maria frowned.

"He has intentions to flee the island in some romantic escapade," Hammond replied.

"I have no intention of leaving," Maxwell protested.

"A certain Louisa would have it otherwise," the Governor gave a look of disdain and handed the letter to Maria. "Perhaps this might enlighten you."

"I am sure it will," Maria replied without looking up.

"Louisa pleads for me to go to her. I intend to reply with a refusal to prevent her harbouring such hope."

"On this occasion I shall not put you ladies through a similar search." Hammond looked at Jane and Maria. "However, I know the king's laundry maids deliver more to him than clean linen. I venture that if he had this army of women at Naseby, then he might not have lost that battle."

"We are merely maidservants," Jane countered.

"And you, Mistress Whorwood, are captain-general of them all, leading my troops astray. Well, no more. Both of you are to leave the island within seven days."

"Please, Governor ..." Jane attempted to intervene.

"Hold thy tongue," Hammond snapped and then pointed at Maxwell. "You shall remain, which in view of your desire to fly to your whore, is punishment enough."

"You wrongly assume such a thing!" This accusation stuck in Maxwell's throat.

"Let your separation prevent any ill-fated union being made before God," Hammond said to Maxwell and Maria. "You both have divided loyalties, which is not conducive to any marriage."

Jane gave a derisive sniff at the remark.

"Something amuses you?" Hammond enquired.

"Men are most unimaginative creatures," Jane replied.

"Maybe so when compared to you and your ingenious intrigues."

"What of your loyalties, Governor?" Jane asked. "You were appointed as governor by Parliament, but soon they will come to blows with their own army. When they do, I wonder which side you will take?"

"How dare you question my motives."

After an order was given to escort the women from the castle, Maxwell quickly got about his duties and laid low. He had no intention whatsoever of joining Louisa. She had merely written upon her arrival in France and implored him to follow – or at very least to retain the passes and not dismiss the notion. Maria's look of detestation bothered him; one that he had experienced numerous times before, but not of late. Might she truly think, like Hammond, that he was about to abscond? If she did, just why did that bother Maxwell so much?

Chapter 24

**Cowes.
30 November 1648.**

It was approaching evening. A splinter of candlelight emphasised the narrow gap of the open window casement. It afforded Maxwell, who stood outside, the discreet opportunity to listen to the conversation within. A new arrival to the island was introducing himself as Major Fox. Maxwell had spotted the man disembark from a ship with some horsemen. Fox's voice was deep, and his brusque words were more suited to his company of men rather than the captain of Governor Hammond's guards.

"We've had enough of the games taking place here. There are two thousand of us on our way to put an end to it all. I have my orders," Fox declared.

"As do I, sir. I am charged by Governor Hammond, who commands this island, to hold it for Parliament and safeguard the king's person."

"Damn the king!" Fox replied. "Far from negotiating with that tyrant, we would have him tried for his crimes."

"On what authority? Parliament has now concluded that the king's concessions are an acceptable basis for peace."

"Peace?" Fox snorted. "There will be none whilst he lives."

"You speak treason!"

"I see you are all under his spell here."

"I remain loyal to Parliament's cause. May I remind you that we are on the same side."

REBELLION

"My men will secure Carisbrooke before morning," Fox declared.

Maxwell drew back from the window upon hearing a noise from behind. The dreaded moment had materialised, and the army had, indeed, come for the monarch.

"Who are you?"

A soldier approached and went for his sword. Maxwell fled, darting through the lanes that he had become so familiar with, but he was relentlessly pursued. He hurried towards the woodland where his horse was tethered. The dying sun slipped beneath the horizon in a bid to escape the events that were unfolding on the island.

It was difficult to run in the wet and muddy conditions. Once amongst the trees, Maxwell made for a large oak that had been toppled by a storm and hid behind the upended roots. After discarding his cloak and hat, he drew his sword. He listened carefully for his foe's approach. There was little time to catch his breath. Upon judging the soldier to be close enough, he went on the attack.

Their blades clashed. During the first few vicious strikes both men attempted to get the measure of the other. Then they fell to circling each other in the woodland shadows, searching for weakness. Searching for a chink in defence. Maxwell kept his nicked blade trained on his foe. As he had foreseen, the man struggled with his wet cloak, casting it over his shoulder.

"Surrender your sword."

"You might have it, but in your gut first," Maxwell cried.

He cut in at the parliamentarian, but the move was adeptly countered. Each of the successive attacks, slashing from left, right or above, were all blocked. The light drizzle plastered Maxwell's fair hair to his face. Their boots splashed in puddles as they lunged at one another, each step churning the mud into an ever more deadly quagmire. The clashes of steel were piercing. Neither did the rain cool their desperation.

As exhaustion increased, their attack reduced in intensity. The swing of swords slowed and then Maxwell slipped, narrowly escaping a direct blow. Now on one knee, he seized his chance that very instant; just as the soldier was about to strike again. Maxwell thrust his sword into his opponent's stomach. The blade pierced the cowhide coat. The man recoiled, and as he bent forward, his cloak flapped around him as if in protective embrace. He released a groan of pain and stumbled backwards.

Maxwell rushed through the trees. His hand was welded to the fish-skin grip of his sword, fingers frozen to the bones. The wet clothes clung to him. The effect hampered his movement, as if he was being held by the grasping hands of an army of demons.

The woodland was so uniformly dull that individual trees barely stood out. As a result, their gnarled forms seemed to merge to block him in. Their clawing branches left pink scratches in the sky above. His horse was a welcome sight. The warm glow of its copper-red coat seemed unaffected by the rain, and soon he was riding along the track and back towards his lodgings. Behind him the shrill cries of a trumpet sounded. It did not augment well. No doubt the soldiers who were spilling onto the island would soon be clamouring to seize the killer swordsman, as well as the king.

***

When a series of muffled thuds echoed from the door, Peter Irwin's body was gripped with fear and shock. His heart almost stopped dead. These were no ordinary raps; the pounding was desperate and continuous. It did not bode well for his escape from the island, which had been planned for that evening. Peter now feared the worst – that the authorities had found him at this last moment. He turned to young Kit, who was wide-eyed. Grace too. He instructed them to go into the back room.

REBELLION

Grabbing a fire iron and brandishing it, his mind returned to Newgate Gaol and the miserable existence of captivity. He threw aside the wood that barred the door and resolved to fight to the end. The figure who rushed into the house was none other than Maxwell.

"They're here!"

"Who?" Peter asked. So many scenarios raced through his mind.

"The army."

"What of my boat?"

"It leaves as planned. But there is one change; take Grace and the boys with you."

As much as the army's coup was unfolding, it was hard for Peter to comprehend, not least because he had been cooped up in this remote hovel for two weeks. The words that Maxwell had just uttered finally sunk in - Grace and the boys? His friend was now talking of passes; documents that had been provided by a French woman. Peter listened, but Maxwell's panting breaths made his speech almost incomprehensible.

"Of what passes do you speak?" Peter yelled and grabbed Maxwell's arm.

"For the boys and Grace. Permitting travel to France."

"But what will you do?"

"You must use my pass and pass yourself off as me. They are all officially sealed. There is much confusion on the island and that will work to your advantage."

"And when they find you?" Peter asked.

"I cannot leave Maria here on her own. Besides, I need to warn the king."

Grace emerged from the back room. Tom and Kit followed her. Maxwell embraced his sons tightly and charged Tom to look after his younger sibling. The boys looked scared and bewildered; Maxwell's bedraggled appearance and his desperate words didn't convince anyone. Their aunt placed her arms about each child.

"I will stay with Maria," Peter persisted.

"You are a wanted man. It's no good, Peter – do as I say, I implore you."

Maxwell took a spare cloak and wrapped it about himself, followed by a Montero Cap, the red wool of which framed his determined features. Nothing Peter could say would alter his friend's resolution. But Peter knew he faced capture if he remained here. There was precious little to be done but acquiesce to what was proposed.

"You must soon convince the army of your new identity. They are pursuing me. I bid thee good luck," Maxwell said.

Maxwell had no sooner fled back into the night than Grace quickly closed the door and barred it once again. She was soon on her knees cleaning the muddy footprints, and then a rush mat was laid over the floor. The boys were instructed to eat some potage in front of the fire. Peter realised just how much Grace held this family together; she was a remarkably selfless woman who had dedicated herself to them – god-fearing and honest. She gave a reassuring smile. It inspired him more than any battlefield war-cry ever could.

It wasn't long before a second pounding came at the door, followed by a deep cry to open up. Peter quickly did so and stood back as several troopers entered, looking around the room.

"Has a rider passed this way?"

"Not that I have seen, though I would be uncertain if they had in this weather."

"Has anyone been here in the last half an hour?

"We have barely enough food for ourselves, never mind entertain anyone else," Peter replied.

"Your name?"

"Maxwell Walker. These are my sons, Tom and Kit, and my sister-in-law, Grace."

The leader stepped forward leaving his beaver-skin hat firmly on his head. His features had a coldness to them. It looked like there was barely enough skin to cover the high cheek bones and contours of his gaunt face. His eyes were sunken. A black cloak made him appear wraith-like, and he looked right through Peter. There was no doubt as to his perceptiveness.

When the officer stepped forward, his soles scuffed at the stone floor. Attention went to the boys and the food they were eating. Gripping the hilt of his sword as he walked, he sauntered towards Grace, sparing a cursory glance at the spitting fire. A damp patch on the floor beside her provoked a frown.

"Pissed yourself?" His voice had a disturbing hoarseness to it.

"The boys dropped some food in their haste. I made them clean it." Grace gave a respectful nod.

"And whipped their backsides, I hope?"

"They will not be so careless again."

Once more, he clenched the hilt of the sword at his side. The groan of his leather gloves broke the silence.

"If you happen across anyone who looks suspicious, or behaves in a like manner, be sure to inform me."

"Of course, sir," Peter replied.

The officer headed back to the door where, after a last glance over his shoulder, he finally left. Peter heard the order to move south to Carisbrooke.

Chapter 25

Newport.
Seven o'clock.

Maxwell neared the house where the king was staying. It dominated the street with a gable crowning the centre of the roof and tall chimneys standing proud on either side. A few soldiers milled around the building and the streets leading to it like flies around a honey pot –New Model Army troops eyeing their prey. Though the island guards remained in place, posted outside the door and brandishing their six-foot-long halberds, it remained unclear if Governor Hammond's men were involved in this coup. There were now as many different strands to a man's loyalty as veins that ran through his body. From religion, politics, and nationality to kinship, or commander. These were dark and confusing days, and none more so than the Thirtieth of November.

"Maxwell Walker, here to speak with the king," he said upon approaching the sentries.

"What business?"

"The king desired a book from the castle."

"He will have more to contend with than reading. Wait here."

"Just let him in," the other soldier muttered. "What's occurring out here is of more importance than a damned book."

Inside, Maxwell found Henry Firebrace, a Groom of the Bedchamber, in deep discussion with one of Hammond's officers from Carisbrooke Castle. Their clandestine whispers ceased. Firebrace's eyes were alert and panicked. His pointed hairline seemed to indicate the concerned frown at his brow.

"Ah, Walker," he said and then introduced Colonel Cook. "What news?"

"They are come to take the king for trial. That much I overheard," Maxwell replied.

"God's wounds, then it is true! Pray follow me." Firebrace beckoned him and tapped at an inner door.

When no reply was forthcoming, he knocked again in slow succession. This time they were given access to the royal bedchamber. The trio bowed. The Duke of Richmond and Earl of Lindsey were already here. The king stood facing them all. In this small room on a remote island that crawled with soldiers, and with a reduced retinue, he seemed more isolated than ever.

Following the dismissal of his barber, King Charles had refused to trust the blade of any other, preferring instead to leave his beard unkempt. His thinning grey hair had all but lost its waves. Instead, it hung limply, and he more resembled a hermit. The men waited with apprehension, as if come to seek his wise counsel, but a forlorn look in the king's eyes betrayed the fact that he had none to give. It was a pitiful sight for Maxwell to behold.

"Colonel Cook," the king said, "Are you are aware of any orders that threaten my person?"

"No, Your Majesty. If I was, then verily I would have informed you."

Cook was another of Hammond's men who had come over to the royal cause. Maxwell entertained some hope that the man could assist even at this late stage.

"Your Majesty, Captain Walker has some news to share," Firebrace spoke up.

The king turned to Maxwell. There was no hint of any recognition – only a pause of expectation.

"I was at Cowes around an hour ago, Your Majesty. I overheard a Major Fox, who by his own admission claims to have come for you … he spoke of a trial."

The king gave a deep sigh and sank onto a chair by the fireside. Leaning forward, he took a fire iron and began poking idly at the charred logs. His actions agitated them to combustion. Only an emerald ring on his finger broke this bleak appearance; the stone resembling a tiny flash of verdant spring amidst this winter's night. It was small as the king's eroding hopes.

"Was anything else said?" There was a hint of reluctance in the monarch's voice, as if he could already sense an affirmative.

"Yes, sir, they have arrested Governor Hammond."

"The great equivocator himself?" The news stirred King Charles and he looked intently at them all. "See, Gentlemen, how these people turn on their own? Like wild dogs, they pull down any who oppose them. Where will they stop?"

Nobody answered. Nobody could answer.

"Pray search out Hammond's deputy," the king ordered Cook. "Enquire of him what he knows. I must discover whether his troops will oppose the army or stand with them."

Maxwell watched as Cook left. He trembled from the coldness that clung to him along with his sodden clothes, exacerbated by the apprehension. It was to be a night of vital consequence to many. The discourse that passed here only heightened Maxwell's concern for the safety of his sons.

"Your Majesty, I would urge you to leave this place," Firebrace pleaded. "If I might remind you, there is a boat near Cowes that continues to wait upon you."

"At this moment, the divisions of my enemies offer more salvation than flight."

REBELLION

"I fear the sea will prove more merciful than your enemies," Firebrace ventured.

"Sire, the army will attempt to seize your person," the Duke of Richmond added. "If you fall into their grasp, it will make the securing of a treaty with Parliament all the more harder."

"I am not confident that escape is feasible." The king shook his head. "I am, in General Fairfax's words, a golden ball passed between all sides. Neither Parliament, nor the army, can prevail without me."

"Pray take heed, Your Majesty, lest the army fail to abide by such rules. They are intent upon using force to override Parliament," the Earl of Lindsey counselled.

"We have seen how easily Cook passes the guards. Were you to wear a leaguer cloak and wrap it about yourself as he does, then I am positive you could to walk out of here entirely unmolested," Richmond said.

"If any escape should miscarry it would unite my enemies and dishearten my friends," King Charles was quick to point out. He then beckoned Maxwell forward. "I think you have more need of the fire than me. Pray dry yourself by it."

Maxwell apologised for his tardy appearance and gritted his teeth in a bid to allay the chill that almost had his jaw trembling. As he peeled off his cloak and hat, the five men settled and waited for Cook's return. Conversation was intermittent. The king turned to Maxwell.

"How fare your family, Captain Walker?"

"I have this night sent them away by ship ... for their safety."

"Alas, I fear nowhere is safe from the rebels. To where are they headed?

"France, sir."

"France?" The king straightened. "I see ..." His eyes seemed momentarily brighter, despite the melancholy that clouded them.

"A friend of mine arranged for passes from London," Maxwell felt the need to explain.

Conversation continued briefly and then the king began writing. An hour or so later, footsteps were heard from outside the bedchamber. There was no knock, nor any voices. Just the acrid smell of smoke – burning musket matches. Upon investigation, sentries were found at the door. Time dragged by until Cook finally returned.

"It is dire, Your Majesty. The army is at Carisbrooke and Hammond's deputy would not speak to me without their leave. He is, as he privately admitted, now a prisoner within his own garrison."

"Then it is confirmed." the king replied. "We can expect no help from that quarter. The army, it seems, will hold the island by sunrise."

"Are the sentries outside part of Hammond's forces?" Richmond queried.

"Aye, sir," Cook replied with a firm nod. "I have their password, and horses are waiting nearby. If the king was to accompany me, I could lead him away from here?"

"I shall not escape," the king answered.

Maxwell noted a sharpness in the king's movement as he turned and picked up a book. It was an obvious sign that all conversation was at an end, and to ensure that this was firmly understood, the monarch announced that he would take some rest while he could. Only the Duke of Richmond was called upon to stay.

"Might I make use of your leaguer cloak?" Maxwell asked of Cook, his own being wet through.

"Take it, Walker," the king interjected. "Take also your betrothed and follow your family. I have noticed how she looks at you, therefore make your marriage real with my blessing. If this turns out to be my last command, let it be one that brings happiness."

"I am humbled and deeply honoured, Your Majesty." Maxwell was profoundly moved by this declaration that he stumbled over words of thanks. He kissed the proffered royal hand.

"If I might make one request of you in exchange?"

"Of course, anything you wish, sir."

"This may be the last chance I have to send a final blessing to my wife. Dawn will bring much uncertainty."

The king stood and retrieved something from his desk. A letter. He paused and looked at it, as if recalling the message word for word. The royal seal held the sheet together.

"I charge you with delivering this to the queen. Pray do your utmost to succeed."

"You have my word that I will do all that is necessary."

The king nodded and then turned away. "Tell her my love is the same now as it has ever been."

Cook handed over the long cloak. Once it was around Maxwell, he was conducted into the dark street and towards a waiting steed. He would collect Maria – a royal command, but also one of his heart.

Chapter 26

A small boat glided across the glassy, black water, leaving Newport behind. This inlet would carry it the three miles to Cowes like an artery that led north from the heart of the island. The boatman's regular exhalations and dip of his oars filled the silence. Maxwell glanced at Maria, whose hooded features were picked out by the golden glow of the wherryman's lamp. She smiled. He reciprocated on impulse.

They could have been getting ferried through the night sky itself. The shadows of trees like blackened storm clouds. Deep inside, Maxwell ached with worry over Tom, Kit, Grace and Peter. Were they safe? The question played over in his mind and he tried to somehow anticipate the answer; to judge the odds, reassuring himself that Peter had a pass and was an able and brave man. That Grace would do anything to protect those boys. He implored God with a silent prayer to have a care for them all, wherever they might be at this moment. With a glance at the sky, he considered that his family might be observing the same sparkling veil; the heavens seemed open and endless, compared to the blinkered earth.

In the distance, beyond the boatman's head, some lights appeared studding the darkness. They emanated from ships of all sizes that were anchored at Cowes, and then the lamp of another ferry darted along. Next, a row of buildings on the waterfront of East Cowes. They looked across the widening expanse of water to West Cowes, where a decaying castle stood on the bank. Maxwell stiffened as they drew closer; the presence of people was palpable in comparison to their solitary journey. He itched to alight and find out whether his loved ones had escaped, as well as the whereabouts of the king's ship. The New Model Army had brought with them momentary confusion as their coup played out. This pivotal point had opened up a brief window that enterprising souls might seize upon. It would be fleeting.

"East or West Cowes?"

"West." Maxwell nodded in response to the boatman.

The timber-framed buildings of West Cowes waterfront were dwarfed by a hill behind them. Further on, the round limestone tower of the castle kept a beady eye on the haven, which led out to the British Sea. Maxwell spotted a lodging house called *The Feathers*. He knew the keeper - a staunch royalist. The boat bobbed as it approached the landing. Maxwell disembarked and held his hand out to Maria.

"Might you wait for us?" Maxwell asked, to which the boatman nodded.

As soon as Maria stepped foot on to the timber planking, they made haste. There were some soldiers near the castle. A couple of drunkards sauntered out of the lodging house and then Maxwell passed the illuminated window. Through it, he was astonished to see his sons with Grace, and hurried inside.

"Tom, Kit!"

He embraced them tightly. Though he was overcome with relief that he had found them, it was tempered by concern that they were not free of the island. What would they do now? He turned to Grace and asked about Peter.

"He's speaking to the keeper," she said discreetly.

"What of the ship?"

"I do not know."

Maxwell cursed under his breath. "Take Tom and Kit to the wherry and wait for me," he told Grace and Maria. "I'll find Peter."

"Might Maria take the boys?" Grace turned to solicit her agreement. "I must speak with you, Maxwell."

As Maria and the children duly left, Grace's cheeks flushed, and her agitation grew more apparent. Her thin eyebrows dipped.

"If they discover Peter's identity he will be arrested again, and I have heard such terrible tales of that prison." Her gaze went to the door as though searching for his friend. "I have vowed not to be parted from him. I love him, Maxwell. We both feel the same."

"Dear Grace," Maxwell replied. "There is another vessel. Let me fetch Peter and we can all be away from here."

Maxwell rushed towards the back room. His heart raced. There he found Peter, whose long face betrayed a haunted look of concern.

"Thank God! I know not what to do, Maxwell."

"Where's the damned ship?" Maxwell asked.

"It has already sailed, due to the army's arrival," Peter replied.

Maxwell paused and turned to the keeper. "What of the *Swift,* is that still here?"

"It is, my friend."

"Praise be to God," Maxwell gasped.

"Some of the crew were in earlier. They will be due to sail soon," the keeper warned.

"Then let us make haste. We must board her now."

Maxwell and Peter hurried back to Grace, whereupon the door was flung open and a cavalryman entered. He wore a long buff coat whose tan colour was broken by a blackened breastplate. There followed a gruff demand about why the place had not closed up. Before any could answer, his blade was drawn.

"Where might you lot be off to?"

"This man and his wife have a ship to catch. They have passes from London," Maxwell replied. He felt ever vulnerable because of the close proximity of his family.

REBELLION

The trooper lifted his visor and turned to Peter, who handed over his travel pass.

"France?" The soldier's eyes narrowed. "You French?"

"No, English. From Leicestershire. I'm a merchant, you see," Peter explained.

"Well, you'll just have to trade with good English Protestants for a while."

"You're not permitting them to board?" Maxwell queried.

"No."

The two-foot-long blade of the trooper's hanger curved menacingly, as though ready to hook itself into Maxwell's innards. An emphasising groove ran its entire length.

"That's signed by the Derby House Committee!" Peter pointed at the paper.

The trooper frowned at Maxwell. "Didn't I see you here earlier, when Adams was killed in the woods?"

"Who?" Maxwell asked, in an attempt to brush off the suspicion.

"Aye, it was you ..."

Peter seized the soldier's helmet, pulled it off and then swung it at the man's head with a crunch. The actions of all three men blurred into one. Maxwell tore off his cloak and smashed his fist into the soldier's face. However quick, he could not stop the parliamentarian from slashing at Peter, whose thigh was cut open. Grace shrieked. Her terrified cry rang in Maxwell's ears and stirred memories of his wife's murder.

Maxwell unsheathed his sword and was at the trooper before a killer blow could be delivered to Peter. The ringing of blades was like a metallic heartbeat. Fast and furious. Maxwell leaped aside to escape the bloody edge of his opponent's sword and was forced onto the defensive. He back-stepped into the room, struggling to hold his own against his oncoming foe. Blood trickled from the trooper's cut face. It gathered in his furrowed brow and emphasised a gritty determination.

In an instant Maxwell was up against a table and fighting for every second. The piercing ring of each parry separated life from death. He leaned back on the table and kicked at the trooper before springing aside. His steps were nimble, and he barely placed his full weight on them. It was a deadly dance that only one would survive.

After Maxwell cut in from the left, the force of the block and the straw on the floor made him stumble. He was soon back at the table and quickly rolled aside. His foe's sword left a groove in the old oak surface. Maxwell fended off a further blow, but realised he was finished. Fear filled him. This was a fear of death - at leaving his sons in danger, and not seeing them grow to manhood.

There was a dull crash. With that moment he was on his feet again, blade held high, only to see the trooper collapse to the floor. Wide-eyed and gasping for breath, sweat beads trickled down Maxwell's face. Grace stood over the parliamentarian, brandishing the handle of what had been a large jug. Pieces lay scattered around the floor. Maxwell stabbed the trooper through the gut. After extracting his sword, he went to Peter, who sat up against the wall. A pool of red had formed under his right leg.

"We're out of practice, are we not?"

Maxwell gave a hollow smile. "A suitable excuse for my poor show."

Grace removed her linen coif, poured some wine on it and began dabbing at Peter's wound. He grimaced with pain.

"It was worth being cut to see her fair locks," Peter said between sharp breaths.

"Can you move?" Maxwell asked.

"No." Peter shook his head. "Leave me here."

"Come, get your arm about my neck," Maxwell insisted. "Once you're on the ship their surgeon can tend to you."

REBELLION

"There will be troops here soon. You must go," Peter replied. "Fight on for your family."

"What of you, Grace?" Maxwell asked.

"I won't be separated from Peter." She did not look up from her work. "I'll tend his wounds and put my trust in God."

"I have found happiness," Peter added. "Are we not put on this earth to love? However brief my joy might be, at least Grace and I are together."

"The boys need you, Maxwell," Grace implored, and then stood. "They'll always be dear to me, but they need their father."

"I can't leave you both like this."

"The keeper will assist us," Peter replied.

"My sister's heart was entirely yours to the end," Grace whispered. "Catherine would want you to be happy. Go to Maria."

Grace handed over the pass with a nod. Peter wished him Godspeed. Maxwell felt numb - as if in some sort of paralysis. Then, as was always the case at such arduous times, the welfare of his sons spurred him on. He blessed the pair and left the lodging house. Into the night he ran towards the ferry. There were tears in his eyes. Thankfully no more soldiers were nearby, and he found Maria and the boys - unharmed - in the boat. He climbed in and gave order to leave. They were soon slipping towards the shadow of the *Swift*.

Chapter 27

Standing on the *Swift's* deck gave separation from the troubled Isle of Wight. The sound of the nocturnal wind, breathing life into the canvas sails, was exhilarating. As the vessel cut through the water, the breeze in Maxwell's ear sang a tune of freedom. But for all this, his eyes remained fixed on Cowes.

The glow of *The Feathers* seeped into the night. The shafts of light reflected in the water like golden fingers reaching out to him. It became an anchor point, and as the distance grew, he felt as though he was being torn apart. The four travel passes had reassured the captain of the vessel. But it was the king's letter, with the wax imprint of the royal arms, that had served as evidence of his mission.

Maxwell realised that Peter was correct about being put on the earth to love. Even amidst the carnage and hate of civil war, it was the love of a king for his queen that had provided an opportunity to escape it. The love between Peter and Grace had united them in the face of adversity. Their selflessness and courage meant that Maxwell and his family were together. And it was love for his boys that had brought Maxwell through hell.

He placed his arms around Tom and Kit. Maria reassuringly stroked his back. In the heavens above them one star seemed to shimmer with particular lustre. The king's cavalier was set upon a fresh course. A new life.

Fictional Characters

Captain Maxwell Walker & family
Maria Wilkins
Peter Irwin
Louisa Laurent
Newgate Gaoler
Major Fox (New Model Army)
Henry Naylor & John Douglas – residents of Selby

Historical Note

After the defeat of King Charles I, the three kingdoms were cast into a fresh battle over the terms of peace. It was, however, fought through diplomacy, intrigue, deals and double-dealing. This had the King, Parliament, Scots and New Model Army vying for the upper hand, despite the outcome of the war. Each wished for a settlement that favoured their interests and religious stance. During this time, the historic Putney Debates took place, in which the Levellers tried to shape a much more democratic outcome. The chapter set at Putney is based on the records of proceedings.

Contrary to what is often stated, it was not King Charles alone that brought about renewed hostilities in 1648. These four factions (each with their own equally entrenched beliefs) attempted to play the others off against one another. Parliament, Scots and the Army tried to use the king as a pawn to give legitimacy to their terms. King Charles used them all too, with the dogged aim of succeeding where he had failed militarily. To divide and conquer. After refusing several offers of military support from the Scots, the king made an alliance with them in December 1647.

The king's escape attempts detailed in this book are all factual. At Hampton Court, Colonel Whalley did show the king various letters that referenced a threat to his life. Whalley dithered before the royal apartments for hours on end, which blessed the initial escape. And the result of the king's flight was a godsend to the New Model Army, unifying it at a crucial moment during a dangerous breach with the Levellers. Amazingly, once the king was free of Hampton Court, it was realised that no decision had been made about his ultimate destination. Was this a sign that the flight was enacted in haste, following rumours of assassination? Through Whalley, could Cromwell and Ireton (who opposed the Leveller manifesto) have been complicit in provoking the king, to end the ever-divisive Putney debates? Acid was collected from London for the erosion of the window bars at Carisbrooke, and the king did get embarrassingly stuck. A ship was provided for his escape, waiting on him at Cowes, and it was perfectly placed for use in the ending of Maxwell's adventures.

During his confinement at Carisbrooke Castle, separated from family, friends, and close advisors, the king's personal character came to the fore. His regal front all but evaporated in this tense period. He could be ever-sanguine, as well as depressed – and at times somewhat deluded. He relished the intrigue but was recklessly indiscreet with his plans. He became argumentative with Governor Hammond and turned in on himself. Here he was reputed to have written much of *Eikon Basilike*, a defence of his actions, which became a bestseller after his death. At Carisbrooke, there are glimpses of humour, such as when the governor stumbled and fell flat on his face during a walk around the walls – Charles playfully called it punishment for Hammond's 'equivocating to me'.

At various points throughout his life, Charles relied on strong and influential figures – Lords Buckingham, Strafford and Digby, for example. At Carisbrooke, bereft of such characters, he was attracted to the indomitable Jane Whorwood. His letters to her are full of highly personal remarks that confirm a closeness and suggest a physical relationship. The final year of his life gave a unique glimpse of the man behind the crown at his most vulnerable. When the New Model Army arrived to take control of the king and the island, Charles refused to escape. No matter the rights and wrongs of his actions, he possessed a courage and inner strength in various moments such as these, which was most famously displayed at his trial and execution.

I hope you have enjoyed reading the three books that make up the *Rebellion* series as much as I have enjoyed researching and writing them. The end of the war is less used in fiction, and I hope the strong factual base for the story brings the various aspects of this tumultuous and fascinating period to life. The characters often took on a life of their own during the writing process and challenged my intentions for the plot. This occurred more than ever in the final chapter of Maxwell's story!

If you'd like to find out more about the period, you can listen to my podcast *CavalierCast – The Civil War in Words* or visit www.1642author.com

Printed in Great Britain
by Amazon